Best English Short Stories V

Best English Short Stories V

EDITED BY GILES GORDON
AND DAVID HUGHES

W·W·NORTON & COMPANY
New York   London

Copyright © 1993 by Giles Gordon and David Hughes
First American Edition 1994
Originally published in Great Britain under the title *Best Short Stories 1993*

Printed in the United States of America

Manufacturing by The Courier Companies, Inc.

ISBN 0-393-03580-8

W. W. Norton & Company, Inc.
500 Fifth Avenue, New York, N.Y. 10110
W. W. Norton & Company Ltd.
10 Coptic Street, Lodon WC1A 1PU

1 2 3 4 5 6 7 8 9 0

Contents

Introduction

There has been talk of recession even in the short story. A noted literary agent told us, in submitting only two (but good) stories for the year, that we must soon change our ground rules, there now being so few magazines, even fewer accepting short fiction. We editors who study the form in both senses see no diminution in the number of outlets, and that increasingly includes BBC Radio as well as an upsurge in new journals. We also note the advent of more young writers who attempt the discipline of the story before moving on to the looser but fiscally sounder rewards of the novel.

Readers of our annual volumes since 1986 will know that we offer you not, of course, the best – the use of the superlative is to woo and win you – but a balance of those stories we regard as among the best published in a given year. On the whole we eschew genre, unless genre is transcended. This year, for instance, we read *Interzone* and *New Worlds* but found no SF story brilliant enough company to join the party. Detective stories, where they existed, creaked. The all-woman edition of *Aquarius*, flourishing four or five stories, seemed less than inspired. Then there is the 'problem' of 'local' magazines. We nearly found room for a story from the *Edinburgh Review* but it was by a Sassenach and the work in

Iron (from the North East) seemed a mite too regional to expand into the universal. Another change: women's magazines now seem to play safe by taking extracts from forthcoming books rather than backing their own fancies.

Once again, with honourable exceptions, the golden oldies are turning out the most imaginative tales, including Christopher Hope, William Trevor and Fay Weldon, all of whom appeared in our first volume. The young, particularly in the little magazines, are very often cautious, tentative and conventional, albeit nicely turned. There are too many dying falls (even in these pages); wit and surprise are at a premium. Yet in this year's cull there are several good and developing practitioners of whom little or nothing has been heard before, except in the enlightened journals, such as *Panurge, Ambit* or *London Magazine*, which have been their first presenters. Meanwhile the brightest single light of enterprise for the short story today is probably Duncan Minshull, who commissions original stories for radio. He has energised a slot dying of blandness into a showcase for the short form where succinctness has to be all.

Far from recession (though nobody seems to be writing directly about that), our experience this year is of optimism, if not wealth. Perhaps, though, there is a feeling on the part of many writers that they can make more sense of a deadish or a waiting time, as these early nineties seem to be, if they confine their comment to the limits of the fairly short narrative. Northern Ireland, for instance, that political insoluble, achieves in this volume two quite remarkably vivid domestic metaphors, just stories round a fire until they release their moment's thought – then expand, all the more for their brevity. In these contexts stories gain profoundly on any amount of ordinary reporting. Whole lifetimes are touched in by more than one of our authors (not least Alice Munro) and someone as astringent as Martin Amis, as surreal as Jonathan Treitel, can seemingly say everything in no more than a sketch. We attempt to choose stories that, once read, inhibit you from wanting to rush straight on to the next one. They ask for digestion.

So these are the ones we both like for this year. We seem rarely to argue. We just discuss a lot. It is plain from our choices that our contributors are well-versed in the work of their predecessors in the art, which is one of the reasons why their contemporary explorations are both relevant and original. Traditional, yes, but in the best sense modern.

Giles Gordon and David Hughes

Career Move

MARTIN AMIS

When Alistair finished his new screenplay, 'Offensive from Quasar 13', he submitted it to the *LM,* and waited. Over the past year, he had had more than a dozen screenplays rejected by the *Little Magazine.* On the other hand, his most recent submission, a batch of five, had been returned not with the standard rejection slip but with a handwritten note from the screenplay editor, Hugh Sixsmith. The note said:

> I was really rather taken with two or three of these, and seriously tempted by Hotwire, which I thought close to being fully achieved. Do please go on sending me your stuff.

Hugh Sixsmith was himself a screenplay writer of considerable, though uncertain, reputation. His note of encouragement *was* encouraging. It made Alistair brave.

Boldly he prepared 'Offensive from Quasar 13' for submission. He justified the pages of the typescript with fondly lingering fingertips. Alistair did not address the envelope to the Screenplay Editor. No. He addressed it to Mr Hugh Sixsmith. Nor, for once, did he enclose his curriculum vitae, which he now contemplated with some discomfort. It told, in a pitiless staccato, of the screenplays he had published in various laptop broadsheets and comically obscure pamphlets; it even told of screenplays published in his university magazine. The truly disgraceful bit came at the end, where it said 'Rights Offered: First British Serial *only*.'

Alistair spent a long time on the covering note to Sixsmith – almost as long as he had spent on 'Offensive from Quasar 13'. The note got shorter and shorter the more he worked on it. At last he was satisfied. There in the dawn he grasped the envelope and ran his tongue across its darkly luminous cuff.

That Friday, on his way to work, and suddenly feeling completely hopeless, Alistair surrendered his parcel to the sub post office in Calchalk Street, off the Euston Road. Deliberately – very deliberately – he had enclosed no stamped, addressed envelope. The accompanying letter, in its entirety, read as follows: 'Any use? If not – w.p.b.'

'W.p.b.' stood, of course, for 'wastepaper basket' – a receptacle that loomed forbiddingly large in the life of a practising screenplay writer. With a hand on his brow, Alistair sidled his way out of there – past the birthday cards, the tensed pensioners, the envelopes, and the balls of string.

When Luke finished the new poem – entitled, simply, 'Sonnet' – he Xeroxed the printout and faxed it to his agent. Ninety minutes later he returned from the gym downstairs and prepared his special fruit juice while the answering machine told him, among many other things, to get back to Mike. Reaching for another lime, Luke touched the preselect for Talent International.

'Ah. Luke,' said Mike. 'It's moving. We've already had a response.'

'Yeah, how come? It's four in the morning where he is.'

'No, it's eight in the evening where he is. He's in Australia. Developing a poem with Peter Barry.'

Luke didn't want to hear about Peter Barry. He bent, and tugged off his tank top. Walls and windows maintained a respectful distance – the room was a broad seam of sun haze and river light. Luke sipped his juice: its extreme astringency caused him to lift both elbows and give a single, embittered nod. He said, 'What did he think?'

'Joe? He did backflips. It's "Tell Luke I'm blown away by the new poem. I just know that 'Sonnet' is really going to happen." '

Luke took this coolly. He wasn't at all old but he had been in poetry long enough to take these things coolly. He turned. Suki, who had been shopping, was now letting herself into the apartment, not without difficulty. She was indeed cruelly encumbered. Luke said, 'You haven't talked numbers yet. I mean like a ballpark figure.'

Mike said, 'We understand each other. Joe knows about Monad's interest. And Tim at TCT.'

'Good,' said Luke. Suki was wandering slenderly towards him, shedding various purchases as she approached – creels and caskets, shining satchels.

'They'll want you to go out there at least twice,' said Mike. 'Initially to discuss . . . They can't get over it that you don't live there.'

Luke could tell that Suki had spent much more than she intended. He could tell by the quality of patience in her sigh as she began to lick the sweat from his shoulder blades. He said, 'Come on, Mike. They know I hate all that LA crap.'

On his way to work that Monday, Alistair sat slumped in his bus seat, limp with ambition and neglect. One fantasy was proving especially obdurate: as he entered his office, the telephone on his desk would actually be *bouncing* on its console – Hugh Sixsmith, from the *Little Magazine,* his voice urgent but grave, with the news that he was going to rush Alistair's screenplay into the very next issue. (To be frank, Alistair had had the same fantasy the previous Friday, at which time, presumably, 'Offensive from Quasar 13' was still being booted round the floor of the sub post office.) His girlfriend, Hazel, had come down from Leeds for the weekend. They were so small, he and Hazel, that they could share his single bed quite comfortably – could sprawl and stretch without constraint. On the Saturday evening, they attended a screen-

3

play reading at a bookshop on Camden High Street. Alistair hoped to impress Hazel with his growing ease in this milieu (and managed to exchange wary leers with a few shambling, half-familiar figures – fellow screenplay writers, seekers, knowers). But these days Hazel seemed sufficiently impressed by him anyway, whatever he did. Alistair lay there the next morning (her turn to make tea), wondering about this business of being impressed. Hazel had impressed him mightily, seven years ago, in bed: by not getting out of it when he got into it. The office telephone rang many times that Monday, but none of the callers had anything to say about 'Offensive from Quasar 13'. Alistair sold advertising space for an agricultural newsletter, so his callers wanted to talk about creosote admixes and offal reprocessors.

He heard nothing for four months. This would normally have been a fairly good sign. It meant, or it might mean, that your screenplay was receiving serious, even agonised, consideration. It was better than having your screenplay flopping back on the mat by return post. On the other hand, Hugh Sixsmith might have responded to the spirit and the letter of Alistair's accompanying note and dropped 'Offensive from Quasar 13' into his wastepaper basket within minutes of its arrival: four months ago. Rereading his fading carbon of the screenplay, Alistair now cursed his own (highly calibrated) insouciance. He shouldn't have said, 'Any use? If not – w.p.b. ' He should have said, 'Any use? If not – s.a.e.'! Every morning he went down the three flights of stairs – the mail was there to be shuffled and dealt. And every fourth Friday, or thereabouts, he still wrenched open his *LM,* in case Sixsmith had run the screenplay without letting him know. As a surprise.

'Dear Mr Sixsmith,' thought Alistair as he rode the train to Leeds. 'I am thinking of placing the screenplay I sent you elsewhere. I trust that . . . I thought it only fair to . . .' Alistair retracted his feet to accommodate another passenger. 'My dear Mr Sixsmith: In response to an inquiry from . . . In response to a most generous inquiry, I am putting together a selection of my screenplays for . . .' Alistair tipped his head back and stared at the smeared window. 'For Mudlark Books. It seems that the Ostler Press is also interested. This involves me in some paperwork, which, however tedious . . . For the record . . . Matters would be considerably eased . . . Of course if you . . .'

Luke sat on a Bauhaus love seat in Club World at Heathrow, drinking Evian and availing himself of a complimentary fax machine – clearing up the initial paperwork on the poem with Mike.

Everyone in Club World looked hushed and grateful to be there, but not Luke, who looked exhaustively displeased. He was flying first class to LAX, where he would be met by a uniformed chauffeur who would convey him by limousine or courtesy car to the Pinnacle Trumont on the Avenue of the Stars. First class was no big thing. In poetry, first class was something you didn't need to think about. It wasn't discussed. It was statutory.

Luke was tense: under pressure. A lot – maybe too much – was riding on 'Sonnet'. If 'Sonnet' didn't happen, he would soon be able to afford neither his apartment nor his girlfriend. He would recover from Suki before very long. But he would never recover from not being able to afford her, or his apartment. If you wanted the truth, his deal on 'Sonnet' was not that great. Luke was furious with Mike except about the new merchandizing clause (potential accessories on the poem – like toys or T-shirts) and the improved cut he got on tertiaries and sequels. Then there was Joe.

Joe calls, and he's like 'We really think "Sonnet"'s going to work, Luke. Jeff thinks so, too. Jeff's just come in. Jeff? It's Luke. Do you want to say something to him? Luke. Luke, Jeff's coming over. He wants to say something about "Sonnet".'

'Luke?' said Jeff. 'Jeff. Luke? You're a very talented writer. It's great to be working on "Sonnet" with you. Here's Joe.'

'That was Jeff,' said Joe. 'He's crazy about "Sonnet".'

'So what are we going to be talking about?' said Luke. 'Roughly.'

'On "Sonnet"? Well, the only thing we have a problem on "Sonnet" with, Luke, so far as I can see, anyway, and I know Jeff agrees with me on this – right, Jeff? – and so does Jim, incidentally, Luke,' said Joe, 'is the form.'

Luke hesitated. Then he said, 'You mean the form "Sonnet"'s written in.'

'Yes, that's right, Luke. The sonnet form.'

Luke waited for the last last call and was then guided, with much unreturned civility, into the plane's nose.

'Dear Mr Sixsmith,' wrote Alistair,

> Going through my files the other day, I vaguely remembered sending you a little effort called 'Offensive from Quasar 13' – just over seven months ago, it must have been. Am I right in assuming that you have no use for it? I might bother you with another one (or two!) that I have completed since then. I hope you are well. Thank you so much for your encouragement in the past.
>
> Need I say how much I admire your own work? The austerity, the depth. When, may I ask, can we expect another 'slim vol.'?

He sadly posted this letter on a wet Sunday afternoon in Leeds. He hoped that the postmark might testify to his mobility and grit.

Yet, really, he felt much steadier now. There had been a recent period of about five weeks during which, Alistair came to realise, he had gone clinically insane. That letter to Sixsmith was but one of the many dozens he had penned. He had also taken to haunting the Holborn offices of the *Little Magazine*: for hours he sat crouched in the coffee bars and sandwich nooks opposite, with the unsettled intention of springing out at Sixsmith – if he ever saw him, which he never did. Alistair began to wonder whether Sixsmith actually existed. Was he, perhaps, an actor, a ghost, a shrewd fiction? Alistair telephoned the *LM* from selected phone booths. Various people answered, and no one knew where anyone was, and only three or four times was Alistair successfully connected to the apparently permanent coughing fit that crackled away at the other end of Sixsmith's extension. Then he hung up. He couldn't sleep, or he thought he couldn't, for Hazel said that all night long he whimpered and gnashed.

Alistair waited for nearly two months. Then he sent in three more screenplays. One was about a Machine hit man who emerges from early retirement when his wife is slain by a serial murderer. Another dealt with the infiltration by the three Gorgons of an escort agency in present-day New York. The third was a heavy-metal musical set on the Isle of Skye. He enclosed a stamped, addressed envelope the size of a small knapsack.

Winter was unusually mild.

'May I get you something to drink before your meal? A cappuccino? A mineral water? A glass of sauvignon blanc?'

'Double decaf espresso,' said Luke. 'Thanks.'

'You're more than welcome.'

'Hey,' said Luke when everyone had ordered. 'I'm not just welcome anymore. I'm more than welcome.'

The others smiled patiently. Such remarks were the downside of the classy fact that Luke, despite his appearance and his accent, was English. There they all sat on the terrace at Bubo's: Joe, Jeff, Jim.

Luke said, 'How did "Eclogue by a Five-Barred Gate" do?'

Joe said, 'Domestically?' He looked at Jim, at Jeff. 'Like – *fifteen?*'

Luke said, 'And worldwide?'

'It isn't *going* worldwide.'

'How about "Black Rook in Rainy Weather"?' asked Luke.

Joe shook his head. 'It didn't even do what "Sheep in Fog" did.'

'It's all remakes,' said Jim. 'Period shit.'

'How about "Bog Oak"?'

' "Bog Oak"? Ooh, maybe twenty-five?'

Luke said sourly, 'I hear nice things about "The Old Botanical Gardens".'

They talked about other Christmas flops and bombs, delaying for as long as they could any mention of TCT's

''Tis he whose yester-evening's high disdain', which had cost practically nothing to make and had already done a hundred and twenty million in its first three weeks.

'What happened?' Luke eventually asked. 'Jesus, what was the publicity budget?'

'On "'Tis"?' said Joe. 'Nothing. Two, three.'

They all shook their heads. Jim was philosophical. 'That's poetry,' he said.

'There aren't any other sonnets being made, are there?' said Luke.

Jeff said, 'Binary is in post-production with a sonnet. "Composed at —Castle". *More* period shit.'

Their soups and salads arrived. Luke thought that it was probably a mistake, at this stage, to go on about sonnets. After a while he said, 'How did "For Sophonisba Anguisciola" do?'

Joe said, "For Sophonisba Anguisciola"? Don't talk to me about "For Sophonisba Anguisciola".'

It was late at night and Alistair was in his room working on a screenplay about a high-I.Q. homeless black man who is transformed into a white female junk-bond dealer by a South Moluccan terrorist witch doctor. Suddenly he shoved this aside with a groan, snatched up a clean sheet of paper, and wrote:

Dear Mr Sixsmith,
It is now well over a year since I sent you 'Offensive from Quasar 13'. Not content with that dereliction, you have allowed five months to pass without responding to three more recent submissions. A prompt reply I would have deemed common decency, you being a fellow-screenplay writer, though I must say I have never cared for your work, finding it, at once, both florid and superficial. (I read Matthew Sura's piece last month and I thought he got you *bang to rights*.) Please return the more recent screenplays, namely 'Decimator', 'Medusa Takes Manhattan' and 'Valley of the Stratocasters', immediately.

He signed it and sealed it. He stalked out and posted it. On his return he haughtily threw off his drenched clothes. The single bed felt enormous, like an orgiast's fourposter. He curled up tight and slept better than he had done all year.

So it was a quietly defiant Alistair who the next morning came plodding down the stairs and glanced at the splayed mail on the shelf as he headed for the door. He recognised the envelope as a lover would. He bent low as he opened it.

> Do please forgive this very tardy reply. Profound apologies. But allow me to move straight on to a verdict on your work. I won't bore you with all my personal and professional distractions.

Bore me? thought Alistair, as his hand sought his heart.

> I think I can at once give the assurance that your screenplays are unusually promising. No: that promise has already been honoured. They have both feeling and burnish.
>
> I will content myself, for now, by taking 'Offensive from Quasar 13'. (Allow me to muse a little longer on 'Decimator'.) I have one or two very minor emendations to suggest. Why not telephone me here to arrange a chat?
>
> Thank you for your generous remarks about my own work. Increasingly I find that this kind of exchange – this candour, this reciprocity – is one of the things that keep me trundling along. Your works helped sustain my defences in the aftermath of Matthew Sura's vicious and slovenly attack, from which, I fear, I am still rather reeling. Take excellent care.

'Go with the lyric,' said Jim.

'Or how about a ballad?' said Jeff.

Jack was swayable. 'Ballads are big,' he allowed.

It seemed to Luke, towards the end of the second day, that he was winning the sonnet battle. The clue lay in the flavour of Joe's taciturnity: torpid but unmorose.

'Let's face it,' said Jeff. 'Sonnets are essentially hieratic. They're strictly period. They answer to a formalised consciousness. Today, we're talking consciousnesses that are in *search* of form.'

'Plus,' said Jack, 'the lyric has always been the natural medium for the untrammelled expression of feeling.'

'Yeah,' said Jeff. 'With the sonnet you're stuck in this thesis-antithesis-synthesis routine.'

Joan said, 'I mean what are we doing here? Reflecting the world or illuminating it?'

It was time for Joe to speak. 'Please,' he said. 'Are we forgetting that "'Tis" was a sonnet, before the rewrites? Were we on coke when we said, in the summer, that we were going to go for the *sonnet*?'

The answer to Joe's last question, incidentally, was yes; but Luke looked carefully round the room. The Chinese lunch they'd had the secretary phone out for lay on the coffee table like a child's experiments with putty and paint and designer ooze. It was four o'clock and Luke wanted to get away soon. To swim and lie in the sun. To make himself especially lean and bronzed for his meeting with the young actress Henna Mickiewicz. He faked a yawn.

'Luke's lagged,' said Joe. 'Tomorrow we'll talk some more, but I'm pretty sure I'm recommitted to the sonnet.'

'Sorry,' said Alistair. 'Me yet again. Sorry.'

'Oh yes,' said the woman's voice. 'He *was* here a minute ago . . . No, he's there. He's there. Just a second.'

Alistair jerked the receiver away from his ear and stared at it. He started listening again. It seemed as if the phone itself were in paroxysm, all squawk and splat like a cabby's radio. Then the fit passed, or paused, and a voice said tightly but proudly, 'Hugh Sixsmith?'

It took Alistair a little while to explain who he was. Sixsmith sounded surprised but, on the whole, rather intrigued to hear from him. They moved on smoothly enough to arrange a meeting (after work, the following Monday), before Alistair contrived to put in: 'Mr Sixsmith, there's just one thing. This is very embarrassing, but last night I got into a bit of a state about not hearing from you for so long and I'm afraid I sent you a completely mad letter which I . . .' Alistair waited. 'Oh, you know how it is. For these screenplays, you know, you reach into yourself, and then time goes by and . . .'

'My dear boy, don't say another word. I'll ignore it. I'll throw it away. After a line or two I shall simply avert my unpained eye,' said Sixsmith, and started coughing again.

Hazel did not come down to London for the weekend. Alistair did not go up to Leeds for the weekend. He spent the time thinking about that place in Earl's Court Square where screenplay writers read from their screenplays and drank biting Spanish red wine and got stared at by tousled girls who wore thick overcoats and no makeup and blinked incessantly or not at all.

Luke parked his Chevrolet Celebrity on the fifth floor of the studio car park and rode down in the elevator with two minor executives in tracksuits who were discussing the latest records broken by "Tis he whose yester-evening's high disdain'. He put on his dark glasses as he crossed the other car park, the one reserved for major executives. Each bay had a name on it. It reassured Luke to see Joe's name there, partly obscured by his Range Rover. Poets, of course, seldom had that kind of clout. Or any clout at all. He was glad that Henna Mickiewicz didn't seem to realise this.

Joe's office: Jim, Jack, Joan, but no Jeff. Two new guys were there. Luke was introduced to the two new guys. Ron said he spoke for Don when he told Luke that he was a great admirer of his material. Huddled over the coffee percolator with Joe, Luke asked after Jeff, and Joe said, 'Jeff's off the poem,' and Luke just nodded.

They settled in their low armchairs.

Luke said, 'What's "A Welshman to Any Tourist" doing?'

Don said, 'It's doing good but not great.'

Ron said, 'It won't do what "The Gap in the Hedge" did.'

Jim said, 'What did "Hedge" do?'

They talked about what 'Hedge' did. Then Joe said, 'OK. We're going with the sonnet. Now. Don has a problem with the octet's first quatrain, Ron has a problem with the second quatrain, Jack and Jim have a problem with the first quatrain of the sestet, and I think we *all* have a problem with the final couplet.'

Alistair presented himself at the offices of the *LM* in an unblinking trance of punctuality. He had been in the area for hours, and had spent about fifteen quid on teas and coffees. There wasn't much welcome to overstay in the various snack parlours where he lingered (and where he moreover imagined himself unfavourably recollected from his previous *LM* vigils), holding with both hands the creaky foam container, and watching the light pour past the office windows.

As Big Ben struck two, Alistair mounted the stairs. He took a breath so deep that he almost fell over backward – and then knocked. An elderly office boy wordlessly showed him into a narrow, rubbish-heaped office that contained, with difficulty, seven people. At first Alistair took them for other screenplay writers and wedged himself behind the door, at the back of the queue. But they didn't look like screenplay writers. Not much was said over the next four hours, and the identities of Sixsmith's supplicants emerged only partially and piecemeal. One or two, like his solicitor and his second wife's psychiatrist, took their leave after no more than ninety minutes. Others, like the VAT man and the probation officer, stayed almost as long as Alistair. But by six-forty-five he was alone.

He approached the impossible haystack of Sixsmith's desk. Very hurriedly, he started searching through the unopened mail. It was in Alistair's mind that he might locate and intercept his own letter. But all the envelopes, of which there were a great many, proved to be brown, windowed, and registered. Turning to leave, he saw a Jiffy bag of formidable bulk addressed to himself in Sixsmith's tremulous hand. There seemed no reason not to take it. The old office boy, Alistair soon saw, was curled up in a sleeping bag under a worktable in the outer room.

On the street he unseamed his package in a ferment of grey fluff. It contained two of his screenplays, 'Valley of the

Stratocasters' and, confusingly, 'Decimator'. There was also a note:

> I have been called away, as they say. Personal ups and downs. I shall ring you this week and we'll have – what? Lunch?

Enclosed, too, was Alistair's aggrieved letter – unopened. He moved on. The traffic, human and mechanical, lurched past his quickened face. He felt his eyes widen to an obvious and solving truth: Hugh Sixsmith was a screenplay writer. He understood.

After an inconclusive day spent discussing the caesura of 'Sonnet''s opening line, Luke and his colleagues went for cocktails at Strabismus. They were given the big round table near the piano.

Jane said, 'TCT is doing a sequel to "'Tis".'

Joan said, 'Actually it's a prequel.'

'Title?' said Joe.

'Undecided. At TCT they're calling it "'Twas".'

'My son,' said Joe thoughtfully, after the waiter had delivered their drinks, 'called me an asshole this morning. For the first time.'

'That's incredible,' said Bo. '*My* son called me an asshole this morning. For the first time.'

'So?' said Mo.

Joe said, 'He's six years old, for Christ's sake.'

Phil said, 'My son called me an asshole when he was five.'

'My son hasn't called me an asshole yet,' said Jim. 'And he's nine.'

Luke sipped his Bloody Mary. Its hue and texture made him wonder whether he could risk blowing his nose without making yet another visit to the bathroom. He hadn't called Suki for three days. Things were getting compellingly out of hand with Henna Mickiewicz. He hadn't actually promised her a part in the poem, not on paper. Henna was great, except you kept thinking she was going to suddenly sue you anyway.

Mo was saying that each child progresses at his own rate, and that later lulls regularly offset the apparent advances of the early years.

Mo said, 'My son's three. And he calls me an asshole all the time.'

Everybody looked suitably impressed.

The trees were in leaf, and the rumps of the tourist buses were thick and fat in the traffic, and all the farmers wanted fertilizer admixes rather than storehouse insulation when Sixsmith finally made his call. In the interim, Alistair had convinced himself of the following: before returning his aggrieved letter, Sixsmith had *steamed it open and then resealed it*. During this period, also, Alistair had grimly got engaged to Hazel. But the call came.

He was pretty sure he had come to the right restaurant. Except that it wasn't a restaurant, not quite. The place took no bookings, and knew of no Mr Sixsmith, and was serving many midday breakfasts to swearing persons whose eyes bulged over mugs of flesh-coloured tea. On the other hand, there was alcohol. All kinds of people were drinking it. Fine, thought Alistair. Fine. What better place, really, for a couple of screenplay writers to . . .

'Alistair?'

Confidently, Sixsmith bent his long body into the booth. As he settled, he looked well pleased with the manoeuvre. He contemplated Alistair with peculiar neutrality, but there was then something boyish, something consciously remiss, in the face he turned to the waiter. As Sixsmith ordered a gin-and-tonic, and as he amusingly expatiated on his weakness for prawn cocktails, Alistair found himself wryly but powerfully drawn to this man, to this rumpled screenplay writer with his dreamy gaze, the curious elisions of his somewhat slurred voice, and the great dents and bone shadows of his face, all the faulty fontanels of vocational care. He knew how old Sixsmith was. But maybe time moved strangely for screen-play writers, whose flames burnt so bright . . .

'And as for my fellow-artisan in the scrivener's trade, Alistair. What will *you* have?'

At once Sixsmith showed himself to be a person of some candour. Or it might have been that he saw in the younger screenplay writer someone before whom all false reticence could be cast aside. Sixsmith's estranged second wife, it emerged, herself the daughter of two alcoholics, was an alcoholic. Her current lover (ah, how these lovers came and went!) was an alcoholic. To complicate matters, Sixsmith explained as he rattled his glass at the waiter, his daughter, the product of his first marriage, was an alcoholic. How did Sixsmith keep going? Despite his years, he had, thank God, found love, in the arms of a woman young enough (and, by the sound of it, alcoholic enough) to be his daughter. Their prawn cocktails arrived, together with a carafe of hearty red wine. Sixsmith lit a cigarette and held up his palm towards Alistair for the duration of a coughing fit that turned every head in the room. Then, for a moment, understandably disoriented, he stared at Alistair as if uncertain of his intentions, or even his identity. But their bond quickly re-established itself. Soon they were talking away like hardened equals – of Trumbo, of Chayevsky, of Towne, of Eszterhas.

Around two-thirty, when, after several attempts, the waiter succeeded in removing Sixsmith's untouched prawn cocktail, and now prepared to serve them their braised chops with a third carafe, the two men were arguing loudly about early Puzo.

Joe yawned and shrugged and said languidly, 'You know something? I was never that crazy about the Petrarchan rhyme scheme anyway.'

Jan said, ' "Composed at —Castle" is ABBA ABBA.'

Jen said, 'So was "'Tis". Right up until the final polish.'

Jon said, 'Here's some news. They say "Composed at—Castle" is in turnaround.'

'You're not serious,' said Bo. 'It's released this month. I heard they were getting great preview reaction.'

Joe looked doubtful. ' "'Tis" has made the suits kind of antsy about sonnets. They figure lightning can't strike twice.'

'ABBA ABBA,' said Bo with distaste.

'Or,' said Joe. '*Or* . . . *or* we go unrhymed.'

'*Un*rhymed?' said Phil.

'We go blank,' said Joe.

There was a silence. Bill looked at Gil, who looked at Will. 'What do you think, Luke?' said Jim. 'You're the poet.'

Luke had never felt very protective about 'Sonnet'. Even its original version he had regarded as no more than a bargaining chip. Nowadays he rewrote 'Sonnet' every night at the Pinnacle Trumont before Henna arrived and they called room service. 'Blank,' said Luke. 'Blank. I don't know, Joe. I could go ABAB ABAB or even ABAB CDCD. Christ, I'd go AABB if I didn't think it'd tank the final couplet. But blank. I never thought I'd go *blank*.'

'Well, it needs something,' said Joe.

'Maybe it's the pentameter,' said Luke. 'Maybe it's the iamb. Hey, here's one from left field. How about syllabics?'

At five-forty-five Hugh Sixsmith ordered a gin-and-tonic and said, 'We've talked. We've broken bread. Wine. Truth. Screenplay writing. I want to talk about your work, Alistair. Yes, I do. I want to talk about "Offensive from Quasar 13".'

Alistair blushed.

'It's not often that . . . But one always knows. That sense of pregnant arrest. Of felt life in its full . . . Thank you, Alistair. Thank you. I have to say that it rather reminded me of my own early work.'

Alistair nodded.

Having talked for quite some time about his own maturation as a screenplay writer, Sixsmith said, 'Now. Just tell me to shut up any time you like. And I'm going to print it anyway. But I want to make one *tiny* suggestion about "Offensive from Quasar 13".'

Alistair waved a hand in the air.

'Now,' said Sixsmith. He broke off and ordered a prawn cocktail. The waiter looked at him defeatedly. 'Now,' said

Sixsmith. 'When Brad escapes from the Nebulan experiment lab and sets off with Cord and Tara to immobilise the directed-energy scythe on the Xerxian attack ship – where's Chelsi?'

Alistair frowned.

'Where's Chelsi? She's still in the lab with the Nebulans. On the point of being injected with a Phobian viper venom, moreover. What of the happy ending? What of Brad's heroic centrality? What of his avowed love for Chelsi? Or am I just being a bore?'

The Secretary, Victoria, stuck her head into the room and said, 'He's coming down.'

Luke listened to the sound of twenty-three pairs of legs uncrossing and recrossing. Meanwhile he readied himself for a sixteen-tooth smile. He glanced at Joe, who said, 'He's fine. He's just coming down to say hi.'

And down he came: Jake Endo, exquisitely Westernised and gorgeously tricked out and perhaps thirty-five. Of the luxury items that pargetted his slender form, none was as breathtaking as his hair, with its layers of pampered light.

Jake Endo shook Luke's hand and said, 'It's a great pleasure to meet you. I haven't read the basic material on the poem, but I'm familiar with the background.'

Luke surmised that Jake Endo had had his voice fixed. He could do the bits of the words that Japanese people were supposed to find difficult.

'I understand it's a love poem,' he continued. 'Addressed to your girlfriend. Is she here with you in LA?'

'No. She's in London.' Luke found he was staring at Jake Endo's sandals, wondering how much they could possibly have cost.

A silence began its crescendo. This silence had long been intolerable when Jim broke it, saying to Jake Endo, 'Oh, how did "Lines Left Upon a seat in a Yew-Tree, Which Stands Near the Lake of Easthwaite, on a Desolate Part of the Shore, Commanding a Beautiful Prospect" do?'

' "Lines"?' said Jake Endo. 'Rather well.'

'I was thinking about "Composed at — Castle",' said Jim weakly.

The silence began again. As it neared its climax Joe was suddenly reminded of all this energy he was supposed to have. He got to his feet saying, 'Jake? I guess we're nearing our tiredness peak. You've caught us at kind of a low point. We can't agree on the first line. First line? We can't see our way to the end of the first *foot*.'

Jake Endo was undismayed. 'There always are these low points. I'm sure you'll get there, with so much talent in the room. Upstairs we're very confident. We think it's going to be a big summer poem.'

'No, we're very confident, too,' said Joe. 'There's a lot of belief here. A lot of belief. We're behind "Sonnet" all the way.'

'Sonnet?' said Jake Endo.

'Yeah, sonnet. "Sonnet".'

' "Sonnet"?' said Jake Endo.

'It's a sonnet. It's called "Sonnet".'

In waves the West fell away from Jake Endo's face. After a few seconds be looked like a dark-age warlord in mid-campaign, taking a glazed breather before moving on to the women and the children.

'Nobody told me,' he said as he went toward the telephone, 'about any *sonnet*.'

The place was closing. Its tea trade and its after-office trade had come and gone. Outside, the streets glimmered morbidly. Members of the staff were donning macs and overcoats. An important light went out. A fridge door slammed.

'Hardly the most resounding felicity, is it?' said Sixsmith.

Absent or unavailable for over an hour, the gift of speech had been restored to Alistair – speech, that prince of all the faculties. 'Or what if . . .' he said. 'What if Chelsi just leaves the experiment lab earlier?'

'Not hugely dramatic,' said Sixsmith. He ordered a carafe of wine and inquired as to the whereabouts of his braised chop.

'Or what if she just gets wounded? During the escape. In the leg.'

'So long as one could avoid the wretched cliché: girl impeded, hero dangerously tarrying. Also, she's supernumerary to the raid on the Xerxian attack ship. We really want her out of the way for that.'

Alistair said, 'Then let's kill her.'

'Very well. Slight pall over the happy ending. No, no.'

A waiter stood over them, sadly staring at the bill in its saucer.

'All right,' said Sixsmith. 'Chelsi gets wounded. Quite badly. In the arm. *Now* what does Brad do with her?'

'Drops her off at the hospital.'

'Mm. Rather hollow modulation.'

The waiter was joined by another waiter, equally stoic; their faces were grained by evening shadow. Now Sixsmith was gently frisking himself with a deepening frown.

'What if,' said Alistair, 'what if there's somebody passing who can take her to the hospital?'

'Possibly,' said Sixsmith, who was half standing, with one hand awkwardly dipped into his inside pocket.

'Or what if,' said Alistair, 'or what if Brad just gives her *directions* to the hospital?'

Back in London the next day, Luke met with Mike to straighten this shit out. Actually it looked OK. Mike called Mal at Monad, who had a thing about Tim at TCT. As a potential finesse on Mal, Mike also called Bob at Binary with a view to repossessing the option on 'Sonnet', plus development money at rolling compound, and redeveloping it somewhere else entirely – say, at Red Giant, where Rodge was known to be very interested. 'They'll want you to go out there,' said Mike. 'To kick it around.'

'I can't believe Joe,' said Luke. 'I can't believe I knocked myself out for that flake.'

'Happens. Joe forgot about Jake Endo and sonnets. Endo's first big poem was a sonnet. Before your time. "Bright star, would I were steadfast as thou art". It opened for like one day. It practically bankrupted Japan.'

'I feel used, Mike. My sense of trust. I've got to get wised up around here.'

'A lot will depend on how "Composed at — Castle" does and what the feeling is on the '"'Tis" prequel.'

'I'm going to go away with Suki for a while. Do you know anywhere where there aren't any shops? Jesus, I need a holiday. Mike, this is all bullshit. You know what I *really* want to do, don't you?'

'Of course I do.'

Luke looked at Mike until he said, 'You want to direct.'

When Alistair had convalesced from the lunch, he revised 'Offensive from Quasar 13' in rough accordance with Sixsmith's suggestions. He solved the Chelsi problem by having her noisily eaten by a Stygian panther in the lab menagerie. The charge of gratuitousness was, in Alistair's view, safely anticipated by Brad's valediction to her remains, in which sanguinary revenge on the Nebulans was both prefigured and legitimised. He also took out the bit where Brad declared his love for Chelsi, and put in a bit where Brad declared his love for Tara.

He sent in the new pages, which three months later Sixsmith acknowledged and applauded in a hand quite incompatible with that of his earlier communications. Nor did he reimburse Alistair for the lunch. His wallet, he had explained, had been emptied that morning – by which alcoholic, Sixsmith never established. Alistair kept the bill as a memento. This startling document showed that during the course of the meal Sixsmith had smoked, or at any rate bought, nearly a carton of cigarettes.

Three months later he was sent a proof of 'Offensive from Quasar 13'. Three months after that, the screenplay appeared in the *LM*. Three months after that, Alistair received a cheque for £12.50, which bounced.

Curiously, although the proof had incorporated Alistair's corrections, the published version reverted to the typescript, in which Brad escaped from the Nebulan lab seemingly without concern for a Chelsi last glimpsed on an operating table with a syringe full of Phobian viper venom being eased into her neck. Later that month, Alistair went along to a reading at the Screenplay Society in Earl's Court. There he got talking to a gaunt girl in an ash-stained black smock who claimed to have read his screenplay and who, over glasses of red wine and, later, in the terrible pub, told him he was a weakling and a hypocrite with no notion of the ways of men and women. Alistair had not been a published screenplay writer long enough to respond to, or even recognise, this graphic proposition (though he did keep the telephone number she threw at his feet). It is anyway doubtful whether he would have dared to take things further. He was marrying Hazel the following weekend.

In the new year he sent Sixsmith a series – one might almost say a sequence – of screenplays on group-jeopardy themes. His follow-up letter in the summer was answered by a brief note stating that Sixsmith was no longer employed by the *LM*. Alistair telephoned. He then discussed the matter with Hazel and decided to take the next day off work.

It was a September morning. The hospice in Cricklewood was of recent design and construction; from the road it resembled a clutch of igloos against the sheenless tundra of the sky. When he asked for Hugh Sixsmith at the desk, two men in suits climbed quickly from their chairs. One was a writ-server. One was a cost-adjuster. Alistair waved away their complex requests.

The warm room contained clogged, regretful murmurs, and defiance in the form of bottles and paper cups and cigarette smoke, and the many peeping eyes of female grief. A young woman faced him proudly. Alistair started explaining who he was, a young screenplay writer come to . . . On the bed in the corner the spavined figure of Sixsmith was gawkily arranged. Alistair moved toward it. At first he was sure the eyes were gone, like holes cut out of pumpkin or blood orange. But then the faint brows began to lift, and Alistair thought he saw the light of recognition.

As the tears began, he felt the shiver of approval, of consensus, on his back. He took the old screenplay writer's hand and said, 'Goodbye. And thank you. Thank you. Thank you.'

Opening in four hundred and thirty-seven theatres, the Binary sonnet 'Composed at — Castle' did seventeen million in its first weekend. At this time Luke was living in a two-bedroom apartment on Yokum Drive. Suki was with him. He hoped it wouldn't take her too long to find out about Henna Mickiewicz. When the smoke cleared he would switch to the more mature Anita, who produced.

He had taken his sonnet to Rodge at Red Giant and turned it into an ode. When that didn't work out he went to Mal at Monad, where they'd gone for the villanelle. The villanelle had become a triolet, briefly, with Tim at TCT, before Bob at Binary had him rethink it as a rondeau. When the rondeau didn't take, Luke lyricised it and got Mike to send it to Joe. Everyone, including Jake Endo, thought that now was surely the time to turn it back into a sonnet.

Luke had dinner at Rales with Joe and Mike.

'I always thought of "Sonnet" as an art poem,' said Joe. 'But things are so hot now, I've started thinking more commercially.'

Mike said, 'TCT is doing a sequel *and* a prequel to "'Tis" and bringing them out at the same time.'

'A sequel?' said Joe.

'Yeah. They're calling it "'Twill".'

Mike was a little fucked up. So was Joe. Luke was a little fucked up, too. They'd done some lines at the office. Then drinks here at the bar. They'd meant to get a little fucked up. It was OK. It was good, once in a while, to get a little fucked up. The thing was not to get fucked up too often. The thing was not to get fucked up to excess.

'I mean it, Luke,' said Joe. He glittered potently. 'I think "Sonnet" could be as big as "—".'

'You think?' said Luke.

'I mean it. I think "Sonnet" could be another "—".'

' "—"?'

' "—". '

Luke thought for a moment, taking this in. ' "—" . . .' he repeated wonderingly.

Life and Art

JOHN BANVILLE

HE ARRIVED IN PARIS for the first time huddled on a hay cart. That was a morning in the May of 1702, blustery and wet, with silk in the air and Dutch clouds piled up and a dull pewter shine on the river. He was on the run: something to do with a woman. The authorities in Utrecht were looking for him. His mother had wept; his father the roofer, that rude man, had swung a punch at him. He was eighteen and already had a cough – Gillot, his first teacher, told him he sounded like a crow. What was his name then? Faubelin, Vanhoblin, Van Hobellijn: take your pick. He changed his name, his nationality, everything, covering his tracks. He never lost those Dutch gutturals though, at which his fancy friends laughed behind their hands.

For a week he lay on a pallet wrapped in his cloak in a dirty little room above Gérin's print shop on the Pont Notre Dame, shaking with fever and grumbled at by the *maître*. Below him the other student hacks copied holy pictures all day long, lugubrious madonnas, St Jeromes with book and lion, ill-proportioned depositions from the cross. The stink of turpentine and pigments seeped up through the floorboards, and he would say that forever afterwards all studios smelled to him faintly of sickness. There was a war going on and the streets were thronged with beggars showing off their stumps.

He worked at the Opéra, painting sets, and even acted in the drama on occasion. Acting did not suit him, though: too much like life for him, who did not know how else to live except by playing parts. He went to the Comédie and stood in the pit amid the ceaseless noise and bustle and the stench of bodies, lost in contemplation of that glowing world above him on the stage. He never followed the plots, those ridiculous farragos, but watched the actors, studying their movements, their stylised, outlandish gestures. Afterwards he sat alone for hours in the Café Procope, sketching from memory. One of his first submissions to the Academy was a harlequinade in oils, very prettily done, he thought, with just the right balance of gaiety and menace. Second prize. Well.

Le grand hiver

It is the winter of 1709, after the disaster of Malplaquet. There was famine in Paris: mothers would not let their children out alone for fear they would be taken and eaten by the poor. Ice on the Seine, and that strange, thin, sour smell in the air for months that everyone said was the smell of the dead on the battlefield, blowing on the wind all the way down from Valenciennes. In the Tuileries one black night a tree exploded in the frost. Vaublin had been studying with Gillot for four years and was sick of it, the nagging and the sneers, the petty jealousies. Gillot was another like himself, watchful and secretive, a misanthrope. In the end they quarrelled, unforgivable things were shouted and Vaublin left and went to work with his friend Claude Audran at the Luxembourg Palace. Audran was the curator of the palace gallery. Vaublin sat every afternoon for hours, until the light faded and his fingers seized up from the cold, copying Rubens's series on the life of Marie de' Medici, plundering all that old master's secrets. Such silence around him there in those vast, gilded rooms, as if the entire city were dead. He stood at the windows and watched the winter twilight coming on, the icy mist turning the same shade of pink as the big-bummed figures on the canvases behind him.

He was living in the rue Dauphine then, with an excitingly sluttish girl he had picked up one night at the Venue Laurent and who had stayed because she had nowhere else to go; he knew that as soon as she could find a rich protector she would leave him. Her name was Léonie: my lion, he called her, in his ironical way. He brought her to the comedies but they bored her; she was deficient in a sense of humour. She complained of having to stand in the pit and spent the time watching with envy and resentment the jewelled ladies with their gallants up in the boxes. He painted her as a court beauty, in a borrowed gown and hat.

She stood before the finished portrait for a long time, wrinkling her nose and frowning, and at last pronounced it bad: her waist was too deep (it is true, his female figures are always long-waisted), and he had got her nose all wrong. Why had he made her expression so mournful? And what was she supposed to be looking back at, with her head turned like that, in that awkward way?

The past he said, and laughed.

That night he coughed blood for the first time, a frighteningly copious flow. Léonie surprised him with her tenderness. She swabbed the blood where it had soaked the sheet, and made a tisane for him, and sat and rocked him like a baby in her arms. Her brother, she said, had suffered from consumption. When he asked her what had become of him she was silent, which was the answer he had feared. He lay against her breast and shivered, light-headed with terror and a sort of shocked hilarity, watching the candle flame shake and sway as if it were the little palpitant flame of his own suddenly frail, enfeebled life.

His friend Antoine La Roque had lost a leg at Malplaquet. Tell me, Antoine, Vaublin asked him, did you think you were going to die? What was it like?

But Antoine only laughed and claimed he could not remember anything except lying on the field and watching a huge thick gold cloud in the zenith floating slowly out of his view. La Roque occasionally contributed art criticism to the *Nouveau Mercure*. Don't worry, Jean, he said gaily, I'll write your obituary.

Fête galante

Living people were too much for Vaublin: he preferred his figures fixed. These strange moments that he painted, so still, so silent, what did they signify for him? He has put a stop to things; here in these twilit glades the helpless tumbling of things through time comes to a halt. His people will not die, even if they have never lived. They exist in stillness; if they were to stir they would vanish.

I like in particular the faint but ever-present air of the perverse that hangs over all his work. From a certain angle these polite arcadian scenes can seem a riotous bacchanal. How lewdly his ladies look, their eager eyes shiny as marbles and their cheeks pinkly aglow, as if from a gentle smacking. Even the props have something tumescent about them, these smooth pillars and tall, thick trees, these pendulous and rounded clouds, these dense bushes where the Marquis's men are lurking, hung like stallions, waiting to be summoned into service.

The parks, the great parks, how he must have loved them, at Anet and Chantilly and Montmorency and Sceaux, above all Sceaux. One summer midnight there he came upon a girl sitting weeping on a stone bench in the park and took her hand without a word and led her through the shrubbery to a little moonlit clearing and made love to her beside a broken statue, smelling her faintly musty, mossy smell and tasting the salt of her tears. She clasped him to her flat little breast and crushed her mouth against his cheek and gasped a word he did not catch – the name of whoever it was she had been weeping for, he supposed – and in a moment it was over and she lay against him in a kind of languorous exhaustion. Over her shoulder he saw in the moonlight an enormous toad come flopping towards them over the grey grass. He never saw the girl again; she remained in his memory only as a scrap of lace, a sharply indrawn breath, the salt taste of tears. The toad he would remember always.

Another war was dragging to a close. The peace was signed at Utrecht. Vaublin was amused; he did not associate his birthplace with peacemaking. He recalled his father standing in the street one summer morning drunk, locked out of the house, in his shirt and boots and no breeches, shouting up abuse at the window of the bedroom where Vaublin's mother cowered on the bed and wept with Vaublin and his little brothers clutched about her (Lancret, Vaublin thought, would do the scene nicely, with his taste for sentiment). That was Utrecht for him.

The Swede Carl Gustaf Tessin called on him and bought a score of counterproofs and ten originals. Vaublin was living then on the quai de Conti, alone, in big, shabby rooms with a good north light. Tessin wrote of him in one of his lively letters home:

> He has promised to paint me a *Festival of the Lenten Fair*, for which I have advanced one hundred livres of the agreed three hundred. It will be his masterpiece, provided he puts the final touches to it, but if he falls into his black humour and his mind is possessed, then away he'll go and it's good-bye masterpiece.

Vaublin went daily to the Fair and wandered among the crowds, looking, looking. He liked the marionette shows and the coarse burlesques, the clumsier the better. He had his favourite characters and painted them again and again: Mezzetin, the scheming valet; poor Gilles, who clowned on the tightrope and always got beaten; and, of course, Polichinelle, that spiteful hunchback. There was something frankly malignant in these spectacles that appealed to Vaublin. He detected the same note, much refined, in the smooth, cruel little comedies of Regnard and Dancourt. The actors from the Comédie sat for him in costume. Paul Poisson, La Thorillière, old Baron, all the leading figures. They were perfect for his purpose, all pose and surface brilliance. They would strike an attitude and hold it for an hour without stirring, in a trance of self-regard. They brought him backstage to the first-night parties, frantic affairs presided over sometimes by Dancourt himself, a plump, self-satisfied cynic. He painted Dancourt's wanton daughter Mimi in the figure of Finette, in a silver gown – how he loved the nacreous sheen and shimmer of those heavy silks! – with a little hat, playing her lute and turning towards the viewer a glance at once wistful and lascivious.

You have made me seem very stout, Mimi said, and looked at him peculiarly, with shining eyes, as if she might be on the point of tears, and gathered up her things and hurried from the studio.

He thought he had offended her, but when next he encountered Dancourt at the theatre the playwright regarded him with cold merriment and said, My daughter, poor doe, is quite smitten with you, you know. Was it a joke? It came to him yet again how little he understood of people.

The double

A curious episode. It was in the summer of 1717, when the dolts in the Academy had at last accepted him as a member – he had presented his *Pèlerinage à l'île joyeuse*; even they could not find much fault with that – and he was moving in exalted company, that he first began to be aware of the presence in the city of this shadowy counterpart. At first it was amusing, when an acquaintance would meet him on the Pont Neuf and stare in surprise, saying he had seen him not five minutes ago in Saint Germain with a lady on his arm and wearing a scarlet cloak. He suspected a conspiracy among his friends to play a hoax on him. Then he began to notice the pictures. There were *Fêtes galantes* and *Amusements champêtres*, and even theatrical scenes, his speciality, the figures in which seemed to look at him with suppressed merriment, knowingly. They were done in a style uncannily like his own, but hastily, with technical lapses and scant regard for quality of surface. Yet they were good – they were alarmingly good, in their hurried, slipshod way. No Lancret or Pater would be capable of such mingled delicacy and power, such dash and daring. They looked like the rushed work of a great master, tossed off in an afternoon or two for an impatient and not very discriminating patron. At times, though, he had the feeling that they were aimed directly at him, an elaborate, monstrous gibe meant to mock his pretensions and the flaws in his technique. But who would be so lavishly gifted that he could afford to squander so much effort on a pointless joke? He tried to get a good look at them, but somehow they always eluded him: he would glimpse a *Récréation galante* being carried between two aproned porters out of a dealer's shop, or a gold and green *Île enchantée* over the fireplace of a fashionable salon just as he was being ushered from the room; when he made enquiries of the collectors that he knew, even the most expert among them could not help him, and only shrugged and said that what he was describing sounded remarkably like his own work. One night at a carnival ball in the Comtesse de Verrue's house on the rue du Cherche-Midi he elbowed his way through the crush and managed to station himself near an interesting little *Fête champêtre*, but the light was poor and the air thick with candle smoke and the fug of bodies, and he could not even make out the signature, a slanted scrawl done with a loaded brush and underscored by a broad black line; at first he thought, with a spasm of something that was almost fright, that the initial was V, but it might as easily have been a U or a W. His nose was almost touching the varnish as he searched for a familiar face among the figures, or a tell-tale quirk of the brush that might reveal the painter's identity, when Madame Verrue, the *Dame de Volupté* herself, came up to him in that languorously suggestive way that she had and took his arm and led him off to talk to some bore about money.

Everyone must have been talking money in those early days of the System. Law's bank had opened on the rue Quincampoix, and cargoes were on their way from the Indies and Africa and China, and suddenly it seemed everyone was rich in paper money. Vaublin, with his peasant's love of substance, preferred gold. He kept it under the floorboards and sewn into the lining of his cloaks. He discovered in himself a distressing inclination towards gambling, though; almost every other night he would find himself seated at cards at the house of the Loyson sisters, watching in a hot sweat, a terrible smile fixed on his face and the air whistling in his papery lungs as the pile of yellow coins at his elbow steadily dwindled. It was an escape from the studio, from the waiting canvas, from that daytime world of meticulous, mad labours. It was risk against caution, abandon against care, chance against rule. Let it go, let it all go; what did he care.

He was thirty-three that year. His health was worse than ever. Someone told him – he would believe anything – that fresh air was debilitating, and for weeks he did not venture out of doors during daylight hours. He was painting pure dreams now, locked in the solitude of his studio. He did not use models, he could not bear the presence of another near him when he worked; it had always filled him with silent fury, the way they sighed and shifted and tried to make idiotic conversation. Now he no longer needed them. When he wanted a face or a gesture he went to his old sketch-books, or cannibalised his finished work from the past. He was not interested in the individual: he would have been content to give the same features to all his figures, it did not matter, a nose, eyes, mouth, all the same. What he was after was something intangible, some simple, essential thing that perhaps was not human at all. He came increasingly to recognise that the centre of a painting, that point of equilibrium from which every element of the composition flows and where at the same time all is somehow ingathered, was never where it seemed it should be. The challenge was to find it and work from there. It could be a patch of sky, the fold of a gown, a dog scratching its ear, anything. He was in a hurry all the time. He had never believed in himself, never thought of what he was doing as art; that was what the masters did, real work, while he played. Now he would leave pieces unfinished, thrust them into a corner face to the wall, disgusted with them, and rush on to new subjects, new scenes. He had a feeling constantly of being hindered; some days he had almost to fight his way to the easel, as if there really were an invisible double there before him, crowding him aside. The light dazzled him, the air rattled like stones in his chest.

He witnessed the deportation of wives for the colonists in Louisiana. Women had been rounded up from the stews and the prisons and given a cotton shift and put on board ship in hundreds at the quayside below his windows. There were riots, all night the sky was red with fires. Next day he began work on the *Embarquement pour l'île d'amour*.

That summer was hot. He went out in the pale nights, mingling with the masked, excited crowds at the public balls in the Palais Royal. He liked crowds, liked the clamour and the crush and the feeling of being in the grip of a vast, shapeless, flowing force. He even enjoyed in his bleak way the breathlessness, the sense of teetering on the very brink of panic and suffocation. He could bear it all only for a little while; often he would end up clinging to a pillar in the tree-scented darkness of the Allée d'Argenson, doubled up and coughing out his life. His friend Madame de Caylus nagged at him to have more care.

Look at you! she would cry, when he came hobbling into one of her soirées at midnight, ashen-faced and panting harshly, look at you, Jean Vaublin, you are killing yourself! And she would take his chill, trembling hands in hers and sit down with him on a divan and smile at him chidingly and peer into his face, until he too smiled despite himself and looked away from her and bit his lip like a little boy scolded by his *maman*. Her sympathy irritated him. Sometimes it frightened him, too. She had a way of turning aside from him and letting her face go hard and blank like the face of one turning aside from a deathbed. She plied him with all sorts of crazy cures; it was ice-cold baths one week and cold compresses the next. He tried them all, of course; they seemed only to make him worse. Once, when she pressed him to let her doctor bleed him – as if he were not bleeding enough already! – he flew into a rage.

There is no help for me! he shouted at her, don't you know that?

The summer ended. Autumn was damp and chill that year, with week-long fogs. His strength was failing. When he stepped to the canvas another, heavier arm seemed to lift alongside his. No help, no help on earth.

L'embarquement

He went to England at the end of 1719. Where did he sail from, where did he land? So many things I do not know about him and never will. That must have been the beginning of his final period of hectic wanderings. He had intended to spend a month in London but stayed for half a year. He saw the celebrated Doctor Mead and allowed himself to believe his lungs could be cured. Mead put him on a regimen of quinine and fresh oxblood and took him to Old Slaughter's in St Martin's Lane where he drank Dutch gin and water and ate a pig's foot boiled in brine.

We must fatten you up, sir, the doctor said, and clapped a big soft hand on his meagre shoulder and laughed in his jolly way.

Vaublin grinned uncontrollably into his glass and blushed; how childish these hearty, capable people made him feel. Will I live, doctor? he asked, direct as ever, and the doctor stared at him in consternation and laughed even louder.

Live, man? he roared. Of course you'll live! But he did not say for how long.

Mead was the author of a scholarly work, *The Influence of the Sun and the Moon on the Human Body*, and bored Vaublin with enthusiastic talk of tides and ecliptics and cosmic harmony.

The moon only reminds me of Pierrot, Vaublin said dreamily – and Pierrot, of course, reminds me of myself. A silence followed and then the doctor cleared his throat and changed the subject.

He was an authority also on poisons.

One bright day in April, when Vaublin had coughed up what seemed to him must be at least a litre of blood, he asked the doctor shyly if he would prepare a fatal draught for him, in concentrated form, so that he could carry it with him for use if life at the last should become unbearable – not worth the candle, he said, smiling wryly, pleased with the English phrase. The doctor refused, of course, and grew quite indignant. Things were never the same between them after that.

In June Vaublin returned to France, sicker now than when he had left. Paris was silent, dazed with the great heat of that summer and the shock of economic collapse: the System had failed, Law's bank was closed, the speculators had been ruined. In July came news of the plague in Marseilles; the city was declared officially dead. Vaublin had thought he would not live to see the decade change, yet here he was, still hanging on while others all around him died. In January his father had succumbed to the purpural fever; in his heart he was glad that man had not outlived him.

Self-portrait

Poor Vaublin at the end dragging himself all over Paris with the angel after him; that was dying, no mistaking it. He was terrified they would bury him before he was absolutely dead, since after all, as he said, he had never been absolutely alive. Wait for the green spot, he urged them, only half in jest, wait for the gangrenous green spot, as they used to do with the ancient kings. And he laughed, on the verge of tears, as he always seemed to be in those last weeks. He experienced strange periods of euphoria standing before that enormous canvas, lost in the picture surface, almost a part of the paint, his hands working faster than his brain could follow. And then the terrible, sweat-soaked nights, and the recurring dream: the figures in the picture coming dazedly to life like the survivors of some huge catastrophe. And in the mornings shivering at the window in the thin dawn-light, amazed it was all still there, large as life, the roofs, the river, the quayside wreathed in mist, all there and not caring anything for him. Paris! he cried, Paris, I'm dying! And wiped his nose on his knuckles. The figure at his back in the corner always now, watching him with quiet interest, waiting.

He had rented a little attic room on the Île in the house of an old Jew who prayed aloud in the night, keening and sighing. In the mornings a girl from the bakery next door brought him bread and apples, a flask of wine, saying nothing, standing big-eyed in the doorway while he delved for pennies in his purse. When she was there he heard his breathing, how bad it was.

What month is it? he asked her one day.

July!

It was hot. He was so tired, so tired. He left the door open and she began to come in, venturing a little farther each day. She stood by the wall with her hands behind her and watched him work. She was so quiet he could forget she was there. She came back in the night and slept with him, held him shaking in her thin, pale arms. When he woke in the mornings she was gone. He put on his smock and walked to the canvas barefoot. It was so much bigger than he. He felt as if he were afloat on some dense, brimming surface. Each brush stroke dragged with a liquid weight. He drifted amongst the figures, bumping softly against this one or that, feeling their insubstantial thereness. Once, working up close against the canvas, he coughed and stippled a patch of sky with blood. He gave Pierrot the girl's face and then painted it over with his own. A self-portrait, the only one he ever did. That night from his pallet, the girl asleep with her bum pressed against his side, he lay and looked at the great pale figure glimmering above him and grinned in the dark. My monster. Me. And then suddenly, without realising it, died.

The author wishes to acknowledge the great catalogue on the life and works of Antoine Watteau, *Watteau: 1684–1721*, by Margaret Morgan Grasselli and Pierre Rosenberg, with the assistance of Nicole Parmantier (National Gallery of Art, Washington, 1984).

Different Ways of Getting Drunk

DAVID BELBIN

THE ROOM IS dark and nearly empty. There's a disco unit set up in a corner but the music coming out is a tape of an old Sister Sledge album. The few women here are brightly dressed. I have on black jeans and a denim jacket covering a tight white shirt. I feel plain. Melanie isn't there yet, so I sit at the bar and order a double vodka with ice. I'm nervous. The drink burns the back of my throat and settles me down. A woman comes over, stands at the bar next to me. She has an earring through her nose and so much black eyeliner I can hardly tell what she really looks like.

'Another?' she asks.

'No. Thanks. I'm waiting for someone.'

'Aren't we all?'

I smile shyly and buy myself a second drink. There's a coat stand and I hang my jacket on it. The room is warmer than it looks.

Black eyeliner leaves and woman in a knitted dress comes up on the other side of me. I don't make eye contact but while the woman's waiting to be served, she slides a cigarette towards me. Rather than shake my head, I leave the bar. I find a seat at an empty table near the door. Somehow I was expecting less obvious pick up gestures, but I was being too optimistic. Or too prissy. You ought to be open about attraction. I hide behind my drink in a corner. I'll be able to see Melanie as soon as she comes in.

The music grows steadily louder. Melanie arrives. She walks straight past me, greets the knitted dress at the bar. It's dark but I can see that Melanie's hair is different from at the office. No, not different. She has on a wig. Blonde. I think she's trying to look like the woman from Eurythmics. Do I fancy her? There are few women who I find arousing and I'm not sure that Melanie is one of them. It's not too late to leave.

But then it is. Melanie's spotted me. She half waves then comes over.

'Alison. I wasn't sure you'd come. Do you need a drink?'

Mine's nearly finished but I shake my head.

'Of course you do. What are you on? Vodka?'

Melanie buys me another double. She sits down, crossing fishnet-stockinged legs. She smiles intently. At work she appears younger than me – twenty-two at most – but here, she's the confident one. I find myself telling Melanie that she looks like Annie Lennox.

'Do you like her?'

'I like dancing to her records. Do you know many people here? Is there a lot of dancing?'

Melanie answers the second question first.

'It varies.'

Then she starts to tell me about some of the other people in the room – a student, a dentist, a Polytechnic lecturer, a hotel receptionist. And us.

Melanie's bought me a drink so of course I have to buy her one and now another double doesn't seem like such a bad idea. I have a warm glow on and most of these people look attractive, friendly: at least they do if I don't look too hard. Anyway, they're more attractive than Brian, who thinks I am out on a 'hen' night. Which, in a way, I am. I tell Melanie some stories about my life. I talk disjointedly at first. I've never been very comfortable talking about myself. But then the booze loosens me up.

I tell Melanie about my father, who I haven't seen for ten years, about the step-brother who I've never met. I tell her about my alcoholic mother who I visit maybe once a year; how she was forced to sell the house and now lives in a complex with a warden and lots of senile old biddies, though she's only fifty-five. And how relieved I was that she got enough money from the house for them to take her in. I was scared that I would end up having to look after her. Now I don't even have to stay overnight when I visit. I don't say that it was Brian who managed all this, not me, because Melanie doesn't know about Brian, doesn't even know that I live with a man.

The music gets louder and it becomes impossible to talk. So we dance. Everybody dances. It's like when I was a girl at school only there are no boys to impress. There are giggles and smiles. The dance floor is small and bodies rub against each other. I've lost count of how many drinks I've had. Sweat drips from Melanie's real hair beneath the blonde wig. On an impulse I reach over and pull the wig off. The music stops.

For a moment I am horrified at what I have done. I have over-stepped some boundary and begin to apologise. But no one is looking, except Melanie. She grins, eyes dilated by booze and poppers. Her short straight hair is scrunched up and darkened by sweat. A slow song begins. Melanie draws me to her and we embrace. Her warm lips meet mine in a kiss so chaste that it reeks of sex. And we dance, cheek to cheek. I have my arm round Melanie's neck. In my hand is her wig, draped over her left shoulder blade like a war trophy. I feel her firm breasts against my flat chest, her thighs grinding against mine. For a moment I entertain a fantasy that I am a man, I'm finding out what it feels like to be a man, holding a woman.

Not that I ever wanted to be a man. Opening my eyes, I watch the other couples dance and think back to teenage discos. Were we all dancing for the boys in those days, or for each other? Were some of us one way even then, or were we all, unknowing, open to everything? Melanie sniffs some more from her small bottle and this time I join her. My heart pounds like an adolescent on her first date.

In the taxi going back to Melanie's flat I tell her that I think maybe I'm bisexual.

'Only straight people are bisexual,' she tells me, as the Asian taxi driver stares discreetly ahead. I am so drunk that I try to kiss her again. Firmly, Melanie fends me off. There are new rules I have to learn.

In bed we go at it like knives. I have heard that sex between women is slow, sensuous, gentle even, but we are too drunk for subtlety. Melanie does me with her hand and her tongue. When I falter she tells me what to do to her. Later, we lie there in the dark, holding each other and, just like with a man, this is the best part. Only, unlike most men I've been with, Melanie doesn't immediately fall asleep.

'You have to go, lover,' she tells me at three in the morning. I nod. I've been dozing. Somehow I expected to stay all night. But tomorrow is a working day. It's hard to sleep soundly in a three-quarter bed with a new partner.

Only when I'm in the taxi do I remember Brian. My drunkenness has gone now, and the afterglow of sex is fading. I feel like a teenager again, sneaking home late after a party. I hope that Brian is fast asleep, won't notice the time when I come in. Really I know that he will be worried and angry, in almost equal measures. I get out of the car. The living-room light is on.

Brian has been drinking too.

'Where've you been, for Christ's sake?'

'We went to a club. I lost track of time.'

'The clubs close at two. It's nearly four!'

'I had to queue for a taxi.'

'Nobody queues for an hour and a half on a Wednesday.'

I match aggression with aggression. We argue. He storms off to bed. I stay in the living room, have another drink, as if that will cure my growing headache. After a while, Brian comes down, apologises. We make up, after a fashion, go to bed. There, Brian tries to have sex with me. I rebuff him, say I'm tired.

'I thought you were with another man,' he confesses in a whisper.

'No,' I tell him. 'Not that.'

Fitfully, we sleep. In the morning he gets up very quietly, goes to work. Without being asked, he calls in sick for me. I don't get up until noon.

I don't go into work on Friday, either. I have this theory that it is more convincing to take two days off than one – people assume that you must really have been sick, especially when there's a weekend in between for you to make a full recovery. On Friday afternoon, Brian rings – a friend has a spare ticket for a concert that night – Eric Clapton at the NEC. Do I mind if he goes? I don't mind. I tell him that I will visit a friend. We may go to a film. I offer him a deal. I won't wait up for him and he won't wait up for me. Laughing, Brian agrees. He thinks that Wednesday was an aberration.

I expect Melanie to be in the pub, to be teased about my skiving. But she isn't. I will have to talk to someone, to dance. Bravely, I sit at the bar. When someone slides a cigarette towards me I turn with a smile, roll it back.

'I don't smoke.'

It's the woman from the other night, only this time she isn't wearing a knitted dress, she has on jeans and a t-shirt. I see she has a figure much like mine – scrawny – only taller. I haven't worked out yet what kind of woman excites me most. I figure I owe it to myself to experiment. We smile at each other.

'Can I buy you a drink?' I ask, confident of the answer.

In bed, later, Paula gets too rough for me, produces toys which don't turn me on. This time, it's she who wants a partner for the whole night, but I tell her I have someone waiting at home. She smirks, a nasty leer in her eyes.

'Don't forget to put your wedding ring back on, dear,' she tells me. I am not as drunk as I was the other night. Very drunk, yes, but not so drunk that I realise I didn't like Paula – she was small-minded and hard, a pick up artist. The excitement of being with her wore off quickly. I've had better sex with Brian.

Once more the living-room light is on. Brian has not kept his promise not to wait up. I brace myself for a conflict. He stands when I walk into the living room.

'Let me get you a drink.'

'I don't need one.'

But he's pouring already. A large vodka. He hands it to me.

'Your mother . . .'

I stare. His eyes meet mine.

'She fell.'

I drink. My mind swims. Brian takes my hand.

'She hit her head. They took her to hospital but she died an hour ago.'

'Drunk,' I mutter, to myself, not to Brian.

'Yes,' he says.

The warden told us there was no point in our coming before the funeral on Tuesday. Mum disposed of most of her stuff when she moved into the flat. I can take what I want and they'll sell the rest for me. I haven't been back to work, and Brian has taken two days off so that he can come with me. He says he feels guilty that he can't drive. I say don't be stupid. Anyway, driving keeps my mind off it.

This is true to some extent, but once we hit the motorway I do a steady seventy in the middle lane and my mind is free to wander. It occurs to me that this is the last time I will make this journey – this once a year pilgrimage to a place I never thought of as home, a place I only lived in for two unhappy years. It is also the last big journey I will make with Brian. He's been so supportive over the last few days, I feel guilty about leaving him. But I'm going to anyway.

Brian is solid and dull but he isn't straight. He might toler-ate me having relationships with women on the side. But I couldn't. I've been sleeping with men for seven years and I want a rest from them. What Brian offered me was security, but security gets boring after a while.

'I was thinking,' Brian says.

'What?'

'After we've got through this, maybe . . .'

I stare at the road straight ahead. Huge grey lorries swerve in and out between each other, dominating the road, forcing me to move into the fast lane, even though I don't want to.

'What?'

'Maybe I should wait until after the funeral.'

I keep my foot on the accelerator. The speedometer registers eighty, ninety. Now I'm leaving the cars in the middle lane behind.

'Alison, you're going really fast.'

The car begins to judder. I put my foot on the brake and, behind me, a large black car switches on its lights, nearly rams me in the back. But the middle lane is crowded. I can't get back in.

We go on like this for what seems an eternity, but is probably only a couple of minutes. At last I find a small gap, signal, then swerve back in to the middle lane. As I do so, the black car speeds past me. I slow down to sixty-five. When I look again the black car has vanished in the distance. I realise that my back is covered in sweat.

'There's a services coming up,' Brian tells me.

Over coffee and a stodgy Danish pastry, Brian asks me to marry him. This doesn't come as a surprise, quite. He's asked me twice before, but both times he was drunk. Essentially, Brian is an old hippy, a seventies person – he believes that living together is more ideologically sound than marriage – but today he is feeling sentimental.

'I don't want to get married,' I tell him. 'I don't even know if I want to stay with you.'

This is called letting him down softly, but Brian looks crestfallen. He stares into his coffee for a while, then asks, 'Is there somebody else?'

I shake my head. 'This is bad timing, Brian. Mum dying and all . . .'

He nods. 'I'm being insensitive. I'm sorry.'

We sit in silence. I feel horrible, exploiting Mum's death

like that, but it was the easiest thing to do and, like most people, I nearly always do the easiest thing.

We continue the drive in silence. I think about who's going to be at the funeral. Mum hardly had any friends. There were the men she had affairs with, but they were married. They wouldn't show up in public. Since she hit fifty her looks went and, as far as I can tell, she had no new boyfriends, unless there was someone from the OAPs in her complex.

There's Dad. He might come. But would the warden have called him? I certainly didn't. I wouldn't know where to find the bastard. It occurs to me that Brian and I might be the only mourners. And Brian hardly knew her. He wanted to come with me when I visited last year but I wouldn't let him. I didn't want him to get that close.

In the end, there's four of us: me, Brian, the warden, and Mrs Hebden, who used to be our next door neighbour when we lived on Beacon Hill.

'She was given a merciful release,' the Warden tells me. 'You know she had cirrhosis of the liver?'

I nod, though I didn't. I'm not surprised. I don't ask, but the Warden tells me exactly how she died. Mum was drunk. She tripped. She banged her head. I stop her there. That's all I need to know.

The service passes quickly. Afterwards, I politely refuse the remains. Brian suggests that we sprinkle her on the fields around the memorial gardens. This is in order. He pays for everything with his credit card. Then, when we have to go back to the flat, he says do I mind if he stays around here? It's a nice day. He wants to walk around for a while. I can hardly refuse, though there are much better places to walk nearby: the sea, for instance. I say I'll come look for him when we're through.

'We cleaned the flat up,' the Warden explains needlessly.

The Warden is a tight-faced, small woman, always very tense. I know that Mum hated her, and would have hated what she's done to the flat now. The place never looked this antiseptic during the two years Mum lived here. Her things are still present, but she is long gone. Yet what did I want?

The smell? The booze spilled on the floor? The blood still spattered across the cabinet she banged her head on?

'Will you take anything?' the Warden asks me.

There is an old photograph on the cabinet. I pick up the frame and slide it out. I am aged three, sitting in a toy car on the paving stone path of our stubbly back garden. I have one hand on the wheel and another over the side. My hair has a lopsided fringe and the car has 'Thunderbolt' written along the side. The expression on my face is odd. I might be happy, or I might be squinting at the sun.

'That's all?'

I look around. My mother didn't keep family albums. She had poor taste in almost everything. The room's few chintzy ornaments are souvenirs of holidays in tourist traps. The only thing here I might have use for is the booze, but even there our tastes were miles apart.

'There might be some financial papers . . .'

'You may remember that our accountant took care of all that . . .'

I remember. Brian sorted it out, one accountant to another, by post.

'He asked me to give you this.'

She hands me an envelope. Quick work, but then I suppose this happens all the time in a place like this. I open the envelope. The letter tells me how much my mother has left me. It's a lot. Enough for me to buy a house and have some left over. I wonder if Brian knew this when he asked me to marry him, knew that I was about to become a woman of independent means.

'Is everything all right?'

The Warden has her hand on my shoulder. Is everything all right? My mother has left me not love, but money. She's given me something I never got from her when she was alive: security. I nod my head. I don't cry.

Brian is wandering in the fields near the Garden of Rest. He is stooped over and has an old carrier bag in one hand. Every few seconds he leans down, picks something up from the grass. I walk over and join him.

'Magic mushrooms,' he tells me. 'The field's full of them.' He smiles, like a boy with a new train set. 'I haven't had any for years. Help me pick them.'

I do as I'm told. Brian's right. The field's full of mushrooms, tiny white liberty caps with a small nipple on top and a black underside. If the underside's white they're the wrong mushroom, Brian explains. Picking them is relaxing. It clears my head. Brian warns me not to eat any. I won't be able to drive. The thought hadn't crossed my mind.

On the drive back he tells me how he used to do mushrooms all the time in the seventies.

'They were like a revelation. Stronger than dope, milder than acid. Organic and free. You ought to try them.'

I'm sceptical. But finding the mushrooms has cheered Brian up and I go along with the idea. He seems so cheerful I think maybe he's taken a few, but I don't ask. As always, the drive back from West Kirby passes quickly, blessed with a sense of relief and release.

Back home, we empty the plastic bag. There must be four or five hundred mushrooms. They're starting to turn dark and slimy. We wash and separate them. Brian clears out the airing cupboard. Then we put the mushrooms on double sheets of newspaper to dry.

'These'll last me ages,' he says. 'But we must have some while they're fresh. They lose half their strength when they're dried.'

I'm not bothered but Brian lulls me into it. Neither of us is going into work the next day – we're still supposed to be in West Kirby.

'Just a few,' Brian says. 'You'll like it.'

I take ten. Then, seeing Brian take twice as many, I eat three more of the little scrawny ones that hardly seemed worth drying. Then we have a cup of tea and wait to see what happens.

I'm not into drugs. I see them as different ways of getting drunk. Why break the law when alcohol is so cheap? The idea of taking acid scares me – I might lose control. But I figure something that grows in a field by a cemetery can't be too dangerous. When the first rush comes, I'm not ready for it. My head feels light. Colours become brighter. It's like there's a wide angle lens between me and the world. Straight lines curve. I can see the dust on the lens, the grain in the glass.

Then my head starts to bubble. I turn to Brian. He's sitting there, watching the nine o'clock news.

'I am scared,' I tell him.

He switches off the TV and turns to me.

'Relax and go with it,' he tells me.

Brian puts on a record – soothing ambient noises. I hear wind, seagulls, the tide coming in.

'We shouldn't have taken them so late. I'm tired. I'm going to be ill,' I moan.

'No you're not.'

Brian puts an arm round me. The bubbles seem to be going through my body now, only they're not so much like bubbles, they're more like warm waves.

'I feel like a human jacuzzi,' I tell Brian.

He laughs.

'That's good.' He keeps laughing. 'That's very funny.'

I start laughing too. We're both laughing. We slide off the sofa and start to roll about on the floor, laughing even more. The lens in my head has become a distorting mirror. Everything looks unreal, and very funny. The laughter fills my body. Brian and I roll about on the floor like tiny children. We're giggling at the very thought of being alive. And my body does feel alive. My head is full of tiny explosions, like the best kind of orgasm, but going on and on and on and on.

The doorbell rings. Brian and I keep laughing.

'Maybe it's the police,' I say.

This makes Brian laugh even harder.

'There's nothing they can do,' he says. 'It's not even illegal.'

The doorbell rings again. Reluctantly, Brian gets up to answer it. I huddle up against the sofa. It will be impossible for me to pretend that I am straight. But then I recognise the voice.

'Does Alison live here?'

Melanie. Brian mumbles something and Melanie is in through the door. She speaks in a rush.

'I hope you don't mind. I got your address from Personnel. I was worried when you didn't show up. It's been nearly a week. I thought maybe I'd . . .'

She looks at Brian, unsure of the relationship. Distorting mirror and all, I can see that his eyes are very dilated. So mine must be too. But Brian is putting on a sober, accountant's face.

'Her mother died,' he explains. 'It was very sudden.'

Melanie misses the dilated eyes, focuses on the tragedy. She comes over to me.

'I'm so sorry,' she tells me. 'If there's anything . . .'

I manage to mumble 'thanks' before I totally lose it and burst into another fit of giggles. This sets Brian off too. He's leaning against the wall letting out these huge guffaws while I am sitting on the floor with Melanie's arms around me, laughing so hard I begin to cry.

Melanie handles all this well. She thinks that it is cathartic, that Brian and I are very upset. She strokes my hair and keeps saying 'It's OK. It's OK.' Brian stops laughing first. The record finishes. I go quiet too. Melanie takes out a tissue and wipes my eyes. She looks very beautiful.

'Thank you,' I say. 'Would you like some mushrooms?'

Later: Melanie and I are in bed, making love very, very slowly. Each tiny caress sends a shiver down my spine. Each kiss moves mountains. In a corner of the bedroom, Brian is watching, a smile on his face. Later, we discover that he is fast asleep. We make love until dawn then sleep until dark.

Or: Melanie leaves and it is Brian and I who are in bed. Again, we make love very, very slowly. The mushrooms wear off but we are still wrapped around each other, tongues and fingers exploring each other. Do I pretend that he is Melanie? No. I don't care what sex he is. Tonight, all I care about is the moment, the sensation, not where it comes from.

When I wake it is nearly dark and I am alone. I don't

remember who I slept with or even what day of the week it is. There's a note from Brian on the dresser. It says 'I've taken a week's holiday. I figure you need some time for yourself. If you're still here when I get back, we'll pick it up from there. I love you. B.'

I have a bath. I know where I will go tonight, and the next night, and maybe the night after that, too. There are four hundred mushrooms in the airing cupboard and there is a cheque on the way. None of this is enough, I know, to make me happy, or fulfilled, or all of the things I've spent the last twenty-seven years trying to find. But it's enough to be going on with. More than enough. More. More. More.

West Wirral Story

MICHAEL CARSON

'*TE ADORO*, ANTON . . .' Mum says.

'*Te adoro*, Maria . . .' I reply automatically, changing to fourth.

'You should have changed the needle oftener . . .' Mum stops, forgetting. I can almost hear the crunch as her brain crashes gears.

'You know Mr Bernstein modelled *West Side Story* on *Romeo and Juliet*, don't you?'

'Yes,' I reply. I ought to.

But she hasn't heard me. She is tuning out the shipping forecast on the radio, watching Wirral pass by flatly, humming 'The Jet Song'.

Then, quite suddenly, she's back. 'If you'd changed the needle oftener I'd still have my *West Side Story* now. It was the first LP your dad bought me to go with the radiogram.' Mum gazes out at the view questioningly. 'We nearly there yet?'

'This is Thornton Hough,' I say.

'Is it?'

'You know it is. You always had a soft spot for Thornton Hough. Your Auntie Dot lived here. The one with the moustache who gave me sloppy kisses.'

Mum nods. 'Daft name, Dot, when you think about it. It was a crime the way that LP deteriorated. It got to the stage where "I Feel Pretty" was unplayable. If you'd changed the needle . . .'

'Come on, Mum! You wore it out.' Like she's worn me out. 'A record can only play so many times, you know. It's got a life span like everything else.'

'Three score years and ten. Well, I've knocked that into a bowl of cherries, haven't I? How much farther?'

'It'll be another fifteen minutes I should think, Mum.'

'Fifteen minutes,' she says. 'That's about what you get on an EP. Have you seen my *Porgy and Bess*? It had Sidney Poitier on the outside. I can't get enough of Sidney Poitier. A pity Mr Bernstein didn't write something for Sidney . . .'

'It's probably in the airing-cupboard. With the Christmas tree.'

'What is? I've kept all your nappies in the airing-cupboard. If you hadn't done what you did, they'd have come in useful.'

Mum seizes her bag, looks at it intently as if it is a strange object that has dropped from the sky on to her lap. She thinks for a moment, then snaps the bag open and delves inside. I can smell rouge, Yardley and old pennies. She takes out a hankie and dabs her nose with it.

'Mum . . .'

'What?'

'You don't have to go, you know. We can turn back and tell them you've changed your mind.'

She snaps the bag shut; then, remembering she's forgotten to put the hankie away – then forgetting that too – she looks at the handkerchief. The sight seems to startle her.

'I said . . .' I begin, wondering how I'll feel if she's changed her mind.

'I know what you said. How much farther?'

'Another ten minutes.'

'Doesn't time fly?' she says. There is contentment in her voice. She has found the bag again, opened it, put the hankie in, snapped it shut. She holds it by the top with both hands.

All is right with the world. She smiles out at it serenely. 'Time. Goes like the clappers!'

The time signal for two o'clock sounds.

'They never used to make one of the boops louder than the others,' Mum says. 'It used to go *boop boop boop boop boop boop*. Life was simple then. You knew where you were. Now it's *boop boop boop boop boop BOOOOP*. I don't call that progress even if you do.'

'The longer boop tells you the exact moment that the clock clicks to the hour,' I say.

'Gee, Officer Krupke!'

I start to reply but she stops me. She wants to listen to the News. I am stuck at a Halt sign, waiting for a gap in the traffic. Behind me a driver keeps rocking his car towards my bumper, pushing me to take risks. I resist him, waiting for a break that does not come.

'Nothing about Mr Bernstein. I won't forget him even if they do,' Mum says as the News gives way to a play and I nose out on to the Chester Road.

There was a time when I would have argued with her faulty reasoning, nudged her back to sense as we used to nudge the pick up of *West Side Story*. But I gave up. Now I wonder if I had kept at her we might have made it through to the end and not be on this journey now.

'There's no real news these days,' Mum says. 'You probably don't remember how Tony met Maria. You see, Tony was convinced something was coming and he went with Riff to the dance at the gym. Maria went with Anita. The gym was neutral territory. Tony was a nice boy. He didn't want the rumble. He was good to his old mum.' She looks round anxiously. 'We nearly there?'

'Five minutes,' I say.

'If only Tony had met Maria and whisked her off straight away. They have all-night vicars in New York, you know.'

'How do you mean?'

'They should have married. Like you should have. If you ask me, it was all that serenading on the fire-escape and the dirty bit that did for Tony. He was weak-willed and easily led. Like someone else I could mention.'

I am silent. I don't want Mum to start on that again. I just do not understand how she can remember *that* and forget her address. Still, life's full of mystery . . .

'Anita and Riff should have helped them when they saw the lie of the land. Your dad and I . . . me and your dad . . .'

'Mum . . .'

'Are we there?' she asks.

'I think I'm lost.'

'It's nice round here,' she says. 'I don't know why me and your dad didn't move out to here when we had the chance. Wallasey's gone down the nick since Tony died. *New York! New York's a hell of a town! The Bronx is up and* . . . Maria's old flame shot him under the motorway.'

I am a rudderless boat adrift on Mum's meanders. The needle in her brain skips, can no longer decode. I keep telling myself that this is not her. But is that right? Perhaps this is really her and everything before was merely concealment. She had always liked Tony, seemed devastated when we broke up and I came back to Wallasey to lick my wounds.

'I know I'm being an imp but you know what I'd really like?' she says.

'What?'

'An ice-cream at Parkgate.'

'It's out of our way.'

'Shh!' she commands, the ice-cream having melted out of her mind. 'It's the play.'

I gladly give up on conversation and let her listen in. I've told the matron we'll be there by two, yet here we are heading into Chester. I've missed the turn-off somewhere.

Mum is excited by the play and adds her opinion on the action. She doesn't like the young American girl who has fallen for a Russian Orthodox seminarian and is confiding to the radio audience that she intends to seduce him.

'Hussy!' Mum calls out. 'Leave him alone! He's promised to Maria! You're all Anybody's these days!'

The seminarian prays for strength. 'That's it, dear!' she

tells him. 'Fight the good fight! Don't give in to that Yank floozie! Keep the faith!'

I have always loved the way she talks back to the radio. I'll miss that. In an hour I'll be driving in an empty car to an empty house.

'Not there yet?' she asks, during a lull in the proceedings. I let my irritation show. 'I'm not niffy, am I? You must tell me if I'm niffy.'

'No, Mum. You're sweet as a nut,' I say.

'I wasn't yesterday, though.'

'No. But you are today.'

' "Sweet as a nut." That's what Butcher Hawkins said about the turkey, wasn't it?'

We both remember that, and laugh. 'At least he had the decency to give us a fresh one,' I say.

'He gave us his. Said he was going to eat that niffy one. Bet he didn't! Remember the pong? God knows how he had the gall. It was probably his stint as mayor of the county borough. It made him cocky. His mince went downhill too after his stint as mayor.'

'It went to his head,' I say. 'Did I tell you that I always took a detour behind his shop after that? I just couldn't face him and his grinning butcher boys.'

'They used to wolf-whistle at you. They provoked you like the Jets provoked Anita.' She cackles and coughs.

'Yes, they did.'

'And you liked it.'

'I did not.'

She looks around. 'Where are we?'

'I don't know.' I do.

'You're taking me to the Home, aren't you?'

We've been through all this before. 'It's you who wanted to go to the Home. "Ring the Home!" you said.'

Mum opens her bag and takes out the hankie again. She dabs her eyes. I glance over and miss a turning that may have been the one we want.

'I only wanted to go because I was niffy. But now you're telling me I'm not niffy. Sweet as a nut, you said.'

'So would you rather we went back home?' I try to speak in a neutral way, not taking sides. Which side am I on? Wouldn't it be wonderful to park the car and enter the house knowing that I will be alone there?

'Did I ever tell you that I did the dusting to "I Want to Be in America." As soon as you were up the road with your satchel out it'd come and on it'd go. Lord, I felt pretty! I . . .' Her voice trails off.

There is a P for Parking sign at the side of the road. I pull over.

'Look, Mum,' I say. 'Do you want to go to the Home or don't you? It's all the same to me.'

'When you talk like that you sound just like you did that time you came home in a mess. Me and your dad just couldn't do anything right . . . I don't know what Tony would have said. I really don't.'

I've had enough. 'Stop it, Mum! You just can't forget it, can you? I had my abortion around the time we put *West Side Story* out for the bin-men. My Tony was over the hills and far away. Now will you try to forget it like you forget everything else?'

'You shouldn't have, you know. He'd have been company for you now. *Womb to Tomb . . . Birth to Earth . . .*'

'Yes . . . well . . .' I say, going all weepy. She can still make me do that.

'Don't create!' she says. 'Worse things happen at sea!'

I tell her that that's as maybe but she's got to make up her mind. We're already late.

'Remember Mr Bernstein's *Kaddish Symphony*? It's dead cheeky to God. Still, I think He deserves it what with one thing and another . . . Fancy Him giving me a daughter who can't be bothered to change the needle and ruins my favourite.'

'Mum . . .'

Now *she* is weeping. 'There's no place for me. Niffy or not niffy, it's all the same to you. If this was Holland you'd tell me I've had enough, stick a needle in me, say bye-bye Mum – weeping big tears – and go and have a party. Well, I haven't had enough. I want to see what's going to happen! I want to see the end!'

I put my arm around her shoulder and squeeze her lightly. I can feel her bones, feel her in my bones. Too much pressure and she'll break. 'I want you to be happy, Mum. Really I do.'

'One hand, one heart,' she says. 'What I can't forgive is you buying me the film version. They all mimed, you know, AND they missed out the ballet section for "Somewhere".'

'At least I got you another copy.'

'I suppose so. But I loved the old one. Maria was running down the street on the cover in that lovely frock with Tony trying to keep up. There were bins in the street! How I danced! Oh, you never knew how I danced!'

It's no good. I can't do it. I suspect there will be a time for me to live – and dance – alone. 'Let's go home,' I say. 'I'll ring the matron and tell her we've changed our mind.'

On the way we call in for an ice-cream at Parkgate. Mum sits on the bench with her cone, looking out across the Dee estuary to Wales. The wind blows wisps of thin hair across her face.

'Could be,' she says. 'Who knows? There's something due any day, something good . . .'

She looks at me, tears in her eyes.

'*Te adoro*, Maria,' I say.

'*Te adoro*, Anton,' Mum replies.

Switchback

RONALD FRAME

ALDERS. BIRCHES. LINDENS.

Yes, I'm back.

The trees of France weren't the same. I couldn't smell this land from there.

Ahead of me is the border, or where the border used to be, because it hardly matters now. In twenty years so much has changed. Imagine this place becoming what it *has*, a hotel. The staff don't show any memories on their faces of what it used to be; they must have heard rumours, surely.

In the magazine kiosk I bought a copy of *Jours de France*. In a six-page colour spread there is Zinaida, there is my wife. Photographed, it says, in a suite at the Raphael. In a tight, short skirt and pencil heels. The new film she's in is top box-office in Paris.

Even here, there's an in-house video film system. At two a.m. they're showing *Switchback*, which was Zinaida's third or fourth. Ballatoire took us up about that time, and we cruised the Mediterranean twice on his yacht, and he offered me a job on one of his Paris newspapers. 'Carte blanche,' he said, 'write whatever you like.' It was too much freedom, being able to dip my pen in vitriol, as it were. All the time it was Zinaida he was interested in. Calls would reach the yacht

or his chateau, for Zinaida, from men as fat as Ballatoire up
in their Bel Air palaces. Zinaida laughed, as if she didn't
believe it, any of it, but she was acquiring a permanent all-
over body tan and she knew, behind the ultra-violet protection creams and the toothpaste-ad wide smiles that showed
off her new caps, she knew that you never let a chance go.
She told me all this was as much for *my* benefit as hers, so
that I could have my mouthpiece – the weekly newspaper
column and its syndications.

Merde, Zinaida.

But I couldn't afford to stop loving you. Only *you* could
help me when I woke up in the night with those dreams.

In the dreams we're crawling on our bellies, both of us,
through scrub and a thorn thicket, in pitch darkness. We
have mud in our mouths, worms wriggle on the backs of our
hands. We're making for the border. It's only twenty metres
away. Then ten. Five. And always – always – at the very last
second the arc-lights are switched on from somewhere above
us, it's brighter than daylight, and suddenly the machine-
guns start up, strafing us.

Beside me in bed, leaning over me, Zinaida pretends not to
understand what's going on inside my head.

'We're safe, Yura,' she says. 'See? It didn't happen like
that. We got away. We're here, we're safe.'

We did get away, across the border, and that was just a
night dream, but I have only her word that we're safe. She
told me over the phone, three weeks ago when I called her on
the Hollywood set in the middle of my Paris night, 'I'm
between takes right now, darling,' She has never called me
'darling', never. For something to say, I told her I was going
back on a visit. Back east. She hesitated; I heard her intake of
breath, from five, six thousand miles away. 'You *are*, Yura?
Back there? Why?'

No reason. Well, every reason. I don't know. Because it's
home, and it always will be. Because I wanted to see the trees
again – birches, alders, lindens – and to smell them. Because
there are no trees quite like them in France. Because I couldn't

believe I might simply book a trip and fly back with a passport.

Maybe there are alders and birches in the United States? Say, in New England? Say, in Virginia? I've heard our captor Livotsky is now lecturing at Richmond for big bucks, on the techniques of state policing that he once practised: he got out just before the regime fell, but he was the cleverest bastard all round. The day they brought us here, Zinaida and me – to this secret internment centre in the woods – I noticed our inquisitor Livotsky was wearing Gucci soft-kid moccasins. I was still in prison clothes, but Zinaida had got her own ones back, because she has always known exactly which strings to pull.

For three days Livotsky put us through it, but separately. He pumped me for everything I could possibly know, about how the students organised themselves, about my fellow journalists, about Zinaida's acting acquaintances. He even asked me why we married, and he smiled slyly when I said I loved her, as I did. He grilled me of course about Solomov, and why Zinaida had given him up – I heard the insinuation in his tone of voice – exchanged such a gifted poet for a mere journalist such as myself. Eventually I couldn't tell what was true in my answers and what I was inventing. And then, at the end of it, miraculously, Livotsky threw open the shutters of the darkened room. There outside was brilliant sunshine. I blinked and blinked at it. The forest was quivering. All the beautiful autumn colours. 'You're free,' he said. 'Both of you. You can go over now.'

He meant it. We had just the clothes we were wearing, and the breath in our bodies. 'You'll be met,' he said. 'On the border. Go now.'

We have to walk through the forest. As we make our way under the sun I'm remembering every childhood nightmare from the Brothers Grimm. I grab Zinaida's hand. I want to run for it. But she's cool, collected. 'We're taking our time, Yura.' I think I'm going to lose my mind as the barbed wire fences loom. We're never going to get there, to the hole we've been told has been cut for us. It must be a trick. I stumble. Zinaida picks me up. She's strength personified. I realise for the first time, today she's wearing lipstick. I can't get that fact out of my mind. I'm waiting to die, for the concealed guns to start firing. But the sun shines down benignly. The voices we can hear from the other side are friendly. Zinaida's scarlet lips smile. Can any of this be happening?

The nightmares only started three years later, when Zinaida was already famous and I had acquired my own (lesser) measure of fame too, writing my first columns for Ballatoire. There was a rumour that they were going to let Solomov out. The PEN organisation was leading the clamour for his release. They asked me to speak at a news conference in Zurich, where the arms talks were taking place. For days, while Zinaida was off filming in Morocco, I agonised about what to do. In Paris I'd recently been seeing Solomov's books in the shops, I would look at the face on the covers and think of those sixteen months when he and Zinaida had been lovers before she suddenly left him and switched to me. In Zurich meanwhile the PEN people kept coming back to me. In the background an exposé journalist from Munich called Kruger was prowling about. One night I slept with a tart, and couldn't make it and knocked her about a bit, and the next day I saw her spilling the beans to Kruger in a café. I knew then I wasn't able to speak at the press call, I wouldn't be supporting Solomov's cause.

After that, I don't know what happened. Solomov didn't come out after all and continued with his 'psychiatric treatment'. I started to lose my touch, in my work I just couldn't get a focus on the old life; my articles meandered, they lost the thread, pussy-footed about the big moral points. Simultaneously newspaper stories appeared carping about the lifestyle Zinaida's film success was bringing us: Ballatoire responded in his own press by puffing up Zinaida, and she was so busy I seldom got a chance to see her. (Now after his death they're saying Ballatoire was a CIA agent, and I'm beginning to lose my way in yet another fairy-tale . . .) I only wanted to be able to write how I used to – earnestly, honestly – but my fingers were stiff on the typewriter keys, they faltered above the letters, the words came out spelt wrongly and not in their proper order. I even felt I was losing my grip on the language, not French but the other one I had continued to think and feel in. I went for longer and longer walks about Paris, along the boulevards and through the parks. I looked to find an alder or birch or linden, a single one, but all the city could offer were plane trees and horse chestnuts.

When Solomov was released at last, for several weeks the Left Bank bookshop windows were filled with books and posters. The fuss died down eventually. He went to Israel, and now he's lecturing in the States, at Princeton and Berkeley, California. Everything's happening in the States, that's where it's at, these days it's like an exiles' club.

There are Yankee voices *here* among the tourists in the hotel, complaining about faulty plumbing and air-conditioning, and room bars that aren't refrigerated enough. I could maybe write this place up for an airline magazine. Forget the building's sinister past and describe the reincarnated hotel version – the locale – the lakes. And the trees, of course. Find words to evoke how the wind runs through them, rattling the leaves, making them rasp. I have to concentrate now on something so simple, so little. The big matters in life can't be understood, but they come and they go, and only the simple and little things are left and endure, like the trees and the sighing of the wind.

Meanwhile Zinaida watches me from the pages of *Jours de France*. Ensconced in luxury, in her gilded Proustian surroundings. Proust floated in a pool of memory, but without his instinctive sense of balance and grace there's a terrible risk – for someone like me – of going under and drowning.

Zinaida's eyes are grey like the Baltic. She had visited the Baltic, she used to tell me. She had visited everywhere, it seemed, presumably sweet-talking travel permits out of those intimate friends in high-places she very vaguely referred to, in the University and in the theatre, but maybe in the police too. How was it that Livotsky knew to give her a packet of her favourite Egyptian cigarettes that last morning, when he clattered the shutters back and opened the windows on the sunlit forest of birdsong? He tossed her the carton, as he'd thrown me mine, of a regular sawdusty sort. I fumbled and dropped my packet: Zinaida, though, she caught hers. He held out a lit match and she leaned forward, cradling her hand to take the flame. It was as if she understood what I then could not, that this also was a theatrical show, *son et lumière*, a chiaroscuro game of clever illusions.

The grey eyes still tell me nothing. She has secrets, she must do, but she won't impart to me what they are. That's the point about secrets. She knows so much – about me, but now I don't count, if I ever really have. She has learned many things about Ballatoire, as she learned so many about the officials she charmed in our old life, and all she has needed to do down the years is name her price.

They're showing her first hit film *Switchback* on the in-house video system tonight. I might watch, or I might not.

I pick up some fallen linden leaves from the cinder path. They are shaped like hearts on a playing card. I shall concentrate on these. It's an easier game than people, than love and hate or indifference. I listen to my slow footsteps on the red cinders and start to count the trees.

Bevis

JANE GARDAM

MY COUSIN, JILLY Willis, a huge, leonine girl of nearly eighteen, arrived in the County Durham town where I had lived since I was born, with her mother, my Auntie Greta, and there was obviously something awful going on.

I knew it as soon as I stepped into the house from school. Something steamy. My mother stuck her head round the front-room door and said, 'Tea in the kitchen. Can't come now.' This was unheard of.

My Ma and Auntie Greta stayed shut in there together for hours. Jilly was not there. She must have been left behind at the boarding house where they'd taken rooms. I sat in the kitchen eating dried-up baked beans. I could half-hear their voices. On and on. Ma's brother, Auntie Greta's husband Uncle Alec, had died two years before. He'd been an optician and worked over towards Northumberland where he'd met and married Auntie Greta and never once come back to see us. He had been a blameless man and when we at last met Auntie Greta, we were silenced. At every meeting afterwards with her, we were silenced with renewed surprise. She was a fierce raw-boned woman who never met your eyes, and always smiled. My mother could not speak of her, for she had come between her and her brother like a rough red wall.

Auntie Greta Willis and Jilly stayed on in our town after the day of the secret conversation and bought a little house over the sand-hills that turned its back on everybody. They appeared to settle, and the following term Jilly started at my school. They hadn't sold their house in Northumberland because they'd left Auntie Greta's old mother in it. There seemed to be no shortage of money. Jilly was nearly six years older than I was and so at school I scarcely saw her. She was very clever. She had already been accepted on the strength of her A-level examinations by the University of Edinburgh where she was to start next year in the Science faculty, and intended to become a vet. This last year at school was to fill in time and she had decided to do an extra A-Level in European History – 'To restore the balance,' my mother said. 'She won't do a year in Europe itself, like anyone else – they can't get her to shift.'

And I scarcely saw Jilly out of school either, though I think she came over to us with her mother sometimes for Sunday dinner. I sort of remember them being invited and all the rushing around to be ready for them after church. My mother and I were church-goers as Uncle Alec had been. He had been a great Christian and sung in his church choir – ethereal Uncle Alec in his nervous metal specs. I don't suppose Jilly and her mother ever went to church with him. (My mother said, 'Ah – Jilly is a pagan lady.') I don't think that Auntie Greta ever went anywhere with him. When Uncle Alec died she wrote us a note well after the funeral and my Ma wept for her brother as much as she had wept for her father. She said, 'Alec died of loneliness.'

'Why've they come here, Ma?'

'There's been a scandal.'

'What scandal?'

'I've sworn never to say.'

'Not even to me?'

'No. She made me promise that. Greta did. I'm very sorry.'

'Why did she?'

'Because you're only twelve.'

'Was it some sort of crime?'

'Not exactly.'

'I know. Jilly's been caught shop-lifting.'

'No. Of course not.'

'People do when they're unhappy.'

'Rubbish,' said my mother. 'You didn't go shop-lifting when your father died.'

When Jilly and her Ma had been living near us for about six months, the abandoned grandmother fell ill and had to be put in a Home and while all this was being arranged by Auntie Willis, Jilly came to stay with us. She seemed very big. When the three of us sat down to meals in our tiny dining-room she filled it like a doll in a box. Yet she was in no way gross, or out of proportion there. All she did was make us feel under-housed. She needed marble halls. She was a foreign body.

'One day,' my mother said, 'you'll be a magnificent Roman matron and you'll wear clothes that hang from the shoulder fastened by a barbaric clip.' Jilly looked startled, rather as if she had known this herself and had been keeping it private. My mother could often say things like this. Jilly looked sharp at my Ma, and blushed. She loved it. All of a sudden she was younger and sillier and began to go floating along to the bathroom at bedtime wrapped in a counterpane tied in a shoulder-knot, tossing her mane. 'Coliseo!' she cried, and my Ma cried, 'Imperatrix.' The house lightened. If only she could have stayed a little I think there might have been jokes. They were not quite in the air, but they were en route.

Her hair was bronzy and her mouth was proud. Her nose however was not Roman in the least but small, broad and flat like a lioness and she had a lion's nobility about the brow. Her teeth when she smiled were small and white and square, like dice. Her eyes were not leonine but like her father's (said my Ma), large and good and grey.

When Auntie Greta came back it was to tell us that the grandmother was very comfortable in the Home now, but failing, and had need of only one thing: a last visit from Jilly.

'We could wait,' the Aunt W said. 'I don't think it's that urgent. But then, you never know. It just might be. I can't go back – it's Bank Holiday and I'm on duty.' Auntie Greta was a nurse.

My Ma said she was on duty then, too. Bank Holidays were her busiest times. She was a Samaritan.

'Well, I'm certainly not letting Jilly go on her own,' I heard the Willis. 'Not by herself. Not next door again.'

'But haven't they all gone now?' said Ma. 'There are new people next door now.'

'I'm not having her anywhere near. Not by herself. Not next door again even if it's empty.'

'Who's moved in there?'

'I've no idea and I don't want to know.'

'Couldn't she stay with the Chalmers? They were nice people. They were good friends to Alec. Before –'

'I'm afraid I never took to them at all.'

I'd been hanging about listening and they found themselves staring at me. Then they started coughing and pouring themselves more tea and behaving as though they'd been saying nothing at all. The Willis gave a sly look at her big bold palms. Ma said, 'I suppose you wouldn't like to go away for a weekend with Jilly, hinney? Back to her old home to see her gran in hospital? Stop her feeling homesick?'

'There'd be nobody else in the house,' said the Willis. 'You could do what you wanted, with Granny in The Gables. You could have plates on your knees and we haven't got rid of the telly yet. I'd maybe stand you a café tea.'

I went on painting my nails. I had my own friends and my own plans for Bank Holiday and I didn't believe that Jilly could still be homesick when I thought of the counterpane.

'Is that my nail-varnish?' asked Ma.

'I'd soon put a stop to that,' said the Willis, 'I'd have given Jilly what-for for nail muck at thirteen.' She turned her empty teacup into the saucer to read the tea-leaves. You could see what her mouth would be like in old age. A drawstring purse tight shut. Everything was ingrowing with Greta. Her chest was concave below her great shoulders. I wondered if her breasts grew inwards too.

'I'm sure she'll go,' said Ma. 'Won't you, hinney? Because of Jilly's grandma – won't you?'

'Would Jilly want me?'

'She's easy,' said Willis. 'There's one thing I'd ask though. You'd have to promise to keep near her. Keep close.'

'Oh I'd be fine,' I said. 'I've been youth-hostelling by myself. I've been on a French exchange.' (I'd hardly seen my French exchange as it happened though they didn't know it. I'd wandered all over Paris alone while Dominique sat looking *soignée* in bars, chain smoking and behaving twenty-five. Her parents fortunately had made no enquiries about our views on the statues in the Louvre and my mother had not yet been made aware of the non-improvement in my French. That was to come.)

'No,' said the W. 'What I mean is that you mustn't let Jilly go off alone. You mustn't leave her for a minute. See?' She was glaring at me like black ice.

'Is something the matter with Jilly?'

'She's not very well,' said Ma. 'Out of kilter. Out of true.'

'Teenage,' said the W and took out her handkerchief. She wiped her hands and dried off the corners of her mouth.

'Whatever did happen?' I asked when she'd gone. 'You'll have to tell me. It's not fair on me if you don't. Or safe. I shan't know the danger signals.'

'Oh, duck,' said Ma. 'Oh my hinney. I promised but I'll –.'

'What?'

'I'll give you a –'

'Clue?'

'No. Not a clue. I promised. I'll give you a whatsit? Example. Metaphor. Little story. Something I once saw and I've never forgotten.'

'Oh Lord.'

'Listen. I was on the top of a tram once long ago. The tram had stopped in the middle of the road, as they did – as they do. It was when I was a student abroad somewhere. Standing on the pavement waiting for someone was a man. Reading a newspaper. He was old. Well, he seemed old to me. He may have been fifty or he may have been sixty – there's no difference when you're eighteen. The fact of him though was that he was most marvellously good-looking. I don't mean Byronic. Don Juanish. Flashy foreigner – he could have been from anywhere in the Western world. But he was a truly handsome man. I can still see him. "Beautiful" sounds soft, but well – he was beautiful. There. I remember thinking, "Like a god. One of the old gods."

'Well, off the bus gets this girl and hinney, she was plain! Not fascinatingly ugly or quaint or arresting – just plain. Very very ordinary, with thick glasses and lank hair and fat little bottle legs. She called out to the man and he looked up and dropped the newspaper on the pavement and smiled and held out his arms and she ran in to them.'

'It was her father.'

'It was not her father.'

'How did you know?'

'I knew. It was huge, romantic love.'

'Oh wow.'

'No. Not oh wow. Don't play tired of life at thirteen. It was love. They stood clasped together with people going round them as if they were a sculpture. Oblivious. After the tram started and swung round to the side at the end of the road I could still see them, still clasped together. And this was Italy. Maybe Holland. Not London. You'll know what that means one day.'

'So then?'

'So then, nothing. It just happened. So think.'

'Think what?'

'Think that there are some queer goings-on.'

I asked, 'Can we have the telly on now?' and Ma said, 'Oh hin. I'm sorry. You're just a bairn. I've been asking a lot.'

'You mean making me go away with Jilly?'

'Yes,' she said. 'Maybe that, too.'

We went first to the Home and it smelled of mince. I said I'd wait for Jilly in the hall and she said, 'It's all right. I don't mind you coming in with me to see her you know. It might even be better.'

'It's you she wants to see. I'd just fuddle her up.'

'Suit yourself,' she said. 'She won't exactly wave the flags when I walk in. That's just Mama. She never liked me and she hated Dad. Pass that mag over.'

'Why can't you go on up now?'

'They said to wait. They're turning her. She's had a stroke. Didn't you know? You can come in with me. Are you frightened?'

'Why should I? She's not mine. Of course I'm not frightened.'

'Can you come now, dearie?' A fat lady had appeared round a cardboard wall that was pressed up against the banister of a coiled mahogany staircase that had once known crinolines. Hair sprouted about round her nurse's cap, pinned on crooked with hair-slides. Whiskers stuck out of her chin and she was smoking. She looked more like an inmate than a nurse but that's England now, as Ma would say.

'I'll be outside,' I said.

'You can bring your friend. She won't mind.'

I fled and kicked the gravel outside until Jilly reappeared, looking glassy. She hadn't been gone ten minutes. She said, 'We may as well walk on then, from here.'

We passed a pub called the Pit Laddie, and then a ramshackle bus passed us full of tired Indians. I said, 'What a lot of Indians all together,' and Jilly said, 'They're miners, fool. It's dirt. Haven't you been anywhere?'

We walked by the grand big clock-works of the coal face and up a steep cobbled street where women leaned against door-frames scratching above their elbows. They looked golden Jilly up and down, saying nothing.

'Gran came from round this way,' she said.

'Did she know who you were?'

'She just looked. She rolled her eye about.'

'Did you talk to her?'

'Listen, shut up. I'll tell you one day when you're older. It's not important anyway.'

'You don't care about anybody Jilly, do you? You don't care about a single human being.'

'Oh, no,' she said. 'Oh, most absolutely no. Miss Angel.'

We left the hilly strip streets and reached the ridge of the town above, where there was a new spread of small red houses and shops with the new-fangled metal window-frames. We came to other new houses built in groups and called after places in the Lake District: Derwent Crescent, Windermere Walk, Esthwaite Close. They were semi-dets, two and two, divided down the middle. The longer we walked the more money had been spent on lawn-mowers, azaleas, plastic ponds, gnarled stumps of Disneyesque plastic trees. Gnomes fished. The last two houses were the finest, a low box hedge separating the gardens. On one side of it the grass was a foot high and full of weeds; on the other shorn and edged with metal strip. On the well-kept lawn a man crouched clipping precisely up to the middle of the hedge in a half knees-bend. Intently. Awkwardly, snip, snip. Jilly wheeled towards the door of the scruffy house and opened the gate, which gave a cry. The man most carefully did not look at us but continued expertly snipping, then rose and went indoors.

Jilly produced a key and entered her old home which lay in semi-darkness and had an airless, old person's smell. She fell across a sofa and shut her eyes.

'What do we do now?' I asked after a bit. 'Jilly?'

'Suit yourself.'

Looking about I saw nothing that suited at all. The furniture of the whole house seemed to have been gathered into the room. A bed stuck out from a wall between a sideboard and a wardrobe. On a gummy dusty dining-table stood pots of marmalade, packets of cornflakes and old library books. Burnt bread-and-milk stood black in a saucepan on the eau-de-nil lounge-tiles of the fireplace. Copper things on leather straps, ornamental bronze shovels, warming-pans and a brass lady who wagged a bell-clapper under her skirts were reminders of more confident times. Uncle Alec's degree in Ophthalmacy hung framed on a wall near a flight of flapping china ducks. There was a knock on the front door.

'Mr Bainbridge just saw you as he was attending to the party hedge,' said the next door Mrs. 'We just wondered if there was any news of Granny.'

'Oh,' I said, 'she's not mine. She's Jilly's.' I turned, but Jilly made signals with her arms, not opening her eyes.

'Anything we can do,' said Mrs Bainbridge. 'Anything,' – she tried not to peer – 'we'd be glad. We've been so worried. We're only newcomers ourselves and we didn't want to impose. And we couldn't make her daughter hear when we rang the bell last week when she came to take her off. Granny got in a terrible state you know. We notified some mutual acquaintances, the Chalmers, and they were the ones sent out the alert to the daughter – that would be' (peering) 'your mother?'

Jilly was continuing to signal. 'Get rid of her. Close the door.'

'Of course it's the old next-door neighbours I blame,' said the woman. 'The people before us. They took no concern for her at all, no matter him being a Latin teacher at the Comp. Useless stuff. And very stand-offish to all round about. Too good for this neighbourhood. Very well-to-do, though how I can't think on teacher's pay. Well *she* had money. And a nice price they got out of us for the house and never a word about painted-over rotten window-sills. Hello dear –?' Jilly had materialised beside me. 'Just the two of you here alone? Well, that does seem a shame on your Bank Holiday.'

'We've been to The Gables to see my grandmother.'

'Well, I'm very glad. I *am* glad. I've just been saying to your sister –'

'Cousin.'

'Sorry dear, cousin – I've just been saying – Could I just step inside? Oh dear – that pan. And all those grease marks round the chair. That'll bring mice. I was saying I blame the neighbours before. The people before us. They could have found out who to contact. We knew nobody crescent-wise and they'd been here for years. Just as you had dear. Born here weren't you? Very cold people you had next door. Southerners I dare say and always away foreign. Would you both like a bite of something?'

'No thanks,' I said, 'we've been told to go to the Chalmers.'

'Actually yes. We would,' said Jilly. 'Thanks, we would.'

'Half an hour then? Give me time to make things nice.'

'I don't want to go,' I said. 'Why ever did you say we'd go? We could have had chips.'

'Or gone to the Charming Chalmers like Mummy said, little lambkin.'

'No – I don't want to go to the Chalmers.' (I was shy with the Chalmers. They sent big presents at Christmas and I never could get my thank-you letters to sound grateful enough. They were gods in the shadows.) 'I just don't want to go in next door. They're busybodies. And if they'd really cared about your Gran they wouldn't have let her eat out of pans.'

'You didn't know my Gran,' said Jilly.

'No,' she said, 'we'll go. We may as well. There'll be hot water and they might let us have a bath. Everything's switched off here.'

'Your mother isn't a very good organiser is she?'

'Well, she's not all over you all the time and she's kept her figure.'

Cold at heart, for I was a retarded thirteen and still believed that all other girls were jealous of me because my mother was so incomparably better than theirs – I spoke not one word as I followed Jilly up the tidy side of the hedge towards Mr Bainbridge who was holding open his front door and looking down at the path in order not to see Jilly's legs. Inside the door, what should have been the mirror-image of Jilly's house was frighteningly different. A forest of new chairs in Jacobean print stood on high-glaze parquet and all was open-plan behind slatted rainbow blinds. 'We had to do a great deal of work here,' said Mrs Bainbridge. 'A lot of knocking through. The last people – well, it hadn't been changed since the war. Finger-plates above the doorknobs with Greek ladies carrying jars and irises and daffodils in plaster-work round the lounge fireplace. And little bits of stained glass. It was a scream.'

'We're told it was an intellectual family,' said Mr Bainbridge, *Readers' Digest* open by his plate. He seemed troubled by something and put his serviette to his face and smelled it.

'It's my scent,' said Jilly, not looking at him.

'The man before – the teacher – he'd had foreign education and a Varsity degree.'

'Oh yes, it's a good neighbourhood,' said Mr Bainbridge. 'I wonder if your mother has had any thought yet – could you ask her – about the selling of the house, strokes being what they are? Naturally it affects us. Pricewise the right people will be important in the crescent. One has to take an interest.'

'Could I go upstairs?'

They looked surprised. Jilly was two bites into her fish pie. Mrs B said, 'Of course, dear. First on the left.'

'I know.'

She disappeared up the spiral staircase for what seemed hours. The Bainbridges were uneasy. They talked brightly on but appeared to be listening. I wondered what they'd heard about Jilly and again I had the random thought about stealing. Why did I always come back to the thought of Jilly as a taker? A danger? A foreigner among us all?

She was back, looming above us over the white wrought-iron. She looked flushed. 'Mr Bainbridge,' she said, 'could I ask you for something very special? A very special favour? A loan?'

He turned pink through his light moustache, 'Of course my d –'

'Have you a bike? Could we borrow a bike for tomorrow? We don't have to be home before evening and we can't spend the whole day sitting with Gran.'

There was a fractional hesitation before Mr Bainbridge

said, 'Yes,' and Mrs Bainbridge said, 'I'm afraid Mr Bainbridge only has his racing bikes. He's been a professional you know. Connected with the Luton Twelve.'

'We'd take great care of it.'

'Yes. Yes of course,' said Mr Bainbridge. After supper he brought ticking through the house a flimsy fine-drawn grasshopper with slim cross-bar and saddle like a whippet.

'Twenty-seven ounces,' he said. 'Hero of the Luton Twelve.'

'*And* the Bedford Four,' said Mrs Bainbridge.

Mr Bainbridge was stroking the saddle and looking at Jilly's legs, starting low, gliding upwards. 'Do you think you can manage it?'

'Oh it's not for me, it's for her,' Jilly said, looking straight at him and smiling. 'Mine's still in Gran's shed. Don't worry, my cousin's a terrific rider.'

'But I've never –'

'You are very kind,' she looked at him again. 'We'll take the greatest care of it.'

'Would you like a practice run?' asked Mr B as we left, looking at my legs quite differently, finding them unreassuring.

'Oh, she's terribly good,' said Jilly.

In the Gran's house I said, 'You're awful, Jilly. You're deceitful. You're mad, too. I can't ride a bike like that.'

'We'll have a dummy run first thing tomorrow. You'll be OK.'

'*You* can ride it.'

'I can't ride it. I'm far too heavy. I can just cope with my own and it's like a sofa. We'll get up early. We'll go to bed now.'

In the morning we wheeled the two bikes respectfully away from Wastwater Crescent and down the cobbled hill to The Gables.

'You keep going round the gravel till I'm out,' she said,

and when she came back I was tottering in zig-zags, heading for easy jumping-off places, but making a little progress.

'How is she?'

'She's a lot better. They've been feeding her gravy.'

'*Gravy*?'

'She likes gravy. Don't look like that. She always liked it. She slurped it up with a spoon. She used to fill up her Yorkshire puddings with it, like a pond and it used to spill out all over her great bits of beef. She liked her beef leathery like tongues in shoes. She used to slap her lips, slap, slap. She dribbled. She always dribbled. Her mouth perpetually watered. She was always foul.'

'Don't look so saint-like,' she said. 'There are horrible people and I hate her.'

We pushed the bikes up cobblestone slopes of little houses and soon came out to open country with high blue hills along the horizon, and a great sky. Clouds rolled over it like tumbleweed in Westerns.

'She used to beat me.'

'*What*!'

'My Gran. She called it "leathering." She used to leather me with a belt. Grow up.'

'But your *mother* was there!'

'She'd been leathered by her, too. Sometimes they both leathered me together. What's the matter? D'you want me to help you up on the bike? Why've you gone white?'

'But your *mother*! She was married to Uncle Alec. My mother's own brother.'

'Oh, Dad used to turn white, too. He used to go and sit in the shed while it was going on. I used to scream. It was when I was little.'

'Shut up, shut up, shut up.'

'It's all right. Dad's dead. He was weak. *Il souffre* but *il est mort*. Gran soon will be, thank God. I don't give a toss for her. Or my mother.'

'But Jilly, there's always a reason for wickedness. *Jilly!*'

She leapt on the lumbering bike and began to push the

pedals down, one-two, with her strong legs until she was away over the hill. After an unpromising start and a fall or two on the lonely road I clenched my teeth and got the hang of it. Soon I was understanding the gears.

I came up alongside Jilly and flew past her. I stopped, one foot on a boulder, balancing with my hand against the stone wall that accompanied us over the moor like a snake, westward towards the Irish Sea.

'Wherever are we going, Jilly?'

She was heaving her bike up the hill towards me, one leg pressing down, then the other, head turning left and then right.

She was like a solemn giant, slowly dancing.

'We're going to his new house. I'm going to see him again.'

'Whose house?'

'Use your empty head. Our old neighbours.'

'D'you know the address?'

'Yes. He told me it. Before we left he managed to get a note to me – God knows how, but he's brilliant. We both knew – we'd always known – I'd have to go the minute they found out. It was a matter of time. We knew that. One of us would have to move. I'd pretty well finished at the Comp. It was his Comp too, but – well, we knew of course it'd have to be me.'

'Jilly – what happened?'

'Do you honestly not know?'

And I did know of course. In the cradle, at the breast, probably in the womb we know. When they announce what they call the facts of life they are never really a surprise.

'No, I don't,' I shouted as she pedalled on past me and away towards the purple, banked-up clouds ahead.

'How far is it, Jilly? How far?'

I caught her up and began to weave about around her and then diagonally in front of her, across and across the road.

'Jilly? Jilly can we stop and have the chocolate? Jilly?'

On she went, and passed me.

'Not far now,' she called as the first big drops fell and the wind began. 'Bloody cold,' she called.

'Where are we *going*? There aren't any houses up here. It's mad. I'm going back.'

'Fine. Go.'

'I promised not to leave you.'

'In case what? Did they say why? In case I went off with him? In case I got kidnapped by him?'

'I don't know what you're talking about, Jilly. Honestly. I don't.'

The rain had become cold and soaking by the time we had climbed the next long hill, Jilly plugging up it slower and slower but never giving up, never getting off to walk. I'd been pushing my bike for some time already. It was so light that I had to walk beside it to hold it down. It was trying to blow away over the wall into the heather.

To the north of our walled road I saw a blacker, higher, more organic looking ridge squirming out of sight. It looked as old as the rock.

'Whatever is it, Jilly?'

'Roman Wall. We're nearly there.'

'Roman this, Roman that. *Jilly*!' Mother going on about Jilly belonging to another country. I had an exhausted, frightened knowledge that she was pedalling me away to it, and out of time – I didn't know whether forward or backward. But I did know where she was going wasn't for me.

She seemed to be almost flying ahead now and the rain flung itself on the shiny, lilac road and the wind struck me in the face. There was a great space of empty moor all round, not a building not a signpost.

'*Jilly*!'

I saw her ahead, turning left, south, down a dirt track, out of sight, and I followed her, bumping over stones into a dip, out of a dip, then as we climbed again one behind the other we were all at once beside a long metal field-gate standing wide open. Just inside and to the right was a tin-roofed Dutch barn and across what once had been an old Northumbrian farmyard but now had flowers planted in its horse-trough was a spruced-up farmhouse painted glittering white. Two stables now fitted with metal up-and-over garage doors stood near. An ornamental wagon wheel, also painted white, was arranged beside a smartened-up old pump and there was the start of a rockery – very sparse – on what had been a midden. No sign of an animal; not a cat, not a chicken, and not one weed in the shining cobbles. I saw all this only after we had both collapsed inside the open-sided barn and could look out at it through rain that fell like silver arrows. Jilly let her bike drop and went round a corner, to sit on a hayblock, knees apart, hands clasped, bowing her wet head. Her hair was plastered against her skull, dark and dripping, as I suppose was mine.

'Jilly?'

I burrowed about, pulling at the hay, trying to get some loose to put it round me like bedclothes. Before us was a great view of sky and fell, the cocky, ravished farmhouse behind. Through the rain, toward the road I saw some flashes of light, like swords, far away. Then the sky cleared, the flashes vanished and the sun came out with ice-cold rain-drops still striking down from clouds blown away. Like light from dead stars, the view, sopped with rain, dazzled and sunlight caught a distant bracelet of Roman Wall, then left it.

'They must have had days like this,' I said.

'Who must?'

'The Romans.'

She said nothing.

I said, 'They must have got ever so depressed. So cold. So far from Italy and nobody talking Latin.'

'They'd been here long enough,' she said. 'They'd prob-ably forgotten Latin. They'd have talked pidgin English – chop-chop and doolally and that. It was like home here. Well, all Europe was home then. Anyway they were soldiers weren't they? They were used to it. It's the girls back home you've to be sorry for – left behind with the wimps. They were the ones to be depressed.'

It was nice she was thinking of all this instead of – 'Jilly,' I said, 'Let's go back. This place is empty. They're all away. They'll be away for Bank Holiday.'

'Yes.' Her voice was dead.

JANE GARDAM

After a while she said, 'They'll be at the boat.'
'Boat?'
'They've a boat. They have everything. Been everywhere.
He has everything. Everything in the world that life can
give.'
'He hasn't got you, Jilly. I bet he misses you.'
She leaned over to her bike and burrowed in the saddle-
bag and brought out a note book and a pencil and scribbled
something.
'Jilly. Jilly – what's his name?'
'Bevis.'
'*Bevis.*'
'Yes,' she said, 'Bevis. Why not?'
'I don't know. It's a bit –'
'It's Latinate,' she said. Solemnly.
Our eyes met across the hay. And held. '*Bevis!*'
Held unblinking.
I had the extraordinary notion that the gods were
assembled and were on my side. I might save Jilly now.
'It's a family name,' she said with hauteur.
I said, 'Coo-er!'
Her lips and nose for a lovely instant twitched. But then –
'And what may I ask does that mean, Po-face?'
'Well, isn't it – a bit sort of comic?'
'*Comic?*' Oh, very proud. Swallowing. Tossing back the
lion's drying mane. Glaring down the lion's flat nose.
'Well, you know. It sounds like some sort of bread.'
'*Bread?*'
'Or some sort of beverage. A sort of wheat-germ drink.'
'*Beverage!*'
Our eyes held steady and then hers flickered and her mouth
trembled and I thought, I've done it!
But no.
She turned her head and sank sideways in the hay and the
wind kicked the tin roof of the barn about and clattered it like
a thunder-sheet. With long plumes of water at its wheels a
long car with a boat behind it on a trolley came rollicking
down the track from the moor and swept through the farm

gate. A great many people shot out of the car and disappeared into the house.

Jilly did not stir.

'Jilly, they're back. The family's back.'

Now down the lane came the flashes I had seen before, far off, a group of cyclists in shiny black-beetle capes, peaked caps and bikes as ritzy as mine. In the tracks of the car they swooped into the yard and over the barn and dismounted all around us, wet through. Ignoring us, they shook themselves like dogs, began removing their capes and mopping their streaming faces. 'She all right?' one of them asked, nodding towards Jilly.

'Yes. She's just tired.'

'Wild day,' said another. 'How far you come? That's a nice bike.'

'I'm just borrowing it. It belongs to someone to do with the Luton Twelve.'

'You coming in with us?'

'In?'

'The house. The geezer in the car said to go in and get dry.'

'But it's stopped raining almost now.'

'Yeah. Look bad though not to go in. After he said.'

They were skinny little people with faces narrowed by continuous slipstream, eyes sharp like birds' eyes, sinews like cords. Under their caps they wore brilliant, proud colours – orange and scarlet and green. Motley, international people. 'Come on. You come on in too.' They made off towards the farmhouse.

'Shall I?' I went over to Jilly as she sat with her back to me. 'Shall I go in with them, Jilly?'

All she did was pass me the note she'd written. On the outside of it she'd scrawled 'Bevis', the tail of the S curled down like a tendril and crossed at the end with a kiss.

'Read it if you like.'

'No. I don't.'

'Read it. I mean it. Give it to him. He'll know it the minute he sees it. I used to leave one for him like this every day. In the rabbit hutches. Until they found one.'

I read it. It said, 'I'm in the hay barn – Jilly.'
'Give it to him. Go on. You'll be too late.'

Someone had in fact already shut the front door behind the last of the cyclists when I reached it and I had to bang hard and at once or I should have faltered. It was immediately opened by a fiftyish sort of man who stood smiling at me. He was shortish, squarish and older than Dad had been but there was a sweet, calm presence all around him as he looked down affectionately at me as I stood soaked through and silent at his door.

'Hullo. One more. Come in. Come in. We're just back from the sea and you look as though you've been in it.' He stood back to let me pass down the flagstones, wetted ahead of me by all the cyclists' feet, 'Come along through, my dear. Get warm. There'll be a fire in a minute but come and stand by the stove first. Are you the last of them?' He peered across the yard.

I couldn't stop looking at him. For the first time since I was a child I wanted to reach out and touch someone. I remembered the feel of my father's clothes again. Such strength, such kindness. Good heavens – old, *old*. And yet I could see the comfort of his arms folding themselves round damaged Jilly. I saw her beautiful head on his shoulder in the house with the Grecian ladies engraved upon the finger-plates; and the fireplaces traced with daffodils.

Then his wife came up alongside and put a hand on his arm. She was a square woman, short, with wiry hair. She was powerful. As powerful as Caesar's wife, as powerful as Volumnia. Her eyes shone.

'Excuse me, dear,' she said to me, and then to him, 'Come in quickly. Great news. *Great* news,' and a sound came floating from a room down the passage that made one think of goals being scored and tidal applause. A wimpish boy and a solid girl came forward flapping letters and the girl flung herself upon her father who swung her round and then put his arm round the boy as well. He hugged both his children together.

'*Well!*' said Volumnia to everyone, and the cyclists all gazed. 'Well, we've come home in style. It's the examination results and we have two heroes. *Heroes!*' She shone with such pride she looked beautiful.

'On the mat,' the boy shouted, waving the letter. 'On the mat. I knew they'd be waiting on the mat. And there they were – yooh, hooh.' The girl was giving long silly shrieks and had laid herself along a window seat.

'What they on about?' one of the cyclists asked me and I said, 'She's happy. Some girls at school do it.'

'Straight As,' said the lovely father, 'Straight As for both of them. Two people climbing to the top of the tree. Right to the top. And all set fair.'

The boy grinning with happiness came loping across to me. 'D'you want a towel? Are you cold? D'you want some cocoa?' But all he meant was 'For me the whole world is set fair.'

The girl went on squealing.

And the sun came out and splashed the wet landscape while the rain still attacked the windows of the house with occasional showers of arrows, as if some ancient little army was bitterly out on the moor. Volumnia led us all to a table in another room and put a bowl of soup in front of each of us as she smiled and smiled. There was nothing, nothing she would not do today, wrapping us all into her magnificent family, for whom all was set fair.

'Shall I relieve you of that?' I heard his voice say over my shoulder as he leaned forward to put a bread basket on the table. My wrists had been propped on the table edge while I waited to see if we were meant to start in on the soup. My left hand had been holding the note marked 'Bevis', with its kiss. The note was no longer there. It had been tweaked away.

Everyone was talking and laughing, gobbling soup and bread, and the cyclist next to me was saying, 'Did you say you were something to do with the Luton Twelve? I'm really more interested in the Bedford Four.'

And Jilly was in the hay barn. Would Bevis go out to her –
oh would he go?

I said 'Excuse me,' to the cyclist, slid off my chair and
went over towards the kitchen where I saw the man standing
gravely beside the stove, with the note. He looked up, not
towards me standing outside the door but at the big fat
bottom of his wife as she bent to the refrigerator: her old
back, her grey wire hair. Then, when she straightened up and
turned to him, he did the thing that ended everything. He
lifted the note and held it out to her.

She put down whatever it was she'd been looking for in
the fridge. I think it was cheese. A great slab of violent cheese.
She walked towards him, took the note and read it, then
they looked hard at each other. The man then touched her
shoulder, lifted off the little round lid of the stove by its iron
handle, took the note back from her hand and dropped it
down in the hot coals. She took his hand and held it against
her face and they both smiled.

'Jilly. Jilly – where are you?'

She had scarcely moved.

'Jilly, we've got to go. We'll be late. For the train. It's
miles and miles.'

'You've gone white again. Did you give Bevis the note?'

'Yes.'

'Well?'

'I don't know. Jilly – let's go. Why are we sitting in this
barn? Jilly – you don't want to get pneumonia.'

'I'm not leaving till I've seen him. He'll come out in a
minute.'

'He won't. No – don't look at me. He won't.'

'He read it?'

'Yes, he read it.'

'And – ?'

'Jilly, I want to go home.'

'Not,' she said, gripping my wrist and I saw for the first
time that she had hands not unlike Auntie Greta, 'not till you
tell me.'

'He threw it in the stove.'

'So that she wouldn't see it?'

'No. She was there. Let go. She saw it, too. She read it, too. They –'

'Yes?' She flung away my wrist and stood up from the hay and the over-large landscape behind looked perfectly right for her. 'Yes?'

'They put it in the stove together. Then they smiled.'

An age later she said lightly, 'Oh, well.'

'OK,' she said. 'Never mind. So what?'

It frightened me more than anything.

'If you like we could wait a bit, Jilly.'

'No,' she said, 'No, I don't think so.'

Her cart-horse sped ahead of my racehorse over the wide terrain. Along the wet purple road we flew, paced to the north by the frontier of the wall, over moors and hills and dykes and ditches, and to the present day country of pits and little houses and hedges and shrubs. 'You'd better dry his bike,' she said.

Mr Bainbridge came out of his house and she undid him with her smile, 'We're just going to dry your lovely bike.'

'Oh, that's all right. I'll see to it. Not necessary at all.' His blush was dark as potted meat. He pleaded with her for some sign.

None.

Half an hour and we were gone.

Because the Bank Holiday was not over until the following day the train home was practically empty and we sat silent in it as far as Sunderland, a Stygian place the train enters and leaves through a black tunnel (like life quoth the preacher) and where Jilly got out and disappeared. She returned, not hurrying – I had been in terror for she had the tickets and the money and knew where we had to change trains – with a big bag of crisps. She ate the crisps slowly, giving none to me,

staring out of the window. We were alone until Middles-
brough.

Then she said, still staring out, 'Ever been had?'

'Had?'

'Had.'

'You mean, made to look silly? Yes. All the time. Oh,
Jilly!'

'Had, had had, *had*,' she said. '*Had*, Miss No-Secrets
Angel. You know perfectly well what I mean.'

'You mean – kissing?'

'*Had*,' she said. 'You know. He *had* me. He had me and
had me and had me. Every morning in his bed for weeks and
weeks and weeks. He HAD me. And how did he have me,
Angel Po-Face? How did he have me? Let me count the ways.
He begged me and begged me and so in the end I climbed
out of my bedroom and into his bedroom next door. Every
morning at five o'clock and back at seven and down eating
breakfast with Gran and Mam, and then walking down the
path either side of the fond hedge – three of them and one of
me, and off to the Comp by eight all together. We never said
a word in the car.'

'But I can't see how. Did he have a bedroom alone then?'

'Yes, he had a bedroom alone. Don't you know anything
yet?'

I thought, I suppose not. I don't. I don't understand anything at all. It must be because there aren't any men in our
house. I didn't know that men don't always sleep with their
wives.

'Jilly. Wasn't it –? Weren't you scared?'

'Getting pregnant? No. I don't know why. He didn't use
anything. Why've you got your hands over your ears, take
them away. Listen. You have to grow up sometime.'

I said, 'Sorry,' but I didn't know what I meant.

'And God was I tired,' she said when we stopped at Cargo
Fleet siding. 'Was I tired at school. But I got an A in every
subject. My mind was as clear –'

'Oh God,' she said, staring at the steel-works through the

rain, 'I was so happy.' At Warrenby some people got in to the carriage and I sat looking at the floor. I heard one of them say to Jilly – righteously, fiercely, like Teesside people do – 'What's your little sister crying for?' But Jilly didn't answer.

'One thing, I suppose,' she said to me the following week at school – it was the day before she left; she'd failed the History – 'One thing –' She had come up behind me in the dark part of the corridor outside the Science rooms and caught hold of the back of my tunic. She twisted it and the knickers underneath it till she hurt. 'I suppose you didn't see anything in him did you? You thought he was nothing. You thought "Who could see anything in that little shit?" '

'Oh, let go Jilly.'

'Don't cry,' she said, 'You're always crying.'

I was crying because I'd expected love to be beautiful but I didn't say so.

'Come on then,' she said. 'Let's hear it. What did you think of him?'

I said, 'He was wonderful.'

Jilly died at forty-two, suddenly in Rome. A brain haemorrhage. Some disc flicked across a lifeline and she was gone. She had not become a vet. She had not even gone to a university. She had gone off on her own at the end of the summer term of the Bank Holiday, first to Paris where she had become a model for a time. Later she took up with a famous Italian photographer and became a beautiful, known face. There were a few films and then one lavish one that for a short moment gave her face to the whole world. The tawny hair blew out beside autostradas and autoroutes and freeways. The grey eyes stared down at Eros in Piccadilly, at the Corso in Rome, the dust of Athens and the severity of Madrid. But soon it was gone.

Later one kept seeing her in hairdressers' society magazines, always with what is called 'the international set', which is to say with those whose names are known only to each other like cyclists, but corrupting. There was a nasty divorce and some hard publicity about money and lovers. But it was not a louche life. If anything, I believe it was rather a dry one. She never grew druggy or raddled or mean, and always her face stayed right.

She never came back.

For a while her mother hung about our town but then without warning she moved away too and we heard of her no more. Sometimes my mother said, 'I feel rather bad about Greta. She *is* my sister-in-law. I suppose we could find her. But she never cared for us. And she left no address.'

But Jilly and I kept in touch always. We wrote at least six times a year and I heard from her the week before she died. I miss her great scrawl, the fat letters with the foreign stamps, heavy on the mat, although they never really said much.

She died just a month before the Chalmers' grandchild's wedding to which our whole family had been invited, very generously I thought, since we hadn't seen any of them for years. Off we set – my mother and step-father, me, my husband and my children in a couple of cars, and very glad to be together for as my mother said, 'There won't be a soul there we recognise except them and maybe not even them.'

'And the *place*!' she said, 'Just look. Oh, poor Alec – look. All the cobbles have gone. D'you remember all the women on the doorsteps? And the pit-heads and the coal dust?' Up the slope where we had pushed the bikes between the grim little houses there was only wasteland and ruins, boards over windows and notices saying 'Demolition'. The Lake District crescents were looking shabby though I thought I saw the box hedge. Only the Chalmers' house, the old rectory over the hill, was bravely surviving beside the unchanged church.

A marquee had been put up on the lawn, approached through the house and the old rector's study. Sensible coconut matting led to the line-up of the bride and groom. And just beyond this I found myself head on to Mr and Mrs Bainbridge, looking little changed. They were smiling nervily over their champagne glasses, looking this way and that for a

familiar face and seemed delighted with me out of all proportion. They swooped forward.

'No, I'm afraid we don't –' Tense wide smiles.

'You hardly would. I was just thirteen. I borrowed your
racing bike, Mr Bainbridge. I was with my cousin, Jilly
Willis.'

They almost took bites out of me. '*Remember!*' they said.
'Remember – of course we do. Remember! *What* a lovely
girl!'

'We saw the obituaries,' said Mrs Bainbridge. Mr Bainbridge said, 'Tragic. And so young. It was a great mistake for
her to travel.'

'The way she swept off on the bike and never on a racing
bike before. Amazing.'

'I often boast about it,' said Mr B. 'That Jilly Willis once
borrowed one of my bikes. I still have it hung up in the shed
by the old hutches. Out of sentiment for her – and of course
for my time with the Luton Twelve.'

'And the Bedford Four,' said his wife.

I introduced them to my mother and heard them saying
that of course they understood that she was no relation to the
grandmother. No blood relation.

Looking down I found myself staring at the wiry and
unthinning hair of Volumnia. She filled her chair and sat in it
as if it were a throne, but there were two sticks with elbow-
pieces propped beside her and her feet were swollen round
the shoe-straps. She was dancing a small child on her knee.

'Hullo,' she said, looking up at me. 'Now, who are you?'
I'm afraid I'm rather blind but I know you don't I? I remember you I think.'

'You couldn't,' I said. 'We met when I was almost a child
and now I'm nearly forty. But I recognise you. We met at
your house in the wilds, one wet Bank Holiday.'

'Oh, *that* house,' she said. 'My word that *was* a romantic
house. Very silly. It didn't last long I'm afraid. Too far out.
You must have been a friend of the children – my dear,
they're both here. The twins. Both behind you.'

Two indeterminate people were laughing nearby and the

one who had been the drippish boy looked round – chinless, red-lipped, white eye-lashed. I remembered him at once.

'He became a vet. I expect you knew?' said his mother, 'Doing so well.'

'The day we met he had just passed all his O-levels. It was a very wild, haunted sort of day.'

'Really?' You could see she thought little of the adjective.

'But how curious –' Then she stopped.

'I came in to shelter. I was with my cousin, Jilly Willis. I was with some cyclists. I was Jilly Willis's cousin.'

She looked down at the grandchild on her knee. She bounced him up and down. 'There we are,' she sang. 'There we are.'

'I except you remember Jilly?'

'That's my baby. Baby boy. Yes I remember Jilly Willis very well.'

'So do I,' said the son joining us, wine glass tipping rather. 'Hullo. Who are you? Ought I to know you?'

'I'm Jilly's cousin.'

'I knew Jilly from being a baby,' he said. 'Bloody sad. So young. She was only a few years older than me you know. We kept rabbits together. It was Jilly started me off wanting to be a vet.' His glass was refilled and he drank. 'Started me off on a lot of things as a matter of fact. Between ourselves.'

'Diddle-de-dee,' sang Volumnia to the baby, 'Bevis, Bevis, Bevis-boy.'

'Is your father here?'

'I'm afraid my father's dead,' he said. 'Do you remember him? Really? Great. Oh – super chap. Lovely man. We miss him.' He drained the glass again.

'Bevis,' I said and saw the sweet-tempered face and Jilly's eyes enlarge with love at the sound of the name. Jilly refusing to mock.

'Yes, Bevis,' he said. 'It's a family name. My son's name.'

'And it was your father's name,' I said.

'Actually, no. No it wasn't. Dad missed out on Bevis for some reason – he was Rodney. No – I'm Bevis.'

The Headscarf

CARLO GÉBLER

MICHAEL WENT OUT the kitchen door, then turned and waved to her through the window. She heard his shoes scuffing on the concrete, and a moment later the van moved off. Then silence, and now the day was hers.

She picked up the newspaper and rearranged the pages. Michael always turned to the sports section first but she liked to read through methodically, starting at the front. She scanned the headlines. A soldier injured by a sniper; a nail bomb defused; a tit-for-tat killing at a Belfast traffic lights. She felt weary, and unmoved; she had read it all before.

Suddenly, she remembered her appointment and looked up. It was half-past eight. She had only forty minutes to get ready. She registered the fizzy, popping feeling which was the first sign of anxiety. It was almost like the tonic in a G and T pricking the back of her throat.

She folded the paper neatly and began to clear up. The crockery was white – a soft-white, not clinical – with a blue band around the edges. The bacon fat on Michael's plate had hardened white as well.

She piled the crockery into a stack. The bubbling sensation of her anxiety became stronger, even painful, as she wondered what checkpoints she would encounter today on the way into town.

From years of struggle she knew activity was the best defence. She stood up and took hold of the plates. For two years before Amanda was born, she had worked as a waitress in the hotel in town. She saw herself suddenly in her smart grey uniform and white apron, rather fetching in a way, running in and out through the green baize door with trays of food. She had enjoyed those days, when she was young and adventurous and capable.

She felt a sharp draught catch the back of her neck and as she turned round a cup flew off her pile of breakfast dishes and crashed on the tiles. Tea stained the front of her brown dressing gown, and round her feet lay a mosaic of white china. The other dishes wobbled in her arms, and fearing they would topple she pulled them against her breast.

She looked down the hall and out through the open front door into the street. Michael had left it ajar; he always did when he came back with the paper. She felt vulnerable and wondered if anyone had seen her.

Plates still in arms, she scuttled down the hall and shut the door, then peered out of the living room window. There was no one at McSpirit's Garage opposite, while on the pavement outside her house, there was just the wee girl, Nellie, absorbed by her bicycle.

She loved where she lived she thought, filling the basin, except for the lack of privacy. Everyone had known about her breakdown after Paddy's death, and her not being able to eat or sleep, and the quite uncharacteristic quarrels she had had, and the crying fits that followed when she had wallowed in self-disgust. Derrybawn had also known when she had gone to Dr Armstrong, and that the pills he gave her did the trick. But what they didn't know, and which she kept even from Michael, was that one symptom of her collapse still remained: an uncontrollable fear of the roving security checkpoints. Nor did anyone know that sometimes, before solo outings, she would spend hours with the map choosing the route she thought was the one least likely to have such a checkpoint, and that sometimes she felt so anxious she cancelled her arrangements rather than go out.

She made her way down the yard to the car and climbed in. It smelt of the blanket on the back ledge which they used when they had their picnics by the sea, a smell simultaneously dusty and salty.

She drove through the gate into the lane, and turned again at the village street in the direction of town. She passed the school, several houses and finally (what she regarded as the village boundary) the old forge with its collapsed roof and the scorch marks up the gable.

Beyond the windscreen she saw that the sky was clear and blue. In the fields a silvery dust of frost coated the grass, and sheep were huddled along the hedgerows. On the side of Hackett's Hill, the wheels of a tractor had left two dark lines in the frost, which reminded her of a vapour trail.

She drove on, watching the blue-black road unfurl under her bonnet, her mind empty. If she could keep it that way the anxiety would trickle away. She had managed to pull this miracle off in the past, although only once or twice. The trick was to concentrate on the outside world . . .

The old sawmill loomed ahead, a big stone building, long abandoned, with gaping, empty windows, and a chimney which leant over at a slight angle, and had an ash tree growing out of the top of it. Some of the wilder local elements used it to fly the Union Flag on the Twelfth of July, but she had never seen this, always being indoors or away.

The road bent round to the right as it passed the mill. A magpie flapped at the side as she followed the curve. One for sorrow, she said to herself, immediately wishing she hadn't, and then straightening the wheel she knew she was in trouble for she saw their unmistakable dark green uniforms fifty yards ahead. Her heart started to race and her hands began to sweat.

She looked in the mirror. There was nothing behind, just the tilting chimney and the empty road bending out of sight. It was too early but her foot went on to the brake and she started to slow down. It was the same pattern every time.

This had all started with Paddy, and whilst she could not control herself, she understood as plainly as she saw the policemen ahead that this was to do with her notion of time. It had been her brother's misfortune to arrive at the checkpoint at precisely the wrong time; he had no sooner pulled up than the mortars had fired. What she feared was that she too was going to arrive at the wrong moment.

She slowed down to nearly a crawl, way in advance of when it was necessary to do so. She realised that this was an utterly illogical action to take, for slowing down could just as easily bring her to the checkpoint at the wrong time as maintaining her speed. But she preferred to dawdle towards her maker, rather than rushing to him.

Peering ahead, and ignoring the part of herself that was somehow above events, looking down at her and hooting with derision, she saw there were two policemen in the road, a soldier behind them in a helmet with foliage looped through the netting and boot polish on his face, and more figures in the field beyond the hedge, with rifles raised. She rolled finally to a halt beside the tripod with the sign, *Stop Checkpoint*. The taller of the policemen came over. She recognised him as Quinlan, from the barracks in town. He had often stopped her.

They said good morning to one another. She was quite calm. From the outside, she knew, nothing showed.

Then he asked, 'Do you have any identification, Mrs Maguire?'

It was all she could do to stop herself shouting, If you know who I am, let me through, and driving away; but she didn't, and instead she handed him her driving licence.

While he studied it, she stared at him. It was funny how observant even objective she was in these situations – impending death, no doubt, concentrating her mind. Quinlan had grey sideburns. Being virulently against hair anywhere except on the head (indeed she was on her way to have various parts of her own body waxed), she was surprised she thought them and him attractive, and found herself wondering if they were the same age. Early fifties. He also had a spot of blood, she saw, on his chin and a tiny trace of shaving cream in his ear. Yes, it was amazing what went on while her heart was fluttering against her ribs. She felt the longing to play with the catch of her handbag, and as a precaution slipped her hands under her legs.

'Thank you very much, Mrs Maguire.'

She took the licence back.

'Are you going into town?' he asked, clearly bored, clearly wanting to get the conversation going.

'I am,' she replied, smiling at him and feeling expansive. Any minute now she'd be off and the ordeal would be over. I'm going to the hairdressers,' she continued. 'A woman's treat, you know.'

He smiled and she drove away, glancing into the rear view mirror where she caught sight of Quinlan, staring after her, gradually growing smaller and smaller. At the next corner he disappeared, and then there was just the empty road behind.

She felt a wave of relief and a modest sense of her own ridiculousness; a grown woman getting into a funk like that. She even managed a half-smile, and then it hit her.

'Oh Christ!' she said aloud, startling herself with the sound of her own voice. Why had she said the hairdressers? It was true she was going there but not to get her hair done. She was going to have her eyebrows plucked and her legs waxed and then, and only then, was she going back to her own village, where she had an appointment at Mrs Cassidy's for her weekly shampoo and set at eleven-thirty.

She put a hand up to her head and felt her hair was greasy. She was bound to meet Quinlan on her way back, and men being so damned literal, he was sure to be deeply suspicious when he saw her unattended head.

She braked abruptly and pulled over. Didn't she have a headscarf? she thought desperately. She opened the handbag and tipped everything on to the seat. Keys, purse, Michael's paying-in book, two brochures from the travel agents, two biros and an *Ulsterbus* ticket. Damn. Damn!

The beauty salon of Cut 'n' Curl was at the rear of the premises, overlooking a tyre store. All over the walls there were photographs of models with immaculate coiffures. The room smelt of lacquer and shampoo.

Usually she enjoyed lying on the couch on the coarse but not unpleasant paper which was pulled out from the big roll at the end to provide a clean surface for each customer. And usually she also enjoyed feeling the wax tightening, while she half-listened to Patsy the beautician, and half-listened to the radio tuned to Jimmy Young. Each time the tweezers pulled an eyebrow hair, she felt a twinge of pain but she was able to ignore it, by getting drowsy in the warm air which wafted from the heater which was always on, and revelling in the sensation of another human being stroking and stretching her skin.

This appointment, however, gave her no pleasure. The wax seemed too hot and she was tormented by the thought that the skin beneath was wrinkling and reddening, and that when the time came to pull it off, it was going to peel away the top layer of skin and leave her legs raw and untouchable, like after a burn. Meanwhile, as these fears were fermenting and the wax was setting, Patsy was plucking and Margaret found her eyes watering, her whole body tense with pain. Patsy sensed it too and the more Margaret winced, the firmer Patsy gripped her head, and then the more Margaret felt trapped, and tied down. She started to swallow and tried to think of other things, to count to ten, to make herself forget about the wax and to concentrate on listening to the music and letting herself grow drowsy, which in turn would relax Patsy. But the more she tried, the firmer the conviction grew that there really was something wrong with the temperature of the wax. It really wasn't her imagination; it really did feel too hot. Patsy had made a mistake and put it on when it was boiling, and with every second the damage was worse. I must say something, she thought, but then she mocked herself. There was nothing wrong. Patsy did not make mistakes.

Her head spun and she felt herself growing breathless, then suddenly she sat up, pulled at the neck of the nylon smock and asked for a glass of water.

'The wax is too hot,' she said, as Patsy handed her the glass.

'Oh'. Patsy lifted a corner and Margaret saw the skin was unharmed, just slightly redder as it always was after a wax.

Margaret left hastily, forgetting to leave her customary tip. She rushed over the road to Dorothy Perkins and hurried past the clothes racks to accessories. Among the lace gloves and bangles, garter belts and evening bags, she found the thickest and biggest headscarf on sale.

'Don't put it in a bag,' she said, as the girl at the till reached for one. 'I want to wear it straight away. It seems it's going to rain.'

'The forecast said fine,' the salesgirl said firmly, a remark Margaret decided to ignore.

With the headscarf tightly around her head, she drove towards home. Her heart was beating, her palms were moist. You won't have to stop, she assured herself ferociously. You'll sail through this. On and on these thoughts went.

Then the chimney of the sawmill appeared with the ash tree growing out of the top of it, and she saw that the police were gone. The empty tarmac glistened in the sun, while the mill with its blank windows looked down on her.

She rounded the corner and emerged on the far side. The tractor marks on the hill had vanished. The frost had melted. She pulled the headscarf off and laughed loudly to herself.

She was early for her hair appointment and Mrs Cassidy gave her a cup of coffee while she was waiting. When she lay back and put her head into the cold porcelain 'U' of the sink, she saw Mrs Cassidy looking at her curiously. 'You look a bit pale. Are you all right?'

Mrs Cassidy was testing the water on the back of her hand, then making minute adjustments to the tap.

Margaret felt the first jet of warm water on her scalp and nodded, indicating that the temperature was right. The hose was held over her head and she felt the water running into her ears, then down over her neck. Any moment she was going to feel the delicious prick of cold shampoo. She squeezed her eyes tight and began to wait for Mrs Cassidy's strong hands to massage her head.

Look-Alikes

NADINE GORDIMER

IT WAS SCARCELY worth noticing at first; an out-of-work
lying under one of the rare indigenous shrubs cultivated by
the Botany Department on the campus. Some of us remembered, afterwards, having passed him. And he – or another
like him – was seen rummaging in the refuse bins behind
the Student Union; one of us (a girl, of course) thrust out
awkwardly to him a pitta she'd just bought for herself at the
canteen, and she flushed with humiliation as he turned away
mumbling. When there were more of them, the woman in
charge of catering came out with a kitchen-hand in a blood-
streaked apron to chase them off like a band of marauding
monkeys.

We were accustomed to seeing them pan-handling in the
streets of the city near the university and gathered in this
vacant lot or that, clandestine with only one secret mission,
to beg enough to buy another bottle; moving on as the
druids' circle of their boxes and bits of board spread on the
ground round the ashes of their trash fires was cleared for the
erection of post-modern office blocks. We all knew the one
who waved cars into empty parking bays. We'd all been
confronted, as we crossed the road or waited at the traffic
lights, idling in our minds as the engine of the jalopy idles, by

the one who held up a piece of cardboard with a message running out of space at the edges: NO JOB IM HUNGRY EVEYONE HELP PLeas.

At first; yes, there were already a few of them about. They must have drifted in by the old, unfrequented entrance down near the tennis courts, where the security fence was not yet completed. And if they were not come upon, there were the signs: trampled spaces in the bushes, empty bottles, a single split shoe with a sole like a lolling tongue. No doubt they had been chased out by a patrolling security guard. No student, at that stage, would have bothered to report the harmless presence; those of us who had cars might have been more careful than usual to leave no sweaters or radios visible through the locked windows. We followed our familiar rabbit-runs from the lecture rooms and laboratories back, forth and around campus, between residences, libraries, Student Union and swimming pool, through avenues of posters making announcements of debates and sports events, discos and rap sessions, the meetings of Muslim, Christian or Jewish brotherhoods, gay or feminist sisterhoods, with the same lack of attention to all but the ones we'd put up ourselves.

It was summer when it all started. We spend a lot of time on the lawns around the pool, in summer. We swot down there, we get a good preview of each other more or less nude, boys and girls, there's plenty of what you might call foreplay – happy necking. And the water to cool off in. The serious competitive swimmers come early in the morning when nobody else is up, and it was they who discovered these people washing clothes in the pool. When the swimmers warned them off they laughed and jeered. One left a dirt-stiff pair of pants that a swimmer balled and threw after him. There was argument among the swimmers; one felt the incident ought to be reported to Security, two were uncomfortable with the idea in view of the university's commitment to being available to the city community. They must have persuaded him that he would be exposed for élitism, because although the pool was referred to as The Wishee-Washee, among us, after that, there seemed to be no action taken.

Now you began to see them all over. Some greeted you smarmily (*my baas*, sir, according to their colour and culture), retreating humbly into the undergrowth; others, bold on wine or stoned on meths, sentimental on pot, or transformed in the wild hubris of all three, called out a claim (Hey man, *Ja boetie*) and even beckoned to you to join them where they had formed one of their circles, or huddled, just two, with the instinct for seclusion that only couples looking for a place to make love have, among us. The security fence down at the tennis courts was completed, reinforced with spikes and manned guard-house, but somehow they got in. The guards with their Alsatian dogs patrolled the campus at night but every day there were more shambling figures disappearing into the trees, more of those thick and battered faces looking up from the wells between buildings, more supine bodies contoured like sacks of grass-cuttings against the earth beneath the struts of the sports grandstands.

And they were no longer a silent presence. Their laughter and their quarrels broadcast over our student discussions, our tête-à-tête conversations and love-making, even our raucous fooling about. They had made a kind of encampment for themselves, there behind the sports fields where there was a stretch of ground whose use the university had not yet determined: it was for future expansion of some kind, and in the meantime equipment for maintenance of the campus was kept there – objects that might or might not be useful, an old tractor, barrels for indoor plants when the Vice-Chancellor requested a bower to decorate some hall for the reception of distinguished guests, and – of course – the compost heaps. The compost heaps were now being used as a repository for more than garden waste. If they had not been there with their odours of rot sharpened by the chemical agents for decay with which they were treated, the conclave living down there might have been sniffed out sooner. Perhaps they had calculated this in the secrets of living rough: perhaps they decided that the Alsatians' noses would be bamboozled.

So we knew about them – everybody knew about them, students, faculty, administrative staff, Vice-Chancellor – and yet nobody knew about them. Not officially. Security was supposed to deal with trespassers as a routine duty; but although Security was able to find and escort beyond the gates one or two individuals too befuddled or not wily enough to keep out of the way, they came back or were replaced by others. There was some kind of accommodation they had worked out within the order of the campus, some plan of interstices they had that the university didn't have; like the hours at which security patrols could be expected, there must have been other certainties we students and our learned teachers had relied on so long we did not realise that they had become useless as those red bomb-shaped fire extinguishers which, when a fire leaps out in a room, are found to have evaporated their content while hanging on the wall.

We came to recognise some of the bolder characters; or rather it was that they got to recognise us – with their street-wise judgement they knew who could be approached. For a cigarette. Not money – you obviously don't ask students for what they themselves are always short of. They would point to a wrist and ask the time, as an opener. And they must have recognised something else, too; those among us who come to a university because it's the cover where you think you can be safe from surveillance and the expectations others have of you – back to play-school days, only the sand-pit and the finger-painting is substituted by other games. The dropouts, just cruising along until the end of the academic year, some-times joined the group down behind the grandstands, taking a turn with the zoll and maybe helping out with the donation of a bottle of wine now and then. Of course only we, their siblings, identified them; with their jeans bought ready-torn at the knees, and hair shaved up to a topknot, they would not have been distinguished from the younger men in the group by a passing professor dismayed at the sight of the intrusion of the campus by hobos and loafers. (An interesting point, for the English Department, that in popular terminology the whites are known as hobos and the blacks as loafers.) If stu-dent solidarity with the underdog was expressed in the wearing of ragged clothes, then the invaders' claim to be within society was made through adoption of acceptable fashionable unconventions. (I thought of putting that in my next essay for Sociology 11.) There were topknots and single ear-rings among the younger invaders, dreadlocks, and one had long tangled blond hair snaking about his dark-stubbled face. He could even have passed for a certain junior lecturer in the Department of Political Science.

So nobody said a word about these recruits from among the students, down there. Not even the Society of Christian Students, who campaigned for moral regeneration on the campus. In the meantime, 'the general situation had been brought to the notice' of Administration. The implication was that they were to be requested to leave, with semantic evasion of the terms 'squatter' or 'eviction'. SUJUS (Students For Justice) held a meeting in protest against forced removal under any euphemism. ASOCS (Association of Conservative Students) sent a delegation to the Vice-Chancellor to demand that the campus be cleared of degenerates.

Then it was discovered that there were several women living among the men down there. The white woman was the familiar one who worked along the cars parked in the streets, trudging in thonged rubber sandals on swollen feet. The faces of the two black women were darkened by drink as white faces are reddened by it. The three women were seen swaying together, keeping upright on the principle of a tripod. The Feminist Forum took them food, tampons, and condoms for their protection against pregnancy and AIDS, although it was difficult to judge which was still young enough to be a sex object in need of protection; they might be merely prematurely aged by the engorged tissues puffing up their faces and the exposure of their skin to all weathers, just as, in a reverse process, pampered females look younger than they are through the effect of potions and plastic surgery.

From ASOCS came the rumour that one of the group had made obscene advances to a girl student – although she denied this in tears, *she* had offered *him* her pitta, which he had refused, mumbling 'I don't eat rubbish'. The Vice-Chancellor was importuned by parents who objected to their sons' and daughters' exposure to undesirables, and by Hope For The Homeless who wanted to put up tents on this territory of the over-privileged. The City Health authorities were driven off the campus by SUJUS and The Feminist Forum, while the Jewish Student Congress discussed getting the Medical School to open a clinic down at the grandstands, the Islamic Student Association took a collection for the group while declaring that the area of their occupation was out of bounds to female students wearing the *chador*, and the Students Buddhist Society distributed tracts on meditation among men and women quietly sleeping in the sun with their half-jacks, discreet in brown paper packets up to the screwtop, snug beside them as hot-water bottles.

These people could have been removed by the police, of course, on a charge of vagrancy or some such, but the Vice-Chancellor, the University Council and the Faculty Association had had too much experience of violence resulting from the presence of the police on campus to invite this again. The matter was referred back and forth. When we students returned after the Easter vacation the blond man known by his head of hair, the toothless ones, the black woman who always called out *Hullo lovey how'you* and the neat queen who would buttonhole anyone to tell of his student days in Dublin, *You kids don't know what a real university is*, were still there. Like the stray cats students (girls again) stooped to scratch behind the ears.

And then something really happened. One afternoon I thought I saw Professor Jepson in a little huddle of four or five comfortably under a tree on their fruit-box seats. Someone who looked the image of him: one of the older men, having been around the campus some months, now, was taking on some form of mimesis better suited to him than the kid-stuff garb the younger ones and the students aped from each other. Then I saw him again, and there was Dr Heimrath from Philosophy just in the act of taking a draw, next to him – if any social reject wanted a model for look-alike it would be from that Department. And I was not alone, either; the friend I was with that day saw what I did. We were the only ones who believed a student who said he had almost stepped on Bell, Senior Lecturer from Math, in the bushes with one of the three women; Bell's bald head shone a warning signal just in time. Others said they'd seen Kort wrangling with one of the men, there were always fights when the gatherings ran out of wine and went on to meths. Of course Kort had every kind of pure alcohol available to him in his domain, the science laboratories: everybody saw him, again and again, down there, it was Kort, all right, no chance of simple resemblance, and the euphoria followed by aggression that a meths concoction produces markedly increased in the open-air coterie during the following weeks. The papers Math students handed in were not returned when they were due; Bell's secretary did not connect calls to his office, day after day, telling callers he had stepped out for a moment. Jepson, Professor Jepson who not only had an international reputation as a nuclear physicist but also was revered by the student body as the one member of faculty who was always to be trusted to defend students' rights against authoritarianism, our old prof, everybody's enlightened grandfather – he walked down a corridor unbuttoned, stained, with dilated pupils that were unaware of the students who shrank back, silent, to make way.

There had been sniggers and jokes about the other faculty members, but nobody found anything to say over Professor Jepson; nothing, nothing at all. As if to smother any comment about him, rumours about others got wilder; or facts did. It was said that the Vice-Chancellor himself was seen down there, sitting round one of their trash fires; but it could have been that he was there to reason with the trespassers, to flatter them with the respect of placing himself in their company so that he could deal with the situation. Heimrath was supposed to have been with him, and Bester from Religious Studies with Franklin-Turner from English – but Franklin-Turner was hanging around there a lot anyway, that snobbish closet drinker come out into the cold, no more fastidious ideas about race keeping him out of that mixed company, eh?

And it was no rumour that Professor Russo was going down there, now. Minerva Russo, of Classics, young, untouchable as one of those lovely creatures who can't be possessed by men, can be carried off only by a bull or penetrated only by the snowy penis-neck of a swan. We males all had understood, through her, what it means to feast with your eyes, but we never speculated about what we'd find under her clothes: further sexual awe, perhaps, a mother-of-pearl scaled tail. Russo was attracted. She sat down there and put their dirty bottle to her mouth and the black-rimmed fingernails of one of them fondled her neck. Russo heard their wheedling, brawling, booze-snagged voices calling and became a female along with the other unwashed three. We saw her scratching herself when she did still turn up – irregularly – to teach us Greek poetry. Did she share their body-lice too?

It was through her, perhaps, that real awareness of the people down there came. The revulsion and the pity; the old white woman with the suffering feet ganging up with the black ones when the men turned on the women in the paranoia of betrayal – by some mother, some string of wives or lovers half-drowned in the bottles of the past – and cursing her sisters when one of them took a last cigarette butt or hung on a man the white sister favoured; tended by the sisterhood or tending one of them when the horrors shook or a blow was received. The stink of the compost heaps they used drifted through the libraries with the reminder that higher functions might belong to us but we had to perform the lower ones just like the wretches who made us stop our noses. Shit wasn't a meaningless expletive, it was part of the hazards of the human condition. They were ugly, down there at the grandstands and under the bushes, barnacled and scaled with disease and rejection, no one knows how you may pick it up, how it is transmitted, turning blacks grey and firing whites' faces in a furnace of exposure, taking away shame so that you beg, but leaving painful pride so that you can still rebuff, *I don't eat rubbish*, relying on violence because peace has to have shelter, but sticking together with those who threaten you because that is the only bond that's left. The shudder at it, and the freedom of it – to let go to assignments, assessments, tests of knowledge, hopes of tenure, the joy and misery of responsibility for lovers and children, money, debts. No goals and no failures. It was enviable and frightening to see them down there – Bester, Franklin-Turner, Heimrath and the others, Russo pulling herself to rights to play the goddess when she caught sight of us but too bedraggled to bring it off. Jepson, our Jepson, all that we had to believe in of the Old Guard's world, passing and not recognising us.

And then one day, they had simply disappeared. Gone. The groundsmen had swept away the broken bottles and discarded rags. The compost was doused with chemicals and spread on the campus's floral display. The Vice-Chancellor had never joined the bent backs round the zoll and the bottle down there and was in his panelled office. The lines caging Heimrath's mouth in silence did not release him to ask why students gazed at him. Minerva sat before us in her special way with matched pale narrow hands placed as if one were the reflection of the other, its fingertips raised against a mirror. Jepson's old bristly sow's ear sagged patiently towards the discourse of the seminar's show-off.

From under the bushes and behind the grandstands they had gone, or someone had found a way to get rid of them overnight. But they are always with us. Just somewhere else.

Nana's Dance

MICHELLE HEINEMANN

PATRICK CAIRN PASSES his wife Inta Levine in the hallway
near the bathroom of their home. He kisses her good morning, then continues to the kitchen where he makes coffee,
cuts oranges for juice, boils water for eggs. When he looks up
from the eggs, Inta stands jack-knifed in the kitchen doorway, struggling with a pair of panty hose. She has one leg in,
but the other side is twisted and won't go on straight. 'Shit.
What a way to start the day,' she sighs, and finally she gets
both legs in.

Patrick waits until she's completely dressed. Then he walks
to her, spatula in hand, and nuzzles into her. He knows her
warmth, his ear to her breast, his free hand at her inner thigh.
'Breakfast is on,' he says.

She purrs deep in her throat. 'You're my man,' she says,
slipping out of her pumps and jumping to straddle him
around his thighs. She purrs into his ear, wriggling her fingers, between his waist and the band on his pyjama bottoms.
They drop to the floor and Patrick Cairn steps out of them. 'I
don't know anybody else in the world who can undress me as
quickly as you can,' he laughs, first alone, then with her.

He carries her to a chair by the kitchen table, leans her
against the table. Light refracts from it, reveals the strands of

red running through her voluminous brown hair. He lifts up her skirt, removes her hose to her knees, then brings her on him in the chair. A fork clatters across the floor.

Her sound is enjoyment. Deep. 'Breakfast,' she manages, in rhythm, 'the most important meal.'

'Eggs,' he says, finally, 'will be getting cold.'

They eat. He in happy, self-absorbed silence. She, hurriedly, then out the door to work.

Patrick Cairn whistles doing the dishes. Hands in hot suds, he feels happiness settled in his blood. He is a man in love: with himself, with his work, with his wife.

He sends her flowers. And a note: 'Meet me at Orestes at 8:30. For supper and the dancer.' Then he goes to his studio and spends his day amidst his paints and brushes, his canvases of various sizes.

Nana Mazoni's first day at her new job with Clarence, Soile, and McKrakin is one filled with too many faceless figures rushing to her desk with work and rushing away just as fast. Her fingers move over the computer keys swiftly, but aimlessly. She processes documents, one after the other of affidavits, letters of intent, last wills, invoices for services rendered. All placed at her desk with the same import. She is too aware it is only 3:12, watching the clock on the wall in front of her moving its shiny digits from second to second. She wants it to be 5:15 and then she will sprint to the subway.

At home, she will prepare her dancing costume. She will rub the sequinned skirt until its polished surface reflects even the shadows from the trees outside her window. She will adjust the halter-strap on the wrap cloth which covers her breasts. She will pack strands of gold arm and ankle bracelets, coils of ear-rings, into a shoulder bag. She will not forget to pack her bag of make-up: colours to paint her dancer's face. Tonight she must impress. Tonight she will dance for Mr Nick Polandras, owner of Orestes. She will dance for his customers too, but first she will dance for him. He will like what he sees and then he will tell her the job is hers.

Inta Levine works late preparing a case she will take to court the next afternoon. She leaves her office and walks the four blocks to her health spa for a shower about the same time as Patrick wraps his brushes in turpentine-soaked rags. He surveys his day before him and then he too leaves his work to take a shower. They arrive promptly, separately, but exactly on time. Years together have taught them not to take the other's time for granted.

Nick Polandras hugs Inta, kisses Patrick on each cheek. 'The best table for you,' says Nick. 'For my most loyal customers. Here, sit.' The wrought-iron chair legs scrape the stone floor. The pop of a cork. Retsina, a bottle, is at their table. Nick pours for Patrick to test. 'Superb, pour away!'

Nick is excited. 'Tonight I try a new dancer. You must tell me what you think.'

Nana touches the bright red lipstick to her mouth one last time, then steps, barefoot, on to the cool stone floor at Orestes. There is music, but she barely hears it. Her mind is now at her belly: it is from there that she moves. Thrusting and revolving, her upper torso straight, but following on its jelly-like foundation. Her legs take the weight, her buttock muscles tight keep her soft belly thrust far forward. She breathes in fresh oxygen, strands of ebony hair fall across her eyes, then move away with the pulsating of her body.

Light splashes diffused colour from the sequins on her skirt to the white walls. Her bracelets and bangles smashing together accentuate the rhythm. She sees colours move by dizzily: people. She moves closer to them. Hot, greedy hands tuck folded bills between her skirt and where it rests low on her hips. There is clapping, whistling, hooting and she has their full attention, dancing along the cool stone floor and out behind the kitchen door.

Patrick Cairn has never seen a body dance as this one does. Each move a separate gesture, yet the slippery smooth transition between each move leaves him wondering if he only imagined a change. He has Inta's hand in his and he is stroking it firmly, with great energy. She offers the dancer money: he is too transfixed by her olive skin, her smell of sweat, her motions. When she is gone, Inta rushes to Nick, telling him he must keep the dancer. Patrick takes a card from his wallet:

'Patrick Cairn. Artist. Viewing by appointment only. Studio phone (416) 837–5521.' On the back, in pencil, he writes: 'Dancer – I would like to paint you. Please phone.' He slips the card to Nick before he leaves for home with Inta.

Nick Polandras hires Nana as the weekend dancer: Thursdays, Fridays, Saturdays, two shifts, 7:30 and 9:00. She turns to leave. He calls her back. 'This is for you,' he says and gives her Patrick's card. 'It is from my good friend Patrick Cairn. You are very lucky.'

She phones him from her desk at work the next day, and arranges to come to his studio that evening. She meets him there promptly at 7:30. 'It will take time. First I need you to model for some drawings. Later, you can dance for me and I will paint you dancing.' Monday and Wednesday, 7:30, until they are done.

Inta Levine notices Nana's full mouth: pregnant and curving low on her face. Above it, the most delicate lift at her nose, then mahogany eyes framed by thick lashes. Inta passes Nana's desk often and stops to chat idly to her at first. 'You are new here.' Yes. 'My name is Inta Levine.' Nana Mazoni. Later, Inta offers compliments. About her face: 'It is very beautiful.' Her choice of colour: 'Red is a stunning colour on you.' Her work: 'So fast. Never any errors.' Then they take coffee together, cozied side by side on the couch in the staff-room looking at fashion magazines and dressing each other. Soon Inta will work late on a Tuesday night, and leaving, will see Nana also working late. They will agree on a movie and after, will talk about it in a coffee shop until there is nothing more to say.

For five weeks Nana has slipped into Patrick's studio and prepared herself for the artist. Dressing, tying her hair in a sweeping knot above her head, and painting her face thickly with colours from her make-up bag. He comes at 7:30 and she stands very still for him. When she is tired, they stop and sip coffee and talk a bit. She tells him of an aunt at home in Greece who taught her to dance. Dancing brings pride. Her mother sewed the costume: each sequin attached by hand.

He paints her again. She sees the slight bulge at the sides of his neck as he moves his head up to see her, then down to the canvas. 'The painting is almost done,' he says and shows it to her. She will look at it long. He leaves her alone in the studio and she will look at her painted self long.

On a rainy Sunday afternoon, Nana opens her door to Inta, standing wet in the hall. 'I was passing by. I came to see if you'd like to join me at the gallery for the Picasso exhibit. I've seen it twice already. Have you?' Instead, Inta comes in. Nana makes hot cocoa and while they sip it on the couch, she rubs Inta's hair dry with a towel. Inta turns to thank Nana, reaches her long arms around the fleshy woman and hugs her. Inta looks into Nana's eyes a moment, sees consent, lips come to lips, and they hold each other in tense excitement, Inta running her hands through Nana's loose hair. They say nothing. Just caress each other in the silence.

Nana's sessions with Patrick go like this: he controls the music. She dances, and when he has seen all he can for the moment, he stops her. She rests while he paints and when he is ready to see her dance again, he starts the music. Tonight, close to 9:00, her foot turns the wrong way and she splashes to the floor. Patrick comes to her quickly and she, flat against the floor now, says she is OK, just wants to rest awhile. He is leaning over her, his hair forward, his face flushed, his breathing fast and heavy. She brings his face to hers. The kiss is not shy. It has been growing stronger from week to week and now it is a brave, acknowledging kiss. She thinks of her mother and takes off her sequinned skirt. He thinks of his wife and locks the studio door.

Inta and Nana sit on the floor in Nana's apartment. Nana feeds grapes to Inta, one at a time, slowly, pushing them between Inta's lips just to feel skin to skin. Later, they will draw the drapes and Inta will move, button by button, down the side of Nana's red dress, exposing the dark skin beneath. Nana will start with Inta's shoes and remove her clothing slow at first, then fast and faster, lunging at Inta's stark breasts with too much energy. They will tumble to the floor: laughing, wanting, having. Nana will be wrapped round by Inta's length, her mouth finding the depressions along Nana's spine. They will fall asleep, and when Inta wakes it will be very late. She will dress quickly and go home to Patrick.

Patrick Cairn tells his wife that his latest painting is almost done. 'Soon I'll show it to you,' he says. They are lying in their bed on this Saturday morning when he turns to her and says how lucky he feels to love her so much. She smiles at him, hugs him to her and tells him the same.

Farthing House

SUSAN HILL

I HAVE NEVER told you any of this before – I have never told anyone, and indeed, writing it down and sealing it up in an envelope to be read at some future date may still not count as 'telling'. But I shall feel better for it, I am sure of that. Now it has all come back to me, I do not want to let it go again, I must set it down.

It is true, and for that very reason you must not hear it just now. You will be prey to enough anxieties and fancies without my adding ghosts to them; the time before the birth of a child one is so very vulnerable.

I daresay that it has made me vulnerable too, that this has brought the events to mind.

I began to be restless several weeks ago. I was burning the last of the leaves. It was a most beautiful day, clear and cold and blue and a few of them were swirling down as I raked and piled. And then a light wind blew suddenly across the grass, scuttling the leaves and making the woodsmoke drift towards me, and as I caught the smell of it, that most poignant, melancholy, nostalgic of all smells, something that had been drifting on the edges of my consciousness blurred and insubstantial, came into focus, and in a rush I remembered . . .

It was as though a door had been opened on to the past, and I had stepped through and gazed at what I saw there again. I saw the house, the drive sweeping up to it, the countryside around it, on that late November afternoon, saw the red sun setting behind the beech copse, beyond the rising, brown fields, saw the bonfire the gardener had left to smoulder on gently by itself, and the thin pale smoke coiling up from its heart. I was there, all over again.

I went in a daze into the house, made some tea, and sat, still in my old, outdoor clothes at the kitchen table, as it went quite dark outside the window, and I let myself go back to that day, and the nights that followed, watched it all unfold again, remembered. So that it was all absolutely clear in my mind when the newspaper report appeared, a week later.

I was going to see Aunt Addy. It was November, and she had been at the place called Farthing House since the New Year, but it was only now that I had managed to get away and make the two-hundred-mile journey to visit her.

We had written, of course, and spoken on the telephone, and so far as I could tell she sounded happy. Yes, they were very nice people, she said, and yes, it was such a lovely house, and she did so like her room, everyone was most kind, oh yes dear, it was the right thing, I should have done it long ago, I really am very settled.

And Rosamund said that she was, too, said that it was fine, really, just as Addy told me, a lovely place, such kind people, and Alec had been and he agreed.

All the same, I was worried, I wasn't sure. She had been so independent always, so energetic, so very much her own person all her life, I couldn't see her in a Home, however nice and however sensible a move it was – and she was eighty-six and had had two nasty falls the previous winter – I liked to think of her as she was when we were children, and went to stay at the house in Wales, striding over the hills with the dogs, rowing on the lake, getting up those colossal picnics for us all. I always loved her, she was such fun. I wish you had known her.

And of course, I wish that one of us could have had her, but there really wasn't room to make her comfortable and, oh, other feeble-sounding reasons, which are real reasons, nonetheless.

She had never asked me to visit her, that wasn't her way. Only the more she didn't ask, the more I knew that I should, the guiltier I felt. It was just such a terrible year, what with one thing and another.

But now I was going. It had been a beautiful day for the drive too. I had stopped twice, once in a village, once in a small market town and explored churches and little shops, and eaten lunch and had a pot of tea and taken a walk along the banks of a river in the late sunshine, and the berries, I remember had been thick and heavy, clustered on the boughs. I'd seen a jay and two deer and once, like magic, a kingfisher, flashing blue as blue across a hump-backed bridge. I'd had a sort of holiday really. But now I was tired, I would be glad to get there. It was very nice that they had a guest-room, and I didn't have to stay alone in some hotel. It meant I could really spend all my time with Aunt Addy. Besides, you know how I've always hated hotels, I lie awake thinking of the hundreds of people who've slept in the bed before me.

Little Dornford 1½ m.

But as I turned right and the road narrowed to a single track, between trees, I began to feel nervous, anxious, I prayed that it really would be all right, that Aunt Addy had been telling the truth.

'You'll come to the church', they had said, and a row of three cottages, and then there is the sign to Farthing House, at the bottom of the drive.

I had seen no other car since leaving the cathedral town seven miles back on the main road. It was very quiet, very out of the way. I wondered if Addy minded. She had always been alone up there in her own house but somehow now that she was so old and infirm, I thought she might have liked to be nearer some bustle, perhaps actually in a town. And what about the others, a lot of old women isolated out here together? I shivered suddenly and peered forwards along the darkening lane. The church was just ahead, the car lights swept along a yew hedge, a lych gate, caught the shoulder of a gravestone. I slowed down.

FARTHING HOUSE. It was a neat, elegantly lettered sign, not too prominent and at least it did not proclaim itself Residential Home.

The last light was fading in the sky behind a copse of bare beech trees, the sun dropping down, a great red, frost-rimmed ball. I saw the drive, a wide lawn, the remains of a bonfire of leaves, smouldering by itself in a corner. Farthing House.

I don't know exactly what my emotions had been up to that moment. I was very tired, with that slightly dazed, confused sensation that comes after a long drive and the attendant concentration. And I was apprehensive. I so wanted to be happy about Aunt Addy, to be sure that she was in the right place to spend the rest of her life – or maybe I just wanted to have my conscience cleared so I could bowl off home again in a couple of days with a blithe heart, untroubled by guilt and be able to enjoy the coming Christmas.

But as I stood on the black and white marbled floor of the entrance porch I felt something else and it made me hesitate before ringing the bell. What was it? Not fear or anxiety, no shudders. I am being very careful now, it would be too easy to claim that I had sensed something sinister, that I was shrouded at once in the atmosphere of a haunted house.

But I did not, nothing of that sort crossed my mind. I was only overshadowed by a curious sadness – I don't know exactly how to describe it – a sense of loss, a melancholy. It descended like a damp veil about my head and shoulders. But it lifted, or almost, the cloud passed after a few moments. Well, I was tired, I was cold, it was the back end of the year, and perhaps I had caught a chill, which often manifests itself first as a sudden change of mood into a lower key.

The only other thing I noticed was the faintest smell of hospital antiseptic. That depressed me a bit more. Farthing House wasn't a hospital or even a nursing home proper and I didn't want it to seem so to Aunt Addy, not even in this slight respect.

But in fact, once I was inside, I no longer noticed it at all, there was only the pleasant smell of furniture polish, and fresh chrysanthemums and, somewhere in the background, a light, spicy smell of baking.

The smells that greeted me were all of a piece with the rest of the welcome. Farthing House seemed like an individual, private home. The antiques in the hall were good, substantial pieces and they had been well cared for over the years, there were framed photographs on a sideboard, flowers in jugs and bowls, there was an old, fraying, tapestry-covered armchair on which a fat cat slept beside a fire. It was quiet, too, there was no rattling of trolleys or buzzing of bells. And the matron did not call herself one.

'You are Mrs Flower – how nice to meet you.' She put out her hand. 'Janet Pearson.'

She was younger than I had expected, probably in her late forties. A small King Charles spaniel hovered about her waving a frond-like tail. I relaxed.

I spent a good evening in Aunt Addy's company; she was so settled and serene, and yet still so full of life. Farthing House was well run, warm and comfortable, and there was good, home-cooked dinner, with fresh vegetables and an excellent lemon meringue pie. The rooms were spacious, the other residents pleasant but not over-obtrusive.

Something else was not as I had expected. It had been necessary to reserve the guest-room and bathroom well in advance, but when Mrs Pearson herself took my bag and led me up the handsome staircase, she told me that after a serious leak in the roof had caused damage, it was being redecorated. 'So I've put you in Cedar – it happens to be free just now.' She barely hesitated as she spoke. 'And it's such a lovely room, I'm sure you'll like it.'

How could I have failed? Cedar Room was one of the two largest in the house, on the first floor, with big bay windows overlooking the garden at the back – though now the deep red curtains had been drawn against the early evening darkness.

'Your aunt is just across the landing.'

'So they've put you in Cedar,' Addy said later when we were having a drink in her own room. It wasn't so large but I preferred it simply, I think, because there was so much familiar furniture, her chair, her own oak dresser, the painted screen, even the club fender we used to sit on to toast our toes as children.

'Yes. It seems a bit big for one person, but it's very handsome. I'm surprised it's vacant.'

Addy winked at me. 'Well, of course it *wasn't* . . .'

'Oh.' For an instant, that feeling of unease and melancholy passed over me like a shadow again.

'Now buck up, don't look wan, there isn't time.' And she plunged me back into family chat and cheerful recollections, interspersed with sharp observations about her fellow residents, so that I was almost entirely comfortable again.

I remained so until we parted at getting on for half-past eleven. We had spent much of the evening alone together, and then joined some of the others in one of the lounges, where an almost party-like atmosphere had developed, with laughter and banter and happy talk, which had all helped to revive my first impressions of Farthing House and Addy's place there.

It was not until I closed the door of my room and was alone that I was forced to acknowledge again what had been at the back of my mind all the time, almost like having a person at my shoulder, though just out of sight. I was in this large, high-ceilinged room because it was free, its previous occupant having recently died. I knew no more, and did not want to know, had firmly refrained from asking any questions. Why should it matter? It did not. As a matter of fact it still does not, it had no bearing at all on what happened, but I must set it down because I feel I have to tell the whole truth and part of that truth is that I was in an unsettled, slightly nervous frame of mind as I got ready for bed, because of what I knew, and because I could not help wondering whether whoever had occupied Cedar Room had died in it, perhaps even in this bed. I was, as you might say, almost expecting to have bad dreams or to see a ghost.

There is just one other thing.

When we were all in the lounge, the talk had inevitably been of former homes and families, the past in general, and Addy had wanted some photographs from upstairs. I had slipped out to fetch them for her.

It was very quiet in the hall. The doors were heavy and soundproof, though from behind one I could just hear some faint notes of recorded music, but the staff quarters down the passage were closed off and silent.

So I was quite certain that I heard it, the sound was unmistakable. It was a baby crying. Not a cat, not a dog. They are quite different, you know. What I heard from some distant room on the ground floor was the cry of a newborn baby.

I hesitated. Stopped. But it was over at once, and it did not come again. I waited, feeling uncertain. But then, from the room with the music, I heard the muffled signature tune of the ten o'clock news. I went on up the staircase. The noise had come from the television then.

Except, you see, that deep down and quite surely, I knew that it had not.

I may have had odd frissons about my room but once I was actually in bed and settling down to read a few pages of *Sense and Sensibility* before going to sleep, I felt quite composed and cheerful. The only thing wrong was that the room still seemed far too big for one person. There was ample furniture and yet it was as though someone else ought to be there. I find it difficult to explain precisely.

I was very tired. And Addy was happy, Farthing House was everything I had hoped it would be, I had had a most enjoyable evening, and the next day we were to go out and see something of the countryside and later, hear sung evensong at the cathedral.

I switched out the lamp.

At first I thought it was as quiet outside the house as in, but after a few minutes, I heard the wind sifting through the bare branches and sighing towards the windows and away. I felt like a child again, snug in my little room under the eaves.

I slept.

I dreamed almost at once and with extraordinary vividness, and it was, at least to begin with, a most happy dream. I was in St Mary's, the night after you were born, lying in my bed in that blissful, glowing, untouchable state when the whole of the rest of life seems suspended and everything irrelevant but this. You were there in your crib beside me, though I did not look at you. I don't think anything happened in the dream and it did not last very long. I was simply there in the past and utterly content.

I woke with a start, and as I came to, it was with that sound in my ears, the crying of the baby that I had heard as I crossed the hall earlier that evening. The room was quite dark. I knew at once where I was and yet I was still half within my dream – I remember that I felt a spurt of disappointment that it had *been* a dream and I was actually there, a new young mother again with you beside me in the crib.

How strange, I thought, I wonder why. And then something else happened – or no, not 'happened'. There just *was* something else, that is the only way I can describe it.

I had the absolutely clear sense that someone else had been in my room – not the hospital room of my dream, but this room in Farthing House. No one was here now, but minutes before I woke, I knew that they had been. I remember thinking, someone is in the next bed. But of course, there was no next bed, just mine.

After a while I switched on the lamp. All was as it had been when I had gone to sleep. Only that sensation, that atmosphere was still there. If nothing else had happened at Farthing House, I suppose in time I would have decided I had half-dreamed, half-imagined it, and forgotten. It was only because of what happened afterwards that I remembered so clearly and knew with such certainty that my feeling had been correct.

I got up, went over to the tall windows and opened the

curtains a little. There was a clear, star-pricked sky and a thin paring of moon. The gardens and the dark countryside all around were peaceful and still.

But I felt oppressed again by the most profound melancholy of spirit, the same terrible sadness and sense of loss that had overcome me on my arrival. I stood there for a long time, unable to release myself from it, before going back to bed to read another chapter of Jane Austen, but I could not concentrate properly and in the end grew drowsy. I heard nothing, saw nothing, and I did not dream again.

The next morning my mood had lightened. There had been a slight frost during the night, and the sun rose on a countryside dusted over with rime. The sky was blue, trees set in dark pencil strokes against it.

We had a good day, Aunt Addy and I, enjoying one another's company, exploring churches and antique shops, having a pub lunch, and an old-fashioned muffin and fruit-cake tea after the cathedral service.

It was as we were eating it that I asked suddenly, 'What do you know about Farthing House?'

Seeing Addy's puzzled look, I went on, 'I just mean, how long has Mrs Pearson been there, who had it before, all that sort of thing. Presumably it was once a family house.'

'I have an idea someone told me it had been a military convalescent home during the war. Why do you ask?'

I thought of Cedar Room the previous night, and that strange sensation. *What* had it been? Or who? But I found that I couldn't talk about it for some reason, it made me too uneasy. 'Oh, nothing. Just curious.' I avoided Addy's eye.

That evening, the matron invited me to her own room for sherry, and to ask if I was happy about my aunt. I reassured her, saying all the right, polite things. Then she said, 'And have you been quite comfortable?'

'Oh yes.' I looked straight at her. I thought she might have been giving me an opening – I wasn't sure. And I almost did tell her. But again, I couldn't speak of it. Besides, what was there to tell? I had heard a baby crying – from the television.

I'd had an unusual dream, and an odd, confused sensation when I woke from it that someone had just left my room.

Nothing.

'I've been extremely comfortable,' I said firmly. 'I feel quite happy about everything.'

Did she relax just visibly, smile a little too eagerly, was there a touch of relief in her voice when she next spoke?

I don't know whether or not I dreamed that night. It seemed that one minute I was in a deep sleep, and the next that something had woken me. As I came to, I know I heard the echo of crying in my ears, or in my inner ear, but a different sort of crying this time, not that of a baby, but a desperate, woman's sobbing. The antiseptic smell was faintly there again too, my awareness of it was mingled with that of the sounds.

I sat bolt upright. The previous night, I had had the sensation of someone having just been in my room.

Now, I saw her.

There was another bed in the opposite corner of the room, close to the window, and she was getting out of it. The room felt horribly cold. I remember being conscious of the iciness on my hands and face.

I was wide awake, I am quite sure of that, I could hear my own heart pounding, see the bedside table, and the lamp and the blue binding of *Sense and Sensibility* in the moonlight. I know I was not dreaming, so much so that I almost spoke to the woman, wondering as I saw her what on earth they were thinking of to put her and her bed in my room while I was asleep.

She was young, with a flowing, embroidered nightgown, high necked and long sleeved. Her hair was long too, and as pale as her face. Her feet were bare. But I could not speak to her, my throat felt paralysed. I tried to swallow, but even that was difficult, the inside of my mouth was so dry.

She seemed to be crying. I suppose that was what I had heard. She moved across the room towards the door and she held out her arms as if she were begging someone to give her something. And that terrible melancholy came over me again, I felt inconsolably hopeless and sad.

The door opened. I know that because a rush of air came in to the room, and it went even colder, but somehow, I did not see her put her hand to the knob and turn it. All I know is that she had gone, and that I was desperate to follow her, because I felt that she needed me in some way.

I did not switch on the lamp or put on my dressing-gown, I half ran to catch her up.

The landing outside was lit as if by a low, flickering candle flame. I saw the door of Aunt Addy's room but the wood looked darker, and there were some pictures on the walls that I had not noticed before. It was still so cold my breath made little haws of white in front of my face.

The young woman had gone. I went to the head of the staircase. Below, it was pitch dark. I heard nothing, no foot-step, no creak of the floorboards. I was too frightened to go any further.

As I turned, I saw that the flickering light had faded and the landing was in darkness too. I felt my way, trembling, back to my own room and put my hand on the doorknob. As I did so I heard from far below, in the recesses of the house, the woman's sobbing and a calling – it might have been of a name, but it was too faint and far away for me to make it out.

I managed to stumble across the room and switch on the lamp. All was normal. There was just one bed, my own. Nothing had changed.

I looked at the clock. It was a little after three. I was soaked in sweat, shaking, terrified. I did not sleep again that night but sat up in the chair wrapped in the eiderdown with the lamp on, until the late grey dawn came around the curtains. That I had seen a young woman, that she had been getting out of another bed in my room, I had no doubt at all. I had not been dreaming, as I certainly had on the previous night. The difference between the two experiences was quite clear to me. She had been there.

I had never either believed or disbelieved in ghosts, scarcely ever thought about the subject at all. Now, I knew that I had seen one. And I could not throw off not only my fear but the depression her presence inflicted on me. Her distress and agitation, whatever their cause, had affected me profoundly, and from the first moment of my arrival at the door of Farthing House. It was a dark, dreadful, helpless feeling and with it there also went a sense of foreboding.

I was due to leave for home the following morning but when I joined Aunt Addy for breakfast I felt wretched, tense and strained, quite unfit for a long drive. When I went to Mrs Pearson's office and explained simply that I had not slept well, she expressed concern at once and insisted that I stay on another night. I wanted to, but I did not want to remain in Cedar Room. When I mentioned it, very diffidently, Mrs Pearson gave me a close look and I waited for her to question me but she did not, only told me, slipping her pen nervously round and round between her fingers that there simply was not another vacant room in the house. So I said that of course it did not matter, it was only that I had always felt uneasy sleeping in very large rooms, and laughed it off, trying to reassure her. She pretended that I had.

That morning, Aunt Addy had an appointment with the visiting hairdresser. I didn't feel like sitting about reading papers and chatting in the lounge. They were nice women, the other residents, kind and friendly and welcoming but I was on edge and still enveloped in sadness and foreboding. I needed time to myself.

The weather didn't help. It had gone a degree or two warmer and the rise in temperature had brought a dripping fog and low cloud that masked the lines of the countryside. I trudged around Farthing House gardens but the grass was soaking wet and the sight of the dreary bushes and black trees lowered my spirits further. I set off down the lane, past the three cottages. A dog barked from one, but the others were silent and apparently empty. I suppose that by then I had begun to wallow slightly in my mood and I decided that I might as well go the whole hog and visit the church and its overgrown little graveyard. It was bitterly cold inside. There were some good brasses and a wonderful ornate eighteenth-century monument to a pious local squire, with florid rhymes and madly grieving angels. But the stained glass was in ugly 'uncut moquette' colours, as Stephen would have said, and besides it was actually colder inside the church than out.

I had a prowl around the graveyard, looking here and there at epitaphs. There were a couple of minor gems but otherwise, all was plain, names and dates and dullness and I was about to leave when my eye was caught by some grave-stones at the far side near to the field wall. They were set a little apart and neatly arranged in two rows. I bent down and deciphered the faded inscriptions. They were all the graves of babies, newborn or a few days old, and dating from the early years of the century. I wondered why so many, and why all young babies. They had different surnames, though one or two recurred. Had there been some dreadful epidemic in the village ? Had the village been much larger then, if there had been so many young families ?

At the far end of the row were three adult sized stones. The inscriptions on two had been mossed over but one was clear.

Eliza Maria Dolly.
Died January 20 1902. Aged 19 years.
And also her infant daughter.

As I walked thoughtfully back I saw an elderly man dis-mount from a bicycle beside the gate and pause, looking towards me.

'Good morning! Gerald Manberry, vicar of the parish. Though really I am semi-retired, there isn't a great deal for a full-time man to take care of nowadays. I see you have been looking at the poor little Farthing House graves.'

'Farthing House?'

'Yes, just down the lane. It was a home for young women and their illegitimate babies from the turn of the century until the last war. Then a military convalescent home, I believe. It's a home for the elderly now of course.'

How bleak that sounded. I told him that I had been staying there. 'But the graves . . .' I said.

'I suppose a greater number of babies died around the time of birth then, especially in those circumstances. And mothers too, I fear. Poor girls. It's all much safer now. A better world. A better world.'

I watched him wheel his ancient bicycle round to the vestry door, before beginning to walk back down the empty lane towards Farthing House. But I was not seeing my surroundings or hearing the caw-cawing of the rooks in the trees above my head. I was seeing the young woman in the nightgown, her arms outstretched, and hearing her cry and feeling again that terrible sadness and distress. I thought of the grave of Eliza Maria Dolly, 'and also her infant daughter'.

I was not afraid any more, not now that I knew who she was and why she had been there, getting out of her bed in Cedar Room, to go in search of her baby. Poor, pale, distraught young thing, she could do no one harm.

I slept well that night, I saw nothing, heard nothing, although in the morning I knew, somehow, that she had been there again, there was the same emptiness in the room and the imprint of her sad spirit upon it.

The fog had cleared and it was a pleasant winter day, intermittently sunny. I left for home after breakfast, having arranged that Aunt Addy was to come to us for Christmas.

She did so and we had a fine time, as happy as we all used to be together, with Stephen and I, Rosamund, Alec and the others. I shall always be glad of that, for it was Addy's last Christmas. She fell down the stairs at Farthing House the following March, broke her hip and died of a stroke a few days later. They took her to hospital and I saw her there, but afterwards, when her things were to be cleared up, I couldn't face it. Stephen and Alec did everything. I never went back to Farthing House.

I often thought about it though, even dreamed of it. An experience like that affects you profoundly and for ever. But I could not have spoken about it, not to anyone at all. If ever a conversation touched upon the subject of ghosts I kept silent. I had seen one. I knew. That was all.

★

Some years afterwards, I learned that Farthing House had closed to residents, been sold and then demolished, to make room for a new development – the nearby town was spreading out now. Little Dornford had become a suburb.

I was sad. It had been, in most respects, such a good and happy place.

Then, only a week ago, I saw the name again, quite by chance, it leaped at me from the newspaper. You may remember the case, though you would not have known of any personal connection.

A young woman stole a baby, from its pram outside a shop. The child had only been left for a moment or two but apparently she had been following and keeping watch, waiting to take it. It was found eventually, safe and well. She had looked after it, so I suppose things could have been worse, but the distress caused to the parents was obviously appalling. You can imagine that now, can't you?

They didn't send her to prison, she was taken into medical care. Her defence was that she had stolen the child when she was out of her right mind after the death of her own baby not long before. The child was two days old. Her address was given as Farthing House Close, Little Dornford.

I think of it constantly, see the young, pale, distraught woman, her arms outstretched, searching, hear her sobbing, and the crying of her baby.

But I imagine that she has gone, now that she has what she was looking for.

Here Come
the Impersonators

JONATHAN HOLLAND

For Sophie Hudson, 1962–1988

LOOKING BACK OVER it now, the boy told Mr Menzies, there were certain episodes, certain feelings in his life which he might have known would lead up to this. As a child of eight, he had escaped getting into a playground fight with Michael Gudd by doing an impromptu impersonation of the headmaster, complete with stammer. His impersonation had stilled Michael Gudd's anger. As he grew older, and got to watch more and more television, it thrilled him to know that the *Mike Yarwood Show*, or *Dick Emery*, was to be shown. 'Oooh, you *are* awful,' he'd said to his mother one night, after they had moved into Prince's Court. 'But I like you!' His mother had laughed and called her boyfriend Geoff through from the kitchen to listen. 'That's good, that,' Geoff had said. 'Just like Dick Emery, that is.' Afterwards, the boy had lain in bed and softly uttered the words, over and over. 'Oooh,' he'd say, thinking of Dick Emery's lady with the glasses, 'you *are* awful.' It had sounded odd, he remembered, in the quiet of his room.

'Dick Emery's dead, of course,' he now said to Mr Menzies, who ran the club at Upton Park called Popsies, in which

127

they were sitting. There were lots of black chairs and tables, and a small stage upon which stood a man in overalls, hands on hips. Mr Menzies wore tinted spectacles and aftershave. Until last year, Popsies had been Klub Kokokabana but, as Mr Menzies explained, Latin America had kicked the proverbial, thanks to the Falklands and that Nicaragua business: 'And if they tell you that showbiz and politics don't mix, don't you believe 'em my son!' The boy quite liked Mr Menzies' voice. It was persuasive and slightly Scottish, a voice with power behind it. He didn't like the sort of people who had voices like that, but the voice itself he liked.

'Let's get a move on,' said Mr Menzies. The boy stood up, cleared his throat and, after a couple of false starts owing to nerves, rapidly delivered four impersonations. He had been a slave to these for the past week, recording from the television when his mother was out and then listening and listening, repeating and repeating. For the moment, as he had tried to explain, he was not concerned with being funny, or original; only with being accurate. He was not poking fun at anybody, just copying. He had got right down to details – vowel sounds, respiratory gaps – and he knew he was good, or he wouldn't have come. He did Terry Wogan, Ronald Reagan, Bruce Forsyth and wound up with the Prime Minister herself, doing something he had seen her say on the News. 'Where you have initiative, talent and ability,' he recited, in Mrs Thatcher's cocksure way, 'the money follows.' Mr Menzies seemed to chuckle at that and the boy, for the first time, thought Yes, I suppose it *is* funny, her saying that, and me doing this. At the end, Mr Menzies clapped, his applause sounding lonely in this usually noisy room. The boy sat down and smiled at the man he hoped would make his day, not knowing that Billy Menzies had not booked a new act for Popsies since Christmas 1978. Sad fact, but your reputation was your living in Clubland, even if it meant tolerating the presence of snotty-nosed adolescent pillocks like this one.

With some awkwardness, Mr Menzies placed the ankle of his right leg atop the knee of his left.

'You got some skill there, my son,' he said, adjusting his

tinted glasses on his nose. 'You want to ally that talent with some good material. You're here for expert advice? Well that's mine. You want to get teamed up with a good writer.' There didn't seem to be much more to say, but since the boy offered nothing by way of reply, merely running his sleeve over his nose, Mr Menzies went on.

'It's like Maggie says, my son, bless her. You got initiative –' he counted them off on his yellowed fingers – 'you got talent, you got ability. Give it a bit of wallop and you could be up there where you want to be. You working now, then?' knowing that the boy would not be here if the answer was Yes.

'I'm on the dole, as a matter of fact,' said the boy. 'Thanks for the advice, Mr Menzies – but what I was looking for was *work*, you understand. I actually need money, Mr Menzies. Badly.'

'Oh-ho dear,' said Mr Menzies, feeling uneasy despite himself, 'you are not alone there, my son. Oh-ho, no.' He smiled in a men–of–the–world way. It was time they parted company.

'I can do others,' said the boy urgently, rising from his chair. 'Other women. Cilla Black. Y'all right darlin's?' he yelped, thinking of Cilla Black, all wavy red hair and hysterical laughter, 'I can even do people we're not sure about, Mr Menzies. Poofters. Shut that door, Mr Menzies.'

Mr Menzies started back and nearly fell off his chair. The brat was accurate, there was no doubt about that. The boy had thought that things might improve if Mr Menzies were to laugh again, but he was not going to. He had nearly been made to fall off his own chair in his own club.

'Very good,' he said. 'Like the others. Give it time. You have a lot of skill up your sleeve there. But believe me, the paying customer sets a high standard. It's good, what you do. But it's not quite exactly right, let's say. Let's say that.'

'It's all about money, isn't it Mr Menzies?' said the boy bleakly, sitting down again like something punctured. 'That's how it is, isn't it?'

Mr Menzies was groping for his response when the boy suddenly continued.

'My impersonations,' he said slowly, 'are exact. You nearly fell off your chair. My impersonations, Mr Ruddy Menzies, are quite – exactly – right.' When he said the last three words, he shifted his gaze up on to Mr Menzies' eyes, and spoke in Mr Menzies' voice. Mr Menzies pushed back his chair and stood up. This was turning chilling.

'Cheek,' he said, 'will get you nowhere. That's more advice. Now adios.'

'Cheek will get you nowhere,' repeated the boy. 'I need *money*, Mr Menzies. Like you.'

'If you need money,' returned Mr Menzies, 'get down to the Job Centre. There are plenty of bloody jobs. It gets my goat, coming in here . . . my old Mum's got more sizzle than some of you lot . . .' He had to watch it with his ticker. He turned and strode towards the stage, overturning a chair with his behind.

'If you need money,' the boy called out, 'get a job, my son. You are not alone there, my son.'

'Jack,' called Mister Menzies. The boy thought it might not be a bad idea to slip out through a fire door.

Outside, it came to him that Mr Menzies hadn't even asked him his ruddy name.

The boy started thinking about things he had never thought about before. That the world was a bastard of a place to live in he had previously known only instinctively – he had known, for instance, that there was something not normal about his wish to sleep eleven hours a night. Now, he realised that life was better in his dreams. He thought about the TV personalities he admired and saw that for them, things were even harder. Natural skill was only the beginning of what they did: without it you had nothing, but with it, only a little. 'One per cent inspiration,' somebody from history had said, 'ninety-nine per cent perspiration.' The boy began to work it out for himself. He studied the television and thought he could see, behind the practised smiles of the performers, something bitter, like a chocolate liqueur filled with vinegar. He tried often, in front of the mirror, to keep it going the way they did, but he tripped up over his words: he tried writing some jokes, but didn't find them funny.

You couldn't do it alone, and yet he had to. You had to be tough and resistant, but he wasn't. He was afraid of things. There must be thousands like him from all over the country, who woke up one morning with a talent, only to take it out into the world to have it stamped out of them. He was, he knew, simply not good enough, not ready. The boy cried, for the first time in ages, because he had hoped for so much, writing a letter to the BBC, enclosing a cassette of his Greatest Impersonations alongside the original voices. It was silly to have sent off those letters. He probably wouldn't even get a reply to them. Those places were probably all run by sharks like Menzies.

He thought of ways to employ his skill. He thought of working for the adverts, and of setting up a business which rang people up on their birthdays, pretending to be someone else: Impersonatograms. But he didn't know how to go about any of these projects without looking a fool.

'When you have initiative, talent and ability,' he said aloud in Mrs Thatcher's voice, 'the money follows.' It sounded simple. It was a simple formula.

In Walthamstow, a woman of seventy-seven peered up at her sitting-room clock, trying to make out the figures through the smoke she had created with her last cigarette of the day. It was time for the *News At Ten*, and she thought that the attractive young presenter whose name she couldn't remember might be on: so she stubbed out her cigarette and turned on the television. The kettle in the kitchen started whistling, reminding the old woman that not a day of her life seemed to pass without her forgetting something more, getting something else wrong. Not only could she no longer tie in her last cup of tea of the day with the beginning of the news: this evening, she was unable even to remember whether or not she had any milk in the house. Perhaps William would remember to bring some along later. Forgetting this, mislaying that, she chided herself. She supposed that this was what getting older must be all about. It was not very nice.

By the time she had made the tea and carried it back to the sitting room, the news was under way. The old woman turned up the sound with her remote control and waited impatiently for the end of a piece about inner-city crime, wondering whether Walthamstow was considered inner-city or not. When it was over, she saw that tonight didn't seem to be one of that nice young presenter's nights. She watched distractedly as international issues were dealt with: the Gulf, Northern Ireland, South Africa, all disaster and gloom, and all strangely even remoter from her now than they had ever been. What was it that Harold had always referred to the television as? 'The old misery-box in the corner.' She remembered that as one of the last comments he had made prior to the stroke which had cost him his speech. Dimly aware that a reporter was speaking from a boat, the old woman allowed her mind to follow her gaze around the sitting room, for five years now quite bare, but still, in her imagination, littered with Harold's objects: his pipe on the mantelpiece, his fishing-rod against the door-jamb. Under the clock, there was a photograph of the three of them standing outside an Aberdeen fish restaurant on William's eighth birthday, she with a headscarf on, William with his kite, Harold in his uniform, That headscarf was quite probably up in the trunk in the glory-hole: she would have to have a good old sort through one day.

The old woman turned off the television and wondered whether that presenter's name wasn't Robert something. She looked up at the clock again, feeling the want of company. If tonight was Friday, which she was sure it was, then William and one of the fellows that worked for him would be popping in about this time, all being well with a drop of milk.

There was a muffled knock at the front door. The old woman went to the window. Pulling back the curtain corner, she could make out their two shapes, rubbing their hands together against the cold. She let the curtain drop.

William knocked again.

'I'm coming,' she called.

'Let's get a move on, Mum,' said William.

'I'm coming as quickly as ever I can, you impatient boy,' said the old woman in the hall. She unbolted the door and opened it.

'Evening, Mum.' A figure with a plastic shopping-bag on its head. Two holes slashed through it for eyes. It pushed past her, stumbled down the hall and mounted the stairs with shocking energy. The old woman made a low noise and turned to follow, when she felt a heavy arm come around her waist and a leathery hand press into her mouth. Her instinct was to struggle, but she did not. From upstairs, a rapid tramping from her room, to Harold's room, to the glory-hole. The familiar noises of her drawers being opened and slammed shut, and then of the trunk being slid out. For the first time the old woman tried to scream, but nothing seemed to come, only a little dribble. She felt very tired, then, and wanted to go to sleep. The creature with his arms round her smelt of the Gents, and his head was right up against hers: she could feel the plastic bag cold against her cheek. He was muttering. The old woman did so want to go to sleep, and closed her eyes.

She heard the first figure come down the stairs and go into her sitting room. There was an odd silence for a moment, then the sound of glass breaking. Then she could feel him close up to her breathing.

'Read this,' he said. The old woman didn't feel like reading anything.

'Open your eyes and read this, Mrs. Menzies,' said the voice, which reminded her of someone. 'And tell your son.' At the sound of her name, Mrs Menzies opened her eyes and saw, on a small white card held in front of her face, the words HERE COME THE IMPERSONATORS. The figure sniffed and threw the card down at her feet. 'Don't hit me,' the old woman mumbled.

'We'll be off, then,' said the one holding her.

'Nice to see you,' said the other.

'To see you, nice. Evening, all.' He pushed the old woman

from him, and she banged her elbow on a picture frame. The front door slammed.

Mrs Menzies waited five minutes in the hallway, not thinking straight and knowing it. Her elbow hurt her, and her neck. She knew she should go through the rooms, but she knew she couldn't. She felt giddy, as though she'd taken too much sun.

She went to the telephone and dialled Popsies. As she was dialling, she felt all her confusion rise in a wave from somewhere deep inside her: and when the girl put her through to her son, Mrs Menzies didn't believe it was him. She continued to ask for him.

'It's me, Mum,' said Mr Menzies. 'It's William.'

'I don't want you,' said his mother. 'I want William. I thought it was Friday. I haven't got any milk.'

The Impersonators had met for the first time in a kebab house in Mile End. They had got drunk: the creature because he had broken up with his girlfriend, the boy because he had just had his first success, an eighty-year-old widow in Shoreditch. They had got talking, which had in itself been a new experience for the boy, and over the course of three meetings, the boy had, with cautious pride, revealed just what he had been driven to in search of an honest penny.

They were getting a small reputation. A handful of local newspapers had carried short reports which the boy had cut out and pasted into his new Impersonators scrapbook. His idea was that one day quite soon, he would call the *Evening Standard* itself for an interview by telephone. He would conduct the entire interview in the voice of Margaret Thatcher, and the Impersonators' fame would spread.

Since Mrs Menzies, they had collected over eleven hundred pounds in cash, plus twenty-eight items of jewellery. They had moved out of the East End into more affluent areas, and the boy would spend the odd afternoon wandering around Hampstead or Chelsea, keeping an eye open. Each job took about three days to prepare. So far, they had avoided violence, apart from Mrs Menzies' arm, and this was important to the boy. It was why he had employed the creature: to hold the oldies while the job was done. It wasn't hooliganism, and as for that bit in the paper about 'breaking and entering', well it was just lies. 'Entering', yes: but the boy wouldn't have 'broken' a house if you'd paid him to. This was smart. This was Art.

Tonight, they were in Camden. It was their second night in this pub: they were keeping an eye on a man called Malcolm Scarfe, who was, as the boy pointed out, easy, with his loud voice and his tendency, after his third scotch, to rattle on in public about the miseries of living with an elderly Scrooge of a Dad, of being overweight, of having an ex-wife. Simply by standing within a fifteen foot radius of Malcolm Scarfe, the Impersonators learned all this about him and more. Malcolm Scarfe, with his club tie and skinny legs, with a different colour each day of carnation in his buttonhole. Malcolm Scarfe, who had read about the Impersonators and didn't know what things were coming to. Scarfe was the target. The boy looked at him as he blabbed away, his colour deepening to match that day's carnation, and thought You are stupid to talk, Malcolm Scarfe. Stupid to believe that people are who they are. Take more care, Malcolm Scarfe.

Each night at about nine o'clock, Malcolm Scarfe would leave the pub to go and check on how the old man was faring. The Impersonators wobbled along on their bikes at a distance of twenty metres. The house was in a mews off to the right of Camden Road. They fixed their bikes to a lamp-post and waited for him to re-emerge, as was his habit: when he passed them, on his way back to the pub, the boy saw that he was looking a little low and humming the tune from an advert for milk. At the front door, the boy made sure that all was quiet before nodding to the creature to get his bag on. Then he rang the bell.

They waited. They were far less nervous now than they had used to be: they had learned that theirs is an easy game to play.

'I'm not letting you in, you know,' came the old man's

voice from inside the house, softened, the boy thought, by luxury. 'Not after what you said to me.'

The Impersonators looked at each other.

'I've forgotten something, Dad,' the boy called out. He thought hard of Malcolm Scarfe.

'Where's your key?' The voice was nearer, but it wasn't pleasant to have to keep it going like this.

'I must have dropped it . . .'

'Really, we're going to have to chat about this, Malcolm . . .'

The bolt slid back. The Impersonators were here.

The door opened, and a lot of sensations came tumbling over the boy and the creature. They saw a figure, curved as a question-mark, with heavy fawn trousers up to his armpits, his Adam's apple in a wrinkled little sack. They saw his eyes, the pupils roving frantically over his eyeballs while the rest of him just hung there in the doorway, limp and old.

The creature took a step back, repelled. The boy didn't know what to do. He realised that what normally enabled him to cross the threshold was the flash of fear on the face. Their fear equalled his power. But here was a face with no ruddy fear whatsoever: and there was the sound of heels coming down the mews.

'Well,' said old Scarfe irritably. 'Come on, then.' He turned and shuffled off down the hall. The boy turned and shook his head. The creature swore quietly, tore off his bag and stepped down into the street. The boy slipped into the house and closed the door softly behind him, escaping from the outside.

'We're going to have to have a chat about this,' said the old man. He walked with one hand touching the wall, and the boy could see where this had left a dirty mark. He raised his eyes and looked up the stairs. There would be drawers of dark, highly polished wood up there. There'd be jewels. Cash. The boy had all the time in the world, and yet he felt oddly lethargic about mounting the stairs. He was quite happy where he was, thinking. There hadn't been that fear. A ruddy blind man, God.

'Come here,' barked old Scarfe from the living room. The boy walked softly down the hall and stood in the doorway of the living room. Malcolm would have to be in a sulky mood tonight.

'What you said earlier,' said old Scarfe, settling himself on a high, hard chair which faced an electric heater, 'it wasn't fair and it wasn't true.' The only other objects in this particular room were a table and a record player. 'Are you there? Don't skulk off, Malcolm. Listen to your father.'

'I'm listening.'

'It is not pleasant to be called a Scrooge, Malcolm. It is a hurtful thing to say. I mean, for the love of God, do you expect me to splash money about at my age? Do you? Malcolm? Are you there?'

'I'm here,' said the boy. So much for the blind being sensitive to sounds. Old Scarfe was half deaf, too. It was strange, watching him: he was just a voice. Like the boy himself, who, he had to admit, was feeling a bit odd about all this.

'All I want,' said old Scarfe, 'is to have my say on the subject of trust. Now I know you consider me a burden. But I also know that when I decided not to go into Holmstead House, I was entrusting my life to you. It was my way of telling you you had grown up . . .' The old man was not used to talking like this, the boy could see. The whole thing was starting to feel downright awkward.

'Do you remember what I said? Soon after your mother?'

'No,' said the boy.

'Too much else going on, I suppose. Too much else going on for your father. I think about what I said, though. I said that everything I had was ours, now. That we had to learn to trust one another. Lord love us, Malcolm, if you and I can't *trust* one another . . .' The old man twisted round on his seat to face the boy and fixed him with a hurtful, sightless stare. The boy's head was sweating inside the Sainsbury's bag, so he quietly slipped it off and put it into his pocket.

'Well?' said the old man urgently. 'Well then, Malcolm? Are you there?'

'I'm here,' said the boy in Malcolm Scarfe's voice. 'Thinking.' He was thinking about Malcolm Scarfe himself, missing all this, missing being lovingly reprimanded by his father. Malcolm Scarfe would come later. He'd still be glum, and his father would say What about our chat earlier . . . they'd both think the other one had gone cuckoo. There'd be hell to pay. Old Scarfe might have an attack or something. The boy hadn't really ever considered this.

'Don't take all this amiss, Malcolm. Just wanted to say my piece. Life goes on.' He turned round to face the heater again.

Being called 'Malcolm' suddenly made something clear to the boy. It sounded stupid, but as far as old Scarfe was concerned, the boy *was* Malcolm. By being there in that room, by listening to all that stuff about trust, about the death of his wife, the boy had temporarily turned into Malcolm Scarfe. He had stolen Malcolm Scarfe, in a way, and along with it, the old man's trust.

Even the boy could see that stealing a blind man's trust was worse than stealing his money. He was right in it now.

'You better go and get whatever it was you forgot,' said old Scarfe. 'Then get back to your pub.' He stretched out an arm. 'Come on. Come and give your old father's hand a squeeze.'

Odd pleasure ran up the boy's spine at that. There was warmth in it, and want. But then he remembered that old Scarfe was not speaking to him at all. He was speaking to his son. A shame. It would be nice to have that said to you.

'Come on,' said old Scarfe.

The boy wanted to run and he wanted to stay. He felt sad.

'Are you there?'

'I'm here,' said the boy in his own voice, and watched with self-pity the effect those two words had on the old man's body. He stiffened and grunted and turned round again.

'Who are you?' he said. 'You're not Malcolm. Who is this?' He was nearly shouting, and the boy had to raise his own voice.

'I'm not Malcolm,' he said. 'I'm one of the Impersonators.'

'Jesus Christ,' said old Scarfe through his teeth. 'Jesus

Christ almighty.' He climbed down from his chair and tried
to glare at the boy.

'I'm blind,' he said. 'I can't see. I knew. I *knew* –'

The boy stepped into the room and interrupted him.

'All that stuff,' he said. 'Trust and that.'

'You keep away,' said old Scarfe. He was working his
mouth into all sorts of odd shapes. 'You please just keep
away, you. Oh Jesus Christ.'

'I don't want to *do* anything, old Scarfe.' Perhaps the old
man would calm down a bit if he heard his name. 'Don't fret,
old Scarfe. Sit down again.' It felt bizarre to be speaking in
his own voice. 'It was good,' said the boy. 'All that about
trust.'

'That was for Malcolm's ears,' said old Scarfe. 'Anyway,
go on, then. I suppose you want to rob me. Go on. He'll be
back soon. To change my music. Go on. You won't find a
lot. Go *on!*'

'Be quiet,' said the boy. 'Be quiet please, Mr Scarfe. Please
sit down.' He didn't want to have to touch old Scarfe. 'You
really don't trust me at all, do you? Please sit down.'

Old Scarfe didn't sit down, but the boy could see that he
was pulling himself together a bit. He waited.

'*Trust* you?' said old Scarfe after a while. 'How can I trust
you? Trust takes a lifetime. Jesus.' His eyeballs continued to
rove as though they didn't know anything was amiss. 'Trust?
All I know is that you deceive people. Lord love us.'

'What sort of music do you want on?' said the boy.

'What?'

'What sort of music?'

The old man's back straightened a little.

'Music? You want to put music on, or rob me? You better
decide, young man.'

'Music,' said the boy. He was squatting by the record
player, reading off the spines. 'Vivaldi?' he said. '*South
Pacific*? Glenn Miller?'

'I do not believe this,' said Old Scarfe. 'I don't. Put some
Glenn Miller on, then. Get some Glenn Miller on there. Go
on.'

He continued to mutter. The boy put the music on. It was total rubbish, but after a while, it seemed to do the trick.

'Please,' said the boy again. 'Sit down.'

'Oh, I'll sit down,' said Old Scarfe. 'I'll sit down, God help me.' Perhaps, the boy thought, this was trust happening.

'I want to be like other people,' said the boy softly. 'I want someone to trust me. I want to be like Malcolm.' Well, he thought, he could say it. The old man couldn't see him anyway.

'You still on about trust?' returned old Scarfe. 'Trust takes a lifetime. How can I trust you? I don't even know your name. Jesus Christ.'

The boy thought about his name. He had almost forgotten he had one.

'Is that how it is, then?' he asked.

'Trust?' said Old Scarfe, and all the boy could hear for a while was the Glenn Miller Orchestra, 'In the Mood'. 'If you gave me your name,' continued old Scarfe, 'perhaps then I could start to trust you a little. How can you trust a body without a name? You can't, can you? Eh?'

The boy wanted to say his name. He wanted to tell it, to hear his own mouth saying it. Without it, he was nobody. Not even Malcolm Scarfe any more. Nobody.

'My name,' he said slowly, as though the words might turn on him if he let them loose all at once, 'is Adrian Shea. Adrian Shea. Yeah. And now you'll call the ruddy cops.'

'Frederick Scarfe,' said the old man. 'And now you can give my old hand a squeeze and you can be getting along. Malcolm will be back.' There was relief in his voice, but he wasn't relaxed. The boy went to Frederick Scarfe's outstretched hand and took it in his own. It was limp and thin, but it was after all someone else's hand, and it was after all him who was holding it.

'You might be a good lad at heart,' said old Scarfe. 'But you're on the wrong road, Adrian.'

Outside again, the boy walked down the road towards his bike, his head buzzing in the cold air. He'd known that something important was happening. He'd known that he'd wanted to be trusted, just as old Scarfe trusted Malcolm, who would just be drowning his last Scotch to come back home. The boy had wanted to leave the house feeling good about things, as he knew he could easily have done, had he given his real name. It would have felt good to have given his real name: he knew that. But the boy also knew that he needed money, and that the more he made, the more he seemed to need. If feeling a bit tacky sometimes was the price you paid for that, then so be it. There would be other chances, when it came to all the spiritual stuff: that was something else the boy knew. For the moment, however, he was an Impersonator, and God, there were plenty worse than him. Pausing by a shop window to examine a nice little personal stereo he'd had his eye on, the boy satisfied himself that, however many hands he may hold, whatever the curious little desires and sadnesses which may course through him, that was how it was.

Maundy

CHRISTOPHER HOPE

A FEW DAYS before Easter, Maggie's father found a man in a
sanitary lane, and took him home. All through Badminton,
our housing estate, sandy, stony sanitary lanes ran between
the houses on Edward Avenue and Henry Street and Eliza-
beth Crescent. They had been built so that the night-soil
men, coming like ghosts after dark, could remove the black
rubber buckets without being seen.

Our fathers returned home from the desert war in Egypt
and Libya and began battling the bare veldt. Every weekend
they wrestled the hard, red earth into gardens. Badminton
was a new housing estate, built outside Johannesburg for
returning soldiers. Its streets were named after English kings
and queens, because we were English South Africans. The
boxy new houses, with their corrugated-iron roofs, ran
down a slope to a small stream and a copse of giant blue
gums. Seven years after the war ended, soldiers who had
gone to fight against Germans had turned into gardeners in
uniform. My father worked in his Army boots. Gus Trupshaw wore a sailor's blue shirt. Nathan Swirsky put on his
leather flying helmet when he took out his motorbike.

Our fathers looked up from their zinnias, mopped their
brows, and said, 'It's hotter down south than it was up north,

make no mistake.' They cursed the African heat. They cursed the stubborn shale that had to be broken up with picks, forked over, sieved, spread and sweetened with rich brown earth, delivered by Errol the topsoil man.

They cursed the burglars. My mother said that there were swarms of burglars hiding among the blue gum trees. They ran down the sanitary lanes at night and slipped into the houses like greased lightning. As I lay in bed at night, I saw the sanitary lanes teeming with burglars and night-soil men, coming and going. Nobody talked about the night-soil men. They came and went in our sleep, though in the morning we caught the scent of something we wished to forget.

Nobody talked about Maggie, either. She lived next door and took off all her clothes from time to time and ran around her house. And we all pretended not to notice. She was the fastest ten-year-old on the estate.

My mother was next door in a flash when she saw the man working in Maggie's garden. He wore old khaki shorts. His legs ended in stumps, inches below the shorts, and the stumps were tied up in sacking. He pulled himself everywhere in a red tin wagon, hauling himself along with strong arms. His muscles were huge. The legless man sat upon a paper bag that he had spread in the bottom of his wagon. It read 'Buy Your Brand-New Zephyr at Dominion Motors.'

'Hell's bells! What could I do? He just followed me home,' said Maggie's father. 'He tells me his name's Salisbury.'

'I don't care if he's the King of Siam,' my mother said to my father a little while later. 'It's bad enough when that little girl tears about the place in the you-know-what, for all the world and his wife to stare. Now they have a cripple in their garden!'

My father was studying the annual report of the South African Sugar Association. 'Figures for 1952 show exports up.'

'Some of us cannot lose ourselves in sugar reports,' my mother said. 'Some of us have to look life in the eye.'

'For heaven's sake, Monica,' my father said. 'The poor

sod's lost his legs. I'm sure he doesn't like it any more than you do. But he's still human. Well, more or less.'

Then Maggie appeared, running around the side of her house. 'Speak of the devil!' my mother said. Maggie was skinny and very brown. Her bare legs flashing, round and round the house she ran. Her dog, a Dobermann called Tamburlaine, ran after her, barking loudly.

'Martin,' said my mother, 'come away from the window. It only encourages her if you stare.'

Maggie's father was chasing her with a blanket. He caught up, and threw it over her. Like a big grey butterfly net.

'You'd hardly think this was Easter,' said my mother. 'I don't know where to put my face.'

Salisbury sat in his red wagon, doing some weeding. 'What on earth do you think is going through his head?' my mother demanded. 'That little girl might be less keen to parade in the altogether if she knew what was going through his head.'

'I see that Henry's been planting out beardless irises,' said my father. 'The beardless iris loves a sunny spot and a good bit of wall.'

'Heavens above, where will it all end?' my mother asked. 'Our neighbours have a cripple in their garden. Easter is almost on us. There are burglars in the blue gums. Soon the streets will be full of servants. Did you know that they've taken to asking for Easter boxes? First Christmas boxes, now Easter boxes. I suppose they'll be asking for Michaelmas boxes next. Dressed to the nines, some of them. And worse for wear.'

I went to bed that night and thought about the burglars down among the blue gums that grew thickly across the road from the big houses in Edward Avenue. All over Badminton our fathers, home from the war, slept with their Army-issue pistols in their sock drawers, ready at any moment to rush naked into the African night, blasting away. The burglars were said to creep up on the houses and cast fishing lines through the burglar bars to hook wallets and handbags from our bedrooms.

We all believed in the burglars. Everyone except for Ruthie

Swirsky, the chemist's new wife. But she was English, from Wimbledon. Swirsky had travelled to Europe and brought her home with him. 'Burglars with fishing rods,' Ruthie Swirsky said to my father just after she moved to the estate. 'I've never heard of anything so absurd. Pull the other one, Gordon.'

'Pull the other what?' my mother wanted to know later.

'How would I know, Monica?' said my father. 'Leg, I suppose.'

'Whatever she had in mind, it wasn't a leg,' said my mother.

'Whatever she had in mind, it wasn't a leg!' sang my friends Tony, Sally, and Eric, and I as we rolled down the steep, grassy banks in Tony's garden that Eastertime in Badminton.

For the rest of the holiday, nothing much seemed likely to happen. The days looming ahead were too hot somehow, even though we were well into autumn. Our fathers worked in their gardens tending to their petunias and phlox and chrysanthemums. They sprayed their rosebushes against black spot, moving in the thick clouds of lime sulphur like refugees from a gas attack in the trenches.

Ernest Langbein had fallen in love with Maggie. Ernest was an altar server at the Church of the Resurrection in Cyrildene, and he told Eric that if only Maggie would stop taking off her clothes, their love might be possible. Maggie was not easy to get on with. When she had no clothes on, she wasn't really there. And when she was dressed she was inclined to make savage remarks. I met her in Swirsky's Pharmacy on Maundy Thursday. She wore a blue dress with thick black stockings. Her brown, pixie face was shaded by a big white panama hat, tied beneath her chin with thick elastic. I was wearing shorts. I'd never seen her look so covered up. She looked at my bare feet and said, 'You have hammer toes, Martin.' It seemed very unfair.

We were standing behind the wall of blue magnesia bottles which Swirsky built across his shop on festive occasions, like Christmas and Easter. We heard Ruthie Swirsky say to Mrs

Raubenheimer of the Jewish Old Age Home across the road, 'I'm collecting Maundy money. It's an Easter custom we have in England. The Royal Mint makes its own money, and the Queen gives it to pensioners and suchlike. The deserving poor. In a special purse.'

Mrs Raubenheimer said that those who could afford it could afford it. Swirsky came around the magnesia wall and grinned at us. He crackled in his starched white coat. His moustache was full and yet feathery beneath his nose. Black feathers, it was. 'Well, kiddies,' he said. 'Can I count on you? Pocket money is welcome for Ruthie's Maundy box. What Ruthie wants she usually gets.' He rattled a black wooden collection box.

My mother said, 'It's appalling. The Swirskys aren't even Easter people. The Queen of England does not live on an estate infested with burglars. Have you seen the collection box Ruthie Swirsky's using? I happen to know that it belongs to St. John's Ambulance. She simply turned it around so you can't see the badge.'

'If you're going to divide the world into those who are and those who are not Easter people,' said my father, 'you may as well go and join the government. They do it all the time.'

'I have no intention,' said my mother, 'of joining the government.'

All the kids gave to Ruthie Swirsky's Maundy-money box. We collected empty soft-drink bottles and got back a penny deposit down at the Greek Tea Room. Swirsky shook the box until our pennies rattled. 'Give till it hurts,' he said. 'Baby needs new booties.'

A deputation arrived at the pharmacy. Gus Trupshaw had been elected to speak for the estate. He wore his demob suit and brown Army boots with well-polished toes. He said that everyone objected to the idea of Ruthie's giving away money to the servants. What would they expect next Easter? It might be difficult for an English person to understand. But the cleaners, cooks, and gardeners of Badminton got board and lodging and wages. 'They might be poor,' Gus Trupshaw explained, 'but they're not deserving.'

'Are you telling me I may not give my Maundy money to whomsoever I choose?' Ruthie asked, her face white beneath her red hair. 'This is outrageous.'

'This isn't Wimbledon,' said Gus Trupshaw. 'When in Rome, do as the Romans do.'

Swirsky leaned over to us and whispered. 'When you're next in Rome, I can recommend the Trevi Fountain. But watch out for pickpockets.'

Ruthie Swirsky tapped the black collection box with her finger after Gus Trupshaw left. She told Swirsky she was so mad she could spit. She asked him to find Errol the topsoil man. 'Tell him I have a job for his wheelbarrow.'

Later, it was my mother who spotted Errol wheeling his barrow into the yard next door. 'There appears to be some movement at the neighbours'. I think I'll go and lie down,' she said.

Errol stopped beside Salisbury with his wheelbarrow. He laid the paper bag from Dominion Motors on the floor of the barrow and lifted Salisbury out of his wagon. Then he set off up Henry Street, wheeling Salisbury, with my friend Sally, her brother Tony, Eric and me tagging along behind them.

We heard the iron wheels scattering gravel in Henry Street.

'Where are we going?' Salisbury asked Errol in a deep, growling voice.

'Boss Swirsky's place. Sit still and don't make trouble.' Errol manoeuvred the barrow right up to the front door of Swirsky's Pharmacy. Papas, the owner of the Greek Tea Room, and Mr. Benjamin, the Rug Doctor, came out of their shops to stare. A couple of ladies from the Jewish Old Age Home also stopped to watch. Ruthie Swirsky came out of the pharmacy. Nathan was next to her. There was sun on his moustache, and it looked as if it had been dipped in oil. Swirsky carried the collection box. He held it carefully, as if it were a baby, and his face when he looked at Ruthie was soft and loving. A crowd of cleaners, cooks, and gardeners gathered across the road. They looked angry.

'I hear you're a poor man, Salisbury,' said Ruthie. 'So I've decided to help you.'

'Yes, Madam,' said Salisbury.

'I hope you're not going to leave him there all day, Mrs Swirsky,' said Mrs Raubenheimer.

Ruthie ignored everyone. 'This box is yours. Take it home with you. Take it back to your family. Take it with my blessings.'

'Yes, Madam,' said Salisbury.

Errol wheeled him home quickly. Salisbury held the box tight to his chest. All over the estate there were servants watching. You could tell the servants were angry because they weren't allowed to have any of the Maundy money. Some of them shouted at Errol as he wheeled Salisbury down Henry Street.

'That's what you get from Africans and Asians,' said my mother. 'That's exactly the sort of thing that led to the Cato Manor Riots. We could be facing more of them. Mark my words.'

Later that night, we were woken by people shouting next door. Tamburlaine the Dobermann began barking. Someone was crying. My father got up and put on his brown woollen dressing-gown. 'Take your hockey stick, Gordon,' said my mother. To me she said, 'Martin, you take the torch. I'm going to call the police.'

We found Maggie and her father trying to lift Salisbury into his red wagon. He was crying and swearing and waving his strong arms about.

'He's as strong as a lion, Gordon,' said Maggie's father. 'Help me. I think Tamburlaine's taken a nip out of him.'

Then Gus Trupshaw arrived and fired several shots. He thought he was using his starting pistol, but it was a flare gun and the sky was like noon for minutes. I could see Salisbury's tears.

'He says somebody has stolen his money,' said Maggie's father. 'People came and robbed him. I let him sleep here last night. I gave him the toolshed to doss down in. In the morning, Errol was going to wheel him to the bus stop. He was going home.'

Salisbury sat in the red tin wagon, rubbing his eyes and crying.

'Lock him in the toolshed,' my father suggested. 'Anything to keep him away from that dog. We'll sort this out in the morning.'

'It's very hard,' said Gus Trupshaw. 'We'll have to replace the money. We'll have a whip round. I just hope Ruthie Swirsky knows what she's done. You can't mess around with Africa.'

But they had reckoned without Salisbury's strong arms.

When they went to the toolshed in the morning, Salisbury was gone. He had torn the door off its hinges. He had levered himself into his little red wagon, and he had vanished.

'Thank heavens for small mercies,' said my mother.

On Good Friday afternoon, Errol found the little tin wagon down by the blue gums. Then a party of men found Salisbury. He was hanging from a branch by his belt. The men made a kind of tent of blankets around him, so that the children shouldn't see.

Ruthie Swirsky waited for the police to come and take Salisbury away. She asked the constable if she might send a little something to his next of kin. The constable laughed at her and said, 'People like Salisbury have no next of kin.' Ruthie Swirsky asked the constable for his number. And he threatened to arrest her.

The police took Salisbury away, and it might have ended there. Except that Ruthie Swirsky found out that he had a brother and a sister in a village sixty miles away. 'This is ridiculous!' said Gus Trupshaw. 'If we had to take responsibility for every soul that dies, where would we be?'

On Easter Saturday, the coffin turned up on the back of Errol the topsoil man's truck. 'Mrs Swirsky, she arranged it,' said Errol.

'She actually believes she's still in Wimbledon,' said my father. But he and Gus Trupshaw offered to drive the coffin back to Salisbury's home village. We all watched as they loaded the coffin on to the back of Gus Trupshaw's new Ford truck. 'If you don't hear from us in a week, send a search party,' said Gus Trupshaw.

'For heaven's sake,' said my mother. 'You're only driving to the other side of Rustenburg. Just explain that you're very sorry about what happened, and don't tell them where you live.'

The men got home at sunset. 'We would've been back earlier,' my father said, grinning. 'But we had a feast with the family. It's tradition. They wanted to thank us for bringing him home.'

'Chicken and rice,' said Gus Trupshaw.

'Quite normal, really,' said my father.

'Normal? My godfathers, Gordon,' said my mother. 'It may be normal to you. But I was worried sick. And there are Easter eggs to be hidden in our garden tonight. The children have waited up while you've been eating chicken and rice.'

You could tell that the men were pleased with themselves. It was as if they had been through some huge adventure at the other end of the world.

'Yes,' said Gus Trupshaw, as though they did such things every day. 'First chicken and rice, and then peaches.'

They came into the kitchen and my mother said to me, 'Your father's been eating chicken, with strangers.'

'Quite normal, really,' said my father again.

My mother held up a hand. 'Please. Not another word. It gives me the heebie-jeebies just thinking about it.'

We were sitting around the house waiting to be sent to bed as soon as our fathers were ready to hide the Easter eggs. They always hid them the night before. On Easter morning, we would go searching for them before the sun was high enough to melt the chocolate. Maggie was saying that dogs always bit black people, because they had different blood.

Sally said, 'But I saw blood on the ground after Tamburlaine bit Salisbury. And it was red. Just like mine.'

'Then why do dogs only bite black people?' Tony asked.

'They don't. Last year, our Aunt Mary got bitten – didn't she? And she's from Kenya,' said Sally. 'Do you know anyone not black who has been bitten, Martin?' Sally wore a dress the colour of apricots. Her shiny yellow hair was held tightly in a blue Alice band. Her brown legs were bare. She had this way of feeding the toes of one foot into the other.

I said, 'I remember Strydom's dog, Attila, bit the postman once.'

'Martin will say anything. Just to please you,' Tony loudly snapped the elastic in the waistband of his brown boxer shorts. 'Because Martin adores you.'

'Rubbish!' said Sally. 'You don't really adore me, do you, Mart?'

'I don't adore anyone,' I said.

'Oh, yes, Mart. Then why are you blushing?' Maggie asked.

Swirsky arrived on his motorbike with Papas sitting in the sidecar. Papas carried a big cardboard box with 'Sundowner Brandy' written on it. We knew that the box held our Easter eggs, which Papas got wholesale from his cousin in Orange Grove. One Easter, Gus Trupshaw had said he could get eggs much cheaper through a connection in Fordsburg. But my father said Papas would not stand for that. The Greeks were very big on Easter.

Other fathers began arriving. They made a barbecue and stood around the fire, watching the meat sizzling on the old garden sieve my father used for a grill. They drank beer. By about eight o'clock, Papas was singing 'She'll be comin' round the mountain when she comes.' My mother stuck her head out the kitchen window and said, 'Excuse me! May I remind you that there are still children present.'

Gus Trupshaw called back, 'Aye, aye, Captain.'

'Right, that's the last straw,' my mother said, and sent us to bed.

Later, for what seemed like hours, I lay in my dark bedroom listening to the men calling to each other. I heard my father saying, 'Go left, Gus, further left! Dead on target now. That's beautiful.' Then Papas would call out, 'Am I on course, Gordon?' And my father would shout back, 'You're at two o'clock, George. Beautiful. Just hold that position.'

Much later, I grew sleepy and it seemed to me that the men

in the garden were not men at all. They were planes and tanks moving across the sand in the desert war in North Africa. While, in the yard next door, Tamburlaine keened and whimpered. His long chain, which had been tied to the steel pole that held the washing line, clashed like the waves of a metal sea.

On Easter morning, we were out in the garden soon after breakfast. Our fathers stood blinking in the early-morning sunshine, rubbing their eyes and yawning. They had not had time to shave. Mr Swirsky brought Ruthie to watch her very first African Easter-egg hunt. She told my mother she would never get used to Easter in autumn. South Africa was all upside down. My mother told her to hang on to her hat. *She'd* been living in South Africa all her life, and there was lots she still was not used to. Swirsky smoothed his moustache with a small, soft white hand. He seemed to be stroking the wings of a special bird. Ruthie wore sunglasses. With her red hair and pale skin, she looked very mysterious. None of us had ever seen anyone in sunglasses.

'Ruthie has sensitive eyes,' Swirsky said proudly. 'Those glasses were specially shipped all the way from England. I kid you not.'

One by one, we set off to find our eggs while the men gave us clues. 'You're ice-cold, Martin! Your right foot's a bit warmer now. Which one is your right foot? Now your knee is getting rather warm. Oh, Martin, your knee is on fire. Can't you feel the heat, boy?'

Swirsky got carried away and tried to take over from my father. He kept shouting out, 'Two o'clock, Martin. Angels at two o'clock!'

When we had all found our chocolate eggs, it was Nicodemus' turn. Nicodemus was our cook and gardener. My father found him in the garage when we moved to Badminton after the war and so we kept him.

'We treat Nicodemus as one of the family,' my mother told Ruth Swirsky. 'At Christmas and Easter, Nicodemus is always included. We don't have to do it. We choose to do it.'

Nicodemus fell on his knees and clapped his hands when my father called him from the kitchen. 'No, no, Nicodemus.' My mother clicked her tongue. 'That's only for Christmas. You have to find your egg in the garden now. Stand up, Nicodemus, and go into the garden.' She explained quietly to Ruthie Swirsky, 'He's a bit touched in the head. Easter must be a real puzzle. Their customs are very different from ours. But I suppose that's something you well understand.'

'You mean, being British?' Ruthie asked.

'Well, that, too,' said my mother.

Nicodemus did not understand the 'hot' and 'cold' directions. He walked about the garden as if he were hunting game. His ears were pricked; his hands were held in little paws in front of his chest. He was very springy on his feet, making little leaps this way and that. He danced across to the rockery. The men shouted, 'You're cold, cold, Nicodemus!' Then he went the other way, and they shouted, 'You're warm, warmer, Nicodemus!' But Nicodemus didn't listen to them. He went back to the rockery and fell on his knees, and my father said, 'Oh God, not another praying session.'

And my mother called out, 'Language, Gordon. This is Easter Sunday.'

When Nicodemus got to his feet, he had found something. But it wasn't wrapped in silver paper like the other eggs. It was square and black. Gus Trupshaw said, 'Now, what the hell have you got there, boy?'

'That's my Maundy-money box,' Ruthie said. 'Give it to me, Nicodemus.' She reached out her hands for it. But Nicodemus fell on his knees again, smiling hugely and happily, and hugged the black wooden box to his chest.

'Happy, happy,' said Nicodemus.

'Hell's bells!' I heard my father say. 'This could be tricky.'

Ruthie said, in her clear English voice, 'But this is absurd! Someone make him give me my box.'

'He thinks it's finders keepers,' Gus Trupshaw said. 'Nicodemus thinks he was meant to find it.'

'But it doesn't belong to him,' Ruthie said. 'Somebody stole that box from Salisbury. They must have hidden it in your garden. Salisbury did away with himself because he thought he'd never see that money again. And all the time it was a few feet away.' And she began crying.

Swirsky said, 'Don't, sweetie. I'll fix it.' But from the sound of his voice we knew that there was nothing much to be done.

'Strictly speaking,' my mother said when the Swirskys had left, 'that box belongs to St. John's Ambulance. It wasn't hers to give away in the first place.'

Nicodemus took the black wooden box to his room. He put it on his table with a photograph cut from a newspaper which showed Mussolini in full-dress uniform. 'Nicodemus is happy,' he told me.

Nobody else was happy. The cooks and cleaners and gardeners from Badminton Estate took to stopping outside our fence and staring. Someone shouted. A stone was thrown. Nicodemus would rush inside when he saw them and hide under his bed.

Then Gus Trupshaw announced that his maid and several other women who had been washing clothes down by the blue gums had been frightened by a vision of Salisbury. Salisbury wore the belt that he'd used to hang himself. He had come back to haunt them, floating above the ground, skimming along the gravel, belt flying from his neck. He had chased the women all the way up Edward Avenue.

'Flying ghosts at Easter!' my mother said. 'What will they think of next? I only hope Ruth Swirsky realises what she's done. Once they get an idea into their heads like this, they don't let go. We'll have the police here. Mark my words.'

In the afternoon, Swirsky arrived and asked to see Nicodemus. Swirsky was wearing a stethoscope and his wife's dark glasses. His chemist's coat was as smooth as an envelope. His moustache was looking oiled again. My mother told him that Nicodemus had locked himself in his room because people were threatening to kill him.

'I intend to fight fire with fire,' said Swirsky. Then he went out to Nicodemus' room and knocked on the door.

When he came back, a long time later, Nicodemus was with him. Swirsky looked pale. His moustache was so black it might have been drawn with charcoal. Somehow, he looked undressed. Nicodemus wore Swirsky's white chemist's coat. He wore Ruthie Swirsky's dark glasses and he had Swirsky's stethoscope around his neck. Nicodemus put the stethoscope to his chest and listened proudly to his heart. 'Boum, boum, boum,' he said.

Swirsky carried the St. John's Ambulance box. 'Fair exchange, no robbery,' said Swirsky. 'But he drives a hard bargain, your Nicodemus. If he had a proper chance, he could run the country.'

'Would you please keep your voice down?' my mother asked, smiling, and speaking without moving her lips.

Later that afternoon, Sally came round to my place and said that there was a religious meeting in the blue gums. We ran down the hill to the little frothing river in the thick bank of enormous trees. Errol the topsoil man was there. Gus Trupshaw stopped in his new truck. 'Is this a church parade?' he asked. 'Where's the bally sky pilot?' A crowd of servants waited under the blue gums. Swirsky and his wife arrived in his blue A40. From the back of the car stepped a tall black woman in a red skirt. She was barefoot. She wore great bracelets of beads around her wrists. There were chicken bladders in her hair, like little yellow balloons. There were rows of beads crossed over her chest.

Ruthie Swirsky held up her hand for silence. 'This is Ethel,' she pointed to the tall woman. 'Ethel is a *sangoma*. A witch doctor.'

Ethel knelt on the ground. She untied a leather bag that was hanging from her waist. She opened the bag and put it on the ground in front of her. Then she closed her eyes and seemed to go to sleep. With her eyes still closed, she tipped some bones from the bag into her palms and blew on them – a long, loud breath. She threw them in the dirt as if she were throwing dice. Then she opened her eyes and studied the bones. Next she took from under her arm the wooden St. John's Ambulance box. Swirsky stepped forward, pulling

Salisbury's red wagon. The crowd groaned and shivered when they saw that it still carried the brown paper with which Salisbury had lined the bottom: 'Buy Your Brand-New Zephyr at Dominion Motors.' Ethel shook the collection box. We heard our pennies and sixpences rattling inside. People began clapping softly. Ethel produced a bottle of petrol and a box of matches. In a moment, the box was blazing in the red wagon. No one said a word. We watched until nothing was left but a smell of paint from the red wagon, ashes, and a pile of glowing, smoking coins.

Ethel leaned over and stirred the money to cool it. Everybody was given a piece of money, black from the fire. I got a sixpence. Sally received a shilling. Even Errol the topsoil man got a florin. Examining the scorched money, Swirsky said, 'King George doesn't look too pleased – he's got a black eye.'

Sally said, 'It's like getting coins out of a Christmas pudding.'

Then Ethel, the witch doctor, stepped back into the A40.

'I was very moved,' Ruthie Swirsky told her.

Ethel lit a Mills cigarette and blew smoke at the roof of the car. 'You're welcome,' said Ethel.

'Will Salisbury be happy, Mr. Swirsky?' Eric asked.

'We had to make contact,' Swirsky said. 'That's Ethel's real forte. Making contact. Apparently, the wandering spirit needs some form of direction. This way or that? It's a bit like looking for Easter eggs. Colder? Or warmer? We made a special fire so the spirit of Salisbury could warm itself.'

'And the Maundy money I collected was given to the deserving poor. If I'd been allowed to do that in the first place, none of this would have happened,' said Ruthie Swirsky.

My mother said, when I showed her my blackened sixpence, 'Don't try and spend it, Martin. Scorched coins are not legal tender. Ask your father.'

Sisters

COLUM McCANN

I HAVE COME to think of our lives as the colours of that place
– hers a piece of bog cotton, mine as black as the water found
when men slash too deep in the soil with a shovel.

I remember, when I was fifteen, cycling across those bogs
in the early evenings, on my way to the dance-hall in my
clean, yellow socks. My sister stayed at home. I tried to avoid
puddles but there would always be a splash or two on the
back of my dress. Boys at the dance-hall wore blue anoraks
and watched me when I danced. Outside they leaned against
my bike and smoked shared cigarettes in the night. I gave
myself. One of them, once, left an Easter lily in the basket.
Later it was men in granite-grey suits who would lean into
me, heads cocked sideways like hawks, eyes closed. Sometimes I would hold my hands out beyond their shoulders and
pretend that I could shape or carve something out of my
hand, something that had eyes and a face, someone very little,
within my hand, whose job it was to somehow understand.

A man with a walrus moustache gone grey at the tips took
me down to the public lavatories in Castlebar. He was a
sailor. He smelled of ropes and disuse and seaport harridans.
There were bays and coverts, hillsides and heather in that
place. Between a statue of Our Lady and a Celtic cross com-

memorating the dead of Ireland, my hand made out the shape of a question mark as a farm boy furrowed his way inside me. My promiscuity was my autograph. I was hourglassy, had turf-coloured hair and eyes green as wine bottles. Someone once bought me an ice-cream cone in Achill Island, then we chipped some amethyst out of the rockbanks, and we climbed the radio tower, then woke up, late, at the edge of a cliff, with the waves lashing in from the Atlantic. There was a moon of white in that water. The next day my father, at the dinner table, told us that John F. Kennedy had landed a man on the moon. It was a shame, he said looking at me, that it had turned out to be heap of ash. My legs were stronger and I strolled to the dance-hall now, aware, the bogs around me wet and dark. The boy with Easter lilies tried it again, this time with nasturtiums stolen from outside the police station. My body continued to go out and around in all the right places. My father waited up late and smoked Woodbines down to the quick. He told me once that he had overheard a man at his printing shop call me 'a wee whore' and I heard him weeping as I tuned in Radio Luxemburg in my room.

My older sister, Brigid, succeeded with a spectacular anorexia. After classes she would sidle off into the bog, to a large rock where nobody could see her, her school sandwiches in her skirt, her Bible in her hand. There she would perch on her feet like a raked robin, and bit by bit she would tear up the bread, like a sacrament, and throw it all around her. The rock had a history – in penal times it had been used as meeting place for mass. I sometimes watched her from a distance. She was a house of bones, my sister throwing her bread away. Once, out on the rock, I saw her take my father's pliers to her fingers and slowly pluck out the nail from the middle of her left hand. She did it because she heard that it was what the Cromwellians had done to the harpists in the seventeenth century, so they could no longer pluck the cat-gut to make music. She wanted to know how it felt. Her finger bled for days. She told our father that she had caught her hand in a school door. He stayed unaware of Brigid's condition, still caught in the oblivion caused, many years before, by the death of our mother – lifted from a cliff by a light wind while out strolling. Since that day Brigid had lived a strange sort of martyrdom. People loved her frail whiteness, but never really knew what was going on under all those sweaters. She never went to the dance-hall. She, naturally, wore the brown school socks that the nuns made obligatory. Her legs within them were thin as twigs. We seldom talked. I never tried. I envied her that unused body that needed so little, yet I also loved her with a bitterness that only sisters can have.

Now, two decades later, in the boot of a car, huddled, squashed, under a blanket, I ask myself why I am smuggling myself across the Canadian border to go into a country that never allowed me to stay, to see a sister I never really knew in the first place?

It is dark and cramped and hollow and black in here. My knees are up against my breasts. Exhaust fumes cough on up. A cold wind whistles in. We are probably still in the province of Quebec. At every traffic light I have hoped that this is the border station, leading into Maine. Perhaps when we're finally across we will stop by a frozen lake, and skim and slide for a long time, out there on the ice, Michael and I. Or maybe not.

When I asked Michael to help smuggle me across the border from Canada he didn't hesitate. He liked the idea of being what the Mexicans call a 'coyote'. It goes, he said, somewhat with his Navajo blood, his forefathers believing that coyotes were the songdogs that howled in the beginning of the universe. Knowing the reputation of my youth, he joked that I could never have believed in that legend, that I must go in for the Big Bang. In the rear of the car I laugh and shudder in the cold. I wear a blue wool hat pulled down over my ears. My body does not sandwich up the way it used to.

I met Michael on a Greyhound bus in the early Seventies not long after leaving the bogs. I had left Brigid at home with her platefuls of food. My father had hugged and cradled me like his last cigarette at Shannon Airport. On the plane I realised that I was gone forever to a new country – I was tired of the knowing way that women back home had nodded

159

their heads at me. I was on my way to San Francisco, wearing a string of beads. In the bus station at Port Authority I noticed Michael first for his menacing darkness, the way his skin looked like it had been dipped into hot molasses. And then I noticed the necklace of teeth that hung over his chest. I learned later that they were mountain-lion teeth. He had found the lion one afternoon on the outskirts of a wilderness area in Idaho, the victim of a road kill. He came and sat beside me, saying nothing, smelling faintly of woodsmoke. His face was aquiline, acned. His wrists were thick. He wore a leather waistcoat, jeans, boots. Later I leaned my head on his shoulder, feigning sleep, and my hand reached over and played with the necklace of teeth. He laughed when I blew on them and I said they sounded like wind chimes, rattling together, though they didn't sound anything faintly like that. We rattled across a huge America. I lived with him for many years on Delores Street, near the Mission, the foghorn of the Golden Gate keening a lament, up until the raid. And after the raid, in 1978, when I was gone and home in Ireland, I would never again sleep with another man.

Once more the car shudders to a halt. My head lolls against the lid of the boot. I would rather hack through a pillar of stone with a pin than ever go through this again. This is dangerous. There is a huge illegal trade going on with cigarettes and alcohol between these two borders. We could be caught. Michael wanted to take me across by floating canoes down the Kennebec River. Something in his eyes had coffined downwards when I had said I would rather just do it in the boot of a car. Now I wish different. 'Up a lazy river with a robin song, it's a lazy lazy river we can float along, blue skies up above everyone's in love . . .' My father had sung that when Brigid and I were very young.

The car pitched forward slowly. I wonder if we are finally there, or if this is just another traffic light in a town along the way. We stay stopped and then we inch up. I wonder what plays in Michael's head. I was shocked when I saw him first, just three days ago, because he still looked much the same after thirteen years. I was ashamed of myself. I felt dowdy and grey. When I went to sleep on his sofa bed, alone, I remembered the new creases on the back of my thighs. Now I feel more his equal. He has cut his hair and put on a suit to lessen the risk of interrogation – giving him some of the time that I have found, or lost, I don't know which.

A muffle of voices. I curl my self deeper into a ball and press my face against cold metal. If the border patrol asks to examine his luggage I am gone once again, I am history come the full circle. But I hear the sound of a hand slapping twice on the roof of the car, a grind of gears, a jolt forward, and we are within moments, in America, the country, as someone once said, that God gave to Cain. A few moments down the road I hear Michael whoop and roar and laugh.

'Greetings,' he shouts, 'from the sebaceous glands. I'll have you out of there in a few minutes, Sheona.'

His voice is muffled and my toes are frozen.

On an August night in 1978 I clocked off my job as a singing waitress in a bar down on Geary Street. Wearing an old wedding dress I had bought in a pawn shop, hair let loose, yellow socks on – they were always my trademark – I got into our old Ford pick-up with the purple hubcaps and drove up the coast. Michael was up, for a weekend, in a cabin somewhere north of Mendicino, helping bring in a crop of California's best. Across the bridge where the hell-divers swooped, into Sausalito, around by Mount Tamalpais, where I flung a few cigarette butts in the wind to the ghosts of Jack Kerouac and John Muir, up along the coast, the sun rising like a dirty red aspirin over the sea, I kept steady to the white lines, those on the dashboard and those on the road. The morning had cracked well when I turned up the Russian River and followed the directions Michael had written on the back of a dollar bill.

The cabin was up a drunken mountain road, parts of old motorbikes perched on by cats, straggles of orange crates, pieces of a windmill, tatters of wild berries and sunlight streaming in shafts through sequoias. Michael and his friends met me with guns slung down by their waists. There had been no guns on Mayo, just schoolgirl rumours of an IRA man who lived in a boghole about a mile from Brigid's rock. They scared me, the guns. I asked Michael to tuck his away. Late that evening, when all the others had gone with a truck-load of dope, I asked him if we could spend a moment together. I wanted to get away from the guns. I got them, though. Four hours later, naked on the side of a creek, I was quoting Kavanagh for some reason, 'leafy with love-banks, the green waters of the canal . . .' when I looked up beyond his shoulder at four cops, guns cocked, laughing. They forced Michael to bend over and shoved a branch of tree up his anus. They tried to take me, these new hawks, eyes open, and eventually they did. Four in a row. This time my eyes closed, arms and hands to the ground, nothing to watch me from my fingerhouse.

Five days later, taking the simple way out – a lean, young lawyer in a white fedora had begun to take an interest in my case – they deported me for not having a green card. Past the Beniano Bufano 'Peace' statue – the mosaic face of all races – at San Francisco International, handcuffed, they escorted me to JFK on to an Aer Lingus Boeing 747. I flung my beads down into the toilet.

Michael is lifting me from the boot. He swirls me around in his arms, in the middle of a Maine dirt road. It is pitch black, but I can almost smell, in the swirl, the lakes and the fir trees, the clean snow that nestles upon branches. A winter Orion thrusts his sword after Taurus in the sky. 'That might be a ghost,' I whisper to Michael, and he stops his dance, questioning. 'I mean, the light hitting our eyes from those stars left millions of years ago. It just might be that the thing is a ghost, already imploded. A supernova.'

'The only thing I know about the stars is that they come out at night,' he says. 'My grandfather sometimes sat in a chair outside our house and compared them to my grand-mother's teeth.'

I laugh and lean into him. He looks around at the sky.

'Teach me some more scientific wonders,' he says.

I babble about the notion that if we could travel faster than the speed of light we would get to a place we never really wanted to go before we even left. He looks at me quizzically, puts his finger on my lips, walks me to the car and lays me down gently into the front seat, saying: 'Your sister.'

He takes off his tie, wraps it around his head like a bandanna, feels for a moment for his gone ponytail, turns up the stereo, and we drive towards New York.

I had seen my sister one day in Dublin, outside the Dawson Lounge. I suppose her new convent clothes suited her well. Black to hide the thinness. Muttering prayers as she walked. The hair had grown thick on her hands and her cheekbones were sculleried away in her head. I followed behind her, up around St. Stephen's Green, and on down toward the Dáil. She shuffled her shoes meticulously, never lifting them very high off the ground. She stopped at the gate of the Dáil where a group of homeless families sat protesting their destitution, flapping their arms like hummingbirds to keep themselves warm. It was Christmas Eve. She talked with a few of them for a moment, then took out a blanket and sat down among them. It shocked me, from the other side of the street, to see her laugh and to watch a small girl leap into her lap. I walked away, bought a loaf of bread, and threw it to the ducks in the Green. A boy in Doc Martens didn't smile at me and I thought of a dance-hall.

'None of these coins have our birthdates on them any more,' I say as I search in my handbag for some money for a toll booth.

'I enjoyed that back there,' he says. 'The danger. Hell of a lot better than hanging from a scaffold. Hey, you should have seen the face of the border patrol guy. Waved me through without a flinch.'

'You think we just get older and then we . . .?'

'Look, Sheona, you know the saying.'

'What saying?'

'A woman is as old as she feels.' Then he chuckles. 'And a man is as old as the woman he feels.'

'Very funny.'

'I'm only kidding,' he says.

'I'm sorry, Mike. I'm just nervous.'

I lean back in the seat and watch him. In his six years of prison notes there is one I remember now the most. 'I wouldn't mind dying in the desert with you, Sheona,' he had written. 'We could both lick the dew off of rocks, then lie in the sun, watch it, let it blind us. Dig two holes and piss in them. Put a tin can in the bottom. Cover the hole with a piece of plastic and weigh down the centre with a rock. The sun'll purify it, let it gather in droplets on the plastic, where it'll run towards the centre, then drop in the tin can, making water. After a day we can drink from each other's bodies. Then let the buzzards come down from the thermals. I hate being away from you. I am dead already.'

The day I received that letter I thought of quitting my secretarial job in a glass tower down by Kavanagh's canals. I thought of going back to Mayo and striking a shovel into a boghole, seeping down into the water, breathing out the rest of my life through a hollow piece of reed grass. But I never quit my job and I never wrote back to him. The thought of that sort of death was way too beautiful.

Days in Dublin were derelict and ordinary. A flat on Appian Way near enough to Raglan Road, where my own dark hair weaved a snare. Thirteen years somehow slipped away, like they do, not even autumn foliage now, but manured delicately into my skin. I watched, unseen as a road sweeper in Temple Bar whistled like he had a bird in his throat. I began to notice cranes leapfrogging across the sky-line. Dublin was cosmopolitan now. A drug addict in a door-way on Leeson Street shocked me when I saw him ferret in his bowels for a small bag of cocaine. The canals carried fabulously coloured litter. The postman asked me if I was lonely. I went to Torremolinos in 1985 and watched girls, whose age I should have been, get knocked up in alleyways.

But I didn't miss the men. I bought saucepans, cooked beautiful food, wrote poems by a single-bar electric heater. Once I even went out with a policeman from Donegal, but when he lifted my skirt I knocked his glasses off. At work, in a ribboned blouse, I was so fabulously unhappy that I didn't switch jobs, always breaking my fingernails on the phone

slots. I watched a harpist in the Concert Hall, playing beautifully on nylon strings. In a fit of daring I tried to find my
sister exactly two years to the day that I had seen her, huddled
with the homeless in a Foxford blanket. 'Sister Brigid,' I was
told, 'is spreading the word of God in Central America.' I
didn't have the nerve to ask for the address. All I knew of
Central America was dogs leaner then her.

We are off the highway now, the darkness being bled into
by the sun in the east, looking for a New Hampshire petrol
station. Michael refuses to go to the ones that lick the big
interstate. He prefers a smaller town. That is still him. That is
still the man who now has a necklace of mountain lion teeth
hanging over an open-necked Oxford. Because I trust him
now, because he still believes in simpler, more honest things,
I tell him about why I think Brigid is sick. I am very simple
in my ideas of Central America. My philosophy comes from
newspapers. She is sick, I tell him, because she was heart-
broken amongst maguey. She is sick because there are soldiers on the outskirts of town who carry either Kalashnikovs
or Ak–47s, hammering the barrels through the brick kilns
that make the dough rise. She is sick because she saw things
that she thought belonged only to Irish history. She is sick
because there is a girl with a bony hand who wanted to be
like her and there was no such thing as a miracle to be found.
She is sick, she is in an infirmary convent on Long Island for
nuns who have, or have not, done their jobs. Though really,
honestly, she is sick, I think because she knew I was watching
when she flung her bread from a rock, and I flung mine into a
pond, shamed by a boy in red boots, and I never said a word.

'You're too hard on yourself,' says Michael.

'I've been hacking through a stone with a pin.'

'What does that mean?'

'Oh come on, Michael, it's not as if we're twenty-one any
more. All those years spat away.'

'It doesn't help to be bitter,' he says.

'Oh, and you're not bitter?'

'I've learned not to think about it.'

'That's worse than being bitter, Michael.'

'Come on,' he says, reaching across to take my hand. 'You can't change the past.'

'No, we can't,' I say. My hand is limp. 'We can't, can we?'

Embarrassed at my anger I tell him once again, for the umpteenth time over the last three days, about how I found out where she was. I decided, only a week ago, to go back and see my father and bring him a carton of Major, because I couldn't find Woodbines. I have no idea what stirred me to see him, except that one of the other secretaries in Dublin had talked all morning long about her pet collie dog throwing up all over her favourite rug and she was actually weeping over it, more for the rug, I imagined, than for the dog. I walked out to the canals and sat watching boys diving in, breaking up the oily slime. Their bravery astounded me. I went to Heuston Station and took a train west.

He was dead, of course. The couple who had bought our old bungalow had three babies now. They said that they had been with my father in a hospital in Galway where, in an oxygen tent, he asked for a nip of Bushmill's and a smoke. The doctors had told him that he would explode and he had said, 'That's grand, give me a smoke, so.' The husband who asked who I was knew exactly who I was, even though I didn't want him to bring out nasturtiums or Easter lilies. I told him, in front of his wife, that I was a distant cousin. In a whisper, at the gate, he told me that he had heard that Brigid was sick and was living now in a convent in the Big Apple. He said the words as if he had just peeled the skin off, then he stole a furtive kiss on my cheek. I wiped it off in disgust, went home to Dublin and made phone calls until I found Michael, a building-site foreman, living in Quebec.

'Michael, I need to get back in. I can get a flight from London into Canada, no hassle.'

'I'll pick you up at the airport in Montreal.'

'Are you married?' I asked.

'Are you kidding? Are you?'

'Are you kidding?' I laughed. 'Will you take me there?'

'Yeah.'

It's one highway, 95, all the way, a torrent of petrol

stations, neon, motels, fast-food spires. Michael talks of a different world, beyond this, where the sun fell and rose and fell again. San Quentin had taught him of windows within walls. The day he got out, in a suit two sizes too big, he learned how to cartwheel again and ended up tearing the polyester knees. He took a bus to Yosemite and got a job as a guide. When my letters stopped coming he had taken a motorbike, a 'riceburner' he called it, from California to Gallup, New Mexico, where his mother and father pissed away a monthly government cheque into a dry creekbed at the back of their house. Michael slept in a shed full of Thunderbird bottles, a hole in the corrugated ceiling where he watched the stars, bitterly following their roll across the sky. He followed the roll. He walked scaffolds to build New York City high-rises. Indian climbers were in big demand for that type of job and the money was good.

Then there was a girl. She brought him to Quebec. They climbed frozen waterfalls in a northern forest. The girl was long gone, but the waterfalls weren't. Maybe, he says, when we get back to Quebec he'll put me in a harness and spiked boots and we'll climb. I finger my thighs and say perhaps.

Floods of neon rushing by.

We stop in a diner and a trucker offers Michael ten dollars for the lion tooth necklace. Michael tells him that it's a family heirloom and, trying to make sure that I don't hear – me, in my red-crocheted cardigan and grey skirt – the trucker offers him a bag full of pills. Michael still has that sort of face. It's been years since I've been wired and I have a faint urge to drop some pills. But Michael thanks the trucker, says he hasn't done speed in years and we drive away.

By late evening, the next day, we snarl into the New York city traffic and head down towards the Village. Michael's eyes are creased and tired. The car is littered with coffee cups and the smell of cigarettes lingers in our clothes. The city is much like any other to me now, a clog of people and cars. It seems appropriate that there is no room for us in the Chelsea Hotel, no more Dylan, no more Behan, no more Cohen remembering us well when we were famous and our hearts were legends. We stay with an old friend of Michael's on Bleeker Street. I have brought two nightdresses in my suitcase. My greatest daring is that I don't wear either of them. Michael and his friend curl on the ends of the sofa. I sleep in a bed, scared of the sheets. Four hawks in badges grunting down from the thermals, red-beaked, by a gentle creek in sequoia sunlight. A bouquet of boys shimmy in from the bogs and glare in brown tweed hats and pants tucked with silver bicycle clips. My father lights a carton of cigarettes and burns in a plastic tent, watching. A nun runs around with dough rising up in her belly. My wrists pinned to pine needles, no light wind to carry me away. Blood running down the backs of his thighs. The talons of a robin carrying flowers off, I toss and turn in sweat that gathers in folds and it is not until Michael finally comes over and kisses my eyelids that I find sleep.

On the drive out to Long Island I buy a bunch of daffodils from a street-corner vendor. He tells me that daffodils mean marriage. I tell him that they're for a nun. He tugs at his hat. 'You never know, hon,' he says. 'You never know these days.'

Michael still gropes for the back of his hair as he drives and every now and then squeezes my forearm and says it'll be all right. The expressway is a vomit of cars but gradually, as we move, the traffic thins out and the pace slows. Occasional flecks of snow get flicked away by the windscreen wipers. I curl into a shell and listen to the sound of what might be waves, remembering a man who perhaps sucked on a reed in a boghole, there to claim his own. I am older now. I have no right to be afraid. I think about plucking the petals from the flowers, one by one. We drive towards the ocean. Far off I can see gulls arguing over the waves. Perhaps they have come from where I have.

The convent, at Bluepoint, looks like a school. There seems little holy about the place except for the statue of Our Lady on the front lawn, a coat of snow on her shoulders. We park the car and I ask Michael to wait. Under his shirt collar I flick out the necklace of teeth and, for the first time since I've seen him, kiss him flush on the lips. 'Go on,' he says, 'don't be getting soppy on me now. And don't stay too long. Those waterfalls in Quebec melt very easily.'

He turns the stereo up full blast on a classical music station and I walk towards the front entrance. Hold. Buckle. Swallow. The words of a poet who should have known: 'What I do is me. For that I came.' I rasp my fingers along the wood but it takes a long time for the heavy door to swing open.

'Yes dear?' says the old nun. She is Irish too, her face creased into dun and purple lines.

'I'd like to see Brigid O'Dwyer.'

She looks at me, scans my face. 'No visitors, I'm sorry,' she says. 'Sister Brigid needs just a wee bit of peace and quiet.' She begins to close the door, smiling gently at me.

'*Is mise a dhreifeur*,' I stutter. The door opens again and she looks at me, askance.

'*Bhfuil tu cinnte.*'

'*Sea*,' I laugh. '*Taim cinnte.*'

'*Cad a bhfuil uait?*' she asks.

'I want to see her, *Se do thoil e.*'

She stares at me for a long time. '*Tar isteach*. Come on, girl.' She takes the daffodils and touches my cheek. 'You have her eyes.'

I move into the corridor where some other old nuns gather like moss, asking questions. 'She's very sick,' says one. 'She won't be seeing anyone.' The nun who met me at the door shuffles away. There are flowers by the doorway, paintings on the walls, a smell of potpourri, a quality of whiteness flooding all the colours. I sit in a steel chair with my knees nailed together, my hands in my lap, watching their faces, hearing the sombre chatter, not responding. A statue of the madonna stares at me. I am a teenager now in a brown school skirt. These are the women amongst whom I flagrantly rode my bicycle to the dance-hall. After *camogie*, in the showers, one or two of them would stand around and watch us. They had seen bruises on my inner thigh and told me about Magdalene. I run now from the school gates. I see her there, on the rock, sucking her finger, making a cross of reeds, the emblem of the saint for whom she was named. Michael walks, sucking the dew off desert rocks. My father puts some peat on the fire. That's grand, give me a smoke, so.

'Will you join us for a cup? She's sleeping now.' It's the old nun who had answered the door.

'Thank you, sister.'

'You look white, dear.'

'I've been travelling a long time.'

Over tea and scones they begin to melt, these women. They surprise me with their cackle and their smiles. They become carragheen, asking of the gone place. Brigid, they say. What a character. Was she always like that? The holy spirit up to the ears?

Two nuns there had spent the last few years with her. They tell me that she has been living in El Salvador in a convent outside a coffee plantation. One day recently three other nuns in the convent were shot, one of them almost fatally, so Brigid slipped out to a mountain for a few hours to pray for their health. She was found three days later, pinned to a rock. They look at me curiously when I ask about her fingernails. No, they say, her fingernails were fine. It was the lack of food that did it to her. Five campesinos had carried her down from the mountain. She was a favourite among the locals. She had always taken her food to the women of the adobe houses, and the men had respected her for the way she had hidden it under her clothes, so they wouldn't be shamed by charity. She'd spent a couple of weeks in a hospital in San Salvador, on an intravenous drip, then they transported her to Long Island to recover. She had never talked of any brothers or sisters, though she had got letters from Ireland. She did some of the strangest things in Central America, however. She carried a pebble in her mouth. It was all the way from the Saragossa Sea. She had learned how to dance. She reared four piglets behind the sacristy in the local church. She had shown people how to skin rabbits. The pebble had made little chips in her teeth. She had taken to wearing some very strange colours of socks.

I start to laugh.

'Everyone,' says one of the nuns in a Spanish accent, 'is allowed a little bit of madness, even if you're a nun. I don't see what's wrong with that.'

'No, no, no, there's nothing wrong with it, I'm just thinking.'

'It does get cold down there, you know,' she replies.

Someone wheezes about the time she burnt the pinto beans. The time the pigs got loose from the pen. The time the rabbit ran away from her. Another says she once dropped a piece of cake from her dress when she knelt at the altar and one of the priests, from Wales, said that God gave his only begotten bun. But the priest was forgiven for the joke since he was not a blasphemer, just a bit of a clown. The gardener comes in, a man from Sligo, and says: 'I've seen more fat on a butcher's knife than I have on your sister.' I leave the raisins on the side of the saucer. I am still laughing.

'Can I see her?' I say, turning to the nun who opened the door for me. 'I really need to see her. I have a friend waiting for me outside and I must go soon.'

The nun shuffles off to the kitchen. I wait. I think of a piece of turf and the way it has held so much history inside. I should have brought my sister a sod of soil. Or a rock. Or something.

An old nun, with an African accent, singing a hymn, comes out of the kitchen carrying a piece of toast and a glass of water. She has put a dollop of jam on the side of the white plate, 'for a special occasion'. She winks at me and tells me to follow her. I feel eyes on my back, then a hum of voices as we leave the dining area. She leads me up the stairs, past a statue, eerie and white, down a long clean corridor, towards a room with a picture of Archbishop Romero on the door. We stop. I hold my breath. A piece of turf. A rock. Anything.

'Go in, child.' The nun squeezes my hand. 'You're shaking.'

'Thank you,' I say. I stand at the door and open it slowly. 'Brigid?' There is a crumple in the bed, as if it has just been tossed. 'Brigid. It's me. Sheona.'

There's no sound, just a tiny hint of movement in the

bedsheets. I walk over. Her eyes are open, but she's not there within them. Her hair is netted and grey. The lines on her face cut inwards. Age has abseiled her cheekbones. I feel angry. I take down the picture of the Sacred Heart that is spraying red light out into the room and place it face down on the floor. She murmurs and a little spittle comes out from the side of her mouth. So she is there, after all, I look in her eyes again. This is the first time I have seen her since we were still that age. A bitterness in there now, perhaps, borne deep. 'I just want some neutral ground,' I say. Then I realise that I don't know who I'm talking to and I put the picture back on the wall.

I sit on the bed and touch her ashtrayed hair. 'Talk to me,' I say. She turns slightly. The toast is growing cold on a plate on the floor. I have no idea if she knows who I am as I feed her, but I have a feeling she does. I'm afraid to lay my hand on her for fear of snapping bones. She doesn't want to be fed. She hisses and spits the bread out of dehydrated lips. She closes her mouth on my fingers, but it takes no effort to pry it open. Her teeth are as brittle as chalk. I lay the toast on her tongue again. Each time it gets moister and eventually it dissolves. I wash it down with some water. I try to say something but I can't, so I sing a Hoagy Carmichael tune, but she doesn't recognise it. If I try to lift her I think I would find a heap of dust in my hand, my own hand, which is speaking to me again, carving out a shape that is in a flux.

I want to find out who is under the bedsheets. 'Talk to me.' She rolls away and turns her back. I stand and look around the room. It all crumples down to a lump in the bed. An empty chamberpot. Some full-bloom chrysanthemums by the window. A white plate with a smear of jam. A dead archbishop on the outside, looking in.

'Just a single word,' I say. 'Just give me a single word.'

Some voices float in from down the white corridor. Frantic, I move to a set of drawers and a cupboard to look at the bits and pieces that go to make her up now. I pull the drawers out and dump the contents on the floor. I cannot understand the mosaic. A bible. Some neatly folded blouses. Long underwear. A bundle of letters in an elastic band. Lots of hairpins. Stamps gleaned from the Book of Kells. Letters. I do not want to read them. A painting of a man sowing seeds, by a child's hand. A photograph of our mother and father, from a long time ago, standing together by Nelson's Pillar, him with a cigar, her with netting hanging down from her hat. A copy of a newspaper from a recent election. A Mayan doll. Lotus-legged on the floor, I am disappointed amongst somebody else's life. I haven't found what I'm looking for.

I shuffle to the end of the bed and lift the sheets. Her feet are blue and very cold to the touch. I rub them slowly at first. I remember when we were children, very young, before all that, and we had held buttercups to each other's chins on the edges of brown fields. I want her feet to tell me about butter. As I massage I think I see her lean her head sideways and smile, though I'm not sure. I don't know why, but I want to take her feet in my mouth. It seems obscene, but I want to and I don't. 'Up a lazy river with the robin song, it's a lazy river, we can float along blue skies up above, everyone's in love, up a lazy river with me.' She mumbles when I lean over her face and kiss her. There is spittle on her chin and she is horribly ruined.

I walk to the window. Far off, in the parking lot, I can see Michael, head slumped forward on the steering wheel, sleeping. Two nuns look in the passenger window at him, curious, a cup of tea and some scones in their hands. I am aware of myself now. I watch him, wondering about the last few days. An old feeling, new now. There is an ocean I know of that laps between here and there, washing. I watch him. Teeth around his neck. I want a bicycle. Sequoia seedlings in the basket. A flurry of puddles to ride through to a place where water is suspended. I will stay here now. I know that. When she recovers, I will go to Quebec and climb. But there is something I need first.

I smile, go away from the window, lean towards Brigid, and whisper: 'Where, Sister, did you put those yellow socks of mine anyway?'

The Wake House

BERNARD MACLAVERTY

AT THREE O'CLOCK Mrs McQuillan raised a slat of the vene-
tian blind and looked at the house across the street.

'Seems fairly quiet now,' she said. Dermot went on reading
the paper. 'Get dressed son and come over with me.'

'Do I have to?'

'It's not much to ask.'

'If I was working I couldn't.'

'But you're not – more's the pity.'

She was rubbing foundation into her face, cocking her head
this way and that at the mirror in the alcove. Then she
brushed her white hair back from her ears.

'Dermot.'

Dermot threw the paper on to the sofa and went stamping
upstairs.

'And shave,' his mother called after him.

He raked through his drawer and found a black tie someone had lent him to wear at his father's funeral. It had been
washed and ironed so many times that it had lost its central
axis. He tried to tie it but as always it ended up off centre.
After he had changed into his good suit he remembered the
shaving and went to the bathroom.

When he went downstairs she was sitting on the edge of

the sofa wearing her Sunday coat and hat. She stood up and looked at him.

'It's getting very scruffy.' she said, 'like a melodeon at the knees.' Standing on her tiptoes she picked a thread off his shoulder.

'Look, why are we doing this?' said Dermot. She didn't answer him but pointed to a dab of shaving cream on his earlobe. Dermot removed it with his finger and thumb.

'Respect. Respect for the dead,' she said.

'You'd no respect for him when he was alive.'

She went out to the kitchen and got the bag for the shoe things and set it in front of him. Dermot sighed and opened the drawstring mouth. Without taking his shoes off he put on polish using the small brush.

'Eff the Pope and No Surrender.'

'Don't use that word,' she said. 'Not even in fun.'

'I didn't use it. I said eff, didn't I?'

'I should hope so. Anyway it's not for him, it's for her. She came over here when your father died.'

'Aye, but he didn't. Bobby was probably in the pub preparing to come home and keep us awake half the night.'

'He wasn't that bad.'

'He wasn't that good either. Every Friday in life. Eff the Pope and No Surrender.' Dermot grinned and his mother smiled.

'Come on,' she said. Dermot scrubbed hard at his shoes with the polishing-off brush then stuck it and the bristles of the smaller one face to face and dropped them in the bag. His mother took a pair of rosary beads out of her coat pocket and hung them on the Sacred Heart lamp beneath the picture.

'I'd hate to pull them out by mistake.'

Together they went across the street.

'I've never set foot in this house in my life before,' she whispered, 'so we'll not stay long.'

After years of watching through the window, Mrs McQuillan knew that the bell didn't work. She flapped the letter-box and it seemed too loud. Not respectful. Young Cecil Blair opened the door and invited them in. Dermot awkwardly shook his hand not knowing what to say.

'Sorry, eh . . .' Cecil nodded his head in a tight-lipped way and led them into the crowded living room. Mrs Blair in black sat puff-eyed by the fire. Dermot's mother went over to her and didn't exactly shake hands but held one hand for a moment.

'I'm very sorry to hear . . .' she said. Mrs Blair gave a tight-lipped nod very like her son's and said:

'Get Mrs McQuillan a cup of tea.'

Cecil went into the kitchen. A young man sitting beside the widow saw that Mrs McQuillan had no seat and made it his excuse to get up and leave. Mrs McQuillan sat down, thanking him. Cecil leaned out of the kitchen door and said to Dermot:

'What are you having?'

'A stout?'

Young Cecil disappeared.

'It's a sad, sad time for you,' said Mrs McQuillan to the widow. 'I've gone through it myself.' Mrs Blair sighed and looked down at the floor. Her face was pale and her forehead lined. It looked as if tears could spring to her eyes again at any minute.

The tea, when it came, was tepid and milky but Mrs McQuillan sipped it as if it was hot. She balanced the china cup and saucer on the upturned palm of her hand. Dermot leaned one shoulder against the wall and poured his bottle of stout badly, the creamy head welling up so quickly that he had to suck it to keep it from foaming on to the carpet.

On the wall beside him there was a small framed picture of the Queen when she was young. It had been there so long the sunlight had drained all the reds from the print and only the blues and yellows remained. The letter-box flapped on the front door and Cecil left Dermot standing on his own. There were loud voices in the hall – too loud for a wake house – then a new party came in – three of them, all middle-aged, wearing dark suits. In turn they shook hands with Mrs Blair and each said, 'Sorry for your trouble.' Their hands were red

and chafed. Dermot knew them to be farmers from the next
townland but not their names. Cecil asked them what they
would like to drink. One of them said:

'We'll just stick with the whiskey.' The others agreed.
Cecil poured them three tumblers.

'Water?'

'As it is. Our healths,' one of them said, half raising his
glass. They all nodded and drank. Dermot heard one of them
say,

'There'll be no drink where Bobby's gone.' The other two
began to smile but stopped.

Dermot looked at his mother talking to the widow.

'It'll come to us all,' she said. 'This life's only a prep-
aration.'

'Bobby wasn't much interested in preparing,' said the
widow. 'But he was good at heart. You can't say better than
that.' Everybody in the room nodded silently.

Someone offered Dermot another stout which he took. He
looked across at his mother but she didn't seem to notice.
The two women had dropped their voices and were talking
with their heads close together.

One of the farmers – a man with a porous nose who was
standing in the kitchen doorway spoke to Dermot.

'Did you know Bobby?' Dermot shook his head.

'Not well. Just to see.' He had a vision of the same Bobby
coming staggering up the street about a month ago and standing in front of his own gate searching each pocket in turn for
a key. It was a July night and Dermot's bedroom window
was open for air.

'I see your curtains moving, you bastards.' A step forward,
a step back. A dismissive wave of the hand in the direction of
the McQuillans. Then very quietly.

'Fuck yis all.'

He stood for a long time, his legs agape. A step forward, a
step back. Then he shouted at the top of his voice.

'Fuck the Pope and . . .' Dermot let the curtains fall
together again and lay down. But he couldn't sleep waiting
for the No Surrender. After a while he had another look but

the street was empty. No movement except for the slow flopping of the Union Jack in Bobby Blair's garden.

Cecil came across the room and set a soup plate full of crisps on the hall table beside Dermot.

'Do you want to go up and see him?'

Dermot set his jaw and said, 'I'd prefer to remember him as he was.'

'Fair enough.'

The man with the porous nose shook his head in disbelief.

'He was a good friend to me. Got my son the job he's in at the minute.'

'Bully for him.'

A second farmer dipped his big fingers in the dish and crunched a mouthful of crisps. He swallowed and said to Dermot, 'How do you know the deceased?'

'I'm a neighbour. From across the street.'

'Is that so? He was one hell of a man. One hell of a man.' He leaned over to Dermot and whispered, 'C'mere. Have you any idea what he was like? *Any* idea?'

Dermot shook his head. The farmer with the porous nose said, 'When Mandela got out he cried. Can you believe that? I was with him – I saw it. Big fuckin' tears rolling down his cheeks. He was drunk, right enough, but the tears was real. I was in the pub with him all afternoon. It was on TV and he shouts, "What right have they – letting black bastards like that outa jail when this country's hoachin' with fuckin' IRA men?" '

He laughed – a kind of cackle with phlegm and Dermot smiled.

The signs that his mother wanted to go were becoming obvious. She sat upright in her chair, her voice became louder and she permitted herself a smile. She rebuttoned her coat and stood up. Dermot swilled off the rest of his stout and moved to join her on the way out. The widow Blair stood politely,

'Would you like to go up and see him, Mrs McQuillan?' she said.

'I'd be too upset,' she said. 'It'd bring it all back to me.'

Mrs Blair nodded as if she understood. Cecil showed them out.

In their own hallway Mrs McQuillan hung up her coat and took an apron off a peg.

'Poor woman,' she said. 'Did they ask you to go up and see him?'

'Aye.'

'Did you go?' Her hands whirled behind her back tying the strings of the apron.

'Are you mad? Why would I want to see an oul drunk like Bobby Blair laid out?'

He went into the living room and began poking the fire. Their house and the Blairs' were exactly the same – mirror images of each other. His mother went into the kitchen and began peeling potatoes. By the speed at which she worked and the rattling noises she made Dermot knew there was something wrong. She came to the kitchen doorway with a white potato in her wet hands.

'You should have.'

'Should have what?'

'Gone up to see him.'

'Bobby Blair!' Dermot dropped the poker on the hearth and began throwing coal on the fire with tongs.

'Your father would have.'

'They asked *you* and you didn't.'

'It's different for a woman.'

She turned back to the sink and dropped the potato in the pot and began scraping another. She spoke out to him.

'Besides I meant what I said – about bringing it all back.'

Dermot turned on the transistor and found some pop music. His mother came to the door again drying her hands on her apron.

'That poor woman,' she said. 'It was bad enough having to live with Bobby.' She leaned against the door-jamb for a long time. Dermot said nothing, pretending to listen to the radio. She shook her head and clicked her tongue.

'The both of us refusing . . .'

As they ate their dinner, clacking and scraping forks, she said, 'It looks that bad.'

'What?'

'The both of us.'

Dermot shrugged.

'What can we do about it?'

She cleaned potato off her knife on to her fork and put it in her mouth.

'You could go over again. Say to her.'

'What?'

'Whatever you like.'

'I don't believe this.'

She cleared away the plates and put them in the basin. He washed and she dried.

'For your father's sake,' she said. Dermot flung the last spoon on to the stainless steel draining-board and dried his hands on the dish towel, a thing he knew she hated.

He slammed the front door and stood for a moment. Then he walked across the street his teeth clenched together and flapped the letter-box. This time the door was opened by a man he didn't know. Dermot cleared his throat.

'I'd like to see Bobby,' he said. The man looked at him.

'Bobby's dead.'

'I know.'

The man stepped back then led the way into the hallway. The farmers were now standing at the foot of the stairs. The one with the porous nose was sitting on the bottom step swirling whiskey in his glass.

'Ah – it's the boy again,' he said. The man led the way up the stairs. Dermot excused himself and tried to slip past the sitting farmer. He felt a hand grab his ankle and he nearly fell. The grip was tight and painful. The farmer laughed.

'I'm only pulling your leg,' he said. Then he let go. It was like being released from a manacle. Somebody shouted out from the kitchen.

'A bit of order out there.'

In the bedroom the coffin was laid on the bed creating its

own depression in the white candlewick coverlet. The man
stood back with his hands not joined but one holding the
other by the wrist. Dermot tried to think of the best thing to
do. In a Catholic house he would have knelt, blessed himself
and pretended to say a prayer. He could have hidden behind
his joined hands. Now he just stared – conscious of the
stranger's eyes on the back of his neck. The dead man's face
was the colour of a mushroom, his nostrils wide black triangles of different sizes. Fuck the Pope and No Surrender.
Dermot held his wrist with his other hand and bowed his
head. Below the rim of the coffin there was white scalloped
paper like inside an expensive box of biscuits. The paper
hid almost everything except Bobby's dead face. Instead of
candles the room was full of flowers. The only light came
through the drawn paper blinds.

From downstairs came the rattle of the letter-box and the
man murmured something and went out. Left alone Dermot
inched nearer the coffin. His father was the only dead person
he had ever seen. He pulled the scalloped paper back and
looked beneath it. Bobby was wearing a dark suit, a white
shirt and tie. Where his lapels should have been was his
Orange sash – the whole regalia. All dressed up and nowhere
to go. Dermot looked up and saw a reflection of himself
prying in the dressing-table mirror. He let the scalloped paper
drop back into place. Footsteps approached on the stairs.

Two oldish women were shown in by the stranger. One
was Mavis Stewart, the other one worked in the paper shop.
Mavis looked at the corpse and her lower lip trembled and
she began to weep. Dermot was caught between the women
and the door. Tears trickled down the woman's face and she
snuffled wetly. The woman from the paper shop held on to
her and Mavis nuzzled into her shoulder. She kept repeating
'Bobby, Bobby – who'll make us laugh now?' Dermot edged
his way around the bed and stood waiting. The women took
no notice. Mavis began to dry her tears with a lavender tissue.

'I never met a man like him for dancing. He would have
danced the legs off you. And he got worse when the rock and

roll came in.' Dermot coughed hoping they would move and let him pass.

'And the twist,' said the woman from the paper shop. 'I think that boy wants out.'

Mavis Stewart said, 'Sorry love,' and squeezed close to the bed to let him pass. Dermot nodded to the stranger beside the wardrobe.

'I'm off.'

'I'll show you out.' The stranger went downstairs with him and went to open the front door. Dermot hesitated.

'Maybe I'd better say hello to Mrs Blair. Let her see I've been up. Seeing Bobby.'

He knocked on the living-room door.

'Yes? Come in.'

He opened it. Mrs Blair was still sitting by the fire. She was surrounded by the three farmers. Dermot said, 'I was just up seeing Mr Blair.'

'Very good, son. That was nice of you.' Then her face crumpled and she began to cry. The farmer with the porous nose put a hand on her arm and patted it. Dermot was going to wave but checked his arm in time. He backed into the hallway just as young Cecil appeared out of the kitchen. It was young Cecil who showed Dermot out.

'Thanks for coming,' he said. 'Again.'

endword

DAVID MACKENZIE

FERRINGS HAS SOLD his television to rid himself of news. He declares that this desperate concern with what other people do is evil and if we all kept ourselves to ourselves then the world would be a happier place. He craves sport now, he admits, and the occasional natural history programme but the benefits of life without television outweigh these minor regrets. He feels freer, he says, than he has ever felt before. He is losing the desire to know.

Six weeks ago he stopped buying newspapers. On trains and buses now he has to avert his eyes to avoid the unwitting capture of a headline or telling picture. There are streets he can no longer walk down as there are newsstands at each end with posters that bark at him, news, news, NEWS! With the aid of street maps he works out routes that mean he need not pass newsagents or television shops. More and more he walks with his head bowed, eyes to the ground. Watching him I feel that maybe there are messages in the pavement, that he is trying to decipher what the cracks in the paving stones might mean, or an arrangement of leaves. But it is just Ferrings on guard, avoiding the chance of a stray hoarding or banner. For he is serious about all this, he says; it is not a whim. I believe him. He *is* serious about it and I am becoming seriously worried about him.

He is under pressure at work. In his office there are seven other people and they all bring in newspapers. Some of his colleagues read these at their desks during coffee breaks. At work then, Ferrings tends to look up rather than down. He has remarked on the state of the ceiling which is not good. There are cracks in it he says, and the elaborate coving is broken in several places.

Of course, there is talk about the news too, but this centres on football and cricket which Ferrings is less interested in. There are conversations about stories from the *Sun* or the *Mirror* to do with the sex lives of film stars or the latest serial killings. To Ferrings these items are not news so he is happy to hear them without listening.

We meet more often now. I seek him out. Over coffee I quiz him about his beliefs, about how he is coping. Is he coping? He admits that it's hard. I ask why this, why news, why is this so important? He says that it has gone beyond an interest in other people's business. He says that this interest must be satisfied at all costs and if it cannot be satisfied by the truth it will be offered lies. The media is no longer concerned with the imparting of knowledge, if it ever was; it is more and more concerned with making money. If the news is not interesting, no one will buy papers or watch TV news shows. So, uninteresting news is changed. It is converted into something interesting or just made up.

I tell him gently that everyone knows this; this, I tell him, is the way it is. But it shouldn't be, he says. Of course it shouldn't be, I reply, but it is. I am making a stand, he says, I am saying no. Good, I say good. Just don't hurt yourself that's all. It's the only thing I can do he says, and I understand from that phrase that maybe, just maybe, he is seeking some sort of martyrdom.

And now we have war. War. It isn't a very big war as wars go, and it is some way away from here but we are involved and everyone knows about it, everyone craves news about it. There are special editions of newspapers, there are magazines, there are extended news bulletins on TV and there is one whole radio channel devoted to it, twenty-four hours a day.

Even Ferrings knows that there is something big going on. Maybe he even knows it's war. One thing is for sure: it's harder for him now, much harder than before. In the office there are more newspapers. There is very little talk about football. Now it is all bombing missions, strike rates, percentage kills, body counts, MIAs, hardware, software, deadware. One of his colleagues has brought in a small pocket TV. This instrument is consulted every half hour for news. The manager himself comes from his office to huddle with the others round the tiny screen. Ferrings goes to the toilet.

He has taken to wearing headphones. These are not small, personal stereo ear-pieces but large rubber-lined cups that enclose each ear completely. The headphones are not linked up to anything; they are not to keep sound in, they are to keep sound out. He wears them all the time when he is not at home and he only takes them off at work when it is necessary for him to communicate with someone on matters related to his job. He always wears them when travelling because people have begun to talk now, openly. The old taboo has gone. On buses, trains and on the Underground people actually talk to each other, total strangers, but only about the war. Ferrings sits among them, ears covered, eyes concentrating hard on the slatted wooden floor. He is aware perhaps that there is a buzz around him, an atmosphere charged with news particles, but he is satisfied that nothing can get past his guard.

I have begun to have dreams about him and they are bad dreams. I see Ferrings walking home late at night. He takes a short cut through an alleyway. Halfway down he sees dark figures at the far end and he knows they are not good men. He turns. At the other end of the alley, the end from which he has just come, there are more dark figures. He is trapped. He begins to feel more than a little afraid. The two groups walk slowly towards him. They know he can't escape so there is no hurry. They take their time. As they get closer he can identify dark grey or black trench coats, hats pulled down over eyes. When they all meet in the middle he is seized and dragged away. Someone takes off his headphones so that he can hear the sound of his own screams. The headphones are bent, the loop of sprung metal that joins the ear-covers pulled until it is straight and then snaps. Ferrings knows he is about to die.

They take him to a house and tie him to a chair. For hours he is tortured. They take it in turns to read to him the front pages of all the dailies. *Troops die in tank battle. Inflation up 2%. Coup in Liberia. Both does it again. Sexy vicar kissed my backside.* They move on to the *Sunday Times* and read him the lot, including the Business Section. *Collapse of Bolivian Tin. Gilts Rise. Treasury Jitters on Eurobond Implications.* He gets everything. After ten hours he is in a state of total exhaustion. They change tactics. They play taped news programmes to him with the volume turned up so high it hurts.

The next day they release him but he is broken, disoriented. He doesn't know where he is. He is in a new world. He goes into a shop to buy a street map. While he is there he also buys a newspaper.

Now he is in trouble, serious trouble. I am in trouble too. It happened like this:

About a week ago we had an argument. It was my fault. I told him that he was too inward looking. If he was really serious about his beliefs he should be telling people about them. He said no. He said he didn't care what other people did or thought. That was up to them: he only cared about himself. I called him selfish.

I told him to get active, tell people, hit the streets. He shook his head. I told him all this because he needs contact, he's turning in on himself and it's bad for him. I told myself that I had his best interests at heart.

But I made things worse.

A few days ago he bought a television set again. Not any television set but the very one he had recently sold. He bought it back. He had to pay more, of course. He lost on the deal and made himself look a fool as well. But neither of these points bothered him. He had to buy the TV back because it was wrong of him to pass on the disease – his word – to someone else.

Then he invited me to join him at Speakers' Corner on Sunday. Yes, he said, he had decided to come out, to declare himself, to launch his campaign. He was about to begin his ministry.

It was just as well that I went along as he needed help to get set up. We struggled in the Underground, he carrying the TV set – fortunately not very large – plus a bundle of newspapers wrapped in brown paper, I half-carrying, half-dragging a small three-step wooden platform which he had built as his soapbox. I had to admit that he seemed quite organised.

It was a warm day and there were lots of people around. Ferrings found a relatively quiet spot and positioned his platform. In front of it he placed the parcel of newspapers with the TV balanced a little precariously on top.

Before he started to speak he sprang a surprise on me. Inside the platform he had stowed a banner and some short wooden rods similar to those that chimney sweeps use to fix on to their brushes. He put up the rods first, producing two poles each about eight feet long. Then I helped him to unfurl the banner and attach it to the top of these poles. He stuck the base of one into some clips at the side of the platform. I stood one side holding the other pole and so the banner was displayed. On a strip of white cloth about ten feet long and eighteen inches wide was written in red letters:

NO NEWS IS GOOD

I smiled when I saw it. The banner alone attracted a small crowd and as he began to speak more people came over until thirty or forty people were gathered round.

'The media is founded on untruth,' he began. 'All the newspapers tell lies . . .'

'Are you any different?' someone shouted.

There was general laughter. Ferrings smiled and I think that was the gesture that earned him a hearing. The crowd was good-natured and willing to listen.

'Yes,' he said, 'I believe I am different and the reason I'm different is that I'm not asking for money. Newspaper editors are there to sell newspapers and they do that by telling us what we want to hear. Generally what we want to hear doesn't involve the truth. I remind you of T.S. Eliot's words: "Humankind cannot bear very much reality".'

A bit of a buzz greeted this. He lost a few at the edge of the crowd who drifted off but some in the main body muttered approvingly.

'So what I'm suggesting is we stop buying newspapers, we stop watching news programmes. If we give up the media, if we reject it because it believes it has to lie to us in order to keep our interest, then maybe the news editors will get the message, maybe they'll begin to understand that the truth is what we want, not lies . . .'

'Hear! Hear!' someone said enthusiastically. Someone else shouted, 'Bollocks.'

'See this lot?' Ferrings went on. He pointed to the bundle of newspapers and the TV in front of him. 'See this lot? There's only one thing to do with this pile of rubbish . . .'

He dug a hand into his pocket and even before I saw the box of matches appear I experienced a sudden moment of unease. Something, I was sure, was about to go horribly wrong.

'No!' I shouted but flame had appeared in his hand and

then sprang out in an arc, out and down, to land on the pile of newspapers.

He must have soaked them in some flammable liquid, though not petrol because I would have smelt it. Anyway, a blue flame scurried across the top and sides of the parcel of papers and in a moment began to lick around the base of the TV set.

The people closest to Ferrings took fright but, because quite a crowd had gathered by this time, they could not immediately move back out of the way. There was a lot of shouting and the first couple of rows of onlookers panicked. An elderly man fell over. I abandoned my pole and ran over to help him up.

He was only a few feet away from me – two quick strides would have got me there, but I didn't make it. Someone else had set off in the other direction. We collided and we both fell over. During the second or two that I was on the ground, watching, almost apart from the action, I saw Ferrings still on his platform, unwilling or unable to move. He was looking hard at the burning TV, the flames quite large now. People in the crowd were shouting and the scene became more chaotic. But Ferrings did not move. Something slanted past him to one side. It was the pole that I had been holding. It seemed a long time ago that I had let go of it. Perhaps it had managed to stay upright for a second or two all by itself. Or maybe things really did happen much faster than I can now remember. But the pole fell, and, took, it seemed, a long time in falling. It side-swiped the TV set and the banner caught fire. The blazing TV toppled from its pedestal of burning paper and bounced a couple of yards across the pale grass. It came to rest on top of the legs of the elderly man I had tried to help.

The old man was not badly burned. I managed to get up and kick the TV away in a matter of two or three seconds. By that time the space in front of Ferrings' platform had cleared so that the TV now lay smouldering on a patch of yellow grass several feet away from the nearest spectator. The bundle of newspapers was still on fire but no one was in danger from that either.

I took off the light jacket I was wearing, rolled it up and put it under the old man's head. He said he was fine, he wanted to get up, but I made him stay down. His trousers were singed and torn but I was sure he was going to be OK. As Ferrings looked on quietly from his platform, a policeman appeared. We both knelt down over the old man. The policeman said that an ambulance was on its way. The old man even managed to smile. Someone took a photograph.

I travelled with the old man to the hospital. When I left the park Ferrings was talking to the policeman. I didn't say anything to Ferrings, not a word. He seemed to be in a daze. He had stepped down from the platform but he didn't seem to be saying very much. It was the policeman's voice I could hear, asking questions that Ferrings obviously found it difficult to answer.

At the hospital they discovered that the old man had a few cuts and bruises on his legs but that was all. They dressed the cuts – no stitches were necessary – and kept him in for an hour or so. They gave him a cup of tea.

He insisted he was fine and wanted to go home. I ordered a taxi. I took his arm and we walked slowly out of the hospital. On the steps down to the taxi he collapsed. We managed to get him back inside the hospital but by the time a doctor from casualty examined him he was dead.

Arsonist Arrested in Hyde Park. OAP Dies in Media Protest. Man Dies at News Demo. Speakers' Corner Tragedy. News Nut Torches TV and Fries Pensioner. Pensioner Burned to Death in Hyde Park. Park Inferno Incinerates OAP. Man Killed by Blazing TV. Man Murdered in Park Protest. Why Did He Die? Death by Fire. Burned to Death! Burned Alive! Burning Man. Face of the

TV Set Killer. Face of the Media Monster. Face of the News Nut.
Fried Park Corner! Face of the Hyde Park Frier.

Ferrings (Ferns/Ferrins/Freens/Ferrine/Herring), who is 28,
29, 31 and 35 years old, is tall, of medium height, six feet
two, six feet three, five feet eight and has pale brown, blonde,
black, no hair. He is an insurance/KGB/ estate agent. He
hears voices. He sees voices. He believes he is a voice. He
believes he is a Martian. He hates TV. He loves TV. Burning
the TV was a wanton act of destruction/a moment of spiritual
uplift/a sacrifice to the god Mars/an attempt to contact his
fellow Martians. He is in the pay of the KGB/the BBC/ITV/
the company that made the TV set/a rival to the company
that made the TV set/the *Sunday Times*/the *Sun*/Mars. He is a
criminal; he is insane; he is criminally insane.

Poor Ferrings. I have told him nothing about this. But I have
the newspapers. I have tapes of the radio reports and videos
of the TV bulletins. I have read them all, listened to and
watched them all. Several times. And I have begun to realise
how right Ferrings was.

Now he has gone a step further. I saw him a week ago, sat
opposite him with a screen between us. He has advanced his
theory. He has come to the conclusion that the offender in all
this is the word. Words, he says, create trouble and he is
going to give them up. He has stopped reading and he allows
no printed material whatsoever inside his cell. He refuses to
fill in any forms or even to read them. I brought him some
books but he asked me to take them away.

The reporters can't wait till Ferrings gets out of jail; they
can't wait to get their claws into him. Right now they are

having great fun making it all up but that phase is coming to an end. They want interviews, photos, in-depth analyses. They need Ferrings.

Meanwhile they have me. I am Ferrings' brother/close friend/lover/accomplice. I fund his campaign. I am a Martian too. I have AIDS (as does Ferrings). He pays me to whip him with radio aerials and electric cable. I am his publicity agent.

They know where I live and they know where I work; they know the route I take from one place to the other. They hover, like mosquitoes. They push and shove each other and me. They fire questions at me and when I tire of saying 'no comment' and lapse into complete silence, they ask me if silence is confirmation. I say nothing. They scribble all this information down and later print it.

News Nut Silent Partner Speaks. Secrets of the Hyde Park Frier by His Lover. Media Monsters Man Reveals All. I Still Love Him Says Frier's Toyboy. Hang Them Both Says Grieving Family. TV Monsters Martian Mate. He Bent Me to His Martian Will. Hyde Park Frier – The Truth at Last.

Ferrings believes that the next step is to give up speech. He is working on it now, limiting himself to fewer and fewer words each day. Later, probably much later, he admits, he will learn to stop himself from listening so that words will no longer reach him by any means at all. I remind him of the words inside his head, the ones he's stuck with whether he likes it or not. He says he's not so worried about those as they are under his control. Anyway, he expects them to leak away slowly, one by one, until there are none left.

He says I can continue to visit him. He says he enjoys my visits but in future it may be that he just sits there and doesn't say much. He asks me if I could maybe not say too much either.

(Lying on the ground, winded, I see the pole toppling over, drawn across in an arc by the burning red words of the banner, **NO NEWS IS GOOD**. Ferrings is up there on his platform, saying nothing. I see the TV set struck by the pole, watch its slow fiery tumble from the pile of burning papers across four or five feet of grass on to the legs of the old man.

I remember that second or so during which I take in what is going on, a tiny expanse of time between the TV's coming to stop and the old man's first cry of pain. But the more I think about it the less I am aware of the old man. It is almost as if he is an irrelevance, a very minor player. It is Ferrings I remember most clearly, trick of memory or not. He is standing there quite motionless and I want to scream at him, 'Do something!' but even then, even during that brief moment, I know that it will do no good. Ferrings is there and he is aware of what is going on but he knows more than I do. He recognises that the immediate events are of little importance, diverting attention from the main theme. But he knows too that the main theme is now lost, it will be swamped by what is happening now and he might as well give up. He might as well do what he has already started to do, keep still. He is already preparing for that long, long silence that he will embark upon one day soon.

After I left the hospital, after the old man was dead, I went back to Hyde Park. I examined the empty space where Ferrings had addressed the crowd. There was very little to see – a bit of scorched grass, the imprint of Ferrings' platform. The platform itself was gone but in a rubbish bin to one side I found the remains of the banner. The poles had been broken up to fit into the bin and only one piece of shredded, singed material was left, clinging to a short length of splintered wood. It bore the first word of the banner, **NO**.)

I ask him a question. It is a bad question and I am a bad man for asking it. But I am curious and angry and sad at the same time. Ferrings is disappearing in front of me. He is thinner and whiter and his eyes tell me that he's not going to get outside again. I'll be visiting him, somewhere, for a long time. It's harder to get through to him now. The words are still there, his and mine, a few of them, but for him the meanings of some are falling away, each leaving behind a shell made up of sound alone.

But I ask my question, if only to get a reaction. If you're giving up speech, I say to him, sooner or later you'll come to your last word, your very last word, *the* last word. What do you think it will be?

He thinks about this for a long time, long enough for me to suspect that my question is only a jumble of sounds to him, an irritating noise. But then he answers. He says, I don't know. I don't know, he says again, but I think it will be very small.

A Real Life

ALICE MUNRO

A MAN CAME along and fell in love with Dorrie Beck. At least, he wanted to marry her. It was true.

'If her brother were alive she would never have needed to get married,' Millicent said. What did she mean? Not something shameful. And she didn't mean money, either. She meant that love had existed, kindness had created comfort, and in the poor, somewhat feckless life Dorrie and Albert Beck had lived together, loneliness had not been a threat. Millicent, who was shrewd and practical in some ways, was stubbornly sentimental in others. She believed always in the sweetness of affection that was untainted by sex.

She thought it was the way Dorrie used her knife and fork that had captivated the man. Indeed, it was the same way he used his. Dorrie kept her fork in her left hand and used the right only for cutting. The was because she had been to Whitby Ladies' College when she was young. A last spurt of the Becks' money. Another thing she had learned there was a beautiful handwriting, and that might have been a factor as well, because after the first meeting the entire courtship appeared to have been conducted by letter. Millicent loved the sound of Whitby Ladies' College, and it was her plan –

not shared with anybody – that her own daughter would go there someday.

Millicent was not an uneducated person herself. She had taught school, she hadn't married early. She had rejected two serious boyfriends – one because she couldn't stand his mother, one because he tried putting his tongue in her mouth – before she agreed to marry Porter, who was nineteen years older than she was. He owned three farms, and he promised her a bathroom within a year, and a dining-room suite and a chesterfield and chairs. On their wedding night he said, 'Now you've got to take what's coming to you,' but she knew it was not unkindly meant.

That was in 1933.

She had three children, fairly quickly, and after the third baby she developed some problems. Porter was decent – mostly, after that, he let her alone.

The Beck house was on Porter's land, but he wasn't the one who had bought them out. He bought Albert and Dorrie's place from the man who had bought it from them. So, technically, they were renting their old house back from Porter. But money did not enter the picture. When Albert was alive he would show up and work for a day when important jobs were undertaken – when they were pouring the cement floor in the barn or putting the hay in the mow. Dorrie had come along on those occasions, and also when Millicent had a new baby or was house-cleaning. Dorrie had remarkable strength for lugging furniture about, and could do a man's work, like putting up the storm windows. At the start of a hard job – such as ripping the wallpaper off a whole room – she would settle back her shoulders and draw a deep, happy breath. She glowed with resolution. She was a big, firm woman with heavy legs, chestnut-brown hair, a broad, bashful face and dark freckles like dots of velvet. A man in the area had named a horse after her.

In spite of her enjoyment of house-cleaning, she did not do a lot of it at home. The house that she and Albert had lived in – that she lived in alone after his death – was large and handsomely laid out but practically without furniture. Furniture would come up in Dorrie's conversation – the oak sideboard, Mother's wardrobe, the spool bed – but tacked on to this mention was always the phrase 'that went at the Auction'. The Auction sounded like a natural disaster, something like a flood and windstorm together, about which it would be pointless to complain. No carpets remained, either, and no pictures. There was just the calendar from Nunn's Grocery, which Albert used to work for. Absences of customary things – and the presence of others, such as Dorrie's traps and guns and the boards for stretching rabbit and muskrat skins – had made the rooms lose their designations, made the notion of cleaning them frivolous. Once in the summer, Millicent saw a pile of dog dirt at the head of the stairs. She didn't see it while it was fresh, but it was fresh enough to seem an offence. Through the summer it changed, from brown to grey. It became stony, dignified, and stable, and, strangely, Millicent herself found less and less need to see it as anything but something that had a right to be there.

Delilah was the dog responsible. She was black, part Labrador. She chased cars, and eventually this was how she got herself killed. After Albert's death, both she and Dorrie may have become a little unhinged. But this was not something anybody could spot right away. At first, it was just that there was no man coming home, and so no set time to get supper. There were no men's clothes to wash – cutting out the idea of regular washing. Nobody to talk to, so Dorrie talked more to Millicent or to both Millicent and Porter. She talked about Albert and his job, which had been driving Nunn's Grocery Wagon, and later their truck, all over the countryside. He had gone to college, he was no dunce, but when he came home from the Great War he was not very well, and he thought it best to be out-of-doors, so he got the job driving for Nunn's and kept it until he died. He was a man of inexhaustible sociability and did more than simply deliver groceries. He gave people a lift to town. He brought patients home from the hospital. He had a crazy woman on his route, and once when he was getting her groceries out of the truck had a compulsion to look around. There she stood with a hatchet, about to brain him. In fact, her swing had already begun, and when he slipped out of range she had to continue, chopping neatly into the box of groceries and cleaving a pound of butter. He kept on making deliveries to her, not having the heart to turn her over to the authorities, who would take her to the asylum. She never took up the hatchet again but gave him cupcakes sprinkled with evil-looking seeds, which he threw into the grass at the end of the lane. Other women, more than one, had shown themselves to him naked. One of them arose out of a tub of bath water in the middle of the kitchen floor, and Albert bowed low and set the groceries at her feet. 'Aren't some people amazing?' said Dorrie. And she also told about a bachelor whose house was overrun by rats, so that he had to keep his food slung in a sack from the kitchen beams. But the rats ran out along the beams and leaped upon the sack and clawed it apart, and eventually the fellow was obliged to take all his food into bed with him.

'Albert always said people living alone are to be pitied,' said Dorrie – as if she did not understand that she was now one of them. Albert's heart had given out – he had only had time to pull to the side of the road and stop the truck. He died in a lovely spot, where black oaks grew in a bottom-land, and a sweet, clear creek ran beside the road.

Dorrie mentioned other things Albert had told her, concerning the Becks in the early days. How they came up the river in a raft, two brothers, and started a mill at the Big Bend, where there was nothing but the wildwoods. And nothing now, either, but the ruins of their mill and dam. The farm was never a livelihood but a hobby, when they built the big house and brought out the furniture from Edinburgh. The bedsteads, the chairs, the carved chests that went in the Auction. They brought it round the Horn, Dorrie said, and up Lake Huron and so up the river. Oh, Dorrie, said Millicent, that is not possible, and she brought a school geography book she had kept, to point out the error. It must have been a canal, then, said Dorrie. I recall a canal. The Panama Canal? More likely it was the Erie Canal, said Millicent.

'Yes,' said Dorrie. 'Round the Horn and into the Erie Canal.'

'Dorrie is a true lady, no matter what anybody says,' said Millicent to Porter, who did not argue. He was used to her absolute, personal judgements. 'She is a hundred times more a lady than Muriel Snow,' said Millicent, naming the person who might be called her best friend. 'I say that, and I love Muriel Snow dearly.'

Porter was used to hearing that, too: 'I love Muriel Snow dearly, and I would stick up for her no matter what.' 'I love Muriel Snow, but that does not mean I approve of everything she does.'

The smoking. And saying hot damn, Chrissakes, poop. *I nearly pooped my pants.*

Muriel Snow had not been Millicent's first choice for best friend. In the early days of her marriage she had set her sights high. Mrs Lawyer Nesbitt. Mrs Doctor Finnegan. Mrs Doud. They let her take on a donkey's load of work in the Women's Auxiliary at the church, but they never asked her to their tea parties. She was never inside their houses, unless it was to a meeting. Porter was a farmer. No matter how many farms. She should have known.

She met Muriel when she decided that her daughter, Betty Jean, would take piano lessons. Muriel was the music teacher. She taught in the schools as well as privately. Times being what they were, she charged only twenty cents a lesson. She played the organ at the church and directed various choirs, but some of that was for nothing. She and Millicent got on so well that soon she was in Millicent's house as often as Dorrie was, though on a rather different footing.

Muriel was over thirty and had never been married. Getting married was something she talked about openly, jokingly, and plaintively, particularly when Porter was around. 'Don't you know any men, Porter?' she would say. 'Can't you dig up just one decent man for me?' Porter would say maybe he could, but maybe she wouldn't think they were so decent. In the summers Muriel went to visit a sister in Montreal, and once she went to stay with some cousins she had never met, only written to, in Philadelphia. The first thing she reported on, when she got back, was the man situation.

'Terrible. They all get married young, they're Catholics, and the wives never die – they're too busy having babies.'

'Oh, they had somebody lined up for me, but I saw right away he would never pan out. He was one of those ones with the mothers.'

'I did meet one, but he had an awful failing. He didn't cut his toenails. Big yellow toenails. Well? Aren't you going to ask me how I found out?'

Muriel was always dressed in some shade of blue. A woman should pick a colour that really suits her and wear it all the time, she said. Like your perfume. It should be your signature. Blue was widely thought to be a colour for blondes, but that was incorrect. Blue often made a blonde look more washed-out than she was to start with. It suited best a warm-looking skin, like Muriel's – skin that took a good tan and never entirely lost it. It suited brown hair and brown eyes, which were hers as well. She never skimped on her clothes – it was a mistake to. Her fingernails were always painted – a rich and distracting colour, apricot or blood ruby or even gold. She was small and round; she did exercises to keep her tidy waistline. She had a dark mole on the front of her neck, like a jewel on an invisible chain, and another, like a tear, at the corner of one eye.

'The word for you is not "pretty",' Millicent said one day, surprising herself. 'It's "*bewitching*".' Then she flushed at her own tribute, knowing she sounded childish and excessive.

Muriel flushed a little too, but with pleasure. She drank in admiration, frankly courted it. Once she dropped in on her way to a concert in Walley, which she hoped would yield rewards. She had on an ice-blue dress that shimmered.

'And that isn't all,' she said. 'Everything I have on is new, and everything is *silk*.'

It wasn't true that she never found a man. She found one fairly often but hardly ever one that she could bring to supper. She found them in other towns, where she took her choirs to massed concerts, in Toronto at piano recitals to which she might take a promising student. Sometimes she found them in the students' own homes. They were the uncles, the fathers, the grandfathers, and the reason that they would not come into Millicent's house but only wave – sometimes curtly, sometimes with bravado – from a waiting car was that they were married. A bedridden wife, a drinking wife, a vicious shrew of a wife? Perhaps. Sometimes no mention at all – a ghost of a wife. They escorted Muriel to musical events, an interest in music being the ready excuse. Sometimes there was even a performing child, to act as chaperon. They took her to dinners in restaurants in distant towns. They were referred to as friends. Millicent defended her. How could there be any harm when it was all so out in the open? But it wasn't, quite, and it would all end in misunderstandings, harsh words, unkindness. A wife on the phone. Miss Snow, I am sorry we are cancelling – Or simply silence. A date not kept, a note not answered, a name never to be mentioned again.

'I don't expect so much,' Muriel said. 'I expect a friend to be a friend. Then they hightail it off at the first whiff of trouble, after saying they would always stand up for me. Why is that?'

'Well, you know, Muriel,' Millicent said once, 'a wife is a wife. It's all well and good to have friends, but a marriage is a marriage.'

Muriel blew up at that – she said that Millicent thought the worst of her, like everybody else, and was she never to be permitted to have a good time, an innocent good time? She banged the door and ran her car over the calla lilies, surely on purpose. For a day Millicent's face was blotchy from weeping. But enmity did not last and Muriel was back, tearful as well, and taking blame on herself.

'I was a fool from the start,' she said, and went into the front room to play the piano. Millicent got to know the pattern. When Muriel was happy and had a new friend she played mournful, tender songs, like 'The Flowers of the Forest'. Or:

> She dressed herself in male attire,
> And gaily she was dressed—

Then, when she was disappointed, she came down hard and fast on the keys, and she sang scornfully some such song as 'Bonnie Dundee'.

> To the Lords of Convention
> 'Twas Claverhouse spoke,
> Ere the King's head go down
> There are heads to be broke!

Sometimes Millicent asked people to supper (though not the Finnegans or the Nesbitts or the Douds), and then she liked to ask Dorrie and Muriel as well. Dorrie was a help in washing up the pots and pans afterward, and Muriel could entertain on the piano.

A couple of years after Albert died, Millicent asked the Anglican minister to come on Sunday, after Evensong, and bring the friend she had heard was staying with him. The Anglican minister was a bachelor, but Muriel had given up on him early. Neither fish nor fowl, she said. Too bad. Millicent liked him, chiefly for his voice. She had been brought up an Anglican, and though she'd switched to United, which was what Porter said he was (so was everybody else, so were all the important and substantial people in the town), she still favoured Anglican customs. Evensong, the church bell, the choir coming up the aisle in meagre state, singing – instead of just all clumping in together and sitting down. Best of all, the words. *But thou, O Lord, have mercy upon us, miserable offenders. Spare thou them, O God, which confess their faults. Restore thou them that are penitent; According to thy promises . . .*

Porter went with her once and hated it.

Preparations for this evening's supper were considerable. The damask was brought out, the silver serving spoon, the black dessert plates painted by hand with pansies. The cloth had to be pressed and all the silverware polished, and then there was the apprehension that a tiny smear of polish might remain, a grey gum on the tines of a fork or among the grapes round the rim of the wedding teapot. All day Sunday

Millicent was torn between pleasure and agony, hope and suspense. The things that could go wrong multiplied. The Bavarian cream might not set (they had no refrigerator yet and had to chill things in summer by setting them on the cellar floor). The angel-food cake might not rise to its full glory. If it did rise, it might be dry. The biscuits might taste of tainted flour or a beetle might crawl out of the salad. By five o'clock she was in such a state of tension and misgiving that nobody could stay in the kitchen with her. Muriel had arrived early, to help out, but she had not chopped the potatoes finely enough, and had managed to scrape her knuckles while grating carrots, so she was told off for being useless and sent to play the piano.

Muriel was dressed up in turquoise crêpe and smelled of her Spanish perfume. She might have written off the minister but she had not seen his visitor yet. A bachelor, perhaps, or a widower, since he was travelling alone. Rich, or he would not be travelling at all, not so far. He came from England, people said. Someone said no, Australia.

She was trying to get up the 'Polovtsian Dances.'

Dorrie was late. It threw a crimp in things. The jellied salad had to be taken down cellar again, lest it should soften. The biscuits put to warm in the oven had to be taken out, for fear of their getting too hard. The three men sat on the veranda – the meal was to be eaten there, buffet style – and drank fizzy lemonade. Millicent had seen what drink did in her own family – her father had died of it when she was ten – and she had required a promise from Porter, before they married, that he would never touch it again. Of course he did – he kept a bottle in the granary – but when he drank he kept his distance, and she truly believed the promise had been kept. This was a fairly common pattern, at that time, at least among farmers – drinking in the barn, abstinence in the house. Most men would have felt there was something the matter with a woman who didn't lay down such a law.

But Muriel, when she came out on the veranda in her high heels and slinky crêpe, cried out at once, 'Oh, my favourite drink! Gin and lemon!' She took a sip and pouted at Porter.

'You did it again. You forgot the gin again!' Then she teased the minister, asking if he didn't have a flask in his pocket. The minister was gallant, or perhaps made reckless by boredom. He said he wished he had.

The visitor who rose to be introduced was tall and thin and sallow, with a face that seemed to hang in pleats, precise and melancholy. Muriel did not give way to disappointment. She sat down beside him and tried in a most spirited way to get him into conversation. She told him about her music teaching and was scathing about the local choirs and musicians. She did not spare the Anglicans, telling about the Sunday-school concert when the master of ceremonies announced that she would play a piece by Chopin, pronouncing it 'Choppin'.

Porter had done the chores early and washed and changed into his suit, but he kept looking uneasily toward the barnyard, as if recalling something that was left undone. One of the cows was bawling loudly in the field, and at last he excused himself to go and see what was wrong with her. He found that her calf had got caught in the wire fence and managed to strangle itself. He did not speak of this loss when he came back with newly washed hands. 'Calf caught up in the fence,' was all he said. But he connected the mishap somehow with this entertainment, with dressing up and having to eat off your knees. It was not natural.

'Those cows are as bad as children,' Millicent said. 'Always wanting your attention at the wrong time!' Her own children, fed earlier, peered from between the banisters to watch the food being carried to the veranda. 'I think we will have to commence without Dorrie. You men must be starving. This is just a simple little buffet. We sometimes enjoy eating outside on a Sunday evening.'

'Commence, commence!' cried Muriel, who had helped to carry out the various dishes – the potato salad, carrot salad, jellied salad, cabbage salad, the devilled eggs and cold roast chicken, the salmon loaf and warm biscuits, and the relishes. Just when they had everything set out, Dorrie came around the side of the house, looking warm from her walk across the field, or from excitement. She was wearing her good summer dress, a navy-blue organdie with white dots and white collar, suitable for a little girl or an old lady. Threads showed where she had pulled the torn lace off the collar instead of mending it, and in spite of the hot day a rim of undershirt was hanging out of one sleeve. Her shoes had been so recently and sloppily cleaned that they left traces of whitener on the grass.

'I would have been on time,' Dorrie said, 'but I had to shoot a feral cat. She was prowling around my house and carrying on so, I was convinced she was rabid.'

Dorrie had wet her hair and crimped it into place with bobby pins. With that, and her pink, shiny face, she looked like a doll with a china head and limbs attached to a cloth body firmly stuffed with straw.

'I thought at first she might have been in heat, but she didn't really behave that way. She didn't do any of the rubbing along on her stomach such as I'm used to seeing. And I noticed some spitting. So I thought the only thing to do was to shoot her. Then I put her in a sack and called up Fred Nunn to see if he would run her over to Walley, to the vet. I want to know if she really was rabid, and Fred always likes the excuse to get out in his car. I told him to leave the sack on the step if the vet wasn't home on a Sunday night.'

'I wonder what he'll think it is?' said Muriel. 'A present?'

'No. I pinned on a note, in case. There was definite spitting and dribbling.' Dorrie touched her own face to show where the dribbling had been. 'Are you enjoying your visit here?' she said to the minister, who had been in town for three years and had been the one to bury her brother.

'It is Mr Speirs who is the visitor, Dorrie,' said Millicent. Dorrie acknowledged the introduction and seemed unembarrassed by her mistake. She said that the reason she took the animal for a feral cat was that its coat was all matted and hideous, and she thought that a feral cat would never come near the house unless it was rabid.

'But I will put an explanation in the paper, just in case. I will be sorry if it is anybody's pet. I lost my own pet three months ago – my dog, Delilah. She was struck down by a car.'

It was strange to hear that dog called a pet, that big black Delilah who used to lollop along with Dorrie all over the countryside, who tore across the fields in such savage glee to attack cars. Dorrie had not been distraught at the death; indeed, she had said she had expected it some day. But now, to hear her say 'pet', Millicent thought there might have been grief she didn't show.

'Come and fill up your plate or we'll all have to starve,' Muriel said to Mr Speirs. 'You're the guest, you have to go first. If the egg yolks look dark, it's just what the hens have been eating – they won't poison you. I grated the carrots for that salad myself, so if you notice some blood it's just where I got a little too enthusiastic and grated in some skin off my knuckles. I had better shut up now or Millicent will kill me.'

And Millicent was laughing angrily, saying, 'Oh, they are not! Oh, you did *not!*'

Mr Speirs had paid close attention to everything Dorrie said. Maybe that was what had made Muriel so saucy. Millicent thought that perhaps he saw Dorrie as a novelty, a Canadian wild woman who went around shooting things. He might be studying her so that he could go home and describe her to his friends in England.

Dorrie kept quiet while eating, and she ate quite a lot. Mr Speirs ate a lot, too – Millicent was happy to see that – and he appeared to be a silent person at all times. The minister kept the conversation going by describing a book he was reading. It was called *The Oregon Trail*.

'Terrible, the hardships,' he said.

Millicent said she had heard of it. 'I have some cousins living out in Oregon, but I cannot remember the name of the town,' she said. 'I wonder if they went on that trail.'

The minister said that if they went out a hundred years ago it was most probable.

'Oh, I wouldn't think it was that long,' Millicent said. 'Their name was Rafferty.'

'Man the name of Rafferty used to race pigeons,' said Porter, with sudden energy. 'This was way back, when there was more of that kind of thing. There was money going on it, too. Well, he said the problem with the pigeons' house, they don't go in right away, and that means they don't trip the wire and don't get counted in. So he took an egg one of his pigeons was on, and he blew it clear, and he put a beetle inside. And the beetle inside made such a racket the pigeon naturally thought she had an egg getting ready to hatch. And she flew a beeline home and tripped the wire, and all the ones that bet on her made a lot of money. Him, too, of course. In fact, this was over in Ireland, and this man that told the story, that was how he got the money to come out to Canada.'

Millicent didn't believe that the man's name had been Rafferty at all. That had just been an excuse.

'So you keep a gun in the house?' said the minister to Dorrie. 'Does that mean you are worried about tramps and suchlike?'

Dorrie put down her knife and fork, chewed something up carefully, and swallowed. 'I keep it for shooting,' she said.

After a pause she said that she shot groundhogs and rabbits. She took the groundhogs over to the other side of town and sold them to the mink farm. She skinned the rabbits and stretched the skins, then sold them to a place in Walley which did a big trade with the tourists. She enjoyed fried or boiled rabbit meat but could not possibly eat it all herself, so she often took a rabbit carcass, cleaned and skinned, around to some family that was on relief. Many times her offering was refused. People thought it was as bad as eating a dog or a cat. Though even that, she believed, was not considered out of the way in China.

'That is true,' said Mr Speirs. 'I have eaten them both.'

'Well, then, you know,' said Dorrie. 'People are prejudiced.'

He asked about the skins, saying they must have to be removed very carefully, and Dorrie said that was true, and you needed a knife you could trust. She described with pleasure the first clean slit down the belly. 'Even more difficult with the muskrats, because you have to be more careful with the fur, it is more valuable,' she said. 'It is a denser fur. Waterproof.'

'You do not shoot the muskrats?' said Mr Speirs. No, no, said Dorrie. She trapped them. Trapped them, yes, said Mr Speirs, and Dorrie described her favourite trap, on which she had made little improvements of her own. She had thought of taking out a patent but had never got around to it. She spoke about the spring watercourses, the system of creeks she followed, tramping for miles day after day, after the snow was mostly melted but before the leaves came out, when the muskrats' fur was prime. Millicent knew that Dorrie did these things, but she had thought she did them to get a little money. To hear her talk now, it would seem she loved that life. The blackflies out already, the cold water over her boot tops, the drowned rats. And Mr Speirs listened like an old dog, perhaps a hunting dog, that has been sitting with his eyes half shut, just prevented, by his own good opinion of himself, from falling into an unmannerly stupor. Now he has got a whiff of something – his eyes open all the way and his nose quivers as he remembers some day of recklessness and dedication. How many miles did she cover in a day, Mr Speirs asked, and how high is the water, how much do the muskrats weigh and how many could you count on in a day and for muskrats is it still the same sort of knife?

Muriel asked the minister for a cigarette and got one, smoked for a few moments, and stubbed it out in the middle of her dish of the Bavarian cream. 'So I won't eat it and get fat,' she said. She got up and started to help clear the dishes, but soon ended up at the piano, back at the 'Polovtsian Dances'.

Millicent was pleased that there was conversation with the guest, though its attraction mystified her. Also, the food had been good and there had not been any humiliation – no queer taste or sticky cup handle.

'I had thought the trappers were all up north,' said Mr Speirs. 'I thought that they were beyond the Arctic Circle or at least on the Precambrian shield.'

'I used to have an idea of going there,' Dorrie said. Her voice thickened for the first time. with embarrassment – or excitement. 'I thought I could live in a cabin and trap all winter. But I had my brother. I couldn't leave my brother. And I know it here.'

Late in the winter Dorrie arrived at Millicent's house with a large piece of white satin. She said that she intended to make a wedding dress. That was the first anybody had heard of a wedding – she said it would be in May – or learned the first name of Mr Speirs. It was Wilkinson. Wilkie.

When and where had Dorrie seen him, since that supper on the veranda?

Nowhere. He had gone off to Australia, where he had property. Letters had gone back and forth between them.

Millicent's questions drew out a little more information. Wilkie had been born in England but was now an Australian. He had travelled all over the world, climbed mountains, and gone up a river into the jungle. In Africa, or South America – Dorrie was not sure which.

'He thinks I am adventurous,' said Dorrie, as if to answer an unspoken question about as to what he saw in her.

'And is he in love with you?' said Millicent. It was she who blushed then, not Dorrie. But Dorrie, unblushing, unfidgeting, was like a column of heat, bare and concentrated. Millicent had an awful thought of her naked, so that she hardly heard what Dorrie said. She amended the question to what she believed she had meant: 'Will he be good to you?'

'Oh – yes,' said Dorrie, rather carelessly.

Sheets were laid down on the dining-room floor, with the dining table pushed against the wall. The satin was spread out over them. Its broad, bright extent, its shining vulnerability, cast a hush over the whole house. The children came, only to stare at it, and Millicent shouted to them to clear off. She was afraid to cut into it. And Dorrie, who could so easily slit the skin of an animal, laid the scissors down. She confessed to shaking hands.

A call was put in to Muriel, to drop by after school. She clapped her hand to her heart when she heard the news, and called Dorrie a slyboots, a Cleopatra who had fascinated a millionaire.

'I bet he's a millionaire,' Muriel said. 'Property in Australia – what does that mean? I bet it's not a pig farm! All I can hope is maybe he'll have a brother. Oh, Dorrie, am I so mean I didn't even say congratulations?'

She gave Dorrie lavish, loud kisses – Dorrie standing still for them, as if she were five years old.

Dorrie said that she and Mr Speirs planned to go through 'a form of marriage'. What do you mean, said Millicent, do you mean a marriage ceremony, is that what you mean? – and Dorrie said yes.

Muriel made the first cut into the satin, saying that somebody had to do it, though maybe if she were doing it again it wouldn't be in quite that place.

Soon they got used to mistakes. Mistakes and rectifications. Late every afternoon, when Muriel got there, they tackled a new stage – the cutting, the pinning, the basting, the sewing – with clenched teeth and grim rallying cries. They had to alter the pattern as they went along, to allow for problems unforeseen, such as the tight set of a sleeve, the bunching of the heavy satin at the waist, the eccentricities of Dorrie's figure. Dorrie was a menace at the job, so they set her to sweeping up scraps and filling the bobbin. Whenever she sat at the sewing machine she clamped her tongue between her teeth. Sometimes she had nothing to do, and she walked from room to room in Millicent's house, stopping to stare out the windows at the snow and sleet, the long–drawn-out end of winter. Or she stood like a docile beast in her woollen underwear, which smelled quite frankly of her flesh, while they pulled and tugged the material around her.

Muriel had taken charge of the clothes. She knew what there had to be. There had to be more than a wedding dress. There had to be a going-away outfit, and a wedding night-gown and a matching dressing gown, and of course an entire new supply of underwear. Silk stockings, and a brassiere – the first that Dorrie had ever worn.

Dorrie had not known about any of that. 'I considered the wedding dress as the major hurdle,' she said. 'I could not think beyond it.'

The snow melted, the creeks filled up, the muskrats would be swimming in the cold water, sleek and sporty, with their treasure on their backs. If Dorrie thought of her traps she did not say so. The only walk she took these days was across the field from her house to Millicent's.

Made bold by experience, Muriel cut out a dressmaker suit of fine russet wool, and a lining. She was letting her choir rehearsals go all to pot.

Millicent had to think about the wedding luncheon. It was to be held in the Brunswick Hotel. But who was there to invite, except the minister? Lots of people knew Dorrie, but they knew her as the lady who left skinned rabbits on doorsteps, who went through the fields and the woods with her dog and gun and waded along the flooded creeks in her high rubber boots. Few people knew anything about the old Becks, though all remembered Albert and had liked him. Dorrie was not quite a joke – something protected her from that, either Albert's popularity or her own gruffness and dignity – but the news of her wedding had roused a lot of interest, not exactly of a sympathetic nature. Her marriage was being spoken of as a freakish event, mildly scandalous, possibly a hoax. Porter said that bets were being laid on whether the man would show up.

Finally, Millicent recalled some cousins, who had come to Albert's funeral. Ordinary, respectable people. Dorrie had their addresses, invitations were sent. Then the Nunn brothers from the grocery, whom Albert had worked for, and their wives. A couple of Albert's lawn-bowling friends and their wives. The people who owned the mink farm where Dorrie sold her groundhogs? The woman from the bake-shop who was going to ice the cake?

The cake was being made at home, then taken to the shop to be iced by the woman who had got a diploma in cake decorating from a place in Chicago. It would be covered with white roses, lacy scallops, hearts and garlands and silver leaves and those tiny silver candies you can break your tooth on. Meanwhile it had to be mixed and baked, and this was where Dorrie's strong arms could come into play, stirring and stirring a mixture so stiff it appeared to be all candied fruit and raisins and currants with a little gingery batter holding everything together like glue. When Dorrie got the big bowl against her stomach and took up the beating spoon, Millicent heard the first satisfied sigh to come out of her in a long while.

Muriel decided that there had to be a maid of honour. Or a matron of honour. It could not be her, because she would be playing the organ. 'O Perfect Love'. And the Mendelssohn.

It would have to be Millicent. Muriel would not take no for an answer. She brought over an evening dress of her own, a long sky-blue dress, which she ripped open at the waist – how confident and cavalier she was by now, about dressmaking! – and she proposed a lace midriff, of darker blue, with a matching lace bolero. It will look like new and suit you to a T, she said.

Millicent laughed when she first tried it on, and she said, 'There's a sight to scare the pigeons!' But she was pleased. She and Porter had not had much of a wedding – they had just gone to the rectory, deciding to put the money saved into furniture. 'I suppose I'll need some kind of thingamajig,' she said. 'Something on my head.'

'Her veil!' cried Muriel. 'What about Dorrie's veil? We've been concentrating so much on wedding dresses, we've forgotten all about a veil!'

Dorrie spoke up unexpectedly and said that she would never wear a veil. She could not stand to have one draped over her, it would feel like cobwebs. Her use of the word 'cobwebs' gave Muriel and Millicent a start, because there were jokes being made about cobwebs in other places.

'She's right,' said Muriel. 'A veil would be too much.' She considered what else. A wreath of flowers? No, too much again. A picture hat? Yes, get an old summer hat and cover it with white satin. Then get another and cover it with the dark-blue lace.

'Here is the menu,' said Millicent dubiously. 'Creamed chicken in pastry shells, little round biscuits, moulded jellies, that salad with the apples and the walnuts, pink and white ice-cream with the cake –'

Thinking of the cake, Muriel said, 'Does he by any chance have a sword, Dorrie?'

Dorrie said, 'Who?'

'Wilkie. Your Wilkie. Does he have a sword?'

'What would he have a sword for?' Millicent said.

'I just thought he might,' said Muriel.

'I cannot enlighten you,' said Dorrie.

Then there was a moment in which they all fell silent, because they had to think of the bridegroom. They had to admit him to the room and set him down in the midst of all this. Picture hats. Creamed chicken. Silver leaves. They were stricken with doubts. At least Millicent was, and Muriel. They hardly dared to look at each other.

'I just thought since he was English, or whatever he is,' said Muriel.

Millicent said, 'He is a fine man, anyway.'

The wedding was set for the second Saturday in May. Mr Speirs was to arrive on the Wednesday and stay with the minister. The Sunday before, Dorrie was supposed to come over to have supper with Millicent and Porter. Muriel was there, too. Dorrie didn't arrive, and they went ahead and started without her.

Millicent stood up in the middle of the meal. 'I'm going over there,' she said. 'She'd better be sharper than this getting to her wedding.'

'I can keep you company,' said Muriel.

Millicent said no thanks. Two might make it worse.

Make what worse?

She didn't know.

She went across the field by herself. It was a warm evening, and the back door of Dorrie's house was standing open. Between the house and where the barn used to be there was a grove of walnut trees, whose branches were still bare, since walnut trees are among the very latest to get their leaves. The hot sunlight pouring through bare branches seemed unnatural. Her feet did not make any sound on the grass.

And there on the back platform was Albert's old armchair, never taken in all winter.

What was in her mind was that Dorrie might have had an accident. Something to do with a gun. Maybe while cleaning her gun. That happened to people. Or she might be lying out in a field somewhere, lying in the woods among the old, dead leaves and the new leeks and bloodroot. Tripped while getting over a fence. Had to go out one last time. And then, after all the safe times, the gun had gone off. Millicent had never had any such fears for Dorrie before, and she knew that in some ways Dorrie was very careful and competent. It must be that what had happened this year made anything seem possible. The proposed marriage, such wild luck, could make you believe in calamity also.

But it was not an accident that was on Millicent's mind. Not really. Under this busy, fearful imagining of accidents, she hid what she really feared.

She called Dorrie's name at the open door. And so prepared was she for an answering silence, the evil silence and indifference of a house lately vacated by somebody who had met with disaster (or not vacated, yet, by the body of the person who had met with, who had *brought about*, that disaster) – so prepared was she for the worst that she was shocked, she went watery in the knees, at the sight of Dorrie herself in her old field pants and shirt.

'We were waiting for you,' Millicent said. 'We were waiting for you to come to supper.'

Dorrie said, 'I must've lost track of the time.'

'Oh, have all your clocks stopped?' said Millicent, recovering her nerve as she was led through the back hall with its familiar, mysterious debris. She could smell cooking.

The kitchen was dark because of the big, unruly lilac pressing against the window. Dorrie used the house's original wood-burning cookstove, and she had one of those old kitchen tables with drawers for the knives and forks. It was a relief to see that the calendar on the wall was for this year.

Yes – Dorrie was cooking some supper. She was in the middle of chopping up a purple onion, to add to the bits of bacon and sliced potatoes she had frying up in the pan. So much for losing track of the time.

'You go ahead,' said Millicent. 'Go ahead and make your meal. I did get something to eat before I took it into my head to go and look for you.'

'I made tea,' said Dorrie. It was keeping warm on the back of the stove, and when she poured it out it was like ink.

'I can't leave,' she said, prying up some of the bacon that was sputtering in the pan. 'I can't leave here.'

Millicent decided to treat this as she would a child's announcement that she could not go to school.

'Well, that'll be a nice piece of news for Mr Speirs,' she said. 'When he has come all this way.'

Dorrie leaned back as the grease became fractious.

'Better move that off the heat a bit,' Millicent said.

'I can't leave.'

'I heard that before.'

Dorrie finished her cooking and scooped the results on to a plate. She added ketchup and a couple of thick slices of bread soaked in the grease that was left in the pan. She sat down to eat, and did not speak.

Millicent was sitting, too, waiting her out. Finally she said, 'Give a reason.'

Dorrie shrugged and chewed.

'Maybe you know something I don't,' Millicent said. 'What have you found out? Is he poor?'

Dorrie shook her head. 'Rich,' she said.

So, Muriel was right.

'A lot of women would give their eye teeth.'

'I don't care about that,' Dorrie said. She chewed and swallowed and repeated, 'I don't care.'

Millicent had to take a chance, though it embarrassed her. 'If you are thinking about what I think you may be thinking about, then it could be that you are worried over nothing. A lot of the time when they get older they don't even want to bother.'

'Oh, it isn't that! I know all about that.'

Oh, do you, thought Millicent, and if so, how? Dorrie might imagine she knew, from animals. Millicent had sometimes thought that no woman would get married, if she really knew.

Nevertheless, she said, 'Marriage takes you out of yourself and gives you a real life.'

'I have a life,' Dorrie said. 'Perhaps I am not adventurous,' she added.

'All right, then,' said Millicent, as if she had given up arguing. She sat and drank her poison tea. She was getting an inspiration. She let time pass and then she said, 'It's up to you, it certainly is. But there is a problem about where you will live. You can't live here. When Porter and I found out you were getting married we put this place on the market, and we sold it.'

Dorrie said instantly, 'You're lying.'

'We didn't want it standing empty to make a haven for tramps. We went ahead and sold it.'

'You would never do such a trick on me.'

'What kind of a trick would it be when you were getting married?'

Millicent was already believing what she said. Soon it could come true. They could offer the place at a low enough price, and somebody would buy it. It could still be fixed up. Or it could be torn down, for the bricks and the woodwork. Porter would be glad to be rid of it.

Dorrie said, 'You would not put me out of my house.'

Millicent kept quiet.

'You are lying, aren't you?' said Dorrie.

'Give me your Bible,' Millicent said. 'I will swear on it.'

Dorrie actually looked around. She said, 'I don't know where it is.'

'Dorrie, listen. All of this is for your own good. It may seem like I am pushing you out, but all it is is making you do what you are not quite up to doing on your own.'

'Oh,' said Dorrie. 'Why?'

Because the wedding cake is made, thought Millicent, and

the satin dress is made, and the luncheon has been ordered and the invitations have been sent. All this trouble that has been gone to. People might say that was a silly reason, but those who said that would not be the people who had gone to the trouble. It was not fair, to have your best efforts squandered.

But it was more than that, for she believed what she had said, telling Dorrie that this was how she could have a life. And what did Dorrie mean by 'here'? If she meant that she would be homesick, let her be! Homesickness was never anything you couldn't get over. Millicent was not going to pay any attention to that 'here'. Nobody had any business living a life out 'here' if they had been offered what Dorrie had. It was a kind of sin, to refuse such an offer. Out of stubbornness, out of fearfulness, and idiocy.

She had begun to get the feeling that Dorrie was cornered. Dorrie might be giving up, or letting the idea of giving up seep through her. Perhaps. She sat as still as a stump, but there was a chance such a stump might be pulpy within.

But it was Millicent who began suddenly to weep. 'Oh, Dorrie,' she said. 'Don't be stupid!' They both got up and grabbed hold of each other, and then Dorrie had to do the comforting, patting and soothing in a magisterial way, while Millicent wept, and repeated some words that did not hang together. *Happy. Help. Ridiculous.*

'I will look after Albert,' she said, when she had calmed down somewhat. 'I'll put flowers. And I won't mention this to Muriel Snow. Or to Porter. Nobody needs to know.'

Dorrie said nothing. She seemed a little lost, absent-minded, as if she was busy turning something over and over, resigning herself to the weight and strangeness of it.

'That tea is awful,' said Millicent. 'Can't we make some that's fit to drink?' She went to throw the contents of her cup into the slop pail.

There stood Dorrie in the dim window light – mulish, obedient, childish, female – a most mysterious and maddening person, whom Millicent seemed now to have conquered, to be sending away. At greater cost to herself, Millicent was thinking – greater cost than she had understood. She tried to engage Dorrie in a sombre but encouraging look, cancelling her fit of tears. She said, 'The die is cast.'

Dorrie walked to her wedding. Nobody had known that she intended to do that. When Porter and Millicent stopped the car in front of her house, to pick her up, Millicent was still anxious. 'Honk the horn,' she said. 'She better be ready now.'

Porter said, 'Isn't that her down ahead?'

It was. She was wearing a light-grey coat of Albert's over her satin dress and was carrying her picture hat in one hand, a bunch of lilacs in the other. They stopped the car and she said, 'No. I want the exercise. It will clear out my head.'

They had no choice but to drive on and wait at the church and see her approaching down the street, people coming out of shops to look, a few cars honking sportively, people waving and calling out, 'Here comes the bride!' As she got closer to the church she stopped and removed Albert's coat, and then she was gleaming, miraculous, like the pillar of salt in the Bible.

Muriel was inside the church, playing the organ, so she did not have to realise, at this last moment, that they had forgotten all about gloves and that Dorrie clutched the woody stems of the lilac in her bare hands. Mr Speirs had been in the church, too, but he had come out, breaking all rules, leaving the minister to stand there on his own. He was as lean and yellow and wolfish as Millicent remembered, but when he saw Dorrie fling the old coat into the back of Porter's car and settle the hat on her head – Millicent had to run up and fix it right – he appeared nobly satisfied. Millicent had a picture of him and Dorrie mounted high, mounted on elephants, panoplied, borne cumbrously forward, adventuring. A vision. She was filled with optimism and relief and she whispered to Dorrie, 'He'll take you everywhere! He'll make you a queen!'

'I have grown as fat as the Queen of Tonga,' wrote Dorrie from Australia, some years on. A photograph showed that she was not exaggerating. Her hair was white, her skin brown, as if all her freckles had got loose and run together. She wore a vast garment, coloured like tropical flowers. The war had come and put an end to any idea of travelling, and then when it was over Wilkie was dying. Dorrie stayed on, in Queensland, on a great property where she grew sugar cane and pineapples, cotton, peanuts, tobacco. She rode horses, in spite of her size, and had learned to fly an airplane. She took up some travels of her own in that part of the world. She had shot crocodiles. She died in the Fifties, in New Zealand, climbing up to look at a volcano.

Millicent told everybody what she had said she would not mention. She took credit, naturally. She recalled her inspiration, her stratagem, with no apologies. 'Somebody had to take the bull by the horns,' she said. She felt that she was the creator of a life – more effectively, in Dorrie's case, than in the case of her own children. She had created happiness, or something close. She forgot the way she had wept without knowing why.

The wedding had its effect on Muriel. She handed in her resignation, she went off to Alberta. 'I'll give it a year,' she said. And within a year she had found a husband – not the sort of man she had ever had anything to do with in the past. A widower with two small children. A Christian minister. Millicent wondered at Muriel's describing him that way. Weren't all ministers Christian? When they came back for a visit – by this time there were two more children, their own – she saw the point of the description. Smoking and drinking and swearing were out, and so was wearing make-up, and the kind of music that Muriel used to play. She played hymns now – the sort she had once made fun of. She wore any colour at all and had a bad permanent – her hair, going grey, stood up from her forehead in frizzy bunches. 'A lot of my former life turns my stomach – just to think about it,' she said, and Millicent got the impression that she and Porter were seen mostly as belonging to those stomach-turning times.

The house was not sold or rented. It was not torn down, either, and its construction was so sound that it did not readily give way. It was capable of standing for years and years and presenting a plausible appearance. A tree of cracks can branch out among the bricks, but the wall does not fall down. Window sashes settle, at an angle, but the window does not fall out. The doors were locked, but it was probable that children got in and wrote things on the walls and broke up the crockery that Dorrie had left behind. Millicent never went in to see.

There was a thing that Dorrie and Albert used to do, and then Dorrie did alone. It must have started when they were children. Every year, in the fall, they – and then, she – collected up all the walnuts that had fallen off the trees. They kept going, collecting fewer and fewer walnuts every day, until they were fairly sure that they had got the last, or the next-to-last, one. Then they counted them, and they wrote the total on the cellar wall. The date, the year, the total. The walnuts were not used for anything once they were collected. They were just dumped along the edge of the field and allowed to rot.

Millicent did not continue this useless chore. She had plenty of other chores to do, and plenty for her children to do. But at the time of year when the walnuts were lying in the long grass she would think of that custom, and how Dorrie must have expected to keep it up until she died. A life of customs, of seasons. The walnuts drop, the muskrats swim in the creek. Dorrie must have believed that she was meant to live so, in her reasonable eccentricity, her manageable loneliness. Probably she would have got another dog.

But I would not allow that, thinks Millicent. She would not allow it, and surely she was right. She had lived to be an old lady, she is living yet, though Porter has been dead for decades. She doesn't often notice the house. It is just there. But once in a while she does see its cracked face and the blank, slanted windows. The walnut trees behind, losing again, again, their delicate canopy of leaves.

I ought to knock that down and sell the bricks, she says, and seems puzzled that she has not already done so.

Bel

TONY MUSGRAVE

'I HAD AN ideal childhood,' she says, kneeling beside him to gently lift his penis and ease off the condom, which she holds in one hand, smoothing the air out of it with the other before expertly tying a knot in its neck. The milky liquid bobs in the teat and base as she springs off the bed and walks through the open bathroom door. 'My parents tried to show me what they knew and something of what they felt.' Out of the mirrored cupboard above the basin she takes a washer from a neat pile, slides it over the condom's knot and throws it in the toilet on which she briefly pauses to pee, looking at him through the doorway as she continues talking. 'What they had discovered for themselves was that we think things about those closest to us that we never dare to express.' She flushes the toilet, waits to be certain that the weighted condom has disappeared along with her warm yellow urine and squats over the bidet to douse her private parts. 'Feelings of hate, rage, jealousy and, oh yes, of boredom are aroused in us by our parents, our partners, our children, our lovers, our friends and we suppress these feelings or redirect them.' She dries herself with an orange bath towel. 'Oh I know it sounds banal. The man has had hell at the office – I fancy a large cup of milky coffee and perhaps a grappa, what about you – and it ends up with the kids tormenting the cat. On the other hand, bread and cheese and grapes would be rather nice and white wine is the accompaniment to that, and anyway the way to celebrate such a glorious fuck is with a chilled bottle of champagne. I keep two or three in the fridge, just in case such a thing should happen to me.'

She comes out of the bathroom with a damp purple flannel and a purple towel. She kneels on the bed again and as he understands what she intends to do, he pushes her away. 'Now, what are you thinking. Am I the mother, come to clean your willy. Am I your conscience, saying that a ritual act of cleansing will absolve you from the guilt of having slept with a woman? Or do I wish to handle you, to peel back your foreskin, to explore you in an unprotected moment? Intimacy is frightening.' He moves heavily off the bed, taking the towel and flannel from her, and goes into the bathroom, shutting, but not liking to lock the door.

She pulls on two thick woollen grey socks and her brown back straight, her bottom broad and firm, she goes into the kitchen.

When she returns, the green wooden tray she carries is heavy. He is sitting up in bed, after some internal questioning still naked, the sheet so draped that his flat stomach and the first few pubic hairs are exposed. 'I couldn't decide what we would like to eat and drink, so I've brought a wide selection.' She observes his gaze travel up from her socks to her thick dark brown pubic hair, the green tray across her middle, her breasts, her short-cropped blonde hair. 'Yes, you've noticed. I dye my pubic hair. Blonde is such an insipid colour.' She sets the tray down at an angle to his hips and sits cross-legged on its other side. 'Help yourself,' she says pouring strong coffee out of one thermos flask and hot milk out of another. There is sugar in oblong cubes and she drops two into her large coffee cup. He picks a sprig of black grapes. She catches his eye and he looks away. 'I wasn't taught as a child that it's rude to stare. A ridiculous commandment. Here, take a really good look.' And she puts down her coffee cup and sits with her legs drawn up to the knees and wide apart, her arms supporting her from behind. 'Is a profound mystery revealed? Am I less than I was before? Can you now read my innermost thoughts? Am I naked before you? Would you like to inspect my nostrils? I found some croissants in the fridge.' And she returns to her cross-legged position and chooses one. 'Flakes of pastry in the bedclothes.'

'My father left me this flat. What I remember most about him were his pauses. As a child, asking him a question, jiggling up and down, there would be this silence. He didn't affect the dead pipe and half a box of matches routine. He simply paused while I waited and he waited for the answer to come. It wasn't that he needed that length of time for his mind to focus on me. I had his full attention from the start. I could sense that. He had his own rhythm of thinking and of talking, that was all. When I was young, I found this very disconcerting, a child needs an instant response, to know immediately that she is loved, that she is accepted. His great passion as a father was to pass on to us children things he had discovered for himself. I don't mean: this evening we will discuss Einstein's General Theory of Relativity and tomorrow be prepared for the unravelling of the mystery of the DNA double helix. It wasn't facts we heard from him. He thought that these could be perfectly adequately taught at school and at university. He had this picture of a West African village, where at the age of fifteen, sixteen, the boys are gathered together and taken by their fathers to a camp in the jungle, where they all live for three months. There they are initiated into the mysteries. They are shown how to hunt and how to survive, they test the limits of their courage and their ability to withstand pain, they learn the secret rites and when they return, they are men. And what do we do, he would ask. He was a great believer in repetition, saying that when an idea fascinated you, it had depth. What do we do, he would ask and although we knew the answer, each time it came out differently, as if he was discovering more and more what he meant. What we do is, – and there would be a long pause – we acquiesce in society's demand that it and it alone should educate our children. Our responsibility is to conceive them, give birth to them, feed them, clothe them, love them and to reinforce society's great myths. Can I remember them all, can I remember what he told me then and what I have discovered for myself since? It doesn't matter. A few will give the flavour for the rest. The myth that the world functions and that we are in charge. That all illness is curable and only those die who are incapable of doing anything else. That universal sanitation means that we actually don't really piss or shit any more. That there is no tension, no contradiction between a marriage contract and the desire for adventure and eroticism. That if the non-existent tension within a marriage becomes unbearable, it is the partner who has failed and we should try again. That children should be taught that their parents are never uncertain, never overwhelmed by emotions they dare not express, never unfaithful to one another. That although young childless adults may enjoy sexual freedom, parents close their bedroom door and NOTHING HAPPENS. In short, he would say and then pause, always looking for a more telling expression of what he meant, in short society demands that we create the same gulf between ourselves and our children that the powerful need in order to control us.

'What would you say to champagne? Yes, open it if you like. Just don't dent my ceiling with the cork. It's good, isn't it? Spanish. I like the cloudy yellow of the bottle.

'My mother? Energetic, a solid body – that I seem likely to inherit – mentally very quick, highly efficient, kind. My father was slightly built, grey eyes, an unruly beard, precise well-kept hands. He explored the word "love" all his life. It never ceased to bewilder him. He was intoxicated by erotic adventures, but knew them to be a game with well-defined rules. Respect, affection, even friendship were the emotions involved, but not love. Trembling on the brink of love he thought had more to do with trembling than with love. Does he find me attractive, will he be considered attractive by my peers, will he want to sleep with me, what if he wants to sleep with me? Falling in love he called an erotic adventure for the inexperienced, who, because they don't know the rules, confuse society's tremendous pressure to take on the unpaid job of bringing up the next generation with the intensity of their feelings and end up with a child or even married. He thought love existed, but as a decision taken, a full acceptance of responsibility. It was the root of our confusion, he felt that we never truly fully believe in the strength of this decision, neither as the one taking it nor as the one for whom it is taken. We need constant reassurance, oh my God we need it. His idea was that within a framework of unshakeable conviction we had the freedom to say exactly what we felt about one another, however unacceptable our feelings might be.

'As small children, my brother and I might be cautioned firmly that something we had done was antisocial, but never once did we ever get told that an emotion we had expressed was "naughty". I can remember screaming and stamping with rage. I must have been four, and my mother smiling encouragement, as if I'd dropped a particularly well-formed turd into my pot. If I flapped at my father and told him I hated him, he was delighted.

'He waited until I was seven or eight, then he began to give us what he later described to me as homoeopathic doses of his emotions, a glimmer of anger, a glint of impatience. I was very frightened and I would run away, but he would follow me and pick me up and hug me and tell me over and over that he loved me, until I almost believed him.

'Oh children are conservative. They want everything always to remain the same. It is not surprising. There is so much that is confusing that some constants are unavoidable. But the depths of conformity that children will aspire to, it isn't necessary, it isn't right. My father's tiny rages, his slight boredom were an attempt not only to free himself from the stifling conventions of parenthood but also to teach us that to live with a little uncertainty was possible.

'Until I was nine or so, I hated him and hid in my mother's trouser legs. She believed, as he did, in letting us express ourselves, but her ideal was to give us room to grow and she must have exercised an iron discipline to remain, always, briskly cheerful. He called this the tolerant parent's tyranny.

He wanted us strong enough to go our own way, not to ignore anger, to see if it had any justification, but not to be destroyed by it. One day, perhaps nearly ten years old, I was in the living room, lying on my stomach, drawing and telling myself a story. He came in, tired, he cursed when he couldn't find the newspaper, he cursed when he found it, because it was crumpled and out of order, he dropped with a sigh into *his* armchair and there was silence; suddenly he stood up, flung down the paper and shouted at me. My stupid droning stopped him reading. I was frightened. After all, he was so much bigger and stronger than I was. But I was also very angry. I'd been there first, I was quiet, I was peaceful and I was usefully occupied. Yes, I said to myself, yes and I let go. I wasn't like a small child, expressing undirected emotions. This was red murderous anger and meant directly for him. Afterwards I was so shocked I cried. He waited until I was finished, then he sat on the floor to be my size and said, "Now, Bel, let's talk." From that day, I began to understand him.

'He was a small professor, my mother's term of the fact that he never progressed beyond his first appointment. Logic and Philosophy at the university here. He was studying mathematics and she psychology when they met. He helped her with the statistics of her experiments. She said, "He was pale, intense and full of wonderful ideas, but I've heard them all now. And he was remarkably good in bed." He said, "She was so good, so kind, so bright and so enthusiastic about fucking." Later, he said, "It took me a long time to realise that she did her fucking as efficiently as she does everything else." It was her becoming a clinical psychologist or him writing his doctorate, so she did what in those days was perfectly possible and became a teacher, maths and social studies. "You know, Isobel," she would say, "it's his slowness I can't stand. That and his endless repetitions," before going off on another of her weekend teachers' conferences. She was far more discreet than my father, who just wasn't there in the mornings. Even so, it wasn't until he was dying that I found out about this flat. "Everyone needs a place of their own, Bel. It's too exhausting trying to discover who you are, living with other people." It was the betrayal in terms of money I minded. "Yes," he said, "I felt the guilt. I knew what I was doing. But this was more important to me than your first holiday in Paris with the school at age 13."

'She left him the day after I passed my A Levels. She got up from the breakfast table and said, "Carl, I'm leaving you. I'm going to live with Hugh (Uncle Hugh!). James, you'll come with me. I could ask you what you want, but it's very cruel for children to have to decide between their parents, so I'll decide for you. If it was the wrong decision, then at least it's me you'll hate later and not yourself. I'm deciding on purely practical grounds. You're sixteen with another two years at school. You still need looking after and I'm not confident that Carl and Isobel will even decide to look after themselves. Isobel, you're legally an adult. Carl, I've faithfully discharged my duties as a wife and a mother. Now I'm going to do what I want. Isobel, if you could have loved me more, things might have been different."

'She presented my father with an entire inventory of their possessions, an asterisk against each item she intended to take. An hour later Hugh arrived with a furniture van. It was terribly frightening how quickly the material accumulation of twenty years of living together could be sifted and separated. We all worked at it, Carl, Hugh, James and I, all so used to my mother's absolute command of practical affairs, that we couldn't even see how we were helping her to behave badly towards us.

'Carl and I stood in the half-empty house and all he said to me was, "Bel, I'm going to disappear for a week." I hated him for that. I told him so often enough, shouted it, screamed it, but the feeling of betrayal does not go away. He would just shrug his shoulders and say, "I'm sorry, but at that moment you weren't important to me."

'I was left with the house and my mother's first unkind statement in eighteen years. "Isobel, if you could have loved me more, things might have been different." How monstrous, blaming her failed marriage on me. It nearly destroyed me, because I knew it was true. I could have loved her more. I could have loved my father less. He could have loved her more and me less. It's amazing that in all those years of caring and providing, she never gave so much as a sign of what she was feeling. It must have been clear to her that it was not her, the provider, the comforter, whom Carl and I loved but one another. The jealousy, the anger and it never showed. She had a hard core of pride, a hard core of perfection. It meant she survived, but how can you learn to love perfection.

'I was left alone for the first time in my life. If I had gone to study at another university in a strange town, of course I would have been lonely, but it would have been my decision and it would have been an adventure. But this wasn't my decision, my parents had left me. It was my mother I missed. She and I got up early, breakfasted together, discussed the shopping, prepared our lunch boxes to avoid the horrors and dietary indignities of school meals, shook James into life, handed him lukewarm coffee and cold buttered toast and bundled him, still dressing, into our car, to drive to our various schools. Carl never got up until after we'd gone.

'In the afternoons she'd keep the car and do the shopping. James and I would come home on the bus. There'd be a cup of tea waiting for us and then we'd do our homework and she'd do the housework. The evening meal was at seven, the table neatly laid, with flowers and a bottle of wine. Carl was always catered for and mostly he was there, but we never knew and he never phoned. There had obviously been bitter quarrels over this at some earlier stage in their marriage, but my mother had by now found what she considered to be an eminently practical solution. The electric clock in the kitchen would click as the minute hand moved to seven, she would say in her briskest voice, "Your father's gone AWOL again," and dish his portion into a metal foil container, which went unlabelled into the freezer. On her teachers' conference week-ends, we would live on "Carl's meals", hilarious occasions with James discovering he had a slab of lasagne, me with last week's none too successful chili con carne and Carl with guilt written right across his plate, as he uncovered the Boxing Day turkey remains he had fled from.

'Our house was big enough for important luxuries, central heating, a bed-sitting room for each of the four of us. As well as the living room with its large dining area, there was a box room to banish the television to. At the end of the evening meal, my mother would say, always say, "Right, I've got work to do," and sit in her room, marking homework and preparing lessons. It was my job to clear the table and stack the washing-up machine. Sometimes, Jimmy sneaking away to watch television, Carl and I would sit talking over the dishes. Sometimes he might leave the table, saying, "Look in later, if you like." That meant a private discussion in his room. Often he'd leave without a word and I would never know, if I knocked on his door, whether he would shout, "Go away," not reply at all or look out, see it was me and welcome me in. I had the freedom to do the same. Our discussions went in phases. When we had talked ourselves out, it might be three or four weeks before we'd begin again and in that period the frozen meals would stack up in the freezer. So I was used to my father's absences. I felt his betrayal, leaving me when my mother left, but it was her daily presence I missed.

'I don't want to think about that time. It was only a week. I lay in bed, the curtains drawn, I didn't go out, except to the take-away and the off-licence. I got drunk. I sat in my father's armchair, my trousers and pants around my ankles, masturbating to News at Ten, abandoned.

'His coming home freed me. I had someone to whom I could announce that I was leaving. I stayed with a girlfriend until the University here found me digs. I started studying anthropology. For a year I pushed him out of my mind. It's not a large town and not a big campus, but somehow we never met.

'Then one morning I woke early and in a waking dream heard him say, "Bel". No one else uses that name. I won't have it. To the world I am Isobel, my mother's sensible name for me. He was telling me the story of the West African tribe and of the initiation rites for their young men. He felt so near, so reassuring that I didn't need to fight; I could let go and trust him. I got up warm and serene, had a cat's wash and went round to our house. He came to the door, an old overcoat over his vest and underpants, half awake and grey with tiredness. I put my arms around him and realised with a shock that I was now his height. I hugged him like a young dog and pressed my hot smooth cheek against the papery dry heat of his beard. "Carl, I've come back."

'I moved back in the same day. I was hurt that he didn't offer to help, but that evening there were flowers and candles on the dining table and a meal he had collected from a local restaurant. He needed wine to get his conversation going and he drank excessively, I was disturbed to see, but his talk was more brilliant and more precise than I ever remember. A whole year of talk to catch up on. I drank little, elated, calm, happy.

'Sometime in the late evening, he lost the thread of his argument, started again, stopped, paused and then said, "I feel very tired." When he tried to get to his feet and failed, I realised indulgently that he must be very drunk. I am physically strong and I got him up into his bedroom and helped him on to the bed. "There's no real intimacy," he said and fell asleep. I undressed him down to his vest and underpants, pulled the bedclothes from under him and over him. I left a bedside lamp burning and sat on a hard chair looking at him. It was late at night and even when very drunk, Carl slept quietly. It was the same room and I was fourteen. It was a Saturday afternoon in August, Carl and I were alone in the house. He was sitting on his bed reading. The door was open and I leaned against the door jamb, bored, a floppy tee-shirt and shorts, scabbed knees and small breasts. He was naked and I leaned against the door-jamb looking at him. We didn't make a cult of nakedness in our house but we were used to the sight of each other's bodies. He looked up from his book, looked at me for a long time and then said, "Here, Bel, let's talk." I pushed myself off the door-jamb, walked to the bed, too tall, awkward, and sat down beside him.

' "Bel, we've explained to you the changes that are taking place in your body and the changes that will soon take place in James's body. You know what happens when a man and woman sleep together, what happens when a woman is pregnant, how she goes into labour and gives birth. What I think though, is that these are things you know in your head, things somehow detached from you. It isn't the mechanics of sex that are so complicated. It's our feelings. We have this obsessional drive to prove, to expose, to know and this deep feeling that sex is private. When I say private, I don't mean holy. Sex is not sacred, people who preach that probably have to, because otherwise they would be forced to admit to finding it animal and anaesthetic. I'm not interested in value judgements like animal and ugly or spiritual and very beautiful, nor, I suspect, is anyone who really enjoys sex. In a private situation, secure surroundings, with a partner you trust and respect, acute pleasure and the rhythm of your sexual drive create the possibility of releasing those hidden irrational sides of your self. A window blows open and out fly bats and larks. Sex like this can be experienced but not expressed. Nor is there any need to express it. It is itself and enough. It is private.

' "That seems a strange statement to make in a world obsessed by sex. In a book on Zen and Psychoanalysis by Erich Fromm and D.T. Suzuki, Suzuki tells the story of the Zen master and the scientist. The Zen master is walking through a field on an early summer afternoon. He stops, sees a particularly beautiful flower, settles into a squatting position near the flower and looks at it for a long time, experiencing its uniqueness, its beauty, its flowerness. He rises, bows to the flower and goes on his way. The next day a scientist is walking through the same field. He sees the same flower. He picks it to possess it. He takes it back to his laboratory. He photographs it, he classifies it, he takes notes, he pulls off its petals to understand its structure and examines them under a microscope. He splits open its stem and performs a chemical analysis."

'He paused and I grew impatient. "What happened then?"

He smiled. "Nothing happened. The story is the two pictures in your mind. Think about it." He paused again. I scratched an itch between my shoulder-blades and said, "All right, I've thought about it."

' "Then I'll tell you another story. During the Second World War, in a cave at Lascaux in the south of France, pre-historical paintings of hunting scenes were found, vivid works of art. When I first saw reproductions of these paintings, they were already labelled in my mind as Stone-age Picassos. It wasn't until much later that I began asking the question, why were they painted at all. The whole concept of artists and art hadn't existed, nobody was going to buy these paintings for the Guggenheim Museum or praise them in the *Sunday Times*. The answer that slowly grew in my mind consisted of the three words Size, Interpretation and Magic. When you draw a picture of a hunting scene, you reduce it in size, the whole scene fits within your field of vision, it becomes more manageable, less frightening. When you draw a picture, you reduce a moving scene to a static one, you reduce three dimensions to two, you simplify, you select, you interpret. Through a reduction in size and an interpretation in terms you can understand, you gain power over the situation. It's now your situation, here, look, it's you leading the tribe and throwing the spear that kills the woolly rhinoceros.

' "The hunter with fear in his heart can never see enough pictures. They frighten him, because hunting is a very frightening activity, and they excite him, because in the pictures he is powerful. He may never leave the cave and still believe that he is potent. He may oscillate between real life disaster and picture triumph. Or, and this is the strangest situation of all, he may have so incorporated the picture that he is able to go out and help slay the mammoth. His fear is such that he doesn't see the real mammoth, the real hunting scene. He sees a flat two dimensional picture world, which behaves as he expects it to and in this world he is not afraid.

' "I used to consider myself a very accomplished lover and could not understand my obsession with pornographic

pictures, pornographic films. It was during intensive psycho-
therapy – no, you wouldn't have known, you were quite
young – that I discovered not just my perfectly normal fear at
sex but also my ridiculous fear of this fear. Me, the campus
casanova, afraid of sex. What a humiliating idea, but one, I
began to realise, that was very plausible.

' "So this is what I want to give to you, Bel, the idea that
sex is private but that before it can become private, you must
let yourself accept whatever deep fears you may have.

' "Now, I want us to try an experiment. Listen carefully to
what I say, give yourself time to think about it and then
decide if it is something you want to do."

'I'll just find a jersey to put on. Perhaps you could pour me
another glass of champagne. This is not something I find easy
to talk about.'

'I hung my head and waited. I could sense his determination,
his tension, his uncertainty. My body said, "Carl, I'm only
fourteen. Don't ask too much of me," but he was too set on
course to register this. "It seems to me that one of the greatest
sexual fears of a young girl must be the fear of the adult male
penis. Bel, I want you to take your time, and when you feel
ready I want you to stretch out your hand and touch my
penis."

'My face burnt. I turned my head slowly to the side, saw
his thighs, sinewy, covered in fine dark brown hairs, his hip
bones, his navel with the hair growing inwards, the curve of
his stomach down to his springy salt and pepper pubic hair,
his fat goose-pimpled testicles on top of which rested his
penis, its violet tip just emerging from the foreskin.

'There was such a short distance between my hand on the
bed beside his thigh and my father's prick that I had trouble
breathing. Transfer the weight to your left arm, lift your
right hand up over his left thigh, stretch out your hand, I
rehearsed in my mind and it seemed utterly impossible. My
desire to leave was very great. I lifted my head, looked at him
looking at me and tried to understand. I looked and saw only

my father looking at me. I reached out and pushed gently with my finger tips against the side of his penis. I hastily withdrew my hand. It had been warm to the touch but had slid off to the right in a helpless manner. It was the movement that had frightened me, the lack of resistance. It lay there at an untidy angle against his thigh and I waited for it to right itself. It lay there and its passivity annoyed me. I picked it up, held it upright by the neck, holding it like a dead plucked chicken, looked at the whiskers on his testicles, the blue veins on his penis, squeezed its top gently and watched the slit in its tip open and close. Then, like a salamander, warmed by the warmth of my hand, it began to move. Began to move, to expand, to stiffen, the soft pulpy tissue turning to cartilage. "Stop it," I cried. "I can't," my father said with an apologetic embarrassed smile. "You must," I said in panic, unable to let go. He sat more upright, removed my hand and held it, to stop me running away. The penis remained upright, not proudly erected but lop-sided and swaying. "It's the natural reaction to your squeezing, blood pumping in and pumping it up. I can exert my will to stop it starting, but sooner or later the involuntary response to the stimulus takes over. Just wait, look, the flow of blood has stopped, the pressure is falling, the process is reversing." The swaying increased, the penis dipped, rose, dipped and settled, still at near full length, a marionette laid aside. Then it shrunk, effaced itself. We looked at one another, Carl and I, and we both laughed. "There it is," said Carl, "the great mystery revealed, the reason why there are so few women professors and why old men dream of executions."

'I sat on a hard chair and the bedside lamp shed its light on Carl, very drunk and quietly asleep. At some much later time I left and went to my childhood room to sleep.

'Carl spent the next two days in bed. A hangover, he said.'

'If you've finished with the tray, I'll clear it away. I think if you don't mind, that I'll join you in bed. Yes, jersey socks and all. Perhaps you'd like to put your arm around me and hold me very tight. Thank you.' And she began to cry, a measured sobbing which went on for a long time. He waited.

'My life with Carl settled down to a careful normality. We minimised the household duties and divided them between us. We came and we went, we talked and we were silent, we ate together and we ate alone, but I felt him to be more and more like the house as I had found it when I first returned, tidy and unlived in. It was no surprise when one evening I got in late to find a note propped up against the telephone. "Gone away, Carl." At first I led my life, attended lectures, went to concerts with friends, but after two weeks, the feeling that he would arrive of an evening and that he would need me grew so strong that I began to stay in. I didn't rush to the window each time a car stopped; my enclosed life of lectures, library, shopping, books and essays was oddly satisfying.

'It was one o'clock in the morning when the taxi-driver rang the doorbell. Carl was outside in his cab and it took the two of us to help him in and to lower him, so pale, so weak, into an armchair. I shut the door on the taxi-driver and knelt by Carl's chair, holding his cold sweating hand. He burst into tears. "Bel, I'm dying."

'It was lung cancer. It killed him quickly and very painfully.'

'I'd like you to fuck me, if you wouldn't mind.'

They drift into sleep, out of sleep, drowse, shift position, sleep again.

Later she kisses his shoulder and asks him a question.

'Do you think it ethical for a psychiatrist to sleep with one of his patients?'

'Client, Bel, we prefer to use the word "client".'

The Guitar
and Other Animals

GEOFF NICHOLSON

The girl bent over her guitar
An axeman of sorts. The day was green.

They said, 'You have a moist guitar
You do not play things as they are.'

The girl replied, 'Jesus Christ, everybody's
a bloody critic these days. Go and make your
own album if you feel that way about it.'

She enters the bar, an end of the world watering hole called
the Paradise Loft. She is carrying a guitar. Its case looks
ordinary enough. It is scuffed and well travelled, her name –
Jenny Slade – is stencilled on the side, and it has a few old
stickers for amp and effects manufacturers, but there is
nothing that gives any hint of what's inside.
　　The bar's decor is early post nuclear holocaust; bare metal,
rotting concrete, smashed furniture. The customers might
have been specially designed to match. The crowd is male,
drunk, aggressive, misogynistic, and adolescent in mind if

not in age. They all lack a certain something, good looks, teeth, fingers. Undifferentiated hostility hangs over them like a cloud of swamp gas.

One of them says, 'Hey, the stripper's arrived,' but even he knows it's not a good joke. She doesn't look at all like a stripper. She doesn't look much like a guitar player either. Oh sure, she has the beat up leather jacket and the motorcycle boots. And she has the cheekbones and the mess of wild hair, but she isn't posing as some kind of guitar heroine. She isn't playing at being tough. She looks strong but not hard-bitten. She looks self-possessed and able to take care of herself, but that hasn't destroyed an essential sensitivity and vulnerability, even a fragility.

Jenny looks her audience over and smiles. She's played far more difficult rooms than this one.

She can't remember a time when she didn't play the guitar. She was always the kind of kid who sat alone in Dad's garage, yanking weird noise out of a cheap Korean copy of a Fender Strat. That might have been considered a strange thing for a girl to be doing, but she had always been far beyond that kind of suburban nonsense.

Even back then she liked to think of herself as a relentless experimentalist. She employed what she liked to call 'extended technique'. Sometimes she played more or less conventionally, other times she hit the guitar with hammers, screwdrivers, drumsticks, egg whisks. She would dangle house keys, paper clips, six inch nails, rusty razor blades, from the strings. She loved feedback, distortion, sheer noise. She liked to abuse both guitar and equipment. She knew this wasn't going to get her into the charts but it made her happy. It seldom made an audience happy, but then again, for a long time she seldom had an audience.

But it all changed after she had a dream. It was one of a series. Often these were dreams full of frustration; she would be on stage playing an electric guitar in front of an audience and something would always be wrong. Sometimes she couldn't get the guitar in tune, sometimes it was too quiet to be heard, sometimes the lead from the guitar to the amplifier was too short to be usable.

But this dream was different in several ways. In this one she didn't even get as far as going on stage, and there was no frustration. She simply arrived at a hall and saw a poster advertising her presence. She was billed as 'The Moist Guitar of Jenny Slade', and there was a crowd of thousands trying to get into the hall.

It was not in the strictest sense a prophetic dream. Yes it did forecast what was to happen, but only because she *made* it happen. But if she hadn't had the dream perhaps it would never have happened at all.

She orders a beer, and props the guitar case against the bar. The barman very slowly brings her drink and asks, 'What kind of axe you got in there?'

'It's custom made.'

'Yeah? Can you play it?'

'Yes, thanks,' she says.

'Tell you what,' he says, with what he takes to be a devilish glint in his eyes. 'The beer's on the house if you can get up on the stage and keep my customers entertained for a couple of numbers.'

'Oh, I can do *that*,' she says, and her face says that she can do a lot more besides.

For a while she was a male impersonator. She impersonated George Formby. She would mimic his toothy grin, his chirpy Lancashire accent. But her ukulele playing lacked a certain authenticity. At the climax of her act she would clutch the instrument to her crotch, use it as a dildo, play it behind her head and ignite it before smashing it to smithereens against the stage. Finally she would quip, 'It's turned out nice again, hasn't it?'

It was an original act but it failed to please the purists.

Then she performed under the name of Juanita and her Musical Snakes. She would come on stage with a Gibson Moderne and half a dozen boa constrictors of various ages and sizes. The more sedate of these would grip themselves around the guitar neck and hold down unresolved chord shapes, while the younger more slender critters would squirm across the strings creating wild atonal arpeggios. The liveliest snake, whom she nicknamed Fidel, would curl himself around the tremolo arm and create a profound and unworldly vibrato. It was good enough as a novelty act, but it wasn't great art and Jenny knew it, and she wanted to make great art.

She says, 'I decided to be my own woman, my own musician. I decided to tear up the rule book, and then I realised there *was* no rule book.'

She says, 'As I get older the appetite for drink and drugs and cheap boys recedes, but the urge to pick up an electric guitar and make a godawful noise just won't go away.'

The barman at the Paradise Loft says she can plug direct into the house p.a. It isn't an ideal arrangement but she guesses it will have to do. She knows that in the end it isn't a matter of equipment.

By now the crowd is taking quite an interest. They're too hip in their malevolence to actively taunt her, but they leave their seats and the pool table and crowd in around the bar's tiny stage, their body language challenging her to impress them.

She stands on the stage, looking suddenly much smaller and younger. She still hasn't taken the guitar out of its case. Now she snaps open the clasps. There's a noise like a sigh, and a wisp of what looks like steam, or maybe even hot breath, billows from the case.

She reaches inside and takes out this *thing*. Well yes, you'd have to admit it was a guitar, but none of these drinkers, these lovers of good ol' rock and roll, has ever seen one like this before. The neck is made out of some kind of unnaturally lustrous metal, so shiny it almost has a glow to it. It is long and thick, and convincingly phallic. The strings run along its length, ultra light, ultra malleable, and end at the machine-heads in a lethal-looking tangle of spikes and cogs and chains.

But this is the orthodox bit of the guitar. It's the body that defies belief. It is shaped like an amoeba, which is to say that it's curvy but essentially shapeless; and it appears at first to be made out of some sort of tan-coloured plastic. But the more you look, the less it looks like plastic at all. In fact it looks more like a piece of soft, malleable, private flesh, and in places there are growths of hair, thick, black, irregular tufts. There are things that on a piece of wood might look like knots, but here they look disturbingly like nipples, and the pickups look like three parallel bands of livid scar tissue.

'Hey what do you call that sucker?' someone yells.

'I call it a guitar,' she answers quietly.

But why the electric guitar at all? Because, she would patiently explain, it is a sexy instrument, of course. And that isn't just because it's simultaneously curvy and phallic. For Jenny it is also a question of language, of vocabulary.

First, there is all that predictable dirty talk about fuzz boxes and truss rods, and 'spanking the plank' as a euphemism for guitar playing.

But there are also all those sexy effects; compressors and enhancers, sustainers and flangers. It sounds as though there is a whole world of erotic possibilities among the pitch shifters, swell pedals, digital delays, something charmingly clandestine in a noise suppressor. There is overdrive and treble boost. There are controls that affect presence, tex-ture, gain, timbre, load impedance. Even a single change in 'volume' can sound like a sexy concept if you're in the right mood.

She straps it on, this instrument that looks part deadly weapon and part creature from some alien lagoon. And she plugs a lead into a deep orifice in the thing's surface, and the barman takes the other end of the lead and runs it into the house p.a.

Without tuning up she grabs the neck at the seventh fret, holds down a fairly straightforward–looking chord, and picks out a lazy arpeggio with her plectrum hand. Well, the guitar isn't in standard tuning, that's for sure. The chord contains all kinds of weird harmonies, unisons, octaves, diminished sevenths, augmented fourths, suspended ninths. In fact it sounds like the richest, most complicated chord anyone has ever heard. And that guitar has the most incredible sustain. She's barely touched the strings and yet the whole room is filled with that dense, ringing fluid sound. It's not so very loud yet it demands absolute attention. It isn't a sound you could dance to exactly but it sure keeps you on your feet.

And as the music hangs in the air it is not a wholly pleasant sound. It has elements of feedback, of white noise, of grunge and skronk. And yet it remains listenable and utterly compelling. Nobody's walking out of this performance.

She says, 'My guitar is a conduit. It connects me with pain and passion, with inspiration and aspiration, with sound waves and electrical charge, with technology and history.

'I feel in touch with Charlie Christian and Eddie Durham. With Muddy Waters and Chuck Berry and Hank Marvin and Duane Eddy, with Beck and Page and Clapton. Sexy boys every one of them.

'Here's Guitar Slim standing in the car park outside the club he's supposed to be playing in. He's got his guitar in his hand and a hundred yard long guitar lead connected to his amp which is inside the club.

'Here's Pete Townshend destroying his guitar in some heroic attempt at self-obliteration. Here's Jimi setting fire to his surrogate phallus. Here's little Stevie Vai inserting the headstock of his seven string Ibanez into the bodily openings of some sad girl called Laurel Fishman. Not very cool Steve. Not very right on at all.

'These are my people. But mostly I feel in touch with all those lonely boys of the future, still sitting in their rooms trying to play guitar, solemnly believing that if only they could coax some music out of this damn machine they're holding then somehow everything would be better, everything would fall into place; their sex lives, their shyness, their bad skin. And you know what fellers, you're right, it would.'

Jenny's guitar continues to fill the Paradise Loft with its song. Her playing remains simple and unostentatious. She hardly seems to be doing anything at all and yet this music continues to spill from the guitar. The music gets ever more complex and darker, gets excruciatingly loud and before long seems to be the sound of planets melting, of glass cathedrals imploding, of mythical beasts being slaughtered.

And as the crowd watches, increasingly spellbound, the guitar seems to develop a life of its own. It seems to be breathing, to be pulsing with its own heartbeat. And then the finale – it starts to bleed. Thick warm blood starts to ooze from the scar tissue of the pickups, trickles down the guitar's body, makes dark, scattered blots on the stage.

It's a hard act to follow. The audience is silent but they give Jenny what she wants and needs; unqualified, undivided attention. And she takes certain energies away from them. But that's okay, it's not as if they were using those energies for anything much. As forms of vampirism go, this one is relatively benevolent.

After the performance she gets a number of offers; of money, gigs, and inevitably sex. But all she will accept is another free beer, and as she drinks it she explains that she doesn't share her bed with anyone or anything except her guitar.

A short while later she leaves the Paradise Loft. There is a vehicle waiting for her outside, a cross between a military tank and a Volkswagen Beetle. She gets in and drives away.

Dust and decay and a new silence hang in the air. Inside the bar the customers are not quite sure what they've heard or seen, but they're suddenly, acutely aware that they're in need of a drink. They crowd around the bar, and the barman has a hard time coping with their urgent demands for more booze.

That night she has a different dream.

If a guitar is cranked up high enough, with the amp, and pickups and fuzz box all set on maximum, even the slightest vibration will produce noise. In one of her earliest radical pieces Jenny's playing consisted of no more than blowing on her guitar strings.

In this new dream, she is strapped into a kind of wheeled electric chair. The wheels fit into some railway tracks, and there is a powerful engine attached to the back of the chair. She is holding a guitar, and it is cranked up so that every breath of wind sets the strings roaring. A wireless transmitter sends signals from the pickups to a mountainous wall of amps and speakers set up some hundreds of yards away.

The idea is that the engine will propel the chair along the track, and the rush of air will make the guitar scream; then the track runs out and she will be propelled into space, still strapped to the chair, still clutching the guitar, and as she falls through the air, she and guitar eventually hit the ground, the most wonderful, wild, eloquent and destructive music will issue from the speakers.

She wakes up before the engine is fired. Next day she

realises how tired she is of playing solo. She decides to form a band called, inevitably the Moist Guitars.

Wilderness

EDNA O'BRIEN

Yes, DEATH STALKED the city that night, stalked the city like a great water wolf. The river – sheer, ruffled, grey, brown, black and khaki – took them into her inhospitable bosom. Why? Why did the river want them, and for what?

All her life Nell had believed that she would have a presentiment if a mishap should befall either of her children. Her bones would tell it. Her bloodstream would tell it. Every hair would stand on end. Often she had half imagined such a thing – indeed, on occasion, went with the delirium of it upon hearing of an accident in this street or that, on a motorway or a leafy lane – and had waited, and the wait had seemed both necessary and ludicrous. She knew the ropes. A policeman, or rather two policemen, came and knocked on one's door. She had heard that somewhere. Yet, as the taxi-driver rattled on about an accident, young people, partying, she had no intimation of anything, just felt glad to be going home to sleep. It was a Saturday. Party night. A pleasure boat had collided with a barge on the Thames, and many were drowned or drowning. She felt a flash of dismay, a mockery of the sadness to come.

When a mother sees two policemen at her front door, she knows. She thought it was her younger son, Tristan, was

certain that a truck had gone off the road in Turkey, where he
and his friends were spending the summer doing relief work.
It was Paddy. He was one of the crowd of young people on
the pleasure boat and, as he was still missing, they had to
inform her. Missing. Missing is not dead. When a mother
knows, she does everything to unknow. She goes to her
bedroom to dress. She discards the old stockings that she had
been wearing in the daytime for a new pair. God knows why.
She says that this is not true, this is a false alarm testing her
last reservoir of strength. She puts on powder, hurriedly,
then returns and, as on any normal occasion, offers brandy or
tea. The policemen say it is better for them to get moving, to
get back to the scene, since all the force is needed. She sits in a
black van with them and slowly and solemnly recites, as her
own chant, the words of Christ in the Garden of Gethsemane:
'O, Father, if it be possible, let this chalice pass from me.'
Missing is not dead. she says that aloud to the policemen and
adds how providential the night is, since it is so still, since
there is scarcely a wind. They recognise that undertow of
hope and look at each other with eyes in which she believes
there are recesses of non-hope. She cannot see their eyes but
she can see them fidget. They have already been there; they
have already seen people crawling out of the water, senseless,
unable to grasp their whereabouts, asking, 'What's
happened? . . . What's happened?' They have heard the
screaming, the disbelief, the shouts of crazed, incensed
people, and they are not in the business of doling out niceties.
She has not seen these things yet. Now she does. Ambulances
bursting from the hospital's steps, their lights whirling round
and round, but no siren sounding. Ghost machines. Inside,
commotion, delirium. People who had been inches from
death asking, asking. Everyone asking; voices charging each
other across the waiting room. Has Alex been found?
'Found'. The word both urgent and wan. A girlfriend has
lost her boyfriend. She calls his name, shouts it. He does not
materialise. She runs, the double glass doors almost swallowing her. A man lost his wife. He stands, a sodden picture
of despair, with a blanket slipping off, saying quietly, 'My

wife . . . My beautiful wife.' A younger man weeps for the woman he swam with. Where is she, where is she? He describes how they held hands – tight, tight – until in the end she slipped away from him, eluded his grasp. Was she dead? Was she still struggling?

Nell is sitting quietly, sitting by herself. She is afraid of these people. They pace, then are still, then give reign to some outburst. This night has dislodged their reserves of sanity. Nurses, who go about with forms and thermometers and blankets, are told to piss off. It has the insubstantiality of a dream but it is not a dream. It is a raw, raucous, unashamed confrontation with life or non-life. The names are shouted incessantly. Samantha and Sue and Paul and Jeff. No one says 'Paddy,' as if no one knew him but her. Outside, the sirens now screech with animal intonations. Inside, coffee, cups of coffee, a voice asking for someone to put another spoon of sugar in, sloshing. Paddy, where are you? She has been told to sit and wait. She will be informed the moment there is news. Rumours bob up the way she imagines, cannot stop herself from imagining, the faces appearing on the water. His face. His alone. A body has been found eight miles upriver at Hammersmith. A woman's. Not a man's. Not him. Should she go to Hammersmith? Did drowned bodies follow one another like shoals of fish? She must go somewhere. Paddy, where are you? She is told again to sit and wait. They know her name and her son's name. It is on a document. Many of the saved are at the hospital. They are weeping, claiming that they do not want to live if their comrades are dead. Their teeth are chattering, they shiver, their features slavered in black mud and ooze.

'Where's my mates? Where's my fucking mates?' a young man shouts as he enters the hospital. His head is gashed, and the blood streaming down his face has black rivulets in it. He is telling everyone how cold it is, how cold and how stupid. She runs from the building and down a narrow footpath to the riverbank, where people are milling and shouting around a posse of police. It is dark and deathlike, everything spectral. The police and the rescue workers are like shadows giving and taking orders, their voices terse. The river is calm but black, a black pit that everyone dreads. Calm, black swishings of water. Looking at it for the first time, looking at it steadily, she thinks it cannot be. He is not in there. He has swum ashore, he is somewhere, he is one of the dazed people in blankets, covered in mud. He is asking someone to telephone her. He is. He is. She hears the tide, its slipslap against the lifeboats, and she thinks, you have not got him. The chains, however, which go clank-clank, tell a different story – a death knell. And the line comes, how could it not: 'A current under sea picked his bones in whispers.' A young policeman loses control, says how the hell does he know what one boat was doing crashing into another. Sirens fill the streets and she thinks that if Paddy is still in the water, which she now thinks he must be, those sirens will be a clarion to him, a reminder that everyone is on the alert, everything is being done.

'Oh, Paddy, we are coming to you, we are coming,' she says, and going over to an officer, she asks if there is any way they could light up the water more, give hope to those who were still struggling in it. For some reason he thinks she is a journalist and tells her to shut her trap. She screams back, screams that she is a mother.

'Why isn't the water lit, the way it's lit for a jubilee or a coronation?' she says, and he looks at her with a kind of murderousness and says that those who are still in there have had it by now. She lets out half a cry – a short, unearthly, broken cry. This shadow, this totem of authority, wishes them dead. A senior officer tries to calm her, says that they are doing everything they possibly can, that any bodies still in the water will be found. 'Found'. There is that word again. She asks him if by any chance she can go to the morgue at Southwark in the police van, since others are going. He looks at her with the candour of a man who has to refuse, and says no, that it would be better for her to go back into the hospital and stay put.

In the hospital, a group of young people is silently weeping, holding one another and rocking back and forth in grief, like children in a play-pen. A boy and two girls. They have lost their mate, their mate. The boy had jumped in the water to search and had to be hauled out. They rock back and forth, like women in labour, giving birth to their grief. Each time they smoke they give Nell a cigarette, too. Some time later one of them, a girl, looks up and screams. A man is coming toward them. She is afraid it is not true. It can't be true. She looks down, she covers her eyes and asks them, Jesus, to look up. It is him. It is Justin. He has been found. Or has he? Is he a spirit? He walks toward them, in his slather of wet clothes, with a strange dazedness. He is holding half a rubber life ring. They get up. They all embrace, four friends, lost for words, unable to speak. They don't believe it. A miracle. Then they do believe it. They cry. They kiss. He cannot speak. He cannot say how he swam ashore. He holds up the bit of black rubber, refuses to let it go. It saved him. It. Then one of them speaks, one of them says that they are going to get out of this hellhole and get in his little banger and drive somewhere and get booze and get fish and chips, and they are going to ring everyone they know and have ever known and give the party of their lives, a party that means welcome home, Justin, welcome home.

Nell shrinks away from them, and they know why. She is still one of the waiting ones. There is nothing to be said. They cannot swap with her. Were she the lucky one she would not swap, either. It is as primal as that.

What she must do is give Paddy strength, send messages to him, urge him, tell him to kick, to kick, not to give in. Her breathing quickens, and it is as if she, too, has dared the water. Then she pauses and says, 'Turn over on your back, love and float.' She does this unendingly, because there is one thing that she cannot unknow: some are trapped in their sunken vessel, were caught in a downstairs suite – corpses side by side, or cleaving to furniture. The vessel cannot be brought up till daylight, when the toll will be taken. He is not among them. She is certain of that. He got out – crawled out and swam and is making his way, is holding on to a raft, is on a little bit of beach, waiting to be picked up. He is that seagull he loves to read about, who flew higher than all the other seagulls, up into the lonely altitudes; hearing herself say 'seagull', she shrieks, glimpsing the maelstroms ahead.

Waiting. Another day. Parents. Relatives. Police. Waiting at the hospital for names to be called out, now for people to go into the morgue in the back and identify their own. Bodies in glass cubicles under sheets – bloated, puffed, disfigured, all prey to the same lunatic fate.

The policeman lifts a sheet, and what she sees is not a face with features but something grey, prehistoric. A purple cowl hides the hair and the body. She does not know if it is a boy or a girl. The hairline is black and eerie, an eerie streak like a charcoal line. Although her name has not been called, she creeps into the morgue furtively, to mettle herself. But now she turns away. Paddy has not been found – he and six others. She goes back to the morgue's anteroom, the chapel of rest where mourners sit silently, too silent by far, praying to a bare altar, a bare God. A mother and a father sit fingering one black rosary. Not long after, a man comes and speaks in a whisper to them, saying yes, it is Jason, their Jason, he recognises the two back fillings he had done the Easter before. In his hand an envelope with the X-ray of the teeth. They confer. The father goes in while the mother stays in the chapel, praying, a tower of strength. Suddenly the silence is shattered – a woman's cry. A different mother insists that the girl they have shown her is not her daughter, Fiona, is not the white maiden, and that no one can tell her so. Fiona is not that lump of disfigurement in there. The policeman tries to reason with the woman, says she had been warned, advised not to go in alone. 'I got to, hadn't I?' the woman says, lashing out at all and sundry, saying it was clear that they were all drunk on the boat except for her Fiona, who had never touched a drop in her life, and was sacrificed, sacrificed for what – scoundrels, brigands, drunks. Looking across at Nell, who is looking at her aghast, she screams and says, 'Who do you think you're looking at?' and Nell shrinks into the corner, hoping the whitewashed wall will absorb her. The woman, while discussing her Fiona, is holding her daughter's jewellery – bracelets, a jingle of them, bone and silver, bracelets and rings. How unfair that these could escape the ravages of the water.

He had no ornaments but an indigo tattoo, and she wonders if this would discolour. 'Oh, please, God, let him be found,' Nell keeps saying over and over again to herself, so she does not break down. Words replace the terror in her mouth and in her windpipe. For him to be found is now all that she asks. She is beginning to lose hope of his being alive.

In the morgue's makeshift refreshment room things are heated, embattled. A small group have already started to rally, to press about fighting for their rights, for compensation, for lolly. She cannot join in. She cannot even be righteous. She says, 'Who can tell what happened in the water in the dark?'

'Now you listen,' a woman says to her, but cannot think what to say next. Rage and grief are battling in her, and her eyes are like wounds from crying. 'I am listening,' Nell says, and the woman throws back her head in a hateful grimace and says she knows exactly the lawyer she'll go to, exactly the shark who will fight her cause. A friend encourages her. Cites shipowners with untold wealth and villas in Spain. The talk seems odd, inappropriate, considering how close they are to the morgue, how the depths of their feelings are just waiting to be met, in there.

At midnight, a detective came to the morgue and asked her to go home and get some sleep. 'I'd rather stay here,' she said.

'It's orders, Ma'am,' he said, and she knew that he hated saying it, because it meant that they had more or less given up. Paddy would not be found. The tears that had been lying in wait came then, unheralded, unannounced, in a burst. She was sobbing. A desecration. Before that she had merely cried like the others, into her sleeve or into her handkerchief, but this was torrents. The few mourners left were stunned into silence. She had allowed the truth to seep into her. The truth was that she would not see him again. That was worse than death. It seemed to be above and beyond death. A rigmarole then of how he would not walk through the door or ride his bicycle or run a comb through his hair again was more significant than death. She was telling them that.

'Squeeze my hand, just squeeze my hand,' a detective kept saying, while the tears poured out of her – baths, basins, buckets, reservoirs of tears that seemed hot and life-giving as blood. Why her? Why her? Why him? Why them? The words flew out of her like bits of old food. Telling them how Paddy believed that seagulls on the river were the souls of dead lightermen. Seagulls. She thought she saw a little brace of them whizzing about, beating the air, then vanishing. She had gone that far. 'You're all right now,' the detective said.

'Yes, I'm all right now,' she said, and remembered that during her outburst he had told her there was a pamphlet by a famous specialist which described death by drowning – how beautiful it was, not a painful death, happy, a kind of ecstasy once the body submitted and allowed the water in.

'Could you find it?' she said.

'I'll try,' he said, and helped her toward the swinging door.

Outside, everyone gone. Her banshee tears had sent them scarpering. Nothing but statues and the shadows they cast. Iron men. Iron women, iron horses, and an iron Boadicea. Fawn clock tower and fawn buildings insubstantial inside these self-same cages.

'Where are my friends now? . . . Where are my friends?' she yelled, hand and arm going up wildly to hail a taxi, missing this one and that, crossing a road, recrossing, waving an overnight bag – Paddy's bag with a few of his childhood effects in it, to put beside him to keep him company, a little tobacco tin and a fob watch which her father had given him, but which never worked.

'You look as if you want the airport,' the driver said.

'No. I want home.' She told him the address.

'So why did I think you wanted the airport?' he said grumpily.

'I want home,' she said weakly.

Home. Once she was there, the doorbell or the phone would ring to say he had been found. He would be found, and the kiss or the clinch or whatever it was would be exchanged between them. She would not quake at the cruel metamorphosis of death, oh no – her son was her son, a little image locked inside her, inviolate, as when he had roamed and sallied inside her womb. And to keep that image company she gave him the voice and the recitation that he had had when he was four or five, his voice like a toy xylophone saying:

> Pam pam pipe
> Plum jam
> Ten bob
> Tip-tip, Peter all the way.

She would bury him. She would bury him as best she could. His friends would come and there would be flowers, lots of flowers – it was summer, after all, high summer, the time of the hollyhocks and the Canterbury bells – and she would have a little party, and then what? Then was a blank in her thoughts, a wall, so to speak, against which memories would be placed end to end, increasing and multiplying like stacks of books. But first he must be found and then he must be buried, because that was fundamental, because earth and not water was the kindest, meetest resting place. Why did she so fear water – water, from whence he came, the waters of herself and of her own mother, womb of waters, known and unknown, nourishing and leeching, giving and taking back. She kept picturing earth, little slants of earth, little mounds, graveyards with things growing out of them, anything, daisies, moss, anything.

The driver was not going fast enough and not going the most direct route and was determined that she suffer the indignities inflicted by his previous fare. Foreigners. Zulus. Couldn't breathe with the four of them in the cab. Under her breath she kept upbraiding him, but she did not want a contretemps. Even one vexed exchange would break her down.

She believed that the moment they could not reach her would be the moment they rang to say he had been found, so she confined herself to her own house, to the pier at Westminster, to the morgue at Southwark – policemen turning away from her in embarrassment. She was understanding, overunderstanding, so as not to rattle them. They had to go on to other things, after all. She felt so alone. No husband, no Tristan. The husband, Walter, long gone, in the West Country, and Tristan travelling in Turkey and as yet not reached. After five days, no word, so she ran to another venue, to her office, where everyone offered to do something for her that was of no use just then. Though she insisted to herself that he would be found, she had a scraping fear, all the time, that he wouldn't, and that this would be the deepest, the most unfinished hurt of all – a hurt incapable of death, of dying, a hole inside her that would grow bigger and sturdier and uglier each day – so that she cursed the God whom hitherto she had implored so passionately.

That night: that drive, that dawn, that mouthful of toast at the pier, the blonde girl at the pier who screamed at her because of the way she described Paddy, every detail, his eyes so very mixed between blue and grey, like gravel, only softer, and his few freckles and his beautiful hands, like a pianist's, and the girl telling her for fuck's sake to belt up, because her boyfriend had had beautiful hands, too, and they were to have been married in September. That night or the next, and that dawn – raw, bleached, drained of light as dawns are – and her own house for an hour or two, then a dash to Paddy's flat, where she should have gone sooner but couldn't, going up the stairs, becoming petrified because Penny might be there. Penny, Paddy's girlfriend and, as she said, soul mate. Penny was not there. Penny was in Spain, working in a pottery. Paddy had moved to a flat to sort himself out, as he put it. Climbing the last bit of steep stairs, Nell remembers how he would have opened the door by then and found her puffing and admitted that he puffed, too, when he hadn't been to the gym and – oh, madness of madness – she thinks, He has not died; the policemen are mistaken, askew; he is here; he is here, either asleep or awake, and the door will open from the inside. Lucky that he has given her a key. They exchanged keys. A sure sign of their reconciliation. Paddy's dog, Charlie, comes toward her with an abject look, a frightened look, and all she can say as she pats him is, 'Charlie, you haven't done number two,' and, saying it, she thinks of her children's youth and of Dixie the dog, years before, years that now seem blithe compared to this inferno. Charlie licks her a lick of thanks, relief, and imprecation. He is hungry. He is desperate to go out. In the front garden, she stands a few yards away from him, disowning him, in case a landlady or a caretaker taps a window and shakes a fist. He takes his time as he squats under a lilac tree. He is nervous, overnervous. His tail and his hind legs shake uncontrollably, but nothing comes; his eyes are fixed on her in case she stirs. Three whole days he has been abandoned. The lilac tree is withered. Dead blossoms like used lavatory brushes. Some rotting smell. What happens to a body in the river? She must look it up in a book. No, she mustn't. Charlie staggers from one spot to another for dribbles, then gives up.

Upstairs, she begins to go through Paddy's things. A diary with entries and little mottoes he copied to better himself. What would he have been? A teacher, she thinks. Yes, a teacher of man, his conscience always smiting him and his pity, pity for those who had not. A teacher of man. There are birthdays. Her birthday is among them. She is not left out. A motto written on a card: 'The lapwing cries loudest when far from its nest.' Why that? Beside the diary are his three pipes and a stack of pipe cleaners, then a photograph of Penny in a pair of shorts, looking so young, so vulnerable, not the needley Penny she knows. The pregnancy that had been mentioned was not. Was not. What happened? Nell would never know. The curtains she gave him are drawn. He drew them before he went out that night. Yes, they are there, and the wooden armchair that he got off a rubbish heap, and a beautiful lapis bowl, the one beautiful thing in the room. She must get some of his clothes, because he will be cold, shivering – madness was taking root, because clothes are for the living. A shroud is for the dead – brown, grey, or off-white. Going shyly to the bedroom she tiptoes, knocks as if he were there with Penny. Traces of them are there and, opening the wardrobe door, she cries at not having given him more money, because his clothes are so spare and so pitiful. There are some secondhand suits, a stack of sweaters, and three gaudy ties, probably birthday presents from friends. His sanctum. She does not touch a thing, or rather touches all of them with a little glide of the fingers, and then she goes out.

It is a mad dash to a shop to get Charlie some sliced ham, which he eats on the street, in a twinkling, and then he tries to eat the greaseproof paper that she is still holding.

Different people at the morgue than the times before, and fewer – new recruits, hopeful, despairing. The others have all gone home, are in their houses now, facing it, resentments piling up in them. She tells a woman she has never seen before that yes, she has another son and that he is in Turkey, that he has gone there with his friends to do relief work but that she has not had him alerted, not yet, not until his brother is found. That will be the time to tell him and have him brought home. She does not mention her husband, the man to whom she has not spoken in over a decade.

Yes, Charlie knew, because the next night he started up his own incantation, his own wake, his own subhuman howl. First it was from the kitchen. She was wakened from a clotted sleep. She took half a sleeping tablet, cut it carefully down the centre, not wanting to be blurry on the morrow yet wanting sleep, even ten minutes of sleep wanting her mind to be borne somewhere else, even to a different nightmare. The phone would ring, and she must not be so asleep that she could not hear it. The nice detective had promised her that the moment the body was found they would summon her, no matter what the hour. He was Welsh, friendlier than the others. He had not yet found the pamphlet, but he assured her that he remembered the line written by the neurosurgeon, the line that said the sensation was ecstatic once the water entered the lungs and the body gave up the fight. Nell was wakened instead by Charlie, with a howl that had a human plaint in it. Her own hysteria speaking back to her, but animalised. Charlie knew. He missed his master. He went around smelling shoes to find the smell of his master. He smelled shoes and Wellingtons; he did not give up. Down to the kitchen to give Charlie a telling off, whereupon he skulked, becoming silent until she went back to her room and the howling started up again. This time she thumped the floor with a broom, the two ends of the broom – the worn, wiry twigs and then the handle as a parting shot. She put her winter coat under the door to shut out all sound. If she did not sleep she would be in danger of going mad. No use. He started again. She dragged him into the garden, thinking it was that, but it was not that, then in the kitchen coaxed him with a sodden ginger biscuit. He spat it out. He was not taking this. She left him again but the howl that started up bit into her brain, and, hurrying back and full of vengeance now, she simply said, as if he could comprehend, 'Charlie, I've had it. I've had it.' His teeth marks on the rungs of the chair told her what she already knew: Charlie was wild, Charlie was unmanageable. The teeth marks on the chair, her bitten coat, the ravelled, grey-white threads, all too much.

She barely saw the streets she drove through with Charlie – the traffic lights, a slice of river as it sauntered upstream to disgorge its prey, or maybe downstream to do the identical thing. How can one plead with water? It is never still, always moving, scheming, eluding. How well she knew its colours. She had lived by it. She had loved it once, claimed to have been moved, oh, so moved by its sheers, its ruffles, its greys, its currents, its debris, and so on. Paddy had loved the water, too, had made a little logbook of the river. She didn't look at

Charlie once. Barely seeing the streets, skimming, the dainty lacelike girders of a bridge an affront.

The building was a smearish colour, mud brown. A man going by with his dog on a leash shouted: no animal of his would set foot there. Inside, baying. A great swell of it that rose and dipped and rerose like the swell of a foaming sea. Multiple bayings. Then individual barks, individual cries saying, 'Find me! Come along down to my little cubby and find me!' She shouldn't be doing it to Charlie. It was to Paddy she was doing it. Passing the cages was the worst. Some of the animals yapped. Others stared in silence. Some dozed in aluminum basins, and everywhere there was fresh and not so fresh shit. Charlie's temperament, Charlie's teeth, and Charlie's hair were all subjects for discussion. Then Nell was by herself, while Charlie was taken off to be examined and vaccinated. Did it hurt? Of course it hurt. Everything hurt. In a little room that adjoined an empty café, she struggled with a form. Where was her heart? It was gone. It was murdered. It was with her son on the bed of the river, trying to find him, two hearts missing each other the way people miss one another in dreams. It was in a sack, like a dead animal – bleeding, the blood oozing out of it. The questions were routine: her name, her occupation, how long she had known Charlie, and could he be trusted with children. Staring at her from the wall, a newsletter about a dog called Patch, who had been badly treated, abandoned twice, and twice brought here, where he made a miraculous recovery. In the end Patch had found a good home, and it was the owners of the good home who wrote this eulogy after his death. Why was she doing this? Only because Charlie howled, a raw howl that cut notches in her.

Back to the chapel of rest that adjoined the hospital, glad to be with others for a moment, or a fraction of a moment, escaping her own stew. Lives that had thought they were booking a holiday, or going to learn to drive, or to plant sweet peas were heading for a voyage of permanent mourning. Everything slashed, every plan and half plan and every dream. The others gave her strength. While she was with them she did not think of how she would tell Tristan, how she would break it to him. She thought only, You do not know yet, sweetheart; you can laugh; you can joke that little bit longer. Had she her way, he would never know; he would live in ignorance of it.

'She was my morning's light and my evening's lamp.' A mother who stood in the pulpit of the Cathedral kept saying it, her voice dramatic, measured, calling her daughter in various intonations. Services and cremations, in the city, in the suburbs, all over the country. Young people having stabs at gaiety – short skirts, blouses and shirts like those worn in a bullring. The draped and decked coffins a far cry from the cold consignments of flesh in the morgue.

A vicar praised those who had come to mourn and those who had died. Talked of the necessity of fun and how no one must fault these young people, stressed the fact that they were not to blame and the skippers were not to blame, either – all were blameless. Then a psalm, then 'Lucy in the Sky with Diamonds' and a short reading from 'The Little Prince'. A man had given her that book once. A lover. Finnish. It came to her that if she were to make love the frostbite of death might be taken away, even momentarily. She had heard that somewhere.

The plots in the cremation grounds were so minuscule. Midget slab-stones as in a doggy's grave, and wan messages, a single yellow iris in a Lucozade bottle. Oh, the paucity of it all. They had to queue for the cremation ceremony. Mourners treated like cattle. A mother in jeans, grumbling because of this. The fact that she was in jeans seemed wrong, seemed inappropriate, worse when she tightened her belt to show how dishy she was. A young man, a thin, sepulchral-looking young man, stepped aside as if to pray. Had the look of Hamlet. Seemed stunned. Everywhere shock and those outbursts and now the woman taking the white belt of her jeans off and using it to hit, to hit out.

Hated going home. Into her dark house. Into sleep and into dreams: searchlights in her innards and men shouting – shouting what? Then a cold, white ship, a liner on to which guests were coming, la-di-da people, oodles of them, with parasols and handbags. Famishing. 'Hold on till I plug in the fire,' she called, not wanting them to shiver, not wanting to be inhospitable. The electric plug going soft in her hand, soft and warmish, turning into a wet tea bag.

Not long after, the people higher up at her office clubbed together to send her to a health farm. Thought it might help. As soon as she crossed the threshold she knew she must leave. It was all too bright and hygienic – that, and a smell of grapefruit. She fled. She went to Paddy's flat so she could not be traced. She slept in Paddy's bed and thought he might appear to her. In a way, he did. A dream, a salve. He came alive in it. It was a strange place, a square flooded in warm golden light, a southern town, yellowish walls, turreted, sun pouring down, white tables. A beautiful girl stood in waiting in leopardskin trousers and high leopardskin boots. Penny waved to the girl. Had an errand for her. The errand was to go to Paddy with a message, to search him out in the monk's room, where he burrowed and where he was praying for guidance. He was to come to the square, the golden square, where he would receive instruction. He agreed. In the dream he looked thin, emaciated, but he smiled at the news of his release. Then it was next day – morning, with the white chairs stacked on the round, white tables, their legs ungainly. He arrived clean-shaven, in praying robes and a white shirt that was threadbare at the cuffs. He looked around to meet his messenger, the woman in leopardskin. Instead, Penny appeared and moved toward him, radiant, then laughing because she had played a joke on him. They danced in the square. The pink stone of the cobbles was dark where it had just been splashed with water, and the music came not in a night-time spasm but in a trickle, like a flute heard across distances of mountains. They danced between the tables and chairs, danced beautifully toward a sign that read 'Tivoli Gardens'. Nell wakened almost happy. She would write to

Penny. Nell would write to tell her this dream and, by telling it, say, 'It means we must be friends.' She posted it to Penny's pottery in Spain. They could bury the hatchet. There was no child, the child was a blind, and there was no Paddy, Paddy was among the perch and the slippery eel, but, as Nell had to keep saying, free of them now, free of all predatoriness, adrift among the algae and the slapping vegetation.

On her kitchen windowpane, a sign – galling, galling. Its appearance brought on by the steam. In a blur of grey, in a fog of steam came his initial, 'P' for Paddy. Pasta boiling over in a saucepan. Long strips of it, a dyed green. A great splutter on the stove, spitting and hopping, beads of water jumping about like translucent insects, the kitchen all foggy, fogbound like a river late at night. In his handwriting, his particular little squiggle. Jesus Christ. She crossed over to it. It was a 'P.' He must have written it once with a crayon while she was cooking dinner, one of the evenings that was either amicable or testy, written it where it lay in hiding, needing only a bit of steam to show up again, apparition-like. She ran her finger along it, tracing it slowly, not wanting to blot it out, and thought that if anything could invoke the dead, it must be this. An afterbirth of hope. Then she rang someone. The bereaved were told to ring each other at moments like this, for counselling, co-counselling. The woman she reached was livid, calling all journalists scum and newspaper proprietors worse scum, millionaires – making packets out of tragedy. There had been an article claiming that her son was gay, that he had lived with a young man, that they had had wedding vows, a wedding ceremony, that they were going to adopt a baby. Lies. Total lies. Garbage. She was going to the editor on the morrow. The next woman Nell rang told her to go to a spiritualist centre. It was the only thing. It did wonders for people, it brought peace of mind. There was a place in Belgravia. This woman would find out the hours, and they would go together. The pasta Nell had made tasted like glue, or like porridge that she had had in Scotland. How long ago was that? Too long ago. 'They're peeing on us from a great height,' the first woman on the phone had said, and suddenly Nell laughed a mad laugh, remembering Paddy and Tristan, two brothers peeing on each other from apple trees and shouting 'Bang, bang, you're dead, I'm not dead,' brothers vying with each other as to who could pee longest and say the most warring things.

She had found it easily in Paddy's address book, under 'F' for 'Father.' Walter was in a home, but she hadn't known where. Lost his marbles, or some of them. She'd lost hers, too, but not the ones that enabled her to remember. Memory weevilling into her every minute, a fresh issue of pain, memory picking, like the hook of a crochet needle, drawing blood. Awful journey. Monotonous. Fields, more fields. Cows. Cattle. Lines of washing. Towns with their miserable little chimney pots. Signs for life insurance. Paddy had made a will and left her everything. Big houses with gates. More fields. Like going across the steppes of Russia. She had brought a book to read: *Light in August*. Sad, stubborn book. The deep, kind of animal sad. Arriving at a neat little railway station, which had won a prize. Hanging baskets and things. Out in the street, affable, smiling faces. Away from the rat race. Recognised her as a stranger in the town. Tea shops. White scones and clotted cream, and barley sugar in twists. Big geranium in the conservatory of the nursing home. Gigantic, clawlike. Bright orange. Flaming orange. The colour of life. Of fire. White is the colour of death. Paddy's friend Baxter had said that. Had written her a beautiful letter. The names of all those missing had been in the paper. Baxter had tried to be manly. Said life had changed a bit since he last met Nell. Paddy and he had done so many things – gone down a pit in Yorkshire, went about half a mile underground and then into a coal tunnel forty-two inches high, just the two of them. In a PS he mentioned Aphrodite coming out of the sea, then apologised for being a bit stoned.

Nell would do anything not to go up those stairs and meet her husband, anything. Slight hitch. He was in the toilet. She must wait. She'd made a bolt for it. Ran down a passage, through a door, into another narrow passage, and found a white door that slid like a trapdoor. Near-naked woman by the lavatory bowl, looking in at it laughing, roaring with laughter. In her shift. Legs like candles, spent candles, white. Age and death. Youth and death. Nurse saying, 'You can come now. Your husband is ready.' Worst would be over in an hour. Stand up to him, fight back if he should say, 'You left me,' or 'You destroyed them,' or 'It's your fault that he went there.' Needn't have worried. Man in pyjamas, vacant, vacant, sitting upright on bed. Shadow of tyrant who had once been, who had exchanged a 'love, honour, and obey' rigmarole. More metamorphoses. Breathing lightly and staring. Staring. She had to sit. A waiting white chair said to her to sit, and she said back to it, with the little gumption that remained in her, 'I am not here . . . I am not here . . . I am not sitting down . . . I was never married to this man . . . And I do not intend to apologise.' Geranium downstairs bursting with life and rage, brushing the old-fashioned glass of the skylight. A waiting taxi. Freedom only two staircases away. His mouth was moving to say something, the something not coming, the sympathy for his son – for surely he must have read the telegram that she had sent; he must know. Lips squashing, unsquashing, then stretching out like rubber bands, a sound of sorts, but no meaning to it. Lips pursing, nearly saying it, but not. Man in the bed across showing no such rectitude. Roaring like a jackass. A roar she well knew – fathers, husbands, mothers all mingling in. Better take the bull by the horns, but not yet. His lips like mauve, trodden-upon fruits. Eyes very sharp, angry eyes, like nails that dig in. His son dead and his not grasping it. She had said it clearly, very clearly. On the bed, beside him, a pen and pad. Maybe she should write it down. No, that was too drastic. His eyes looking daggers at her. He knew. He was about to pontificate. 'Do you sleep?' she asked. 'I slee . . . eee . . . eee . . . ppppppp,' the words like mince. Getting out the gifts she'd brought. Shades of love, or would-be love. Flowers from the station. Red carnations sunk in a white haze of gypsophila. Red and white. She would give the things

Paddy left her to Tristan. Tristan would save her, as he had before. His birth had saved her when she was in the dumps – his little kisses, the teeth he cut, the teeth he lost, and the sixpences she put in eggcups as rewards. She had brought flowers and a bottle of pink champagne.

Impossible to think she and Walter were once married. He was unrecognisable, and yet recognisable by that sneer, that disdain. Otherwise a stranger, a stranger with parchment skin. No trace of his other self, his gallant self, his dash. They had stood together, proud to be married, a ceremony in the sacristy of a church where a priest grudgingly tied the knot. Workmen as witnesses. Paddy kicking away like blazes, saying, Let me out, let me out of here. Her firstborn. She was too afraid, afraid of his fragility, the little well in the crown of his bare head giving her the shivers. Two lines of bone, opening and closing like a mouth, saying something. Still, she tried. Got the pepper the day he put pebbles up his nose. He was crawling then. Thought the stones were boiled sweets. She ran and got pepper so that he sneezed like billy-o and then she hugged him and then delivered a bit of a scolding, which he was impervious to. Rascals. They were Walter's, too, his and hers. Sitting upright now, he was telling her slowly but determinedly that he refused hospital food because it was poison. She should have brought baby food. Each word, each bit of word, taking an eternity to get out. Had to be wrenched out.

'Paddy got drowned,' is what she heard herself say, calmly but bluntly.

'You got drowned,' was what she heard back. A smile. Vengeance even in dementia.

'You . . . got . . . drow . . . ned.' A smile within a smile, in the recesses of blur. The eyes, both tortured and torturing, wished to nail her. Man opposite deciding to shout louder and louder for the nurse. The worst was uttered.

'No – Paddy, not me.'

'You got drowned,' he said, triumphant. The speech quite quick, quite clear, and the meaning. The hate he had for her was like a pilot light, waiting not for extinction but to be relit.

She hated him, too, remembered a whole nest of wrongs, yet more than anything she wished that they could throw a crumb to each other, they who never had. Why did they mate? What stars had caused such a strange conjunction? What, now, was the fresh bafflement in his eyes? Hearing others go down to tea, she rose to fetch him some, but once outside she knew that she would not cross that threshold again.

At first it seemed to her that Tristan was breaking, spilling in her arms, his sobs punctuating the little things he was saying so as not to seem so broken. He had gained some hours on the flight from Istanbul, he said. The difference in time between Turkey and home was a difference of hours. At moments she thought he was going to retch. She held him. He held on. It was a clumsy embrace. He would have come sooner, the very instant it happened. She should not have borne it alone. She should not have had to bear it alone. Did she know the people who had given the party? Of course not. Sorry. Sorry. He should not have asked that. He would not ask anything else. Questions were cruel. Everything was said to comfort, to show solidarity. He had gained three hours and that was something. He had brought gifts. He did not say for whom, apart from her. It was a goatskin, dappled, luxurious, a brown that had suffered the scorching heat of the animal's life, so it was almost black. She laid it on the stairs where she and Tristan sat making plans. Plans of a sort. He would go to Paddy's flat and move the things, give them for a jumble sale. Paddy had a little insurance policy, which she said Tristan could have. He didn't want it. He didn't want anything. 'You could live there if you wanted, my pet.'

'No. I'll stay with you, stay with my mother.' In every syllable, in every thought, in every fresh bout of grief he grew closer to her, snatching with one hand at the fringeing of the rug for comfort, his other arm shielding his eyes from the light. A window smothered in creeper looked in on them, each leaf of it smarting in the heat. He inquired about the summer. It had been warm, though not as warm as where he had been. He had eaten a lot of yogurt – grown fond of it, to his surprise. Been invited into houses that were out in the wilds, dogs following the truck, big dogs with muzzles, leaping up; the women in the houses were veiled, veiled and spinning. Got drunk with his friend Andy on his last night in Istanbul. Met many carpet merchants, in one tavern after another; got back to his lodgings somehow, his pockets full of business cards, replete with the names and addresses of numerous carpet dealers.

'Where's Charlie?' he said, looking around, ready to whistle.

'Charlie . . .' she said, flustered, knowing that he had known before she even started to speak. Charlie's crying had got to her, 'bitten into' her, as she said, using the word 'banshee' more than once. He did not say 'How could you?' but, as he suddenly stood, a brute determination seemed to rise in him, and he trembled with hate.

'I couldn't sleep, I was going mad,' she said, and tried to make him imagine the house empty, the hoping, the ebbing of hope, and then Charlie, and then Charlie. It seemed a long pause, too long, as Tristan's tongue sought words to annul the spleen that had just entered him, but finally he said he would go straight to the Dogs' Home and find Charlie, no matter what.

Find him he did, so there was a truce of a kind as Charlie pattered around, much quieter now, much more subdued, almost speaking to them – so happy was he to be back, so abjectly happy, licking even her who had consigned him to exile. A tick under Charlie's ear had to be removed. She fetched her tweezers and watched Tristan filch it out, deftly and with love; he showed her the fat, squat belly of blood, Charlie's blood, which had supplied the tick's homestead for the week. Charlie mewled with excitement, relief; he showed not a trace of venom as she held him. Then he was ensconced in the bath, a thing she would normally have objected to. They took turns soaping him. She thought, Tristan doesn't hate me now – it was a passing thing. Later, he poured boiling water on to a soup plate, dunking the tweezers into it to sterilize them. Tristan and she were near now. They would hold each other up, be props for each other. She did not know then that he, too, would go. She did not know the change that would take place in him once the death had sunk in, how dark and troubled he would become. She did not know that he would not shave for weeks, or eat, and that he would not talk or be talked to.

Penny had still not appeared. After Nell had sent her the account of her dream about the Tivoli Gardens, and appropriate condolences, she got a letter back with somewhat similar sentiments except that it ended with 'I knew him better than anyone in the world and yet I didn't know him.' Ending with that. Others had written such beautiful things, heartfelt things. A girl who had done group therapy with him had written a poem for Nell, a poem that said, 'It was only a dream that I had a son.' A cleaner from Paddy's school, saying he had visited her after she had an operation. Tributes from his teachers. Getting to know him through his friends. Baxter asked if he could have his pipe as a keepsake – his awful, smelly old pipe.

In the two weeks that followed Tristan's arrival, the two of them tried to be buoyant, tried to make jokes, had suppers in front of the television. He made a point of talking about Paddy – of plays he had directed at school and leading ladies he had fallen in love with. He had been sent home once for drink, she said, he and a friend called Norrie, and she described the two boys going to a Turkish bath to sweat out their guilt. She kept urging Tristan to see friends, his own and Paddy's. Tristan left notes, such as 'Gone to mow a meadow.' Charlie followed him like his shadow, lay in wait behind the front door. Charlie knew his footstep two streets away. Charlie was bounced in his arms, flung up to the ceiling, caught on the way down, and then tossed up again like a pancake. Tristan had arranged with his university for permission to bring Charlie and put him in a kennel nearby. He had not discussed it with her. That was the first wedge in their nearness. She thought, To the outside world we seem near, but something has happened; he is disappointed in me, he thinks I am wallowing in my grief, but he doesn't know what it is to be older and to be a mother. She bought him gifts, bribes. She thought about a time long ago, in the country, when she had crossed a meadow to pick a few rhododendrons that took her fancy, the deep-red ones. From afar they looked massed, each flower brushing against its neighbouring cluster of petals, but close up that was not the case at all; each flower was on its own little stalk – separate, surviving, the way it is with every living thing.

The memorial service was to be a grand event, which many dignitaries were to attend. She had her ticket, a yellow ticket ornamented with the crest of the Cathedral. The mourners were invited to gather in the Glaziers' Hall afterward. She shrank from the pomp and stoicism of it: 'The Lord is my shepherd, I shall not want.' Untruer words never spoken. Tristan decided at the last minute that he would not come up from university, though he did not say why. His grief had become darker, and he was having quarrels with people. He and another boy had had a fistfight in chambers. 'Please do not write to me for the time being,' Tristan had written. Her tribulations were getting to him. He didn't shave. He didn't eat. The proctor believed Tristan's grief would run its course. Tristan kept Charlie in his room – was allowed to, in clemency.

On the steps of the chapel she saw the relatives, whom she had last seen so squashed and numb, now loquacious, rallying. They wore hats or head scarves in bright colours. Few were in black. Why hadn't she come to the meetings? Why had she gone into the woodwork? Why? She must know that it was important that everyone fight the fight, that it was not the time for wallflowers.

'I wasn't able,' she said, pleading ill health. Ill health! Men on drink, women on tranquillisers, families wrecked beyond redemption, and she couldn't give her support. As she turned to escape, a young man approached, touched her sleeve, and at that touch she felt a premonition. He was thin, wore a threadbare gabardine coat, and had the bluest eyes she had ever seen. They reminded her of school ink. His hair – soft brown and closely cropped – was like the bristles of a shaving brush upon his meek skull. Everything about him was crushed, shorn.

'I was the last person with your son. We met on that boat.'

'Don't,' she said. It pierced. A quite different stab from when the news was first broken to her.

'I have wanted to talk to you. I have phoned but I didn't have the guts to speak.'

'So it's you,' she said, inflamed. At first she had thought the hang-ups were journalists; later she believed it was Tristan, wanting to give her a pasting, a piece of his mind.

'How could you?' she said.

'Nerves,' he said, and laughed skittishly. How she disliked him. How she took that laugh for insolence and hated his little blackheads.

People were passing on either side, and she wanted to join them, to go inside, to suffer the sermons, the fugues, and the hymns, to get it over with because a rage engulfed her, a rage at this young man who had just told her he met her son on the boat, had hit it off with him because of their interest in the theatre. He was an actor – yes, an actor, he stressed. He was determined that she should listen. He had to tell her. Like it or lump it. For six weeks he had been preparing his confession, and here it was: he and Paddy had gone down to the loo together, both dying for a leak, so they decided to toss for it.

'A leak,' she said, affronted.

'Yes, a leak, and we tossed for the loo, and he went in, and next thing I know it's happening. I see black, blackness. I am being sucked into it and all I hear is screaming – somebody saying, "Elsa can't swim! Elsa can't swim!" and I don't know if I'm swimming, but I must be, because I'm moving through this black hellhole. I bump into something; it thumps me and – would you believe? it's a barrel – so I cling to it, or it clings to me . . . This barrel and myself in the wilderness, and "Elsa can't swim" in my bloody head . . . Then a bridge, a fucking bridge, the stone base; I touch it, my tombstone, and I'm so fucking wet and winded that I am thankful to be about to die, thankful to give it all up.'

'Except that you didn't,' she said, her eyes now on the wobble of his Adam's apple, which looks like a goitre.

'No, I didn't,' he said sadly, and withdrew for a second into some corner of his thinking before describing the mercy ship that was lit up like a bus, the arms – several arms – hauling him through, though he didn't want to go, he wanted to be dead. Once on board, a bloody sight, shivering and shaking. He needed a brandy, but the barman said, 'if he needs a brandy, someone's got to pay for it,' and at first no one did. Then a girl called them all shits, throwing her biker's jacket on the counter, saying she'll pay for the drink. He can still see the studs on her jacket, blinking at him.

'Why in Christ's name did you tell me all this?' Nell said and ran, ran past the people, down the steps, and into a taxi that has just disgorged some smartly dressed mourners. She asked to be taken to the river.

November again, the holy souls, the rain. She would pray that she might pray in earnest. The rain beat slantwise down the long office window and soaked into the woodwork. Soaked into the bricks of the houses, too, altering the shades of colour, so they were like abortive frescoes. She had promised herself that she would go back to Italy, she hoped with Tristan. Something about seeing frescoes. She dreamed one night that Tristan had written her a letter of forgiveness, on parchment, and that it was headed by a Leonardo da Vinci painting. She dreaded Christmas, breaking-down time. There were invitations, oodles of invitations, including one from a family in Guildford, one from an author whose book she had worked on, and one from her boss and his mistress, Miss Flite. Yes, he had made the break – rather, had made it three times, and each time before had gone back to his wife, each time taking a holiday with her – a 'second honeymoon', as it was called – and the last time, in the Lake District, they had almost frozen to death and had not had the heart left to warm each other. Miss Flite had won. A bitter divorce and smears in the newspapers and his getting suddenly older, much older-looking – the shame of it all being too much, too wounding. They were welcome, she and her son, to stay overnight. The one thing that could not happen was for them to be alone. When you are empty and depleted, being alone with someone you love is quite the worst, most ghastly thing. When she asked Tristan on the phone, he said, 'We'll see, we'll see.' He seemed not to want to go. Probably a girl. Normally, he talked about the girls – their beauty or their prettiness, their little ways, such as who was shy, or who loved horseback riding – but this girl, whoever she was, was an enigma.

It was a manor house, with open fires and plenty to drink. Neighbours called throughout the day. A big tin of caviar was opened after Mass. People were so nice to her; even Miss Flite had taken special trouble with her gifts. Miss Flite had given her a woolly, but a very special woolly, a grey shawl that was half cashmere. Tristan was a success with them all. He carried in logs, he mended the record-player, he put on the records that Miss Flite loved – the jazz records she danced to so beautifully that people looked and thought, What carriage, what carriage! Nell kept having to disappear in order to cry. Secret crying, like secret drinking. Someone or other called her, called her name, because they knew. Christmas was not a time to brood. At midnight Mass she had prayed both for Paddy and to him, but went awry. Luckily, Nell and Tristan had got there late and had to squash in anywhere they could, so that she was with strangers; it was strangers' hands that she shook and wished peace upon, though she was in torment. The turkey was delicious, the stuffing a triumph. Stuffing from a recipe in a French magazine, with unusual things in it – smoked oysters and angelica. She drank champagne, glugged it. Tristan watched her drinking and gave a little cautionary wag of a finger. Upstairs she cornered him to give him his present – mistake; it meant that she was recalling to him her asylum of woe. What she gave him was a leather briefcase with his initials and, inside, a little photo album of Paddy and himself from infancy on. There were too many words on her card, endearments. He was edging from the room toward the door, down to the others, down to Charlie, and the pheasants for tomorrow that he was to help Miss Flite with, to pluck.

'Are you cold, love?'

'I think they want us downstairs.' Dancing attendance on Miss Flite, helping with the fire, the Christmas crackers, carrying the box of truffles around. When he kissed her good-night and she asked if there was anything wrong, he said, 'Tush.' 'Tush' was his word now, both a propitiation and to ward her off. She heard him on the phone to the railway station, making an inquiry about trains to Exeter. In a way she was relieved. They must each grapple with it alone. Each in his dripping cell.

Easter. Soon the Easter bells would be ringing out, masculine and feminine, pewter and lead, bongs of resurrection. Oh, to meet the risen! She and Tristan were going to a Russian Mass. She had asked him on the phone. He lost no time with her as he came in, with only a small bag. He was saying something as he came through the kitchen door, his jacket slung over his shoulder. It was warm as summer, with gnats in little swarms outside.

'I think you had better know –' he began, his eyes fixed firmly on her, saying, by their expression, 'Don't interrupt and don't try to make it easy.' She was thinking that he had come home to say that, in fact, he would rather spend Easter with friends, and that she would retaliate by saying what a good thing that would be, and how it was not healthy to be hatching indoors with her, and how she understood, understood.

'Penny and I are going to live together.'

'Penny,' she said, and although she had not shrieked, it seemed as if she had. 'Have you been seeing Penny?' she asked, with as much composure as she could muster. Her heart was beating against her blouse, beating wildly.

'Yes,' he said quietly.

'How did you run into her?' she asked, trying to hide the scalding curiosity that gripped her. Why hadn't she known? Why hadn't she been told? In deference or distractedness, she was also offering a plate of hot cross buns.

'She wrote to me after Paddy died,' he said, and then blurted out that Penny was having a baby, his voice a little shy and a little solicitous and, above all, concerned.

'His,' Nell said, unable to say Paddy's name, unable to join them together.

'Maybe his,' he said, and looked away.

'Maybe his, but maybe not his – what does that mean?'

'She's not sure,' he said, his face still turned away, obviously wishing that she would not make it as brutal as this.

'She's a slut,' she said. The word had tumbled out of her.

'She's not a slut,' he said, with a cold look.

She gripped his arm, deciding that somehow she must reach him, she must reason with him, point out that he was young, at university, and that he did not have to take on this legacy, this lie. Then, in a terrible instant, she saw his resemblance to Paddy, the transmitted resemblance of his face when he hated her.

'We can always have the bloods tested,' she said, waspishly, her voice octaves high.

'What would be the point?' he said, gall in his voice.

'So you're going to live with her?' Nell said – her turn now to walk away, to swallow the curd of banishment. He said yes, that for now Penny could not be alone – she had nightmares, she was racked with guilt, she was frightened and going to have a child.

'Do you love her?' she asked, each word cutting him like a hacksaw. He didn't answer. He had taken on his brother's mantle and, possibly, his brother's love. Or was it sacrifice, needless sacrifice?

'Is it pity you feel?' she asked, unable to hold her tongue.

'It's not pity, Nell,' he said, and the tart way he pronounced her name made her feel that he was finished with her. In desperation, she heard herself reverting to Penny's previous pregnancy – the 'high on poetry, short on prams' scenario, as Nell put it. Would that she had not voiced it. Would that she had not.

'If you saw her you'd believe her,' he said, then shouted, in case she needed to know, the lyrical name of the maternity ward where Penny was to be admitted, and the name of her obstetrician, who was a woman. Nothing more. When he left the kitchen, it was obvious that he was going to his room, to pack some of the things he had left at home, and obvious, too, that this was the final breach.

She walks now with a vengeance, with the malice of the destinationless and the pounding of someone who will not concede that she has nowhere to go. She believes it to be her last walk. She cannot go on. She might as well never have had children or a husband or parents – phantoms all. She thinks that no one will ever know or should know the spleen within her. This walk is her last. In the shop-windows she knows so well are the things she knows too well. A necklace from Africa, each pendant a golden acorn, the gold dun-coloured like that of icons. Then the wedding dresses in the dry cleaner's, the same batch or an identical batch, dispatched by the newly wed. Successions of them each week. Lifelike, ghostlike. Hanging from the ceiling – cream and ivory and white, creations stuffed with tissue, ready to float. The tissue gives the arms and the chest a sturdiness, so they seem to breathe. The little white arms are asking to be picked up.

Walking, racing, her glance on the ground mostly, seeing cigarette butts, swirls of dust, and, here and there, carbuncles in the pavement where the cement had bulged up. In a restaurant window little meringue cases, not quite sallow and not quite white. A tiny dish of raspberries catches her eye, each one like a rosebud, moist. Only nature can touch her now, a fleeting touch at that. Was he going to Penny for the sake of his brother, or was he going for the sake of himself? Passing a half-finished block of buildings, she reads a sign chalked on hardboard: 'Lads, no work today, go to yard.' Cruelty. Lashings of it. A sudden brain wave, a ruse. She will buy a bottle of champagne and bring it to Tristan and Penny's flat, a bribe to patch things up.

'You see,' she says to herself, 'you are even prepared to lie, simply to cling to him, to cling; you have become as craven as that.'

'But I am doing my best,' she answers, and in an oblong of mirror at the side of a shut shoe shop, she sees a face that bears no resemblance to the face of even half a year ago. A wounded face, eyes stark, upbraiding, all traces of beauty gone. The shoe shop has closed for good, but there are shoes left in the window. They stand, like solitary props, on glass plinths, with a little tag in front of each one of them. Circulars and letters cram the passage inside.

'You don't remember me,' a voice says. She is in the wine shop now, having decided to go the whole hog of hypocrisy. She does not recognise the face or the very blue eyes or the short, brown, upthrust hair, like the hairs of a shaving brush. She should. The man repeats himself and gives his little laugh, his laugh of insolence. Suddenly she does remember and gasps at the sheer galling coincidence of it. He is working here. The actor Paddy met on the fatal night. Why is she here? Why did she cross the road at that point? Only because the other light was green, and she wanted to walk as fast as she could, and she saw a glut of bottles crammed into wooden barrels, plus, as she sees now, lore about wine and wine tasting, which gives her the pip.

'I thought you were an actor,' she says, tartly.

'Not at the moment,' he says, and she detects the same little mendacious sneer from which she retreated on the oratory steps. She inquires about wine. He is fluent with description – adjectives rolling off his tongue, false confidence in his narrow, hurt eyes as he says, in a blasé voice, 'South African, Bulgarian, Italian, Californian, Lebanese.' As if she didn't know. As if she couldn't read. He points to the barrels, and she knows why. A barrel saved him. She remembers that. The iron hoop of the barrel cutting his neck. Part of her – indeed, an almost vanished part of her – wishes to throw the gauntlet down and tell him her latest bombshell and weep. Ridiculous. Feelings have died. Not so – feelings are alive and bucking in her, vicious feelings, growing, like a child that swells but does not come out, an alien battering the walls of her mind.

'I'll have the Mâcon,' she says, to which he asks officiously if she wants the Villages or the Lugny. 'Whichever is cheaper,' she says, and detests the remark, as if she were asking him to take pity on her straits. He pounces on it. He has the advantage. He will give her the better one at the lesser price. She doesn't want that. She does not want charity, especially not his. When they tossed the coin, did he choose heads or tails? His eyes are more cavernous than when they last met. The blue is all fear, droplets of fear. She feels that if she and he were opened up liquid would spill out, gurglings of it; his would be this vitiated blue and hers a viscous black-red. She vows to smash the bottle on the way home and carry the jagged neck like a weapon, a weapon she is no longer afraid to brandish. He wraps it and hands her warm coins, coins so warm that they are perspiring. They disgust her.

'So you don't act any more?' is her parting shot.

'No. I don't act any more. The thing is, I just don't sleep,' he says, and he says it softly, and if there were a moment in this world for a person to forgive another or to initiate a gesture of reconciliation it is this moment, except that she can't – she is all balk, blunder, stammer, umbrage, woundedness and hate – so she flees.

In the luxury and hush of a chapel, she moves among blues and golds, among pews and escutcheons, around the myriad altars, holding the bottle, skulking. She sees the guttering candle flame heaving this way and that, teetering, recovering, swelling, like air being pumped into a bellows; sees the brown oak of the confessionals, the dropsical expressions of martyrs overlooked by sages with sage hands and sage, punitive eyes; she sees virgins like queens, like whores, and in recesses angels, naked, determined to frisk. In the blue dome of the rotunda a vapourish light, the smell and smokiness of the quenched altar candles still linger. A barricade of flowers to one side on an iron rest. Mass has finished. The smell of incense a floating presence. Oddments have been forgotten – gloves, rosary beads, a baby's knitted boot. Candles have been lit, to beam and intercede for those who have fled to their lunches or their copulations or their tennis courts or their gymnasiums.

Plumes of light, spiring, aspiring as in a theatre. She kneels by St. Anthony, he who once brought gleanings of hope. The bottom of the infant Jesus fits snugly, fleshily into the hollow of St. Anthony's outstretched palm. Comical. Both man and child are smiling, as if they shared a joke. She cannot pray and yet she waits, the way someone waiting to be sick waits. There are two black boxes on metal stands. One for alms and one in His honour. She cannot give. That is the truth of it. That is her plight. Her sin. She cannot give. Too much has been taken away from her, everything, her sons, first one and now the other. Galling to see necklaces and lockets and trinkets in the oblong case next to St. Anthony, offerings from those who can give – mothers such as herself, wives such as herself, daughters such as herself. Hers not the only tragedy, except to her. She cannot give. She will not give. She would steal the barricade of flowers from the altar, but they seem so vulgar, so secular, so vast, so overblown. To think that she thought she might pray. What does one do with grief? What does one do with hate? She thinks of refuse dumps. They are everywhere, only a mile or two from your stately manor or your green-grow-the-rushes lake. A phantasmagoria of ashes, plastic, paper, food, condoms, flowers, mush – the afterbirth of all hope, toil and aspiration merged into a grotesqueness that cannot be destroyed. She thinks that she is like that, and calls out to her dead mother – the pity, the raw pity that they had never known that milky oneness, each alone in her slough of dark.

How could the actor have known? At any rate, he is there, chaining his bicycle to the church's black railing. The blue of the chain transparent, the metal inside like a series of snakes, each coil snug in its socket.

'Mass is finished,' she says, harshly, harshly.

'I've just come to say my little prayers.'

'Oh, you're religious.'

'Let me tell you,' he says, and he moves toward her, his hackles out now, his moment for retribution. She may think he killed her son. She may think he cadged a ticket to life. She has another guess coming. He would gladly have died. Yes, lady, to relive the moment before the toss of the coin, the heave-ho, the black, watery hole that he squirmed in is worse. He has been there. Knowing that everyone else has forgotten it, the shemozzle has died down, and that you're alone and that you've lost your three lifelong friends isn't a picnic. He laughs, a strange, metallic laugh, and says evidently it was his fate, his karma. His outburst does not frighten her, merely makes her pause for a moment to think.

'Your three lifelong friends?'

He nods. He fears that he has said too much, babbled.

'Say anything, say anything,' she whispers.

'Well, we have dinner sometimes,' and he looks to see if this is too fantastic, but it isn't. 'Jim loved soup, so I make soup, tomato or lentil. We have it in mugs, brown pottery mugs. Pasco and I go swimming – he was a great swimmer, the best swimmer of us all – he's teaching me to dive. Then Hugo, the ringleader, the king, wants diversion. He was going to be a rock star, he had all the makings. He left a song. Well, a bit of a song – "Love Is Gonna Cut You Down". We put different lines to it, different beginnings, different ends. "Love Is Gonna Cut You Down". I make him an omelette, and he throws it back in my face, and he says "Jeeves, it's runny – it's not the way I like it," so I add this and that to it, a bit of grated cheese, herbs, then I whisk it, put it back in the pan, and I brown it and toss it and say, "Is that the way you like it, Hugo?" He loves it. He tells me he loves it. I put a few flowers in a pot on the window-sill, and I say, "They're for you, and they're for you, and they're for you." '

Suddenly he stops, and she sees that he is about to cry and

that he does not want her to see him. She shrinks from pity.
She thinks, How childlike and how beautiful. So this is what
he does with his pain. He regards the dead friends as living,
or at least living in the spot inside him that matters. Most
likely Hugo and he were lovers – yes, they were lovers,
because he now singles him out and says that Hugo did not
want to go to the party, that he woke up and said he'd had a
dream in which his boots were too clumsy for swimming.
They had gone to bed, they had made love, then Hugo's
dream, then Hugo ignoring his dream, then down to the pier
and meeting others, being introduced to Paddy.

'So that's how you manage,' she says quietly.

'Sometimes. Some days are worse. I haven't been to the
bottom yet, the very bottom,' he says. But she already
knows. Then she asks his name. He is called Mitch, short for
Mitchell.

'Maybe you'll visit me sometime, Mitch,' she says, and
gives her address in a voice that falters.

'Or if I'm in a show you'll come and we'll have supper.'
Supper, symbol of another world, a world so far behind both
of them, suave and light-hearted.

'So you will be acting.'

'I hope to. The thing is . . . at the moment, I just don't
sleep.'

Their bodies more or less collide into each other in a
sudden embrace. He is all vertebrae, so it is like holding a
musical instrument that is about to break yet won't. He will
keep faith with something within – innocence, perhaps.

At home there was no barking. Tristan and Charlie had both
left. What met her on the hallway floor were the gifts that she
had left for him – 'necessities', as she called them. A radio, a
blender, a coffeepot, and a packet of fresh coffee beans.
Seeing them as he had put them, in a heap, she thought, He
has not even acknowledged them; he has left them there to
show his anger and confirm his separateness. The note had
slipped down behind. She read it many times. She read, 'Ta
for these things but I don't need them yet. I am never far from

you and always at the other end of the telephone. Thanks too for everything.' He had signed it with love and a little flourish of hasty kisses. It was the PS that touched her most of all: 'Do you remember one summer we all went to Arezzo?' A stab of memory. A wash of words, baptism. They were not like words at all, they were like something animate, touching her, a hand, a voice, a presence from long, long ago, a presence within absence and, yes, within pain, within death. Everything radiant for a moment, as if she reached or was reached beyond the boundaries of herself, as if she had known him, and he her, before – a friendship that transcended time and place and even those little ruses by which we lay claim on one another.

'I can bear it,' she said, and looked around at the air, so harmless, so flaccid, and so still – a stillness such as she had not known since it had happened, or maybe ever. In the stillness there was a silence, but there was no word for that yet, because it was so new, a pale sanctuary devoid at last of all consolation.

'You can bear it,' the silence said, because this is all there is – this now that then, this present that past, this life this death, and the involuntary shudder that keeps reminding us we are alive.

The Gymnasium

KATHY PAGE

MALCOLM WAS HANGING upside down from the bars in the gymnasium at Winhampton. He could feel the veins pushing beneath the skin of his chest, forehead and neck as he pulled himself up. Abdominals. Up and down, up and down . . . The thing was to keep the movement smooth. In about six months he would be free. He was frightened and he needed to be strong. He was waiting for the voice in his head to speak, telling him what to do. He had been waiting a long time. The bar bit into the backs of his knees; he spat out his breath. The muscles of his abdomen screamed and hated him; he hated them back. He counted out an extra five, ten, fifteen – but the voice inside was obstinate and silent.

Often, though not always, it had spoken to him in a gymnasium. Amongst the other sounds – the whine of a pulley that needed oil, the slap of a skipping rope, the thud of weights coming to rest, the grunts of effort, the hiss of his own breath – all regular and muffled in the echoing space, all outside – it would speak itself in the hollow of his skull, very clear. It was a male voice, far firmer than his own. He would have obeyed it if it had ordered him to lead an army against the Queen or walk naked in a shopping mall. When Malcolm looked back, what he remembered about particular times of his life was whether his inner voice had spoken and which gymnasium he had been using. In amongst the weights and machines and mirrors he had experienced the most acute events of his life – every startling insight, decision, mistake – such as to marry Sandra – and moment of truth. After, he'd carried them outside with him like trophies.

It came first when he was fifteen, in the barber's as he paid for his fortnightly haircut. As his right hand scooped up the change, he thought he heard a voice say, 'Go on – ' and he reached for one of the cards stacked by the till. Outside, he examined it. *Boswell's Gymnasium*, it said, in solid Gothic letters, *River Road*. A cold wind tightened his newly exposed scalp and he slipped the card carefully into his wallet.

At that time Malcolm was perhaps slightly shorter than average, and certainly softer and more shapeless than other boys his age. He had never been to a gymnasium, other than the school one, which only consisted of a few ropes, a set of bars and two greasy suede vaulting horses. His nickname was 'coleslaw', everlasting punishment for knowing and once using such a fancy word. But at home, his mother let him do more or less as he pleased. He decided to go to Boswell's Gymnasium after school on Friday.

Just before he set out, he went to the kitchen. His mother seemed almost to be still listening to the radio she'd switched off when he entered: her face was flushed, but absent; her hands steadily kneaded a lump of currant dough. The kitchen air smelled of cinnamon and caught in his throat. He watched her from the threshold, dimly aware of a kind of disgust growing inside him. The heavy hot stickiness of the dough, the formlessness and lack of edge it had – after cooking, the loaf would be crisp, but inside treacherously sweet and soft – it was not proper food, but a trick, made you fat, it turned you into itself, dough – he needed to eat hard, chewy things with substance, flesh, to make flesh – more of it, of him.

'I'm going,' he told her, 'to the gymnasium.' Perhaps he half-expected her to be pleased. She took off her glasses and wiped them on her apron. It wasn't often he saw her eyes.

The skin around them was very pale, softly crinkled as if it had been washed and then dried in a bundle instead of being hung out. There were two reddish dents from the glasses either side of the bridge of her nose.

'In town?' she said, Town was twenty hilly miles away, reached by a bus which stopped running at 5pm. Boswell's Gymnasium was at the furthest extremity, near the docks. She put her glasses back on. 'That'll be a long cold ride,' she commented.

'It's not that far.' He turned to go. Mind over matter, he thought. What I want to do, I can do – and somewhere he'd heard a phrase, I think therefore I am, and that seemed to sum it up. In the hall he took some money from her purse without asking.

The dynamo moaned softly as he cycled across the damp lawn and out, holding himself steady with one hand while he unlatched the gate. His football kit was in a plastic duffle bag, clipped to the carrier of his bike. The first stretch was downhill: he gripped the bars and set himself into the throat of the wind. The sky was a soft deep indigo, the land in silhouette. By the time he reached the town, everything would be lit up. The sound of the dynamo rose in pitch and then merged with the whirr of wheels and the wind in his ears.

His legs were heavy by the time he reached the docks, where only a few intermittent street lights remained. Men, forklifts and vans gathered in a welter of diesel fumes and shouts which faded slowly as he left them behind. Further up, the river narrowed. The big warehouses to his right loomed in the dark, their windows broken or boarded up. He could hear dogs barking.

Inside the gymnasium he stood watching. The lighting came from far above, where dark green metal shades guarded yellow bulbs suspended in a row along the centre of the ceiling. There was a taint of gas from two heaters mounted high on the walls. Several men lay on their backs on benches upholstered in red vinyl, pushing bars of weights from a trestle into the air. Green mats were set at irregular intervals on the floor, and on one of them a thickset man, stripped to the waist, was doing press-ups. Another sat beneath one of several contraptions of wire, rope and pulleys, his feet braced against a wooden frame; another stood loading a bar with huge circular weights, then crouched straining at the loaded bar, his face screwed tight, his stomach bulging above a thick leather belt. Weights lay on the floor like a scattering of giant coins. Belts and several skipping ropes hung from a neat row of hooks. Opposite, the wall was covered in horizontal wooden bars, and hanging upside down from them by the knees, with dumbbells in either hand, was Mr Boswell. Malcolm knew it must be him. Regular as the beat of a clock, he pulled his body up towards his knees, pushing his breath out with a hiss and then let himself evenly down. The muscles of his torso stood out as if someone had outlined each one with a pen. He was perhaps fifty, with a short trimming of mid-grey hair around a bald pate – this, as well as his face, neck and chest, was deep red and glistened with sweat.

When he had finished, Mr Boswell threw a towel over his shoulders and took Malcolm into a small office that reeked of cigarette smoke. He squeezed behind the desk and took out a notebook bound in maroon leather. His hands held the ballpoint pen as if it was something impossibly fiddly, like a needle or tweezers. He printed Malcolm's name in capitals.

'Do I know your dad?' he asked.

'No,' Malcolm said.

'Work round here, does he?'

'No.'

'What's he do then?'

'He's dead.' *Probably* dead, was what Malcolm's mother always said, *if he went on the way he was going.* Mr Boswell wrote out the address.

'That's some distance,' he said, 'how d'you get here?'

'Biked it,' said Malcolm, and Mr Boswell nodded approvingly.

'Good on you,' he said, 'Get kitted out and I'll show you the ropes. Call me Bobby, everybody does.'

'Breathe out,' Bobby Boswell said. 'Yell if you want. Sets

285

of ten. Push it, or you won't get anywhere.' Malcolm pushed; at first it was hard, and then he felt a hot prickling rush of energy fingering its way through him and it seemed as if he could go on forever. He could feel his eyes shining in their sockets. He felt like God; he was among men. Bobby Boswell had lent him a pair of fingerless leather gloves. He pushed what seemed impossible and crushing right above his head, shuddering, time and time again. And afterwards the muscles felt sore but it was a good feeling, a tenderness, as if someone had kneaded and pummelled each one with a rough kind of love.

His mother had gone to bed and her baking was set out on its wire trays, the crusts glazed dark sticky brown. A cheese sandwich lay between two enamel plates on the kitchen counter, alongside a note suggesting he might toast it. Too tired for that, he stood with his back against the stove and clamped his teeth through the soft bread till they met the thick slices of salty cheddar. He chewed slowly, feeling the power of his bite. Bobby Boswell had explained to him how a muscle grew by being used; how he must eat protein; how pain must be overcome; had said he should visit the gymnasium three times a week. But he would go four, five, six if he could. His flesh would transform itself, resist. He would become a metal man; he would slam doors and houses would fall down.

For many years afterwards the orders the voices gave were nothing out of the ordinary. It didn't come often and it never uttered more than half a dozen words. For instance, when Bobby Boswell retired, Malcolm began using another gym in the town centre. There, as he thought about the effect Sandra had on him, how tense he was, waiting for her in Marco's coffee house, how she loosened his tongue, lost him sleep, filled his thought – it had interrupted him with: 'Marry her, then.' And when Sandra left him six years later the voice had said: 'You must get back in the gym.' His attendance had dwindled because he was working and Sandra had liked him to spend evenings with her. Yes, he thought, as he stood in the over-warm, pinkish bedroom of what had been their house, of course I must.

If I want to find someone else, he told himself, I'd better look better than this. He had become a large man, pale as dough, and now it seemed that even his face had gone soft, the freckles and pale lashes adding to the effect. He imagined the loose flesh quivering when he moved, and panicked. She's made me soft, he thought, I've got to get it back, got to. It seemed almost impossible: everything, the whole damn world, the universe was bearing down, bearing down on top of him – he could feel it physically: it wanted to reduce him to nothing – dissolve him and sweep him down a drain in the floor. But he would go back to the gym and try to beat it.

'I need to be strong,' Malcolm said aloud, looking at himself in the empty wardrobe mirror. He pulled back his shoulders, jutted out his chin, 'I need to be strong.'

Sandra had thought the same thing in that room as she'd pondered and plotted and finally managed her departure. But she had had enough of mirrors by then, and instead looked out through the undersize window that gave on to the gardens of Mabel Close, where everything was perfect and neat but so very small, as if someone had decided what space on average was just enough, and if you or your desires grew one centimetre more then it would be too small, no, you would be too big and you would be exiled from Mabel Close and the area and everything. There was nothing good, nothing bright or inventive that didn't look too much in that house, but what could you do? And the exactness of the space was the exact same feeling you'd get from wearing a too-tight skirt – it said: Stay how you are. It said: Be still or you'll hurt yourself and look right stupid. For years she had kept herself from being too large – with diets, with television and pills and prejudice and platitudes – but now she had given up exhausted, and she needed to be strong. There was no one else, she had no money of her own, and she had just come off anti-depressants.

On the morning she was to leave she stood behind the

door and wondered if she would have the strength to open it and step out. But once she was out, she closed the door gently, because suddenly she was afraid her own strength might send the place down like a pack of cards. Thank Christ there were no kids, she thought, as she slipped into the taxi. *We* were just kids, she thought, forgiving everything in the pleasure of her escape, I'm still young.

The gym had changed. The piles of weights had been replaced with shining multi-purpose machines, and music played. Malcolm had to be taught how to use the equipment, and a young man in a turquoise track-suit asked politely whether he wanted to build or tone.

'Build,' he'd said. On days when he didn't feel like going, the voice would come, commanding him. He knew he was building up for something. A change. Once he had wanted to be in the army, but Sandra – and she, he heard, now had a permanent job in the new Community Centre, and had moved into a flat – she had taken that away from him and put him in an office where every day the tasks he had to perform itched at him like mites or flies, tiny, but too many of them to ever shake off, and all for nothing. There must be something, he thought, as he worked the pec deck, the lateral pull down – trapezius, triceps, deltoid; as he did the maximum weight on the lag press – quadriceps, sartoris, extensors – first with both legs, then with one, shuddering the machine – there must be something he could do to stop himself from feeling so bad. His voice would tell him.

About halfway through his workout on the evening of the day in which he'd learned that Sandra was seeing someone else and that his name was Neil, his voice finally did speak. It just said: 'Go there.' It was cunning: if it had told him the whole thing at once, he might have balked. But it went in little stages. It was quiet while he showered and dressed himself, as he drove round to the big Victorian mansion block and sat outside, looking at where Sandra lived; silent as he got out and crossed the road. Then it spoke: 'Put your shoulder to it.' And he obeyed, running up the chequered path and crashing into the wood, once, twice, until he was in and turning left – he'd seen where the light was from the car – into the sitting room with its old-fashioned fireplace and a little table with a bottle of wine and two glasses and the television which laughed and cheered as the two of them stood rigid, open-mouthed, and then Sandra said, reaching for Neil's arm, 'It's Malcolm,' and Neil took a step forward saying, 'Look here,' and the voice said to Malcolm, 'Do him,' and so he hit Neil twice, on the chin from below and then on the side of the head as he fell. Sandra phoned the police and he was arrested.

The prosecution called Sandra, who wore a white blouse and no make-up. At first she burst into tears, and the court had to adjourn. But she came back at the new time and spoke in a steady, low voice which made people crane forwards to listen. 'I thought the house was going to fall down,' she said, 'and then he burst into the living room, and wham, just like that, one minute I was happy and the next everything was gone. I still have nightmares,' she said. A psychiatrist had pronounced Malcolm normal, so his defence did not mention the voice. All through the trial, and ever since, it had been silent.

Eight years later, here he was, still waiting. He was beginning to get angry with it. He was beginning to feel it owed him one, after bringing him here to Winhampton to be crushed by the weight of the walls within walls around him, concrete and brick and wire, the sheer bulk and strength of that which had been built to stop him getting out – that voice owed him, the things it made him do, which seemed like mistakes but must, must have some reason, some plan.

'Tell me,' he said to himself as he strapped the belt around his waist. 'Tell me. What is going to happen to me when I get out? What can I do?' And he loaded the bar with what he knew he could lift, and then a bit more and then a bit more than that, crouched, strained – 'Tell me!' He could feel his gut pushing into the belt, his back elongating dangerously, his thighs trying to bunch up, his shoulders pulling from their sockets; he could feel the strings on his neck standing out and the blood in his veins trying to escape from his body. 'You'll do yourself in,' the gym screw said sourly, walking by with a clatter of keys. 'Piss off,' Malcolm said under his breath. He lifted the weights a few inches, but couldn't get himself under it, to push up, and it bounced heavily on the floor.

'You've got to make the most of what you've got,' they told him that afternoon at Welfare as he bent despairingly over a questionnaire designed to find out what kind of job he might do on release. It was a new initiative. 'Put down what you're good at.' His hands felt shaky; the pen was difficult to control. The letters had to be written in separate boxes. He nearly put NOTHING, but then wrote GOOD AT WEIGHTS. He waited to see what their computer would say to that.

It sent him on a course. He passed his instructor's certificate with distinction; he was released. He went to work in the gymnasium – now called a fitness centre – at Beckenham Leisure. He showed people how to use fitness machines even more gleaming and sophisticated than he remembered – machines which calculated time and rpm and calories burned total and per sec and which he secretly thought were rubbish. There were pictures of the human body on the wall, the muscles and the bones and the tendons, and a drinking fountain by the door. Young women in leotards came into the fitness centre as well as men, and, as he had been taught, he reassured them that it was impossible for them to become unduly muscular, and wrote REDUCING on the top of their programme cards. Malcolm was careful in his dealings with people – polite but distant; he was scrupulous in his obeying of rules – even when two years had passed he remembered Winhampton almost every day. He worked out whenever he could.

In the quiet time just after lunch, an elderly woman wearing court shoes and a beige coat entered the gymnasium.

'Excuse me, this is the gym,' Malcolm called to her from the rower where he was warming up.

'Yes,' she said, prising her shoes off then walking without asking towards the machine designed to build pectoral muscle. He unstrapped his feet and followed her.

'Have you got a membership card?' he asked.

'It's in my bag,' she said as she removed her beige coat, folded it and put it on the floor next to a large handbag. She settled her ample behind on the small plastic seat. She adjusted the weight and angle of the machine.

'It's all right,' she reassured him as she set her hands in position and gripped the foam-covered handles. 'I used one of these at the hospital.'

Malcolm watched, bewildered, as she brought her arms slowly together in front of her face, let them gently back, and explained, slightly breathlessly: 'I need to build up after my operation.' After about five lifts she stopped, searched for a handkerchief, and removed her glasses. They left two red dents either side of her nose.

'You see, dear,' she said as she wiped the lenses carefully, 'I need to be strong.'

Malcolm returned her gaze, He saw that beneath the short-sleeved blouse her chest was perfectly flat, like a man's. He saw that the skin around her eyes was paler than the rest, softly crinkled. Her face was damp. Powder clogged the lines around her mouth and spittle had coagulated in the corners. Malcolm sat down suddenly on the leg press. He smiled. And all at once, as he surrendered to a sudden and curious rushing inside – as if instead of everything being on top of him bearing him down, everything was inside him trying to get out, he knew that his voice had left him for good.

Stalin, Stalin, and Stalin

JONATHAN TREITEL

THE FIRST ANNUAL meeting of the Stalin's Doubles (Ret.) Association took place in the banquet chamber of the Great Hall of the Union, Moscow, in the autumn of 1953. An historic occasion. Columns of porphyry and marble flanked the dining space. An electric chandelier bestowed its myriad lights. The long, burnished table was set with gilt-rimmed crystal glasses, stiff napkins monogrammed with the hammer and sickle, and silver caviar dishes. And, of course, occupying one entire wall, looming over us, a larger-than-life full-length portrait of Him.

Since He had passed away only a few months earlier, this was the first opportunity we had to meet one another in a social setting. Some of us, who had worked in the more isolated regions of the country, had never encountered another Stalin before, and indeed it was not rare for an individual to believe he was the unique specimen in existence (apart from the original, that is).

It should be stressed that we were not literally identical in appearance. After all, His image was known only through idealised portraits and touched-up photographs, plus the occasional blurry news film, so no one expected a Stalin in person to resemble the iconic version too exactly. Besides, several of us had already shaved off the moustache and restyled the hair. To take an extreme example, the lone woman present (Stalin XXVII; real name Olga Kirov, from Vladivostok) would scarcely have been recognisable as a former look-alike at all, now that she had ungummed her moustache and gone in for a blonde perm, were it not for a certain squareness about the jaw and coldness in the eyes.

General conversation, first. We mingled. We did our best to work out who was who, and what aspect of His life (military, agricultural, penological, etc.) we had each been involved in. Fortunately a course in mnemonic techniques had been an integral part of our training – it is vital for a double to know whom to shake hands with, whom to salute, whom to kiss on both cheeks, whom to stride by without a glance – so we were able to link names to faces without too much difficulty. Amazing little coincidences kept coming to light: for example, Stalin XI had addressed a conference of five-year-plan-surpassing peasants in Tselinograd at precisely the same moment as Stalin III had favoured a similar gathering with his presence in Semipalatinsk!

Time to take our places around the long mahogany table. The organiser of the event, Stalin IV (real name Moshe Segal, from Vitebsk), gave a short speech. He was, it turned out, the only one among us still employed in the old profession. He assured us he was kept busy posing for deathbed scenes, and what with the motherland being perpetually threatened by imperialists and traitors, and given that the succession was disputed between Malenkov and Khrushchev, he had every expectation that the demand for busts, dioramas, and so forth would remain strong for some years to come. While his present work (he conceded) could scarcely be compared with the thrill of standing in for the live Leader, he felt honoured to have been and to continue to be of service, and he was confident we all shared in this emotion. (*Applause*.) It was the logic of history that had brought Stalin to the forefront and it was the logic of history that demanded Stalin should have doubles. (*Loud cheers and unanimous cries of affirmation.*)

We rose to our feet. Vodka was distributed; the carafes

were passed always to the left. Glasses were raised. 'Comrades. To Him!' The toast was drunk; then, as one man, we hurled the crystal over our shoulders, and it smashed against the walls and the pillars and littered the floor with iridescent shards.

Now we were more at ease. Each of us in turn narrated: My Most Memorable Experience. The Stalin voice (a raspy Georgian accent) was employed by some, while others preferred to use their everyday voices. And in any case certain doubles had been purely visual, such as Stalin XVI (real name Rahim Muhamadov, from Baku), a simple soul, who knew just a few words of Russian: *Hello. Comrade. Thank you.* In many cases the reminiscences were touching. Stalin V had visited a military hospital in the aftermath of the siege of Leningrad: wounded soldiers had cheered him to high heaven; there had been tears in his eyes. Others partook of the comic. Stalin XXI had been patting a baby in a collective-farm kindergarten near Krasnoyarsk when the baby had turned and bit him on the webby part of his hand between index finger and thumb. He had had to restrain himself from crying out, lest an overzealous bodyguard dispose of the baby and its family. Still others shed a novel light on Him. Few people know, for instance, that throughout the Potsdam Conference He suffered from a painful boil on His back (so Stalin IX informed us), or that (according to Stalin XXII) He sometimes chewed His toothbrush. A handful of Stalins seemed to misunderstand the point of sharing these testimonies. Stalin XV sang a little song about the beauties of the birch forest. Stalin XXX told us how much he loved his wife.

Then the organiser recited: 'Ode to Iosif Vissarionovich Dzhugashvili.' More toasts were drunk: 'To the Party!' 'To Malenkov!' 'To Khrushchev!' 'To History!' The caviar was eaten. Georgian champagne fizzed eloquently. A simple but satisfying meal appeared on the table and was consumed.

And at the end the organiser stood up and declared that though originally this meeting had been planned as a one-time event, since it had been such a roaring success, why should we not come back the following year, and the year after that, and so on *ad infinitum*? *(Resounding applause.)* 'His spirit lives on!'

Some of the Stalins who hailed from the more distant republics suggested that the next session should convene outside Moscow. The point was well taken. Where, then? Stalingrad was mooted, as symbolically appropriate. Also proposed were Stalinsk and Stalino. However, the three locations that seemed to command the widest support were the cities known subsequently as Brasov, Varna, and Donetsk, but named at that time, respectively, Stalin, Stalin, and Stalin. After much discussion, it was agreed that we should reconvene the following year in Stalin.

The 1954 meeting was on a smaller and in some ways more intimate scale than the previous year's. The table was round. A plaster bust of Him was arranged as a centrepiece on a bed of dried ferns and thorny foliage. Hardly so many doubles showed up, since the travel distance was prohibitive for some, and others had more pressing engagements. As for those who did come, their resemblance to the original had decreased, partly owing to the ageing process (Stalin XIV had developed alarming jowls, and Stalin XIX was halfway bald) and partly to changes in masculine fashions. But such things are only to be expected: if Stalin Himself were alive today, He would not be so very much like Stalin.

The usual toasts were drunk: 'To the Party!' 'To Khrushchev!' 'To Malenkov!' 'To Stalin!' 'To History!' The lumpfish caviar was much appreciated. The white wine was poured into elegant, slender glasses. For all the air of bonhomie, however, the meeting was not going with quite the swing of the previous year's – it is always a mistake, arguably, to try to repeat past successes – until Stalin XII (real name Sergei Balin, from Moscow), currently employed as a telephonist at the Institute for Agronomical Development, revealed the outcome of his researches. He explained he had been working on a hunch that Stalin surely could not have been the only statesman to have possessed doubles: he had been undertaking an investigation to contact the stand-ins for other world leaders.

We held our breath. We glanced toward the swinging doors: two butlers stood on duty with grenades in hand. At any moment, we fantasised, a score of Churchills and Roosevelts could march in, re-creating the Yalta Conference many times over. Or might there still be some surviving Lenins – even a handful of mock Trotskys hiking in from Siberia?

Balin held up his hand. He regretted that, for all his diligence, he had been unable to find evidence of visual doubles, but – and here he switched on a loudspeaker system connected to the international switchboard – he had on the line a certain Norman Jones from London. Jones came over loud and clear for the most part – just a little crackly sometimes, and accompanied by a strange, watery echo. He greeted us in Russian and then announced that he had been a Churchill in his time. Nothing too grand, mind you – he just used to read speeches on the wireless, and record orations previously given by the real Prime Minister, for subsequent retransmission to the United States and the colonies. He delighted us with a medley of his all-time favourites: 'Blood, toil, tears, and sweat,' 'Some chicken. Some neck,' 'We shall fight on the beaches,' and so forth. His 'An iron curtain has descended across the Continent' was perhaps not altogether in the best of taste . . . But even those of us who could not understand English were duly impressed by Jones' immaculate growl and lisp, and his virtuoso imitation of the sucking of saliva through false teeth.

And what about the American? Surely Roosevelt, that poor invalid, must have sent in stuntmen to cope with his more pressing engagements? But apparently not. At least no deutero-Roosevelt had so far come to light. Besides, as Stalin VIII (real name Boris Backev, from Kiev) pointed out, if Roosevelt had possessed a double, the President would never have been permitted to 'die' at such an inconvenient moment in 1945 – the double would have stood in until the conclusion of the war, at least.

At this suggestion, the same thought ran through all our heads: why did *He* have to die? Surely any one of us in this room could have done a passable job as Chairman of the Party and Leader of the State. We could have carried on the torch. Why, indeed, need He ever die? New generations of doubles could be selected and trained – rendering Him virtually immortal.

The connection from England had been cut, and the wine had run out. It was time for us all to go home.

The third meeting took place in a back room in the regional Party headquarters at Stalin (not the same Stalin as the previous year's location) in October of 1955. Perhaps it had been poorly advertised, or there were difficulties with the hotel reservations, for only a dozen or fifteen doubles showed up. A colour reproduction of Stalin was framed on the wall above the samovar. In some ways, you could say, this was a more friendly, a more confidential occasion. The toasts were repeated several times ('To the Party!' 'To Krushchev!' 'To Stalin!' 'To History!'). Caviar was not available this year, but the bortsch was exceptional. Some of the more jovial, not to say rowdy, Stalins participated in an informal competition to imitate His facial expressions – the generous smile, the air of concern at the fate of His people, the jolly-worker-just-like-you chuckle, the grim glare. The prize, supplied by Stalin XIII, was a cut-throat razor still clotted with soap and a few bristles from His chin. It was won by Stalin XV, largely on the strength of the almost frightening verisimilitude of his stern stare-into-the-middle-distance.

Stalin XXII (real name Iosif Zaharudov, from Ulan Bator) stood up and cleared his throat. He declared he felt called upon to say a few words lamenting the comparative lack of interest in Stalin among the youth of today. For instance, the heroic acts He performed in His childhood (combatting the hoarder, foiling the incipient capitalist, denouncing the spy) are no longer taught to schoolchildren as paradigms of socialist behaviour. Although the spirit of this contribution was in accord with our general thinking, it was felt by many of us that it was perhaps too serious, too melancholy even, for what was, after all, supposed to be a festive occasion.

We departed early.

The 1956 session was the last. We all knew that. Originally, it had been scheduled for September in a police barracks in one of the cities called Stalin, but the city had changed its name the previous month – a bad omen, surely – and, besides, the prospective attendance was down.

So on a wintry October evening we came, less than ten of us, up the three flights of stairs and along the narrow corridor into the cramped living room of Stalin IV's apartment in a Moscow suburb. We sat on the acid-green sofa and on rickety kitchen chairs; a few latecomers had to slump on the rug. A black-and-white photograph of Stalin was stapled to the side of the bookcase.

What had happened was that in February Khrushchev had denounced Stalin's 'crimes' in the course of a long, fiery speech at a closed session of the Twentieth Party Congress. To be sure, this speech had officially remained secret, but everybody knew.

No one wanted to be the first to break the silence. Eventually Stalin IV, who had arranged the first triumphal meeting of our association three years earlier, mumbled, 'I never said He was perfect.' And we all agreed that everybody is human, and mistakes will happen, and no doubt even He made the occasional error of judgement.

Stalin XII recalled that he had delivered a fiery speech in court denouncing Sirin as a Trotskyite agent, and probably Sirin was innocent after all. Well, it is easy to be wise in retrospect.

And each of us had similar anecdotes. Stalin VI had played his part in several show trials of officers in the vicinity of Vladivostok in 1937–38, knowing full well they could not *all* have been Japanese spies, monarchists, sodomites, and so forth.

Stalin XXX, who had told us three years before how much he loved his wife, had had to denounce his father-in-law.

Stalin XVII had even been responsible for the arrest of another double (Stalin XVIII [deceased]) as a Zinovievite deviationist.

In fact, not one of us could claim to have doubled for only the better side of Stalin's personality. We all were tainted. But it is not as if (we argued) we were individually responsible. Doubtless, had we been acting *in propriis personis*, we would not have dreamed of behaving so brutally, but we had simply been doing what Stalin Himself would have done, had He been able to spare the time.

But was that really the whole story? Stalin VI recalled how several times, when he had been given only the vaguest instructions – for example, to attend a show trial and give the usual kind of testimony – he had fulminated viciously against the defendant, whereas, in fact, a milder reproof might well have been acceptable. And each of us could think of similar instances from his own experience. Indeed, looking back, we realized we had been given quite a free hand in the construction of the role, and possibly we had exaggerated the bloodthirstiness.

In fact, on reflection, we doubles had been responsible for a number of the more tragic aspects of that sorry era. It might have been that Stalin Himself was reasonably gentle. If only we had not misunderstood!

The bottle of vodka had rolled under the sofa, so it had to be kicked into the open. Shots were poured into glasses and cups and tooth mugs and bowls. Nobody felt like toasting Stalin or Khrushchev or the Party. Finally somebody blurted, 'To History!' and we all drank to that.

Two of Them

ROSE TREMAIN

WE USED TO be a family of three: my mother, Jane, my father, Hugh and me, Lewis. We lived in a house in Wiltshire with a view of the Downs. At the back of the house was an old grey orchard.

Then, we became a family of two and three-quarters. I was fourteen when this happened. The quarter we lost was my father's mind. He had been a divorce solicitor for twenty years. He said to me: 'Lewis, human life should be symmetrical, but it never is.' He said: 'The only hope for the whole bang thing lies in space.' He said: 'I was informed definitively in a dream that on Mars there are no trinities.'

My mother searched for the missing bit of my father's mind in peculiar places. She looked for it in cereal packets, in the fridge, in the photographs of houses in *Country Life*. She became distracted with all this searching. One winter day, she cried into a bag of chestnuts. She said: 'Lewis, do you know what your father's doing now?'

She sent me out to find him. He was on our front lawn, measuring out two circles. When he saw me he said: 'Capital. You're good at geometry. Hold this tape.'

The circles were enormous – thirty feet in diameter. There were two of them. 'Luckily,' said my father, 'this is a damn large lawn.' He held a mallet. He marked out the circles by driving kindling sticks into the grass. When he'd finished, he said: 'All right. That's it. That's a good start.'

I was a weekly boarder at my school. In the weekdays, I didn't mention the fact that my father had gone crazy. I tried to keep my mind on mathematics. At night, in the dormitory, I lay very still, not talking. My bed was beside a window. I kept my glasses on in the darkness and looked at the moon.

My mother wrote to me once a week. Before we'd lost a quarter of one third of our family, she'd only written every second week because my father wrote in the weeks in between. Now, he refused to write any words anywhere on anything. He said: 'Words destroy. Enough is enough.'

My mother's letters were full of abbreviations and French phrases. I think this was how she'd been taught to express herself in the days when she'd been a débutante and had to write formal notes of acceptance or refusal or thanks. 'Darling Lewis,' she'd put, 'How goes yr maths and alg? Bien, j'espère. Drove yr f. into Sibury yest. Insisted buying tin of white gloss paint and paint gear, inc roller. Pourquoi? On verra bientôt, sans doute. What a b. mess it all is. You my only consol. and hope now.'

The year was 1955. I wished that everything would go back to how it had been.

In mathematics, there is nothing that cannot be returned to where it has been.

I started to have embarrassing dreams about being a baby again – a baby with flawless eyesight, lying in a pram and watching the sky. The bit of sky that I watched was composed of particles of wartime air.

I didn't want to be someone's only consolation and hope. I thought the burden of this would probably make me go blind. I wished I had a sister, someone who could dance for my parents and mime to their favourite songs.

When I got home one weekend, there were two painted crosses inside the circles on the lawn. They were white.

My father had taken some of the pills that were supposed to give him back the missing part of his mind and he was asleep in a chair, wearing his gardening hat.

'Look at him!' said my mother. 'I simply don't know what else is to be done.'

My mother and I went out and stood on the white crosses. I measured them with my feet. 'They're landing pads,' said my mother, 'for the supposed spaceship from Mars.'

I said: 'They're exactly sixteen by sixteen – half the diameter of the circles.'

We sat down on them. It was a spring afternoon and the air smelled of blossom and of rain. My mother was smoking a Senior Service. She said: 'The doctors tell me it might help if we went away.'

'Where to?' I asked.

'I don't know where to. I don't suppose that matters. Just away somewhere.'

I said: 'Do you mean France?'

'No,' she said. 'I think he might be worse abroad. Don't you? And the English are better about this kind of thing; they just look the other way.'

'Where, then?'

I was thinking of all the weekends I was going to have to spend alone in the empty school, if my parents left home without me. Sometimes, boys were stuck there with nothing to do for two days. A friend of mine called Pevers once told me he'd spent a total of seventeen hours throwing a tennis ball against a wall and catching it.

'What about the sea?' said my mother. 'You'd like that, wouldn't you?'

'You mean, in the summer?'

'Yes, darling,' she said. 'I couldn't manage anything like that without you.'

So then it was strange. What I thought next was that it might be better to throw a ball against a wall for seventeen hours than to be by the sea with my father watching the horizon for Martians and my mother reminding me that I was her only hope and consolation.

I got up and measured the crosses again. I said: 'They're absolutely symmetrical. That means he can still do simple calculations.'

'What about Devon or Cornwall?' said my mother. 'They get the Gulf Stream there. Something might blow in. One can never tell.'

My father woke up. The pills he was taking made his legs tremble, so he sat in his chair, calling my name: 'Lewis! Lewis! Boy!'

I went in and kissed his cheek, which was one quarter unshaved, as if the razor had a bit of itself missing. He said: 'Seen the landing sites, old chap?'

'Yes,' I said. 'They're brilliant.'

'*Two*,' he said triumphantly.

'How did you know how big to make them?'

'I didn't. I'm guessing. I think there'll be two craft with four fellas in each, making eight. So I doubled this and came up with sixteen. Seems about right. Everything with them is paired, perfectly weighted. No triangles. No discord. No argy-bargy.'

I waited. I thought my father was going to tell me how the Martians could set about saving the world after they'd landed on our front lawn, but he didn't.

'What do they eat?' I asked.

My father took off his gardening hat and stared at it. 'I don't know,' he said. 'I overlooked that.' And he began to cry.

'It won't matter,' I said. 'We can drive into Salisbury and buy masses of whatever it turns out to be. It's not as though we're poor, is it?'

'No,' he said. He put his hat back on and wiped his eyes with his fists.

My mother found a summer holiday house for us in north Cornwall. It was out on a promontory on a wild hill of gorse. From the front of it, all you could see was the beach and the ocean and the sky, but from the back – the way my bedroom faced – you could see one other house, much larger than ours. It was made of stone, like a castle. It had seven chimneys.

On our first day, I found that a narrow path led up from our house directly to it. I climbed it. I could hear people laughing in the garden. I thought, if I was a Martian, I would land on this castle roof and not on our lawn in Wiltshire; I would go and join the laughing people; I would say, 'I see you have a badminton net suspended between two conveniently situated trees.'

My parents didn't seem to have noticed this other house. Wherever they were, they behaved as though that spot was the centre of the universe.

On our first evening, they stood, hand in hand at the french windows, looking out at the sunset. I sat on a chair behind them, watching them and hearing the sea far below them. My mother said to my father: 'Do you like it here, Hugh?'

My father said: 'Beach is ideal. Just the place. Better than the bloody lawn.'

That night, when I was almost asleep, he came into my room and said: 'I'm counting on you, Lewis. There's work to be done in the morning.'

'What work?' I said.

'I'm counting on you,' he repeated. 'You're not going to let me down, are you?'

'No,' I said. 'I'm not going to let anybody down.'

But then I couldn't sleep. I tried throwing an imaginary tennis ball against an imaginary wall until the morning came.

We made circles in the sand. I was supposed to calculate the exact spot where the sun would go down, as though we were building Stonehenge. My father wanted the sun to set between the two circles.

My mother sat in a deckchair, wearing a cotton dress and sunglasses with white frames. My father took some of his pills and went wandering back to the house. My mother went with him, carrying the deckchair, and I was left alone with the work of the circles. They had to have sculpted walls, exactly two feet high. All that I had to work with was a child's spade.

I went swimming and then I lay down in the first half-made circle and floated into one of my dreams of previous time. I was woken by a sound I recognised: it was the sound of the castle laughter.

I opened my eyes. Two girls were standing in my circle. They wore identical blue bathing costumes and identical smiles. They had the kind of hair my mother referred to as 'difficult' – wild and frizzy. I lay there, staring up at them. They were of identical height.

'Hello,' I said.

One of them said: 'You're exhausted. We were watching you. Shall we come and help you?'

I stood up. My back and arms were coated with sand. I said: 'That's very kind of you.' Neither of them had a spade.

'What's your name?' they said in unison.

I was about to say 'Lewis.' I took my glasses off and pretended to clean them on my bathing trunks while I thought of a more castle-sounding name. 'Sebastian,' I said.

'I'm Fran,' said one of them.

'I'm Isabel,' said the other.

'We're twins,' said Fran, 'as if you hadn't guessed.' And they laughed.

They were taller than me. Their legs were brown. I put my glasses back on, to see whether they had a bust. It was difficult to tell, because their swimming costumes were ruched and lumpy all over.

'We're fourteen,' said Fran. 'We're actresses and playwrights. What are you, Sebastian?'

'Oh,' I said, 'nothing yet. I might be a mathematician later on. What are your plays about?'

'You can be in one with us, if you like,' said Isabel. 'Do you want to be in one?'

'I don't know,' I said.

'We only do it for fun,' said Fran. 'We just do them and forget them.'

'I don't expect I've got time,' I said. 'I've got to get these circles finished.'

'Why?' said Isabel. 'What are they for?'

'Oh,' I said, 'for my father. He's doing a kind of scientific experiment.'

'We've never met any scientists,' said Isabel. 'Have we, Fran?'

'We know tons of sculptors, though,' said Fran. 'Do you like sculpture?'

'I don't know,' I said. 'I've never thought about it.'

'We'll go and get our spades,' said Isabel, 'shall we?'

'Thanks,' I said. 'That's jolly kind.'

They ran off. Their difficult hair blew crazily about in the breeze. I watched them till my eyesight let them vanish. I felt out of breath – almost faint – as though I'd run with them into the distance and disappeared.

That night, my mother got drunk on Gin and It. She had never explained to me what 'It' was. She expected me to know thousands of things without ever being told them. She said: 'Listen Lewis, the tragedy of your father is a tragedy of *imagination*. N'est-ce pas? You see what I mean, darling? If he'd just concentrated on the Consent Orders and the Decrees and so on, this would never have happened. But he didn't. He started to imagine the *feelings*. You see?'

She was scratching her thigh through her cotton dress. Some of the Gin and It had spilled on to her knee. 'So, listen,' she said. 'In your coming life as a great mathematical person, just stick to your *numbers*. Okay? Promise me? You're my only hope now, darling, my only one. I've told you that, haven't I? So don't *start*. Promise me?'

'Start what?'

'What I'm saying is, stick to your own life. *Yours*. Just stay inside that. All right? Your mathematical life. Promise?'

'Yes,' I said. 'What does "It" stand for, Mummy?'

'What does what?'

' "It". What does it stand for?'

' "It"? It's just a *name*, sweetheart. A name for a thing.

And names can make Mummy so happy, or so, you know . . . the other thing. Like your father, Hugh. Darling Hughie. Mostly the other thing now. All the time. So promise and that's it. Understood.'

'I promise,' I said.

The next day my father came to inspect the circles. Only one was finished. Just beyond the finished one was a sand sculpture of a bird. Fran and Isabel and I had stayed on the beach for hours and hours, creating it. They had made its body and wings and I had made its feet.

The bird was huge. It had a stone for an eye. My father didn't notice it. He was admiring the circle. 'Good,' he said. 'Now the other one. I'll give you a hand. Because the time's coming. I can feel it. I've been watching the sky.'

I worked with the child's spade and my father worked with his hands. The sight of his red hands scooping and moulding the sand made me feel lonely.

I waited all day for Fran and Isabel to come. At tea time, it began to rain and I knew they'd be up in the castle, doing a play to pass the time. The rain fell on the bird and speckled it.

It rained for two days. My parents tried to remember the rules of Ludo. I walked in the rain up the path as far as the castle shrubbery, where I sat and waited. I stared at the droopy badminton net. I counted its holes. And then I walked back down the path and went into the room where my mother and father sat and closed the door. They'd abandoned the Ludo game. They were just sitting there, waiting for me to return.

That night, I wrote a note to Isabel and Fran:

> Dear Isabel and Fran,
> When is your next play? I would like to be
> in it, if you still want me to be.
> Yours sincerely,
>   Sebastian

I set my alarm for four o'clock and delivered the note as the sky got light and the larks in the gorse began singing.

When the good weather came back, my father and I mended the circle walls beaten down by the rain. My mother watched us from her deckchair, wearing shorts. Her legs looked very pale. Sometimes, she went to sleep, behind her glasses.

My father seemed very restless and excited. He said: 'It's going to be soon, Lewis. And at night. I'm going to peg down two sheets in each of the circles, I've checked the moon. Visibility should be fair.'

'Good,' I said.

'I'm as prepared as I can be, thanks to you. Bar the food question. But your mother will cope with that. And there's always fish. Fish is a universal; it must be. But there's one other important thing.'

'What?' I said.

'You've got to be there. Your mother thinks this is a lot of drivel, so she won't come. So I'm counting on you. They want to see two of us. I'm as certain of that as I can be of anything. If there's only me, they'll take off again and go back to Mars.'

'Right,' I said.

But I wasn't really listening to him. My mind was on Isabel and Fran who had sent me an answer to my note:

> Dear Sebastian,
> The first rehearsal for our next play is going to be in a tent we've pitched between our house and yours. Friday evening. Ten o'clock. Bring a glass.
> Yours faithfully,
> Isabel and Fran

Ten o'clock was the bedtime of our family of two and three quarters. When we'd been three, it had been later. Now, my parents preferred sleep to life. In a dream, you can be transported back in time.

I tried to imagine saying: 'Goodnight, Mummy. Good night, Dad. I'm going to a play rehearsal now,' but I couldn't. If you are the hope and consolation of anyone alive, you can't go to play rehearsals without warning.

So, I knew what I would have to do. I would have to wait until the house was silent and then creep out of it without being heard and find my way to the tent in the moonlight, remembering first to go into the kitchen and find a glass. The thought of this made me feel very hot and weak. I sat down on the sand, with my arms on my knees.

'What are you doing, boy?' said my father.

'Resting,' I said. 'Only for a moment.'

I stood at my bedroom window. There was a thin moon. Bright but thin.

It was 10.18 by my watch.

I could hear my mother coughing. She said the cough came from the sea air.

At ten thirty exactly, I let myself out of my room and closed my door. I stood on the landing, listening. There was no coughing, no sound of anything.

I went downstairs, holding my shoes. I tried to glide soundlessly, like filmstars glide into rooms.

I got a glass from the kitchen and unlocked the back door and went out into the night. I was wearing a grey shirt and grey flannel trousers and the thing I could imagine most easily was all my grey veins going into my heart.

I moved up the path. I couldn't see the tent, but I could hear laughing – castle laughter. My mind seemed to be in holes, like a badminton net.

The tent was small. I'd imagined a kind of marquee. This tent was low and tiny. It was pitched on a little clearing in the gorse.

I bent down and called softly: 'Isabel? Fran?'

The laughter stopped. I could hear them whispering. 'I've come for the rehearsal,' I said.

There was silence. Then they giggled. Then Fran stuck her frizzy head out. 'You're late,' she said.

I began to explain and apologise.

'Ssh,' said Fran. 'Sound carries. Come inside.'

She opened the little flap of the tent and took hold of my hand and pulled me in.

It was pitch dark in the tent and very hot. I felt blind. Fran said: 'Did you bring a glass?' Isabel said: 'Can you see us, Sebastian?'

There was a familiar smell in the little bit of air left in me to breathe in; it was the smell of gin.

'You like gin, don't you?' said Isabel.

'I don't know,' I said. 'My mother drinks Gin and It.'

They began giggling again. Now, I could see two soft white shapes, one either side of me. One was Fran and one was Isabel. They were wearing identical white nightdresses. Isabel handed me a glass of gin. She said: 'It's quite comfortable, don't you think? We stole masses of cushions. Try the gin.'

'And lie down,' said Fran. 'Relax.'

I took a sip of the gin. I felt it go into my veins.

I lay down, holding my glass in the air. I felt a hand on my face. I didn't know whether it was Fran's or Isabel's. The hand removed my spectacles.

'Don't,' I said.

'We've got to,' said Isabel.

'Why?' I said.

'That's the rehearsal,' said Fran.

'What do you mean?'

'Well,' said Fran, 'don't you want to rehearse?'

'You mean the play?'

'Yes. It's a kind of play, isn't it, Isabel?'

'Yes,' said Isabel.

'Except that there are two of us and only one of you and in the real future, when it's no longer a play, it won't be like that. But it's okay, because we're so alike that in the dark you won't be able to tell which of us is which.'

'What do you mean?' I said. I let my glass tilt deliberately, splashing gin on to my face. The taste of it was beautiful.

They giggled. I felt the skirts of their nightdresses cover my legs, like feathers. Then I saw both their faces above mine and their crazy hair touched my forehead and my cheek.

'Come on, Sebastian,' they whispered. 'There's nothing difficult about it.'

I walked back to our house just as it was getting light.

From high up, I could see my parents on the little front lawn, wearing their dressing gowns and clinging together.

When they saw me, they stared at me in horror. Then my father broke away from my mother and came roaring at me. My mother followed, trying to catch him and hold him back.

'Hughie!' she screamed. 'Don't! Don't!'

But she couldn't catch him. He hit me on the jaw and I fell to earth.

I woke up in hospital, with a wire like a dog's muzzle round my face. I couldn't utter a word.

My mother was sitting by me. She looked pale and tired.

Later, she said: 'It wasn't only that we were worried, Lewis. There was the Martian business. He told me he saw them land. He saw them from his window. And he went running to find you and you weren't there, and then, as soon as he arrived on the beach, they took off again. He thought it was because there was only one of him. And then he was in despair. He felt you'd let him down and let the world down.'

I went back to school. I could move my jaw. Autumn came.

My head had emptied itself of equations and filled up with the faces and bodies of Isabel and Fran.

My father went away. My mother wrote: 'They say it's just for a while, until all's well. But I know that the only *all's well* is you.'

The night after I got this letter, I had a dream. I was at home in Wiltshire. standing in the old, grey orchard.

I saw something come out of the sky and land on the lawn. It was a shadowy thing, without shape or measurable angle, and I knew what it was: it was my life and it was a thing of no hope and no consolation. I wanted to send it into the clouds, but it stayed there, just where it was, blotting out all the further hills.

Lost Ground

WILLIAM TREVOR

ON THE AFTERNOON of September 14th, 1989, a Thursday, Milton Leeson was addressed by a woman in his father's upper orchard. He was surprised: if the woman had been stealing the apples she could easily have dodged out of sight around the slope of the hill when she heard his footfall. Instead she came forward to greet him, a lean-faced woman with straight black hair that seemed too young for her wasted features. Milton had never seen her before.

Afterwards he remembered that her coat, which did not seem entirely clean, was a shade of dark blue, even black. At her throat there was a scarf of some kind. She wasn't carrying anything. If she'd been stealing the apples she might have left whatever contained her takings behind the upper orchard's single growth of brambles, only yards from where she stood.

The woman came close to Milton, smiling at him with her eyes and parted lips. He asked her what she wanted: he asked her what she was doing in the orchard, but she didn't reply. In spite of her benign expression he thought for a moment she was mad and intended to attack him. Instead the smile on her lips increased and she raised her arms as if inviting him to step into her embrace. When Milton did not do so the woman

313

came closer still. Her hands were slender, her fingers as frail as twigs. She kissed him and then turned and walked away.

Afterwards Milton recalled very thin calves beneath the hem of her dark coat, and narrow shoulders, and the luxuriant black hair that seemed more than ever not to belong. When she'd kissed him her lips hadn't been moist like his mother's. They'd been dry as a bone, the touch of them so light he had scarcely felt it.

'Well?' Mr Leeson enquired that evening in the farmhouse kitchen.

Milton shook his head. In the upper orchard the Coxes were always the first to ripen. Nobody expected them to be ready as soon as this, but just occasionally, after a sunny summer, the first of the crop could catch you out. Due to his encounter with the stranger, he had forgotten to see if an apple came off easily when he twisted it on the branch. But he had noticed that not many had fallen, and guessed he was safe in intimating that the crop was better left for a while yet. Shyness prevented him from reporting that there'd been a woman in the orchard: if she hadn't come close to him, if she hadn't touched his lips with hers, it would have been different.

Milton was not yet sixteen. He was chunky like his father and his brothers, one of them much older, the other still a child. The good looks of the family had gone into the two girls, which Mrs Leeson privately gave thanks for, believing that otherwise neither would have married well.

'They look laden from the lane,' Mr Leeson said, smearing butter on to half a slice of bread cut from the loaf. Mr Leeson had small eyes and a square face that gave an impression of determination. Sparse grey hair relieved the tanned dome of his head, more abundant in a closely-cropped growth around his ears and the back of his neck.

'They're laden all right,' Milton said.

The Leesons' kitchen was low-ceilinged, with a flagged floor and pale blue walls. It was a rambling, rectangular room, an illusion of greater spaciousness created by the removal of the doors from two wall-cupboards on either side of a recess that for almost fifty years had held the same badly stained Esse cooker. Sink and draining-boards, with further cupboards, lined the wall opposite, beneath narrow windows. An oak table, matching the proportions of the room, dominated its centre. There was a television set on a corner shelf, to the right of the Esse. Beside the door that led to the yard a wooden settee with cushions on it, and a high-backed chair, were placed to take advantage of the heat from the Esse while viewing the television screen. Five unpainted chairs were arranged around the table, four of them now occupied by the Leesons.

Generations of the family had sat in this kitchen, ever since 1809, when a Leeson had married into a household without sons. The house, foursquare and slated, with a porch that added little to its appeal, had been rebuilt in 1931 when its walls were discovered to be defective. The services of a reputable local builder being considered adequate for the modifications, no architects had been employed. Sixty years later, with a ragged front garden separating it from a lane that was used mainly by the Leesons, the house still stood white and slated, no tendrils of creeper softening its spare usefulness. At the back, farm buildings with red corrugated roofs and breeze-block walls were clustered around a concrete yard; fields and orchards were on either side of the lane. For three-quarters of a mile in any direction this was Leeson territory, a tiny fraction of Co Armagh.

'There's more, Milton.'

His mother offered him salad and another slice of cold bacon. She had fried the remains of the champ they'd had in the middle of the day: potatoes mashed with butter and spring onions now had a crispy brown crust. She dolloped a spoonful on to Milton's plate beside the bacon, and passed the plate back to him.

'Thanks,' Milton said, for gratitude was always expressed around this table. He watched his mother cutting up a slice of bacon for his younger brother Stewart, who was the only other child of the family still at home. Milton's sister Addy had married the Reverend Herbert Cutcheon, his other sister was in Leicester, married also. His brother Garfield was a butcher's assistant in Belfast.

'Finish it up.' Mrs Leeson scooped the remains of the champ and spooned it on to her husband's plate. She was a small, delicately-made woman with sharp blue eyes and naturally wavy hair that retained in places the reddish-brown of her girlhood. The good looks of her daughters had once been hers also and were not yet entirely dispelled.

Having paused while the others were served – that, too, being a tradition in the family – Milton began to eat again. He liked the champ best when it was fried. You could warm it in the oven or in a saucepan, but it wasn't the same. He liked crispness in his food – fingers of a soda farl fried, the spicy skin of a milk pudding, fried champ. His mother always remembered that. Milton sometimes thought his mother knew everything about him, and he didn't mind: it made him fond of her that she bothered. He felt affection for her when she sat by the Esse on winter's evenings or by the open back door in summer, sewing and darning. She never read the paper and only glanced up at the television occasionally. His father read the paper from cover to cover and never missed the television News. When Milton was younger he'd been afraid of his father, although he'd since realised that you knew where you were with him, which came from the experience of working with him in the fields and the orchards. 'He's fair,' Mrs Leeson used to repeat when Milton was younger. 'Always remember that.'

Milton was the family's hope, now that Garfield had gone to Belfast. Questioned by his father three years ago, Garfield had revealed that if he inherited the farm and the orchards he would sell them. Garfield was urban by inclination: his ambition during his growing-up was to find his feet in Belfast and to remain there. Stewart was a mongol.

'We'll fix a day for the upper orchard,' his father said. 'I'll fix with Gladdy about the boxes.'

That night Milton dreamed it was Esme Dunshea who had come to the upper orchard. Slowly she took off her coat, and then a green dress. She stood beneath an apple tree, skimpy underclothes revealing skin as white as flour. Once he and Billie Carew had followed his sisters and Esme Dunshea when they went to bathe in the stream that ran along the bottom of the orchards. In his dream Esme Dunshea turned and walked away, but to Milton's disappointment she was fully dressed again.

The next morning that dream quickly faded to nothing, but the encounter with the stranger remained with Milton, and was as vivid as the reality had been. Every detail of the woman's appearance clung tightly to some part of his consciousness – the black hair, the frail fingers outstretched, her coat and her scarf.

On the evening of that day, during the meal at the kitchen table, Milton's father asked him to cut the bramble patch in the upper orchard. He meant the next morning, but Milton went at once. He stood among the trees in the twilight, knowing he was not there at his father's behest but because he knew the woman would arrive. She entered the upper orchard by the gate that led to the lane and called down to where he was. He could hear her perfectly, although her voice was no more than a whisper.

'I am St Rosa,' the woman said.

She walked down the slope toward him, and he saw that she was dressed in the same clothes. She came close to him and placed her lips on his.

'That is holy,' she whispered.

She moved away. She turned to face him again before she left the orchard, pausing by the gate to the lane.

'Don't be afraid,' she said, 'when the moment comes. There is too much fear.'

Milton had the distinct impression that the woman wasn't alive.

Milton's sister Hazel wrote every December, folding the pages of the year's news inside her Christmas card. Two children whom their grandparents had never seen had been born to her in Leicester. Not once since her wedding had Hazel been back to Co Armagh.

We drove to Avignon the first day even though it meant being up half the night. The children couldn't have been better, I think the excitement exhausted them. On the third Sunday in December the letter was on the mantelpiece of what the household had always called the back room, a room used only on Sundays in winter, when the rest of the year's stuffiness was disguised by the smoke from a coal fire. Milton's sister Addy and Herbert Cutcheon were present on the third Sunday in December, and Garfield was visiting for the weekend. Stewart sat on his own Sunday chair, grimacing to himself. Four o'clock tea with sandwiches, apple pie and cakes, was taken on winter Sundays, a meal otherwise dispensed with.

'They went travelling to France,' Mr Leeson stated flatly, his tone betraying the disappointment he felt concerning his older daughter's annual holiday.

'*France?*' Narrow-jawed and beaky, head cocked out inquisitively, the Reverend Herbert Cutcheon dutifully imbued his repetition of the word with a note of surprised disdain. It was he who had conducted Hazel's wedding, who had delivered a private homily to the bride and bridegroom three days before the ceremony, who had said that at any time they could turn to him.

'See for yourself.' Mr Leeson inclined his tanned pate toward the mantelpiece. 'Have you read Hazel's letter, Addy?'

Addy said she had, not adding that she'd been envious of the journey to Avignon. Once a year she and Herbert and the children went for a week to Portrush, to a boarding-house with reduced rates for clergy.

'France,' her husband repeated. 'You'd wonder at that.'

'Aye, you would,' her father agreed.

Milton's eyes moved from face to face as each person spoke. There was fatigue in Addy's prettiness now, a tiredness in the skin even, although she was only twenty-seven. His father's features were impassive, nothing reflecting the shadow of resentment in his voice. A thought glittered in

Herbert Cutcheon's pale brown eyes and was accompanied by a private nod: Milton guessed he was saying to himself it was his duty to write to Hazel on this matter. The clergyman had written to Hazel before: Milton had heard Addy saying so in the kitchen.

'I think Hazel explained in the letter,' Mrs Leeson put in. 'They'll come one of these years,' she added, although she, more than anyone, knew they wouldn't. Hazel had washed her hands of the place.

'Sure, they will,' Garfield said.

Garfield was drunk. Milton watched him risking his observation, his lips drawn loosely back in a thick smile. Specks of foam lingered on the top of the beer can he held, around the triangular opening. He'd been drinking Heineken all afternoon. Mr Leeson drank only once a year, on the occasion of the July celebration; Herbert Cutcheon was teetotal. But neither disapproved of Garfield's tippling when he came back for the weekend, because that was Garfield's way and if you raised an objection you wouldn't see him for dust.

Catching Milton's eye on him, Garfield winked. No one in the room said Garfield was the reason why Hazel would not return, although it might have been said quite naturally, Hazel being the subject of the conversation.

'Hi!' Stewart suddenly exclaimed, the way he often did. 'Hi! Hi!' he shouted, his head bent sideways to his shoulder, his mouth flopping open, eyes beginning to roll.

'Behave yourself, Stewart,' Mrs Leeson sternly commanded. 'Stop it now.'

Stewart took no notice. He completed his effort at communication, his fat body becoming awkward on the chair. Then the tension left him and he was quiet. *Give Stewart a hug from all of us*, Hazel's letter said.

Addy collected her husband's cup and her father's. More tea was poured. Mrs Leeson cut more cake.

'Now, pet.' She broke a slice into portions for Stewart. 'Good boy now.'

Milton wondered what they'd say if he mentioned the woman in the orchard, if he casually said that on the fourteenth of September, and again on the fifteenth, a woman who called herself St Rosa had appeared to him among the apple trees of the upper orchard. It wouldn't have been necessary to say he'd dreamed about her also: the dream was just an ordinary thing, a dream he might have had about any woman or girl. 'Her hair was strange,' he might have said.

But Milton, who had kept the whole matter to himself, continued to do so. Later that evening, alone in the back room with Garfield, he listened while his brother hinted at his city exploits, which he always did when he'd been drinking. Garfield belonged to an organisation that kept an eye on things. Milton watched the damp lips sloppily opening and closing, the thick smile flashing between statements about punishment meted out and premises raided, youths taken in for questioning, warnings issued. There was always a way to complete the picture, Garfield liked to repeat, and would tell about some Taig going home in the rain and being given a lift he didn't want to accept. Disposal completed the picture, you could call it that: you could say he was in the disposal business. When the phone rang in the middle of the night he always knew at once. No different from dealing with the side of a cow, a professional activity. Garfield always stopped before he came to the end of his tales; even when he'd had a few he left things to the imagination.

Every year Mr Leeson gave the six-acre field for the July celebration. Bowler-hatted and sashed, the men assembled there, their drums and flutes echoing over the Leeson lands. At midday there was the long march to the village, Mr Leeson himself prominent among the marchers. He kept a dark serge suit specially for the July celebration, as his father had also. Before Garfield had gone to Belfast he'd marched also, the best on the flute for miles around. Milton marched, but didn't play an instrument because he was tone deaf.

Men who had not met each other since the celebration last year came to the six-acre field in July. Mr Leeson's elderly Uncle Willie came, and Leeson cousins and relatives by marriage. Milton and his friend Billie Carew were among the younger contingent. It always pleased Mr Leeson and the other men of his age that boys made up the numbers, that there was no falling away, new faces every year. The Reverend Cutcheon gave an address before the celebration began.

With the drums booming and the flutes skilfully establishing the honoured tunes, the marchers swung off through the iron gate of the field, out on to the lane, later turning into the narrow main road. Their stride was jaunty, even that of Mr Leeson's Uncle Willie and that of Old Knipe, who was eighty-four. Chins were raised, umbrellas carried as rifles might be. Pride was everywhere on these faces; in the measured step and the music's beat, in the swing of the arms and the firm grip of the umbrellas. No shoe was unpolished, no dark suit unironed. The men of this neighbourhood, by long tradition, renewed their loyalty and belief through sartorial display.

Milton's salt and pepper jacket and trousers had been let down at the cuffs. This showed, but only at close scrutiny – a band of lighter cloth and a second band, less noticeable because it had faded, where the cuffs had been extended in the past. His mother had said, only this morning, that that was that, what material remained could not be further adjusted. But she doubted that Milton would grow any more, so the suit as it was should last for many years yet. While she spoke Milton had felt guilty, as many times he had during the ten months that had passed since his experience in the upper orchard. It seemed wrong that his mother, who knew everything about him, even that he wouldn't grow any more, shouldn't have been confided in, yet he hadn't been able to do it. Some instinct assured him that the woman would not return. There was no need for her to return, Milton's feeling was, although he did not know where the feeling came from: he would have found it awkward explaining all that to his mother. Each of the seasons that had passed since September had been suffused by the memory of the woman. That autumn had been warm, its shortening days mellow with sunshine until the rain came in November. She had been with him in the sunshine and the rain, and in the bitter cold that came with January. On a day when the frost remained, to be frozen again at nightfall, he had walked along the slope of the upper orchard and looked back at the long line of his footsteps on the whitened grass, for a moment surprised that hers weren't there, miraculously, also. When the first primroses decorated the dry warm banks of the orchards he found himself thinking that these familiar flowers were different this year because he was different himself and saw them in some different way. When summer came the memory of the woman was more intense.

'They'll draw in,' a man near the head of the march predicted as two cars advanced upon the march. Obediently the cars pressed into a gateway to make room, their engines turned off, honouring the music. Women and children in the cars waved and saluted; a baby was helped up, its small paw waggled in greeting. 'Does your heart good, that,' one of the men remarked.

The day was warm. White clouds were stationary, as if pasted on to the vast dome of blue. It was nearly always fine for the July celebration, a fact that did not pass unnoticed in the neighbourhood, taken to be a sign. Milton associated the day with sweat on his back and in his armpits and his thighs, his shirt stuck to him in patches that later on became damply cold. As he marched now the sun was hot on the back of his neck. 'I wonder will we see the Kissane girl?' Billie Carew speculated beside him.

The Kissane girl lived in one of the houses they passed. She and her two younger sisters usually came out to watch. Her father and her uncles and her brother George were on the march. She was the best-looking girl in the neighbourhood now that Milton's sisters were getting on a bit. She had glasses, which she took off when she went dancing at the Cuchullain Inn. She had her hair done regularly and took pains to get her eyeshadow right; she matched the shade of her lipstick to her dress. There wasn't a better pair of legs in Ulster, Billie Carew claimed.

'Oh, God!' he muttered when the marchers rounded a bend and there she was with her two young sisters. She had taken her glasses off and was wearing a dress that was mainly pink, flowers like roses on it. When they drew nearer, her white sandals could be seen. 'Oh, God!' Billie Carew exclaimed again, and Milton guessed he was undressing the Kissane girl, the way they used to undress girls in church. One of the girl's sisters had a Union Jack, which she waved.

Milton experienced no excitement. Last year he, too, had undressed the Kissane girl, which hadn't been much different from undressing Esme Dunshea in church. The Kissane girl was older than Esme Dunshea, and older than himself and Billie Carew by five or six years. She worked in the chicken factory.

'D'you know who she looks like?' Billie Carew said. 'Ingrid Bergman.'

'Ingrid Bergman's dead.'

Busy with his thoughts, Billie Carew didn't reply. He had a thing about Ingrid Bergman: whenever *Casablanca* was shown on the television nothing would get him out of the house. For the purpose he put her to it didn't matter that she was dead.

'God, man!' Billie Carew muttered, and Milton could tell from the urgency of his intonation that the last of the Kissane girl's garments had been removed.

At ten to one the marchers reached the green corrugated-iron sheds of McCourt's Hardware and Agricultural Supplies. They passed a roadside water pump and the first four cottages of the village. No one was about. No face appeared at a window. The village was a single wide street, at one end Vogan's Stores and public house, at the other Tiernan's grocery and filling station, where newspapers could be obtained. Next door was O'Hanlon's public house and then the road widened, so that cars could turn in front of the Church of the Holy Rosary and the school. The houses of the village were colour-washed different colours, green and pink and blue. They were modest houses, none of more than two storeys.

As the marchers melodiously advanced upon the blank stare of so many windows, the stride of the men acquired an extra fervour. Arms were swung with fresh intent, jaws were

more firmly set. The men passed the Church of the Holy
Rosary, then with abruptness halted. There was a moment of
natural disarray as ranks were broken so that the march might
be reversed. The Reverend Herbert Cutcheon's voice briefly
intoned, a few glances were directed at, and over, the nearby
church. Then the march returned the way it had come, the
music different, as though a variation were the hidden vil-
lagers' due. At the corrugated sheds of McCourt's Hardware
and Agricultural Supplies the men swung off to the left,
marching back to Mr Leeson's field by another route.

The picnic was the reward for duty done, faith kept. Bottles
appeared. There were sandwiches, chicken legs, sliced beef
and ham, potato crisps and tomatoes. The men urinated in
twos, against a hedge that never suffered from its annual
acidic dousing – this, too, was said to be a sign. Jackets were
thrown off, bowler hats thrown down, sashes temporarily
laid aside. News was exchanged; the details of a funeral or a
wedding passed on; prices for livestock deplored. The Reverend Herbert Cutcheon passed among the men who sat easily
on the grass, greeting those from outside his parish whom he
hadn't managed to greet already, enquiring after womenfolk.
By five o'clock necks and faces were redder than they had
earlier been, hair less tidy, beads of perspiration catching
the slanting sunlight. There was euphoria in the field, some
drunkenness, and an occasional awareness of the presence of
God.

'Are you sick?' Billie Carew asked Milton. 'What's up with
you?'

Milton didn't answer. He was maybe sick, he thought. He
was sick or going round the bend. Since he had woken up
this morning she had been there, but not as before, not as a
tranquil presence. Since he'd woken she had been agitating
and nagging at him.

'I'm OK,' he said.

He couldn't tell Billie Carew any more than he could tell
his mother, or anyone in the family, yet all the time on the
march he had felt himself being pressed to tell, all the time in

the deadened village while the music played, when they turned and marched back again and the tune was different. Now, at the picnic, he felt himself being pressed more than ever.

'You're bloody not OK,' Billie Carew said.

Milton looked at him and found himself thinking that Billie Carew would be eating food in this field when he was as old as Old Knipe. Billie Carew with his acne and his teeth would be satisfied for life when he got the Kissane girl's knickers off. 'Here,' Billie Carew said, offering him his half bottle of Bushmills.

'I want to tell you something,' Milton said, finding the Reverend Herbert Cutcheon at the hedge where the urinating took place.

'Tell away, Milton.' The clergyman's edgy face was warm with the pleasure the day had brought. He adjusted his trousers. Another day to remember, he said.

'I was out in the orchards a while back,' Milton said. 'September it was. I was seeing how the apples were doing when a woman came in the top gate.'

'A woman?'

'The next day she was there again. She said she was St Rosa.'

'What d'you mean, St Rosa, Milton?'

The Reverend Cutcheon had halted in his stroll back to the assembled men. He stood still, frowning at the grass by his feet. Then he lifted his head and Milton saw bewilderment, and astonishment, in his opaque brown eyes.

'What d'you mean, St Rosa?' he repeated.

Milton told him, and then confessed that the woman had kissed him twice on the lips, a holy kiss, as she'd called it.

'No kiss is holy, boy. Now, listen to me, Milton. Listen to this carefully, boy.'

A young fellow would have certain thoughts, the Reverend Cutcheon explained. It was the way of things that a young fellow could become confused due to the age he was and the changes that had taken place in his body. He reminded Milton that he'd left school, that he was on the way

to manhood. The journey to manhood could have a stumble
or two in it, he explained, and it wasn't without temptation.
One day Milton would inherit the farm and the orchards,
since Garfield had surrendered all claim to them. That was
something he needed to prepare himself for. Milton's mother
was goodness itself, his father would do anything for you. If
a neighbour had a broken fence while he was laid up in bed,
his father would be the first to see to it. His mother had
brought up four fine children, and it was God's way that the
fifth was afflicted. God's grace could turn affliction into a
gift: poor Stewart, you might say, but you only had to look
at him to realise you were glad Stewart had been given life.

'We had a great day today, Milton, we had an enjoyable
day. We stood up for the people we are. That's what you
have to think of.'

In a companionable way the clergyman's arm was placed
around Milton's shoulders. He'd put the thing neatly, the
gesture suggested. He'd been taken aback but had risen to the
occasion.

'She won't leave me alone,' Milton said.

Just beginning to move forward, the Reverend Cutcheon
halted again. His arm slipped from Milton's shoulders. In a
low voice he said:

'She keeps bothering you in the orchards, does she?'

Milton explained. He said the woman had been agitating
him all day, since the moment he awoke. It was because of
that he'd had to tell someone, because she was pressing him
to.

'Don't tell anyone else, Milton. Don't tell a single soul. It's
said now between the two of us and it's safe with myself.
Not even Addy will hear the like of this.'

Milton nodded. The Reverend Cutcheon said:

'Don't distress your mother and your father, son, with talk
of a woman who was on about holiness and the saints.' He
paused, then spoke with emphasis, and quietly. 'Your
mother and father wouldn't rest easy for the balance of their
days.' He paused again. 'There are no better people than your
mother and father, Milton.'

'Who was St Rosa?'

Again the Reverend Cutcheon checked his desire to rejoin the men who were picnicking on the grass. Again he lowered his voice.

'Did she ask you for money? After she touched you did she ask you for money?'

'Money?'

'There are women like that, boy.'

Milton knew what he meant. He and Billie Carew had many a time talked about them. You saw them on television, flamboyantly dressed on city streets. Billie Carew said they hung about railway stations, that your best bet was a railway station if you were after one. Milton's mother, once catching a glimpse of these street-traders on the television, designated them 'Catholic strumpets'. Billie Carew said you'd have to go careful with them in case you'd catch a disease. Milton had never heard of such women in the neighbourhood.

'She wasn't like that,' he said.

'You'd get a travelling woman going by and maybe she'd be thinking you had a coin or two on you. Do you understand what I'm saying to you, Milton?'

'Yes.'

'Get rid of the episode. Put it out of your mind.'

'I was only wondering about what she said in relation to a saint.'

'It's typical she'd say a thing like that.'

Milton hesitated. 'I thought she wasn't alive,' he said.

Mr Leeson's Uncle Willie used to preach. He had preached in the towns until he was too old for it, until he began to lose the thread of what he was saying. Milton had heard him. He and Garfield and his sisters had been brought to hear Uncle Willie in his heyday, a bible clenched in his right hand, gesturing with it and quoting from it. Sometimes he spoke of what happened in Rome, facts he knew to be true: how the Pope drank himself into a stupor and had to have the sheets of his bed changed twice in a night, how the Pope's own mother was among the women who came and went in the papal ante-rooms.

Men still preached in the towns, at street corners or anywhere that might attract a crowd, but the preachers were fewer than they had been in the heyday of Mr Leeson's Uncle Willie because the popularity of television kept people in at nights, and because people were in more of a hurry. But during the days that followed the July celebration Milton remembered his great-uncle's eloquence. He remembered the words he had used and the way he could bring in a quotation, and the way he was so certain. Often he had laid down that a form of cleansing was called for, that vileness could be exorcised by withering it out of existence.

The Reverend Cutcheon had been more temperate in his advice, even if what he'd said amounted to much the same thing: if you ignored what happened it wouldn't be there any more. But on the days that followed the July celebration Milton found it increasingly impossible to do so. With a certainty that reminded him of his great-uncle's he became convinced beyond all doubt that he was not meant to be silent. Somewhere in him there was the uncontrollable urge that he should not be. He asked his mother why the old man had begun to preach, and she replied that it was because he had to.

Father Mulhall didn't know what to say.

To begin with, he couldn't remember who Saint Rosa had been, even if he ever knew. Added to which there was the fact that it wasn't always plain what the Protestant boy was trying to tell him. The boy stammered rapidly through his account, beginning sentences again because he realised his meaning had slipped away, speaking more slowly the second time but softening his voice to a pitch that made it almost inaudible. The whole thing didn't make sense.

'Wait now till we have a look,' Father Mulhall was obliged to offer in the end. He'd said at first that he would make some investigations about this saint, but the boy didn't seem satisfied with that. 'Sit down,' he invited in his living room, and went to look for Butler's *Lives of the Saints*.

Father Mulhall was fifty-nine, a tall, wiry man, prematurely white-haired. Two sheepdogs accompanied him when he went to find the relevant volume. They settled down again, at his feet, when he returned. The room was cold, hardly furnished at all, the carpet so thin you could feel the boards.

'There's the Blessed Roseline of Villeneuve,' Father Mulhall said, turning over the pages. 'And the Blessed Rose Venerini. Or there's St Rose of Lima. Or St Rosalia. Or Rose of Viterbo.'

'I think it's that one. Only she definitely said Rosa.'

'Could you have fallen asleep? Was it a hot day?'

'It wasn't a dream I had.'

'Was it late in the day? Could you have been confused by the shadows?'

'It was late the second time. The first time it was the afternoon.'

'Why did you come to me?'

'Because you'd know about a saint.'

Father Mulhall heard how the woman who'd called herself St Rosa wouldn't let the boy alone, how she'd come on stronger and stronger as the day of the July celebration approached, and so strong on the day itself that he knew he wasn't meant to be silent, the boy said.

'About what though?'

'About her giving me the holy kiss.'

The explanation could be that the boy was touched. There was another boy in that family who wasn't the full shilling either.

'Wouldn't you try getting advice from your own clergyman? Isn't Mr Cutcheon your brother-in-law?'

'He told me to pretend it hadn't happened.'

The priest didn't say anything. He listened while he was told how the presence of the saint was something clinging to you, how neither her features nor the clothes she'd worn had faded in any way whatsoever. When the boy closed his eyes he could apparently see her more clearly than he could see any member of his family, or anyone he could think of.

'I only wanted to know who she was. Is that place in France?'

'Viterbo is in Italy actually.'

One of the sheepdogs had crept on to his feet and settled down to sleep. The other was asleep already. Father Mulhall said:

'Do you feel all right in yourself otherwise?'

'She said not to be afraid. She was on about fear.' Milton paused. 'I can still feel her saying things.'

'I would talk to your own clergyman, son. Have a word with your brother-in-law.'

'She wasn't alive, that woman.'

Father Mulhall did not respond to that. He led Milton to the hall door of his house. He had been affronted by the visit, but he didn't let it show. Why should a saint of his Church appear to a Protestant boy in a neighbourhood that was over-whelmingly Catholic, when there were so many Catholics to choose from? Was it not enough that that march should occur once a year in July, that farmers from miles away should bang their way through the village just to show what was what, strutting in their get-up? Was that not enough without claiming the saints as well? They closed the village down, they kept people inside. Their presence was a reminder that beyond this small, immediate neighbourhood there was a strength from which they drew their own. This boy's father would give you the time of day if he met you on the road, he'd even lean on a gate and talk to you, but once your back was turned he'd come out with his statements. The son who'd gone to Belfast would salute you and maybe after-wards laugh because he'd saluted a priest. There was no one who didn't know that Garfield Leeson belonged in the gang-lands of the Protestant back streets, that his butcher's skills came in handy when a job had to be done.

'I thought she might be foreign,' Milton said. 'I don't know how I'd know that.'

Two scarlet dots appeared high up in Father Mulhall's

scrawny cheeks. His anger was more difficult to disguise now; he didn't trust himself to speak. In silence Milton was shown out of the house.

When he returned to his living room Father Mulhall turned on the television and sat watching it with a glass of whiskey, his sheepdogs settling down to sleep again. 'Now, that's amazing!' a chat-show host exclaimed, leading the applause for a performer who balanced a woman on the end of his finger. Father Mulhall wondered how it was done, his absorption greater than it would have been had he not been visited by the Protestant boy.

Mr Leeson finished rubbing his plate clean with a fragment of loaf-bread, soaking into it what remained of bacon fat and small pieces of black pudding. Milton said:

'She walked in off the lane.'

Not fully comprehending, Mr Leeson said the odd person came after the apples. Not often, but you knew what they were like. You couldn't put an orchard under lock and key.

'Don't worry about it, son.'

Mrs Leeson shook her head. It wasn't like that, she explained; that wasn't what Milton was saying. The colour had gone from Mrs Leeson's face. What Milton was saying was that a Papist saint had spoken to him in the orchards.

'An apparition,' she said.

Mr Leeson's small eyes regarded his son evenly. Stewart put his side plate on top of the plate he'd eaten his fry from, with his knife and fork on top of that, the way he had been taught. He made his belching noise and to his surprise was not reprimanded.

'I asked Father Mulhall who St Rosa was.'

Mrs Leeson's hand flew to her mouth. For a moment she thought she'd scream. Mr Leeson said:

'What are you on about, boy?'

'I have to tell people.'

Stewart tried to speak, gurgling out a request to carry his two plates and his knife and fork to the sink. He'd been taught that also, and was always obedient. But tonight no one heeded him.

'Are you saying you went to the priest?' Mr Leeson asked.

'You didn't go into his house, Milton?'

She watched, incredulous, while Milton nodded. He said Herbert Cutcheon had told him to keep silent, but in the end he couldn't. On the day of the celebration he had told his brother-in-law when they were both standing at the hedge, and later he had gone into Father Mulhall's house. He'd sat down while the priest looked the saint up in a book.

'Does anyone know you went into the priest's house, Milton?' Mrs Leeson leaned across the table, staring at him with widened eyes that didn't blink. 'Did anyone see you?'

'I don't know.'

Mr Leeson pointed to where Milton should stand, then rose from the table and struck him on the side of the face with his open palm. He did it again. Stewart whimpered, and became agitated.

'Put them in the sink, Stewart,' Mrs Leeson said.

The dishes clattered into the sink, and the tap was turned on as Stewart washed his hands. The side of Milton's face was inflamed, a trickle of blood came from his nose.

Herbert Cutcheon's assurance that what he'd heard in his father-in-law's field would not be passed on to his wife was duly honoured. But when he was approached on the same subject a second time he realised that continued suppression was pointless. After a Sunday-afternoon visit to his in-laws' farmhouse, when Mr Leeson had gone off to see to the milking and Addy and her mother were reaching down pots of last year's plum jam for Addy to take back to the rectory, Milton followed him to the yard. As he drove the four miles back to the rectory, he repeated to Addy the conversation that had taken place.

'You mean he wants to *preach*?' Frowning in astonishment, Addy half shook her head, disbelief undisguised.

He nodded. Milton had mentioned Mr Leeson's Uncle

Willie. He'd said he wouldn't have texts or scriptures, nothing like that.

'It's not Milton,' Addy protested, this time shaking her head more firmly.

'I know it's not.'

He told her then about her brother's revelations on the day of the July celebration. He explained he hadn't done so before because he considered he had made her brother see sense, and these matters were better not referred to.

'Heavens above!' Addy cried, her lower jaw slackened in fresh amazement. The man she had married was not given to the kind of crack that involved light-hearted deception, or indeed any kind of crack at all. Herbert's virtues lay in other directions, well beyond the realm of jest. Even so, Addy emphasised her bewilderment by stirring doubt into her dis-belief. 'You're not serious surely?'

He nodded without taking his eyes from the road. Neither of them knew of the visit to the priest or of the scene in the kitchen that had ended in a moment of violence. Addy's parents, in turn believing that Milton had been made to see sense by his father's spirited response, and sharing Herbert Cutcheon's view that such matters were best left unaired, had remained silent also.

'Is Milton away in the head?' Addy whispered.

'He's not himself certainly. No way he's himself.'

'He never showed an interest in preaching.'

'D'you know what he said to me just now in the yard?'

But Addy was still thinking about the woman her brother claimed to have conversed with. Her imagination had stuck there, on the slope of her father's upper orchard, a Catholic woman standing among the trees.

'Dudgeon McDavie,' Herbert Cutcheon went on. 'He mentioned that man.'

Nonplussed all over again, Addy frowned. Dudgeon McDavie was a man who'd been found shot dead by the roadside near Loughgall. Addy remembered her father coming into the kitchen and saying they'd shot poor Dud-geon. She'd been seven at the time; Garfield had been four,

Hazel a year older; Milton and Stewart hadn't been born. 'Did he ever do a minute's harm?' she remembered her father saying. 'Did he ever so much as raise his voice?' Her father and Dudgeon McDavie had been schooled together; they'd marched together many a time. Then Dudgeon McDavie had moved out of the neighbourhood, to take up a position as a quantity surveyor. Addy couldn't remember ever having seen him, although from the conversation that had ensued between her mother and her father at the time of his death it was apparent that he had been to the farmhouse many a time. 'Blew half poor Dudgeon's skull off': her father's voice, leaden and grey, echoed as she remembered. 'Poor Dudgeon's brains all over the tarmac.' Her father had attended the funeral, full honours because Dudgeon McDavie had had a hand in keeping law and order, part-time in the UDR. A few weeks later two youths from Loughgall were set upon and punished, although they vehemently declared their innocence.

'Dudgeon McDavie's only hearsay for Milton,' Addy pointed out, and her husband said he realised that.

Drawing up in front of the rectory, a low brick building with metal-framed windows, he said he had wondered about going in search of Mr Leeson when Milton had come out with all that in the yard. But Milton had hung about by the car, making the whole thing even more difficult.

'Did the woman refer to Dudgeon McDavie?' Addy asked. 'Is that it?'

'I don't think she did. But to tell you the truth, Addy, you wouldn't know where you were once Milton gets on to this stuff. For one thing, he said to me the woman wasn't alive.'

In the rectory Addy telephoned. 'I'll ring you back,' her mother said and did so twenty minutes later, when Milton was not within earshot. In the conversation that ensued what information they possessed was shared: the revelations made on the day of the July celebration, what had later been said in the kitchen and an hour ago in the yard.

'Dudgeon McDavie,' Mrs Leeson reported quietly to her

husband as soon as she replaced the receiver. 'The latest thing is he's on to Herbert about Dudgeon McDavie.'

Milton rode his bicycle one Saturday afternoon to the first of the towns in which he wished to preach. In a car park two small girls, sucking sweets, listened to him. He explained about St Rosa of Viterbo. He felt he was a listener too, that his voice came from somewhere outside himself, from St Rosa, he explained to the two small girls. He heard himself saying that his sister Hazel refused to return to the province. He heard himself describing the silent village, and the drums and the flutes that brought music to it, and the suit his father wore only on the day of the celebration. St Rosa could mourn Dudgeon McDavie, he explained, a Loughgall man who'd been murdered ages ago. St Rosa could forgive the brutish soldiers and their masked adversaries, one or other of them responsible for the shattered motor-cars and shrouded bodies that came and went on to television screens. Father Mulhall had been furious, Milton said in the car park, you could see it in his eyes: he'd been furious because a Protestant boy was sitting down in his house. St Rosa of Viterbo had given him her holy kiss, he said: you could tell that Father Mulhall considered that impossible.

The following Saturday Milton cycled to another town, a little further away, and on the subsequent Saturday he preached in a third town. He did not think of it as preaching, more just telling people about his experience. It was what he had to do, he explained, and he noticed that when people began to listen they usually didn't go away. Shoppers paused, old men out for a walk passed the time in his company, leaning against a shop window or the wall of a public lavatory. On the fourth occasion Mr Leeson and Herbert Cutcheon arrived in Mr Leeson's Ford Granada and hustled him into it. No one spoke a word on the journey back.

'Shame?' Milton said when his mother employed the word.

'On all of us, Milton.'

In church people regarded him suspiciously, and he noticed

that Addy sometimes couldn't stop staring at him. When he smiled at Esme Dunshea she didn't smile back; Billie Carew avoided him. His father insisted that in no circumstances whatsoever should he ever again preach about a woman in the orchards. Milton began to explain that he must, that he had been given the task.

'No,' his father said.

'That's the end of it, Milton,' his mother said. She hated it even more than his father did, the Papist woman kissing him on the lips.

The next Saturday afternoon they locked him into the bedroom he shared with Stewart, releasing him at six o'clock. But on Sunday morning he rode away again, and had again to be searched for on the streets of towns. After that, greater care was taken. Stewart was moved out of the bedroom and the following weekend Milton remained under duress there, the door unlocked so that he could go to the lavatory, his meals carried up to him by his mother, who said nothing when she placed the tray on a chest of drawers. Milton expected that on Monday morning everything would be normal again, that his punishment would then have run its course. But this was not so. He was released to work beside his father, clearing out a ditch, and all day there were never more than a couple of yards between them. In the evening he was returned to the bedroom. The door was again secured, and so it always was after that.

On winter Sundays when his sister Addy and the Reverend Cutcheon came to sit in the back room he remained upstairs. He no longer accompanied the family to church. When Garfield came from Belfast at a weekend he refused to carry food to the bedroom, although Milton often heard their mother requesting him to. For a long time Garfield had not addressed him or sought his company.

When Milton did the milking his father didn't keep so close to him. He put a padlock on the yard gate and busied himself with some task or other in one of the sheds, or else kept an eye on the yard from the kitchen. On two Saturday afternoons Milton climbed out of the bedroom window and set off on his bicycle, later to be pursued. Then one day when he returned from the orchards with his father he found Jimmy Logan had been to the farmhouse to put bars on his bedroom window. His bicycle was no longer in the turf shed; he caught a glimpse of it tied on to the boot of the Ford Granada and deduced that it was being taken to be sold. His mother unearthed an old folding card-table, since it was a better height for eating off than the chest of drawers. Milton knew that people had been told he had become affected in the head, but he could tell from his mother's demeanour that not even this could exorcise the shame he had brought on the family.

When the day of the July celebration came again Milton remained in his bedroom. Before he left the house his father led him to the lavatory and waited outside it in order to lead him back again. His father didn't say anything. He didn't say it was the day of the July celebration but Milton could tell it was because he was wearing his special suit. Milton watched the car drawing out of the yard and then heard his mother chatting to Stewart in the kitchen, saying something about sitting in the sun. He imagined the men gathering in the field, the clergyman's blessing, the drums strapped on, ranks formed. As usual, the day was fine: from his bedroom window he could see there wasn't a cloud in the sky.

It wasn't easy to pass the time. Milton had never been much of a one for reading, had never read a book from cover to cover. Sometimes when his mother brought his food she left him the weekly newspaper and he read about the towns it gave news of, and the different rural neighbourhoods, one of which was his own. He listened to his transistor. His mother collected all the jigsaw puzzles she could find, some of which had been in the farmhouse since Hazel and Garfield were children, others of a simple nature bought specially for Stewart. She left him a pack of cards, with only the three of diamonds missing, and a cardboard box containing scraps of wool and a spool with tacks in it that had been Addy's French-knitting outfit.

On the day of the celebration he couldn't face, yet again, completing the jigsaw of Windsor Castle or the Battle of

Britain, or playing patience with the three of diamonds drawn on the back of an envelope or listening all day to cheery disc-jockeys. He practised preaching, all the time seeing the woman in the orchard instead of the sallow features of Jesus or a cantankerous-looking God, white-haired and bearded, frowning through the clouds.

From time to time he looked at his watch and on each occasion established the point the march had reached. The Kissane girl and her sisters waved. Cars drew courteously in to allow the celebration to pass by. McCourt's Hardware and Agricultural Supplies was closed, the village street was empty. Beyond the school and the Church of the Holy Rosary the march halted, then returned the way it had come, only making a change when it reached McCourt's again, swinging off to the left.

Mrs Leeson unlocked the door and handed in a tray, and Milton imagined the chicken legs and the sandwiches in the field, bottles coming out, the men standing in a row by the hedge. 'No doubt about it,' his father said. 'Dr Gibney's seen cases like it before.' A nutcase, his father intimated without employing the term, but when he was out of hearing one of the men muttered that he knew for a fact Dr Gibney hadn't been asked for an opinion. In the field the shame that was spoken about spread from his father to the men themselves.

Milton tumbled out on the card-table the pieces of a jigsaw of a jungle scene and slowly turned them right side up. He didn't know any more what would happen if they opened the door and freed him. He didn't know if he would try to walk to the towns, if he'd feel again the pressure to do so or if everything was over, if he'd been cleansed, as his father's old uncle would have said. Slowly he found the shape of a chimpanzee among the branches of a tree. He wished he were in the field, taking the half bottle from Billie Carew. He wished he could feel the sun on his face and feel the ache going out of his legs after the march.

He completed the top left-hand corner of the jungle scene, adding brightly-coloured birds to the tree with the chimpanzees in it. The voices of his mother and Stewart floated up to him from the yard, the incoherent growling of his brother, his mother soothing. From where he sat he saw them when they moved into view, Stewart lumbering, his mother holding his hand. They passed out of the yard, through the gate that was padlocked when he did the milking. Often they walked down to the stream on a warm afternoon.

Again he practised preaching. He spoke of his father ashamed in the field, and the silent windows of the village. He explained he had been called to go among people, bearing witness on a Saturday afternoon. He spoke of fear. It was that that was most important of all. Fear was the weapon of the gunmen and the soldiers, fear quietened the village. In fear his sister had abandoned the province that was her home. Fearful, his brother disposed of the unwanted dead.

Later Milton found the two back legs of an elephant and slipped the piece that contained them into place. He wondered if he would finish the jigsaw or if it would remain on the mildewed baize of the card-table with most of its middle part missing. He hadn't understood why the story of Dudgeon McDavie had occurred to him as a story he must tell. It had always been there; he'd heard it dozens of times; yet it seemed a different kind of story when he thought about the woman in the orchard, when over and over again he watched her coming towards him, and when she spoke about fear.

He found another piece of the elephant's grey bulk. In the distance he could hear the sound of a car. He paid it no attention, not even when the engine throbbed with a different tone, indicating that the car had drawn up by the yard gate. The gate rattled in a familiar way, and Milton went to his window then. A yellow Vauxhall moved into the yard.

He watched while a door opened and a man he had never seen before stepped out from the driver's seat. The engine was switched off. The man stretched himself. Then Garfield stepped out too.

'It took a death to get you back.'

On the drive from the airport Hazel did not reply.

'It's broken up your mother.' Her father's voice softened, as if begging for Hazel's sympathy by way of her mother's distress, as if his own distress was less fittingly exposed. 'You'll see.'

'She'll never recover.' With satisfaction Hazel heard reflected in her tone the bitterness there had been in his when he'd said it took a death to get her back. She wanted to be harsh, she wanted her opinion to be clear: that her mother would go to her own grave with the scalding pain of what had happened still alive within her. None of them would recover, it was not right that they should: that sounded also in Hazel's uncompromising tone.

Hazel was twenty-six, a year younger than Addy, small and dark-haired, as Addy was too. Ever since the day she had married, since her exile had begun, the truth had not existed between her and these people she had left behind. The present occasion was not a time for prevarication, not a time for pretence, yet already she could feel both all around her. Another death in a procession of deaths had occurred; this time close to all of them. Each death that came was close to someone, within some family: she'd said that years ago, saying it only once, not arguing because none of them wanted to have a conversation like that.

Mr Leeson slowed as they approached the village of Glenavy, then halted to allow two elderly women to cross the street. They waved their thanks, and he waved back. Eventually he said:

'Herbert's been good.'

Again Hazel did not respond. 'God took him for a purpose,' she imagined Herbert Cutcheon comforting her mother. 'God had a job for him.'

'How's Addy?'

Her sister was naturally distressed also, she was told. The shock was still there, still raw in all of them.

'That stands to reason.'

They slid into a thin stream of traffic on the motorway, Mr Leeson not accelerating much. He said:

'I have to tell you what it was with Milton before we get home.'

'Was it the Provos? Was Milton involved in some way?'

'Don't call them the Provos, Hazel. Don't give them any kind of title. They're not worthy of a title.'

'You have to call them something.'

'It wasn't them. There was no reason why it should have been.'

Hazel, who had only, up to now, been told that her brother had died violently – shot by intruders when he was alone in the house – heard how Milton had insisted he'd received a supernatural visitation from a woman. She heard how he had believed the woman was the ghost of a Catholic saint, how he had gone to the priest for information, how he had begun street-corner preaching.

'He said things they didn't like?' she suggested, ignoring the more incredible aspect of this information.

'We had to keep him in. I kept him by me when we worked, Garfield wouldn't address him.'

'You kept him in?'

'Poor Milton was away in the head, Hazel. He'd be all right for a while, maybe for weeks, longer even. Then suddenly he'd start about the woman in the orchard. He wanted to travel the six counties preaching about her. He told me that. He wanted to stand up in every town he came to and tell his tale. He brought poor Dudgeon McDavie into it.'

'What d'you mean, you kept him in?'

'We sometimes had to lock his bedroom door. Milton didn't know what he was doing, girl. We had to get rid of his bicycle, but even so he'd have walked. A couple of times on a Saturday he set off to walk, and myself and Herbert had to get him back.'

'My God!'

'You can't put stuff like that in a letter. You can't blame anyone for not writing that down for you. Your mother didn't want to. "What've you said to Hazel?" I asked her one time and she said nothing, so we left it.'

'Milton went mad and no one told me?'

341

'Poor Milton did, Hazel.'

Hazel endeavoured to order the confusion of her thoughts. Pictures formed: of the key turned in the bedroom door; of the household as it had apparently become, her parents' two remaining children a double burden, Stewart's mongol blankness, Milton's gibberish. 'Milton's been shot,' she had said to her husband after the telephone call, shocked that Milton had apparently become involved, as Garfield was, drawn into it no doubt by Garfield. Ever since, that assumption had remained.

They left the motorway, bypassed Craigavon, then again made their way on smaller roads. This is home, Hazel found herself reflecting in that familiar landscape, the reminder seeming alien among thoughts that were less tranquil. Yet in spite of the reason for her visit, in spite of the upsetting muddle of facts she'd been presented with on this journey, she wanted to indulge the moment, to close her eyes and let herself believe that it was a pleasure of some kind to be back were she belonged. Soon they would come to Drumfin, then Anderson's Crossroads. They would pass the Cuchulainn Ballroom, and turn before reaching the village. Everything would be familiar then, every house and cottage, trees and gateways, her father's orchards.

'Take it easy with your mother,' he said. 'She cries a lot.'

'Who was it shot Milton?'

'There's no one has claimed who it was. The main concern's your mother.'

Hazel didn't say anything, but when her father began to speak again she interrupted him.

'What about the police?'

'Finmoth's keeping an open mind.'

The car passed the Kissanes' house, pink and respectable, delphiniums in its small front garden. Next came the ruined cowshed in the middle of Malone's field, three of its stone walls standing, the fourth tumbled down, its disintegrating roof mellow with rust. Then came the orchards, and the tarred gate through which you could see the stream, steeply below.

Her father turned the car into the yard of the farmhouse. One of the dogs barked, scampering back and forth, wagging his tail as he always did when the car returned.

'Well, there we are.' With an effort Mr Leeson endeavoured to extend a welcome. 'You'd recognise the old place still!'

In the kitchen her mother embraced her. Her mother had a shrunken look; a hollowness about her eyes, and shallow cheeks that exposed the shape of bones beneath the flesh. A hand grasped at one of Hazel's and clutched it tightly, as if in a plea for protection. Mr Leeson carried Hazel's suitcase upstairs.

'Sit down.' With her free hand Hazel pulled a chair out from the table and gently eased her mother toward it. Her brother grinned across the kitchen at her.

'Oh, Stewart!'

She kissed him, hugging his awkward body. Pimples disfigured his big forehead, his spiky short hair tore uncomfortably at her cheek.

'We should have seen,' Mrs Leeson whispered. 'We should have known.'

'You couldn't. Of course you couldn't.'

'He had a dream or something. That's all he was on about.'

Hazel remembered the dreams she'd had herself at Milton's age, half-dreams because sometimes she was awake – close your eyes and you could make Mick Jagger smile at you, or hear the music of U2 or The Damage. 'Paul Hogan had his arms round me,' Addy giggled once. Then you began going out with someone and everything was different.

'Yet how would he know about a saint?' her mother whispered. 'Where'd he get the name from?'

Hazel didn't know. It would have come into his head, she said to herself, but didn't repeat the observation aloud. In spite of what she said, her mother didn't want to think about it. Maybe it was easier for her mother, too, to believe her son had been away in the head, or maybe it made it worse. You wouldn't know that, you couldn't tell from her voice or from her face.

'Don't let it weigh on you,' she begged. 'Don't make it worse for yourself.'

Later Addy and Herbert Cutcheon were in the kitchen. Addy made tea and tumbled biscuits on to a plate. Herbert Cutcheon was solemn, Addy subdued. Like her father, Hazel sensed, both of them were worried about her mother. Being worried about her mother was the practical aspect of the grief that was shared, an avenue of escape from it also, a distraction that was permitted. Oblivious to all emotion, Stewart reached out for a biscuit with pink marshmallow in it, his squat fingers and bitten nails ugly for an instant against the soft prettiness.

'He'll get the best funeral the Church can give him,' Herbert Cutcheon promised.

Garfield stood away from them, with a black tie in place and his shoes black also, not the trainers he normally wore. He had to be there; no way he could have avoided it.

'*I am the resurrection and the life, saith the Lord . . .*' His brother-in-law's tone was special, solemn with the churchiness that was discarded as soon as his professional duties ceased, never apparent on a Sunday afternoon in the back room of the farmhouse. A hymn was sung, *My times are in Thy hand . . .* Then there was the address.

'*I will keep my mouth as it were with a bridle,*' Herbert Cutcheon proclaimed, and Garfield was reminded of his great-uncle Willie, whose preaching had been peppered with intentions that were similar. *Out of thine own mouth will I judge thee . . .* and *Cleansed with blood, thy servants wait.*

When the moment came Garfield stepped forward with his father to bear the coffin. Billie Carew stepped forward also, with one of the undertaker's men. There was a way of doing it, the shoulder of your partner firmly gripped, and being gripped yourself in turn. More than once, in Belfast, Garfield had borne a coffin.

'*Forasmuch as it hath pleased Almighty God,*' Herbert Cutcheon continued at the open grave, the coffin now in position for its lowering. *Cometh the wrath of God,* the old man had reminded in a very different tone of voice, thunderous and bleak, *upon the children of disobedience.*

Milton had been told not to. You had all kinds of fancies when you were sixteen and seventeen years of age. He'd been told that; it had been explained to him. They'd tried to keep it from old Willie, but he'd heard, the way everyone had heard. 'This'll kill Uncle Willie,' Garfield remembered his father saying when it all came out, when everyone was talking about Milton and a Papist saint, saying it was the same as the Romans seeing one of their idolatrous statues move. Prominent among the mourners, Garfield's great-uncle Willie's granite features displayed no emotion.

Earth was thrown on to the coffin, which had descended into the grave. *'Our Father, which art in heaven,'* Herbert Cutcheon suitably declared, and Garfield watched the old man's lips, in unison with Addy's and Hazel's and their parents'. Stewart was there too, now and again making a noise. Mrs Leeson held a handkerchief to her face, clinging on to her husband in the bright sunshine of the churchyard. *'And forgive us our trespasses.'* Mechanically Garfield mouthed the words too.

He didn't believe in funerals. When you were dead you were dead, a sheep became mutton. But he believed a person should be shown respect; he understood that there had to be all the paraphernalia, that there had to be the decencies if it was how family and relations felt. Garfield didn't feel revulsion for his brother any more, as he'd felt it first of all in the back room, knowing Milton was upstairs, a brother of his sickening the whole house with what he'd brought to it; as he'd felt it when people knew, when it got around and people talked about it.

'Amen,' Herbert Cutcheon prompted, and the mourners duly murmured.

He had had no option, Garfield reflected, still standing in the sunshine, for no one yet had moved. He had had no option; he had no regrets. Loyalty had been displayed; it was known the length of certain streets, in certain clubs and bars, that Garfield Leeson had been in the car that day, that he had pointed out the way through the country lanes, had chosen the day and the time because he knew the workings of the house. The ground had been regained. In no other way could shame be lifted, in no other way could the family's heads be raised again. 'Your body's a living sacrifice,' the old man used to thunder, steadfast in his certainty.

Mrs Leeson sobbed, the only sound at the graveside now. Both daughters moved closer to her, receiving her from their father's care. They knew too, Garfield reflected, though in a different way. All of them knew without sharing their knowledge as the knowledge was shared in the Belfast streets and clubs. His father knew, and Addy, and Herbert Cutcheon. His mother knew; the knowledge was there in Hazel's face, wanting to break out, not doing so because everything would be worse if she permitted that. It was talked about in the neighbourhood, as it was further afield, but the family could not do that and the family never would.

'You'll come to the house,' Garfield heard his father inviting someone. He would not go back himself. He'd drive off quickly, stop for a drink as soon as he was far enough away. 'Hi, Garfield,' Milton had said that day, his talk about the woman in the orchard beginning all over again.

He didn't say good-bye. He'd done his bit, a day off specially, the sober clothes to show respect; he couldn't do more, there was nothing honest he could say. He drove through the village, past Tiernan's grocery and filling station, O'Hanlon's public house. He stopped half an hour later, beyond Portadown. In an empty bar he ordered a Bushmills and water, and then had another, and a packet of crisps. He moved from the bar and sat at a table, drinking, and nibbling the crisps, smoking. It couldn't be helped. You could have a few moments of regret, with all the funeral stuff still echoing, and his black tie and shoes, and the memory of Milton, and how he used to tell him a thing or two in the back room on a Saturday night when the others were all in bed. You could have a few moments of regret, natural that you should, but next year, on the anniversary of that day, his father would hold his head up on the march from his field, and in the field itself when there was the celebration picnic. By then his mother would have ceased to weep, and would know that Milton's death was only the way things were, the way things had to be. Addy knew it already, Hazel knew it in her bones. They would none of them survive if they ever gave an inch, if lost ground was not regained.

Fallen by the Wayside

BARRY UNSWORTH

ON FINDING HIMSELF thus accidentally free, Sullivan's only idea was to get as far as he could from Newgate Prison while it was still dark. He set off northwards, keeping the river at his back. In Holborn he lost an hour, wandering in a warren of courts. Then an old washer-woman, waiting outside a door in the first light of day, set him right for Gray's Inn Lane and the northern outskirts of the City.

Once sure of his way he felt his spirits rise and he stepped out eagerly enough. Not that he had much, on the face of things, to be blithe about. The December morning was bitterly cold and he had no coat, only the ragged shirt and sleeveless leather waistcoat and cotton trousers issued to him on the ship returning from Florida. His shoes had been made for a man with feet of a different calibre, on him they contrived to be too loose at the heel and too tight across the toes. He was hungry. He was penniless. He was assailed by periodic shudders in this rawness of the early morning.

All the same, Sullivan counted his blessings as he walked along. He had his health and strength still. He had friends in Liverpool if he could get there. And there was a blessing on him – it was not given to many just to stroll out of prison like that. Strolling through the gates . . . His teeth chattered.

'Without so much as a kiss my arse,' he said aloud – in Florida he had developed a habit of muttering to himself, as had most of the people of the settlement. No, he thought, it was a stroke of luck beyond the mortal, the Blessed Virgin had opened the gates to him. A sixpenny candle, if I get through this. Best tallow . . . He thought of the beautiful flame of it and tried in his mind to make the flame warm him.

He did not think of the future otherwise except as a hope of survival. There was an element missing from his nature that all wise men are agreed is essential for the successful self-governance of the individual within society, the basic requirement of civilisation in fact: the ability to make provision, to plan ahead. But this is the doctrine of the prosperous. The destitute and dispossessed are lucky if they can avert the mind from a future unlikely to offer them benefit. Sullivan knew in some part of his mind that evading recapture would put him at risk of death in this weather, with no money and no shelter. But he was at large, he was on the move, the threat of the noose was less close. It was enough.

An hour's walking brought him to the rural edges of London, among the market gardens and brick kilns north of Gray's Inn Fields. And it was now that he had his second great stroke of luck. As he was making his way through narrow lanes with occasional low shacks on either side, where the smallholders and cowkeepers slept during the summer months, at a sudden turning he came upon a man lying full length on his back across the track.

He stopped at some paces off. It was a blind bend and an early cart could come rounding it at any time. 'This is not the place to stretch out,' he said. 'You will get your limbs destroyed.' But he did not go nearer for the moment because he had remembered a trick like that – you bend over in emulation of the Good Samaritan and get a crack on the head. 'I am not worth robbin',' he said. A half-choked breath was the only answer. The man's face had a red and mottled look. His mouth hung open and his eyes were closed. Across the space of freezing air that separated them an effluvium of rum punch came to Sullivan's nostrils.

'I see well that you have been overtaken by drink,' Sullivan said. 'The air is dancin' with the breath of it over your head. We will have to shift you off the road.' He took the man under the armpits and half-lifted, half-dragged him round so that he was lying along the bankside, out of the way of the wheel ruts. While this was taking place he grunted once, uttered some words of indistinguishable startlement and made a deep snoring noise. His body was heavy and inert, quite helpless either to assist or obstruct the process of his realignment.

'Well, my friend,' Sullivan said, 'you have taken a good tubful, you have. You have been celebratin' Our Lord's Nativity a bit ahead of yourself.' The exertion had warmed him a little. He hesitated for a moment, then sat down on the bankside close to the recumbent man. From this vantage point he looked around him. A thin plume of smoke was rising from somewhere among the frozen fields beyond the shacks, but there was no other sign of life anywhere, no human stirring. A faint sun swam among low clouds; there was no warmth in it but the touch was enough to wake a bird to singing somewhere – he could hear it but not see it.

The man was well-dressed, in a square-cut bottle-green coat with brass buttons, worsted trousers and stout leggings and boots. 'Those are fine buttons,' Sullivan said. 'I wonder if you could make me a loan now. I am hard-pressed just at present, speakin' frankly, man to man, I beg your parding, did you utter some words?'

The man did not answer this but when Sullivan began to go through his pockets he sighed and choked a little and made a motion with his left arm as if warding off some incubus. There was sixteen shillings and eightpence in his purse. Sullivan extracted eight shillings and returned the purse to its pocket. 'I leave you the greater half,' he said. Again, at this intimacy of touch, the man stirred and this time his eyes opened briefly. They were bloodshot and vague and sad. He had lost his hat in the fall; it lay in the road beyond him. His goat's-hair wig had slipped sideways. It glistened with wet and the sparse, gingerish wisps of his own hair curled damply out below it.

'I have nothin' to write with an' neither have you,' Sullivan said, 'an' we have niver a piece of paper between us, or I would leave you a note of hand for the money. Or yet again, if you were in a more volatile state, you could furnish me with your address. As things are, we will just have to leave it unsatisfactory.'

The man's face had returned to sleep. Sullivan nodded at it in valediction and set off again along the lane. He had not gone far however, when it came to him that he had been the saviour of this man and that eight shillings was hardly adequate. To rate a man's life at only eight shillings was offensive. Any man with self-respect would set a value on himself higher than that. Even he, Sullivan, who had no fixed abode and no coat to his back, would think eight shillings too little. If this man's faculties were not so much ravaged and under the weather, he would be bound to agree that sixteen shillings met the case better.

Full of these thoughts, he retraced his steps. The man appeared to have made some brief struggle in the interval, though motionless again now. His wig had fallen off completely and lay bedraggled on the bankside, like a bird's nest torn from the bare winter hedge and flung down there. His hair was thin on top, pinkish scalp showed through the flat crown. His breath made a slight bubbling noise.

'I do not want you to go through life feelin' convicted of ingratitude,' Sullivan said. 'You may take the view that death was problematical, but that I rescued you from the hazard of mutilation, you are bound to agree on.' He found the purse again and took out another eight shillings. 'In takin' this money I am doublin' your value,' he said. 'It is little enough after all. But I will leave you the eightpence, seein' that the season of goodwill is bearin' down.'

He was silent for some moments, listening intently: he thought he had heard the rattle of wheels. He went to the bend and surveyed the long curve of the road: no sign of anything. His eyes watered and he was again racked with shudders from the cold. He clutched at himself and slapped his arms and sides in an effort to get some warmth in them. He returned to the victim of his kindness. 'I had a coat once with fine brass buttons on it,' he said, 'but the coat was stole off me back aboard ship on the false grounds it was verminous an' the bosun kept the buttons, though they brought him no luck. It is only justice you would reinstate me buttons, having saved you from injury or worse. If I had a knife about me I could snip them off, but looking at it another way I am not the man to desecrate a fine coat . . . Here, hold steady.' Feeling the coat being eased off him, the man struggled up to a sitting position, glared before him for some moments, then fell back against the bank.

The coat was rather too big at the shoulders for Sullivan, a fact which surprised and puzzled him, conflicting with his sense that this encounter by the wayside was perfect in all its details of mutual benefit. 'You will be a local man,' he said. 'You will not have far to go. I am bound for Liverpool an' the New World. That is a tidy step.' He had been unlacing the boots as he spoke. Now he raised the man's legs to pull them off, first right, then left. The thick legs fell heavily to earth again when released.

The boots fitted Sullivan perfectly. He slipped his shoes on to the other's feet. 'Each man will keep to his own trousers,' he said magnanimously. In fact he had grown hasty in the lacing of his new boots and was eager to be off. He straightened up and moved away, into the middle of the lane. 'The morning is not só cold as it was,' he said. 'I am your benefactor an' I will remember you as mine.' No sound at all came from the man now. He was slumped back against the bank. His head had fallen forward and slightly sideways, towards his left shoulder. He had the look of total meekness that the hanged possess, and perhaps it was this that brought a sudden tightening to Sullivan's throat. 'At another time I would have saved your life free of charge,' he said. The hat was still lying there. He took it up and set it firmly on the man's lowered head. Then he began to walk quickly away.

He walked for an hour or so in the sullen light of the

morning. Nothing passed him on the road and he met no one. At a junction of lanes there was a huddle of houses and a small inn, but he did not dare to stop. A mile further on he came up with a wagon setting off north with a load of shoring posts. Sixpence got him a place up beside the driver. As the wagon jolted along, he thought of his luck again and of the meekness of the hanged. After a while he slept.

Through a Dustbin, Darkly

FAY WELDON

'OH, SERENA,' THEY said. 'Serena! Serena was quite mad, you know. She would have made the finest surrealist painter of the twentieth century, only she ended up in a dustbin.' And the little circle of ex-art students filled up their glasses and rolled a smidgen more dope and stared exhausted and melancholy into their mutual past. They wore sandals although it was cold outside.

'You mean,' said Philly, 'her paintings ended up in a dustbin?' 'Oh no,' they said, whichever one of them it was – Harold or Perse or Don or Steve – Philly found them hard to tell apart, so information about Basil's past seemed to come from some communal centre – 'Serena ended up in the dustbin. She left Basil when she found him upstairs in the studio in bed with Ruthy Franklyn, and shacked up with some frame-maker she met in a squat, who then committed suicide. She must have gone completely bonkers after that because she broke in to Basil's studio upstairs: burned all her own paintings in the stove – five years' work gone in five hours – and had begun on Basil's when luckily Ruthy came by and stopped her.

'So poor Basil changed the locks and Serena went and lived in the alley at the house for a week or so, shouting and

screaming, selling herself to passers-by, and then OD'd on
heroin. She fell headfirst into a dustbin from whence she was
carted off to the booby hatch, where she died. That was four
years ago.'

'Poor Basil,' they chorused.

Philly envisaged Serena's thin, white legs waving out of a
big, black, plastic bin: a rag doll thrown away.

'He'd married her to calm her down and help her paint, but
it didn't work,' said Harold, Perse, Don or Steve. 'Serena
was always completely mad, perhaps even because she was
so talented. More talented even than Basil.'

'Completely mad,' agreed the Jean, Holly, Ryan and Olive
who went with the men. 'Way, way over the top. OTT.
Poor Basil. Better luck next time!'

They were all thirtyish; Basil was fortyish; Philly was
twenty-one. In her family people only married once. What
did she know?

They were all in Basil's house, which had been left him by
his grandmother. It had been designed in the Thirties, and
was made of functional and brutalist concrete: a long, low,
expensive building with portholes where other people would
have had windows. Philly had moved in a week ago. She was
pregnant with Basil's baby. The house was cold because the
gas bill had not been paid. No one seemed to mind. Philly
could see she'd be the one who'd have to attend to such
matters.

Basil came down from the studio to join his friends, to join
Philly. He had worn out his talent for the day. Now they
could all party. He had a gentle manner, a sweet smile and a
reputation as a major painter. His father had been an RA,
his grandmother had slept with Augustus John. Dark green
foliage surged up against the portholes, as if the house was
under water. A sudden wind must have got up outside. The
place was crowded in by trees. Philly would have risen to
turn on the lights, but there was no electricity. Those bills
had not been paid either.

So many things about the house, Philly could see – glamor-
ous though it was, more exciting than anything she had ever

known – which needed seeing to, organising, fixing, changing, cheering up. Then it could be a home. But not yet, not yet: better to offer no judgements. Philly knew the friends accepted her, or why would they talk about Serena? But perhaps to Basil she was just another item of changing human scenery. Wait and see. She sat quiet in the half dark.

'Let's not talk about Serena,' Basil said, 'ever again. This is Philly's home now. A new life starts for her and me. Let's forget Serena.'

So everyone forgot Serena, including Philly.

That was in September. Philly set about making the house her own.

The kitchen door was stuck. It had not been opened for years. But since the back garden had at some time been sold off to keep creditors at bay, and the door led almost directly into the loading bays and alleys which backed a shopping complex, who would want to open it anyway? Better, Basil said, to use the front door, walk up the garden path and go round to the shops. Philly did.

How did you unstick a door, anyway? It seemed better closed. The back of the complex was sunless by day, poorly lit by night. It always seemed deserted but if ever you opened the windows at the back you could smell stale urine and hear a scuttling sound – rats or cockroaches, no doubt startled by the noise. So Philly kept the back windows closed: she let fresh air blow in from the front. Hardly windows, anyway; hinged portholes. And you had to force foliage back in order to get them open.

By November the trees on windy days were bare and the portholes easier to open although branches scratched up against the glass, and there was never a silence. Philly's father came to visit her. Philly's mother had died that same month only a year ago, and left her daughter £11,000. Perhaps Philly had got pregnant to forget the grief, sorrow and shock, to lose herself in a new life: the thought hung between father and daughter. 'I'd have those trees cut down,' said Philly's father. 'They make the house dark and damp. Personally, I'd rather live in a bungalow. Shall I come over and get rid of a few thousand branches for you?'

But Basil liked trees. The worst offender, when it came to opening the studio window, was an elm which had escaped Dutch elm disease, and was apparently as rare as it was beautiful. Basil was shocked at the notion that there could be a leaf, a twig less of the tree than nature suggested. But what did Philly know? To Philly, according to Basil, one leaf was much like another. She was a barbarian: but hadn't they always known that: Harold, Perse, Don and Steve, Jean, Holly, Ryan and Olive, too? Philly was the new blank canvas on which Basil could imprint his taste, his knowledge, his guidance.

'But don't you need as much light as possible to paint?' asked Philly.

'This house is perfectly light and cheerful,' Basil said, and discouraged her father from visiting thereafter, on the grounds that he made Philly gloomy.

Philly was six months pregnant and didn't like to argue with Basil, since she only got upset and never won. The fact was that it was a dark, cold house, no matter how much was spent on gas and electricity, how much wine was drunk by the friends. Basil encouraged her to put in new radiators: she'd turn them up full but the concrete walls seemed to swallow warmth and give none back. She put in wall lights to supplement the stark central bulbs; she washed the concrete walls with white; she brought halogen uplighters, but, even by night, light seemed not to be doing its proper job of banishing gloom. A stubborn month. Well, November is never the brightest of months: just grey, grey.

Basil didn't like spending money on the house: she used her own, and was happy to. He was pleased with what she did. 'It's your home,' he'd say. 'Have it the way you want.'

That encouraged her. She did what she could. She called in a carpenter to plane down the back door, and he freed it, but damp must have swelled the wood again, because within a week it was stuck once more. She had an electrician in to fix the oven, which always either burned or cut out at the worst

357

possible time, but its thermostat stayed unreliable. It was only five years old. Basil balked at the cost of a new one. Philly couldn't make the floors 'come up', to use her mother's phrase. Over and over she'd washed the wide stretches of dark green floor tiles, and polished them too, but some of the tiles must have been unusually porous: the result was always patchy. Unsightly lines of what seemed like white salt kept rising up to spoil the finish. The whole floor should by rights have shone and gleamed; perhaps it was something about the pattern of light from the porthole windows which managed to give it a ridged effect. Philly would scrub and polish on her hands and knees. It was a comfortable thing to do. When she was upright, pressure on her sciatic nerve gave her continual pain. It was not an easy pregnancy.

When Philly was seven months pregnant, in December, Basil suggested they got married. Twelfth Night, he said, would be the right kind of day: a special day: one you wouldn't forget when it came to anniversaries.

January, and Philly was Basil's second wife. Harold and Perse, Don and Steve came to the party after the wedding, in the house, along with Jean, Holly, Ryan and Olive. One of them observed, 'Serena's birthday was Twelfth Night,' and Philly said, 'Who's Serena?' a moment before she remembered. A rather strange thing happened. A box of indoor fireworks somehow caught fire inside its wrappings: blackish ash erupted from the box, swelled and burst the plastic: a series of tiny explosions then sent the ash flying and whirling through the air, so all the surfaces in the room were soon covered with a soft film of grey. It was not unpretty; and the event had not even been dangerous, just extraordinary, watching the box jump up and down as if of its own volition, puffing out ash. But when someone else said, 'Philly, you forgot to take down the Christmas decorations: that's unlucky,' she worried at once. She feared for her baby. Dear God, let me be lucky, prayed Philly. Babies got born with all kinds of things wrong with them. She vacuumed carefully every day, into every corner, and felt better. Cleaning was a kind of talisman. Amazing how Christmas tree needles hung around and got everywhere, no matter how sure you were you'd finally got rid of the last of them. But you could clean and clean in this house and it just never looked as if you'd done a thing. She couldn't understand it.

Basil laughed when she complained. 'It looks just fine to me,' he said. 'But thank God you have proper domestic ambition. You are the right wife for me, Philly.'

Philly's father hadn't been invited to the wedding. He'd written to ask if Philly would hand back the £11,000 from her mother for his safekeeping. He'd invest it for her, to her advantage. Basil had understandably taken offence. Philly felt her loyalties were to her husband, not her father, and Harold, Perse, Don and Steve, Jean, Holly, Ryan and Mattie agreed.

'The thing to do with Basil,' all agreed, 'is not to make waves. He can be ruthless if you do. Poor Olive!'

Olive had been taken on at the same gallery as Basil. She had had a one-person show and instead of being a failure, was now a success. She was no longer in the group of friends. Steve had taken on Mattie instead: it was that, or be out of the circle too. Mattie was a pleasant, daft girl, good at the Benefit Game, and no one spoke much about Olive any more, and within weeks she, too, was forgotten.

February, and there was only £4,000 left of Philly's legacy. Basil needed better frames for his paintings than his gallery was prepared to provide: anything looks better, sells better, if surrounded by real gold leaf: that had been Olive's one trick – Basil had said – unfairly used. Nothing to do with talent. Then the roof had to be re-tiled. Rain had leaked down from the ceilings, corrugating the studio walls with lines of damp. The studio was where Basil and Philly slept, in the large brass bed which was there when Philly moved in. They slept surrounded by canvas, rags, easels, paints, brushes: his hand companionable on her thigh. The famous hand: how she loved it! Completed paintings were stacked against the walls. These days Basil painted, to the despair of his gallery, only swirls of grey and black: gold leaf helped, but not enough. Philly could get quite depressed, looking at the swirls. The smell of paint and turps lingered in the studio all night through, although tubes and jars were closed, sealed; she once tried wrapping them in plastic to stop the fumes, but it didn't help. Sometimes they made her feel quite sick. It was as if morning sickness, which she had not suffered from in early pregnancy, had stored itself up till now, when she had just a few weeks to go.

Basil's baby! Oh, she was lucky. So was he; he said so, lucky second time round. He'd always wanted a baby; someone to inherit the family's genes. A pity he had to be away so often now, in Edinburgh, commissioned to paint a mural on a town hall wall. But times were hard: an artist did what he could. If he had to be a man of the people, so he would be. Philly would be OK; polishing and scouring away. When he called on the phone, its ring sounded oddly echoey: his voice would babble, as if he were under water.

Eight-and-a-half months' pregnant and who should turn up for tea one day, while Basil was away, but someone who announced herself as Ruthy Franklyn, an old friend of Basil's? Ruthy just stood on the doorstep, a total stranger, and asked herself in for tea. She was fortyish, smart, small, thin and lively and made Philly feel bulky, stupid and slow. Ruthy wore a silk turban in green and had a yellowy chiffon scarf at her wiry neck. Ruthy owned a small gallery. She'd come to collect an early painting of Basil's for a show she was mounting. She looked a little death's headish to Philly, as if the Reaper had come calling. Ruthy drank Earl Grey and took lemon: always a problem to provide. You had to use a teapot, not teabags, and slice the lemon thinly, and serve the whole thing properly.

'Nice rock cakes,' said Ruthy, 'if on the crispy side.'

'It's one of those ovens,' said Philly, 'you can never quite get to understand. Always leaping out of control.'

'Serena never had any trouble with it,' said Ruthy.

Philly had not quite realised the oven had once been Serena's. Presumably Serena had slept in the brass bed with Basil. Philly cooked in Serena's kitchen: slept in Serena's bed:

Philly replaced Serena. Ruthy had slept in the brass bed with Basil too, by all accounts.

'Did you use Serena's recipe?' asked Ruthy, yellowy teeth scraping away at the hard little cake, which seemed the best Philly could contrive. 'She was hopeless at housework but always a wonderful cook. Just generally creative, I suppose.'

'I'm not a very creative person,' said Philly. 'But I wish I could make the house look better.'

'It looks perfect to me,' said Ruthy Franklyn, surprised. 'You must make Basil very happy. All this and pregnant too! The famous genes will survive. Serena only ever miscarried. Four times in five years. Basil thought she somehow did it on purpose to annoy, but he would, wouldn't he? Basil likes a woman to be a woman: simple and sweet and fertile; up to her elbows in soap suds. That's why he likes you so much, no doubt.' And Ruthy laughed. Why does she dislike me so much, wondered Philly. What went on? Ruthy in Basil's bed while Serena, out in the rain, banged and pummelled at the back door, stuck forever, swelled in the damp.

White snow hit against the portholes and turned bitter black. It was a storm at sea: foam and black water. How could you tell earth from sea, plant from person? Even the baby seemed to be tossing inside her.

'Do you see much of Basil?' asked Philly. 'I know you did in the past, but now?'

'From time to time,' said Ruthy. 'But only when he wants something. Right now he wants me to sell an early painting, and his current gallery not to know. Don't take any of it seriously. I don't any more. It's you and the baby he wants,' and Ruthy Franklyn laughed. She went up to the studio, and took the painting she wanted. It was a nude: one of Basil's very early works: face to the wall for years: its plain wooden frame blackened by smoke.

'Since he started swirling the greys and blacks,' said Ruthy as she left, 'he's hardly sold a thing. Sometimes I think it's Serena's curse. I get myself checked over pretty carefully for cancer, I can tell you that. Serena might have been mad but she had a strong personality. She loved Basil. A pity he didn't

361

love her. But then, he probably can't love anybody. Not really.' And she looked at Philly with the drop-dead look women sometimes do give pregnant women. You have what I don't. Die, then!

Ruthy left before the blizzard got worse. Philly felt, and was, alone in the world, and the washing machine, on its fast spin, tipped itself forward on to a loose tile which vibrated and made an echoing sound, worse than the phone, worse than anything she'd ever known, right inside Philly's head. She thought she'd go deaf. Presently it faded and she could think again. She called Basil at his hotel in Edinburgh but they said there was no guest under that name, and she didn't have the strength or the will to argue. The walls of the room closed in to encircle her, ridged and streaked; ash filled her nostrils. It was an old tin dustbin she was in, she realised, not the black plastic one she'd somehow envisaged: she was head-down in a bin, half-filled with water, and what Serena saw, Philly saw, and always would. What Serena heard, clang, clang, so would Philly, for ever. As for the first wife, so for her successors.

Philly took a couple of packets of firelighters up to the studio, placed them under the brass bed and fired them. The white valance caught; the mattress smouldered and flared; the turpentine went up satisfactorily: so did the paints. The wooden stretchers of a hundred canvases flickered merrily: the canvas itself puckered, blackened, shrivelled to nothing. Gold leaf, Philly discovered, burns in a series of little spurting explosions.

When there seemed to be no possibility of bed or paintings surviving, Philly went downstairs; the fire came with her. Concrete would not burn, the house itself would survive. Philly watched while streaks of fire raced over the tiled floor, feeding themselves on layer after layer of polish: generations' worth, as woman after woman had tried to erase the gritty, salty patches of grief and anger that past and future met to create.

'OK, Serena?' she said, leaving by the kitchen door, the

one which led out to the alley, and which today opened perfectly easily; the alley where the old tin dustbins stood and the homeless lingered, and the lager louts peed, and Serena had howled and screamed, day after day, night after night, while Basil and Ruthy waited for her to just go away. 'OK now?' she asked.

Biographical Notes
on the Authors

MARTIN AMIS was born in 1949. His publications include *The Rachel Papers* (1973), which won the Somerset Maugham Award; *Dead Babies* (1975); *Success* (1978); *Money* (1984); *Einstein's Monsters*, a collection of short stories; *London Fields* (1989); and *Time's Arrow* (1991). A collection of his essays will be published in autumn 1993. He lives with his wife and family in London.

JOHN BANVILLE was born in Wexford, Ireland, in 1945. His books include *Long Lankin* (1970); *Dr Copernicus*, which won the James Tait Black Award 1976; *Birchwood*; *Kepler*, which won the Guardian Fiction Prize 1981; *The Newton Letter*; *Mefisto*; *The Book of Evidence*, which was shortlisted for the 1989 Booker Prize and won the 1989 GPA Book Award; and *Ghosts* (1993). He is literary editor of the *Irish Times*, and lives with his wife and family in Dublin.

DAVID BELBIN was born in Sheffield in 1958. He has written several novels for teenagers, including *The Foggiest* and *Shoot the Teacher*. His short stories, a number of which feature the 'Alison' narrator, were first published by *Ambit* in 1989, and have appeared in many magazines and anthologies since then. He lives in Nottingham.

MICHAEL CARSON was born in Merseyside just after the Second World War. Educated at Catholic schools he became a novice in a religious order, but decided the religious life was not for him. University followed, then a career teaching English as a foreign language. His first novel was *Sucking Sherbet Lemons*. This was followed by *Friends and Infidels*, *Coming Up Roses*, *Stripping Penguins Bare* and *Yanking Up the Yo-Yo*. Michael Carson now lives in Wales.

RONALD FRAME was born in 1953 in Glasgow, and educated there and at Oxford. His tenth book, *Walking My Mistress in Deauville*, was published in 1992. His next, *The Sun on the Wall* – comprising three short novels – will appear in 1993. His first television play won the Samuel Beckett Award, and his radio plays have earned a number of Sony nominations.

JANE GARDAM is the author of many collections of short stories, the first being *Black Faces, White Faces* (1971), about Jamaica. *The Pangs of Love* won the Katherine Mansfield Award. *The Hollow Land* won a Whitbread Award as did her seventh and latest novel *Queen of the Tambourine*. She reads her stories to audiences in many parts of the world. She lives in North Yorkshire, above the River Swale.

CARLO GÉBLER is a highly acclaimed novelist and travel writer. His novels comprise *The Eleventh Summer, August in July, Work and Play, Malachy and his Family* and *Life of a Drum*. His travel writing includes *Driving through Cuba* and most recently *The Glass Curtain*, an anecdotal account of a year spent in the Enniskillen community in Northern Ireland – he and his family live nearby. He has also written and directed several television dramas and documentary films.

NADINE GORDIMER was born and lives in South Africa. She has published ten novels, the most recent being *My Son's*

Story (1990), and seven collections of short stories. Amongst many literary awards, she has won the Booker Prize for *The Conservationist*. In 1991 she was awarded the Nobel Prize for Literature.

MICHELLE HEINEMANN is a graduate of the University of East Anglia writing course. Her short stories have been published widely in magazines and anthologies. She lives in the Canadian North West Territories where she is working on a novel.

SUSAN HILL was born in Scarborough, North Yorkshire, in 1942. She was educated at grammar schools there and in Coventry, and studied at King's College, London. Her works include *I'm the King of the Castle*, which won the Somerset Maugham Prize; *The Albatross and Other Stories* (John Llewellyn Rhys Memorial Prize); *The Bird of Night* (Whitbread Award); *The Woman in Black*; *Lanterns Across the Snow*; *Air and Angels* and *The Mist in the Mirror* as well as two autobiographical books, *The Magic Apple Tree* and *Family*. She is married to the Shakespeare scholar Stanley Wells; they have two daughters and live in the Oxfordshire countryside.

JONATHAN HOLLAND was born in Macclesfield, Cheshire, in 1961 and studied at the Universities of London and East Anglia. He lived in Italy for four years and now lives in Madrid, teaching and doing occasional book reviews. Three of his stories are in *First Fictions, Introductions 11* (Faber, 1992). His first novel is to be published by Faber in 1994.

CHRISTOPHER HOPE was born in Johannesburg in 1944, grew up in Pretoria and was educated at the Universities of Witwatersrand and Natal. His novels include *A Separate Development*, *My Chocolate Redeemer* and, most recently, *Serenity House*, which was shortlisted for the 1992 Booker Prize. *The Love Songs of Nathan J Swirsky* will be published by Macmillan in September 1993.

COLUM MCCANN was born in Dublin in 1966. He has been

working in the USA, and travelled its breadth on a bicycle, for two years and is currently spending a year in Japan. This is his first published story. His first collection will be published by Phoenix House in 1993. He'is married.

BERNARD MACLAVERTY was born in Belfast in 1942, and lived there till 1975. He now lives in Glasgow. He has published three collections of short stories and two novels. He has also written versions of his fiction for other media – radio plays, television plays and screenplays.

DAVID MACKENZIE was born in Easter Ross and worked as a social worker before becoming an English teacher overseas. He now works as a systems analyst in London. His first novel, *The Truth of Stone*, was published in 1991.

ALICE MUNRO was born in Wingham in southern Ontario in 1931. She is a gifted contemporary author best known for *Dance of the Happy Shades* (1966), *The Beggar Maid* (1977), *Progress of Love* (1986) and *Friend of My Youth* (1990). Almost all her stories are set in the towns and countryside of southern Ontario.

TONY MUSGRAVE was born in Bath, grew up on Merseyside, and has lived in Berlin since 1973. A computer consultant until 1990, he now writes full time, living modestly. He has had short prose published by *London Magazine* and *Panurge*; his first novel and a collection of stories are as yet unpublished.

GEOFF NICHOLSON is the author of six novels: *Street Sleeper*, *The Knot Garden*, *What We Did On Our Holidays*, *Hunters and Gatherers*, *The Food Chain* and *The Errol Flynn Novel*. He is also the author of a travelogue called *Day Trips to the Desert*. His work has been translated into German, Japanese and Polish. He lives in London.

EDNA O'BRIEN is the author of five collections of short stories and twelve novels, including *The Country Girls*, *A Fanatic Heart*, *Lantern Slides* (which won the Los Angeles Times fiction prize) and most recently, *Time and Tide*. She has written several plays, including *Virginia* (A life of Virginia Woolf) and *A Pagan Place*. Edna O'Brien was born in the west of Ireland and now lives in London.

KATHY PAGE was born in 1958 and lives in London. She studied at the Universities of York and East Anglia. She has worked variously as a carpenter, copywriter, and writer-in-residence and now teaches literature and writing part-time. Her most recent novel is *Frankie Styne and the Silver Man* and her short stories have been collected in *As in Music*.

JONATHAN TREITEL was born in London in 1959. He was educated mainly in California, where he worked as a physicist. Stories of his have appeared in four out of the five most recent editions of *Best Short Stories*. He has put together a book length collection of his stories, and is now working on a novel.

ROSE TREMAIN, born in 1943, is a novelist, short-story writer and playwright. Her books include *Sadler's Birthday*, *The Cupboard*, *Letter to Sister Benedicta*, *The Swimming Pool Season*, *The Colonel's Daughter*, *The Garden of the Villa Mollini*, *Restoration* and, most recently, *Sacred Country*. *Restoration* was shortlisted for the Booker Prize and won the Sunday Express Book of the Year Award in 1989. *Sacred Country* won the James Tait Black Prize in 1992. She won the Dylan Thomas Short Story Award in 1984.

WILLIAM TREVOR was born in Cork in 1928, and educated at Trinity College, Dublin. He has spent much of his life in Ireland. His novel, *The Old Boys*, won the Hawthornden Prize in 1946, since when he has received many honours for his work including the Royal Society of Literature Award, the Allied Irish Banks Prize for Literature, and the Whitbread

Prize for Fiction. He edited *The Oxford Book of Irish Short Stories* (1989), and his *Collected Stories* were published in 1992.

BARRY UNSWORTH was born in Durham in 1930. He has published ten novels including *Mooncranker's Gift*, which won the Heinemann Award; *Pascali's Island*, which was shortlisted for the Booker Prize in 1980 and made into a successful film; *Stone Virgin* and *Sacred Hunger*, which shared the Booker Prize in 1992. He has spent much of his life living abroad in Greece, Turkey, Finland and now Italy.

FAY WELDON was born in England in 1931, raised in a family of women in New Zealand, and took a degree in psychology and economics at the University of St. Andrews. Her twenty-one novels and collections of stories include *Praxis*, *Puffball*, *The Lives and Loves of a She-Devil*, *The Hearts and Lives of Men*, *The Cloning of Joanna May*, *Growing Rich* and, most recently, *Affliction*. She has four sons and lives in London.

ACKNOWLEDGEMENTS

cast on BBC Radio 4, 19 February 1992, and is printed here for the first time by permission of the author and A P Watt Ltd, 20 John Street, London WC1N 2DR.

'Bevis', copyright © Jane Gardam 1992, was first published in *Discovery Magazine*, Vol 20/9, 1 September 1992, and is reprinted by permission of the author and David Higham Associates, 5–8 Lower John Street, Golden Square, London W1R 4HA.

'The Headscarf', copyright © Carlo Gébler 1992, was first published in *Critical Quarterly*, Vol. 34/2, summer 1992, and is reprinted by permission of the author and Curtis Brown & John Farquharson, 162–8 Regent Street, London W1R 4HA.

'Look-Alikes', copyright © Felix Licensing BV 1992, was first published in *Granta*, summer 1992, and is reprinted by permission of the author and A P Watt Ltd, 20 John Street, London WC1N 2DR.

'Nana's Dance', copyright © Michelle Heinemann 1992, was first published in *Whetstone*, spring 1992, and is reprinted by permission of the author and Richard Scott Simon Ltd, 43 Doughty Street, London WC1N 2LF.

'Farthing House', copyright © Susan Hill 1992, was first published in *Good Housekeeping*, December 1992/January 1993, and is reprinted by permission of the author and Richard Scott Simon Ltd, 43 Doughty Street, London WC1N 2LF.

'Here Come the Impersonators', copyright © Jonathan Holland 1992, was first published in *Stand Magazine*, Vol. 34/1, winter 1992, and is reprinted by permission of the author.

'Maundy', copyright © Christopher Hope 1992, was first published in the *New Yorker*, 1 June 1992, and is reprinted by permission of the author and Rogers, Coleridge and White Ltd, 20 Powis Mews, London W11 1JN.

'Sisters', copyright © Colum McCann 1992, was first published in *Analecta*, the Student Literary Journal of the University of Texas, and is reprinted by permission of the author and Sheil Land Associates Ltd, 43 Doughty Street, London WC1N 2LF.

'The Wake House', copyright © Bernard MacLaverty 1992, was first published in American *GQ*, October 1992, and is reprinted by permission of the author and Rogers, Coleridge and White Ltd, 20 Powis Mews, London W11 1JN.

'endword', copyright © David Mackenzie 1992, was first published in *Stand Magazine*, Vol. 33/2, spring 1992, and is reprinted by permission of the author and John Johnson Ltd, Clerkenwell House, 45/47 Clerkenwell Green, London EC1R OHT.

'A Real Life', copyright © Alice Munro 1992, was first published in the *New Yorker*, 10 February 1992, and is reprinted by permission of the author, Virginia Barber Literary Agency Inc., 353 West 21st Street, NY 10011, and Abner Stein, 10 Roland Gardens, London SW7 3PH.

'Bel', copyright © Tony Musgrave 1992, was first published in *Panurge* 15/16, April 1992, and is reprinted by permission of the author.

'The Guitar and Other Animals', copyright © Geoff Nicholson 1992, was first published in *Ambit 130*, autumn 1992, and is reprinted by permission of the author.

'Wilderness', copyright © Edna O'Brien 1992, was first published in the *New Yorker*, 16 March 1992, and is reprinted by permission of the author and Aitken & Stone Ltd, 29 Fernshaw Road, London SW10 OTG.

'The Gymnasium', copyright © Kathy Page 1992, was first published in *Passport 4*, and is reprinted by permission of the author.

'Stalin, Stalin and Stalin', copyright © Jonathan Treitel 1992, was first published in the *New Yorker*, 21 September 1992, and is reprinted by permission of the author.

'Two of Them', copyright © Rose Tremain 1992, was first published in *Marie Claire*, August 1992, and is reprinted by permission of the author and Richard Scott Simon Ltd, 43 Doughty Street, London WC1N 2LF.

'Lost Ground', copyright © William Trevor 1992, was first published in the *New Yorker*, 24 February 1992, and is reprinted by permission of the author and Peters, Fraser and Dunlop, 503/4 The Chambers, Chelsea Harbour, London SW10 0XF.

'Fallen by the Wayside', copyright © Barry Unsworth 1992, was first published in *The Times*, 24 December 1992, and is reprinted by permission of the author and Sheil Land Associates Ltd, 43 Doughty Street, London WC1N 2LF.

'Through a Dustbin, Darkly', copyright © Fay Weldon 1992, was first published in *Options*, December 1992, and is reprinted by permission of the author and Sheil Land Associates Ltd, 43 Doughty Street, London WC1N 2LF.